TIM SHOEMAKER

ESCAPE
FROM THE
EVERGLADES

A HIGH WATER NOVEL

S0-BRW-595

FOCUS
ON THE FAMILY

A Focus on the Family Resource
Published by Tyndale House Publishers

27	26	25	24	23	22	21
7	6	5	4	3	2	1

To my three sons . . . Andy, Mark, and Luke . . . who encouraged me to write in the first place. Fiction is one of the most powerful ways to teach truth—because it reaches directly to the heart. I loved reading to you as you grew up . . . watching your eyes grow wide with the suspense and adventure. And when it was time to stop—I loved how you begged me to "read just a little bit more." May you have the joy of reading to your kids. And always, always . . . read just a little bit more.

CHAPTER 1

Everglades National Park
Saturday, June 13
6:55 p.m.

PARKER BUCKMAN STOOD ON the airboat deck and searched the surface of the water. He didn't actually see any alligators, but they were here. Watching. Reminding him that he was an intruder in their world. He was pretty sure the gators didn't mind, though. A visitor could become a meal for some lucky alligator in one careless moment.

An uneasiness clung to him like the muggy air itself. It worked its way inside and wouldn't let go. He couldn't shake the creepy sense that he shouldn't be in the Everglades today.

Which was crazy. He loved the outdoors. Even he had to

1

admit that Everglades City and the neighboring island town of Chokoloskee were pretty much the armpit of America. But he still found things to love about the place—once you got past the mosquitoes, that is.

And Everglades National Park itself, the swampy wetlands that dominated some 7,800 square miles of southern Florida, was never boring. A place of contrasts. Bright sun that could burn your eyeballs out quicker than a solar eclipse, yet water so dark you'd think there was no bottom. Hardly a speck of ground above water in the wet season, yet trees and brush and grasses grew high above the surface as if there were no water at all. A place as wild and uncivilized as anyplace Parker had ever been, yet there was still an order to it. No streets, no signs, but a seemingly endless maze of watery paths crisscrossing the Everglades. Narrow alleys and routes beat through the sawgrass. As a park ranger's son, he got to explore them as often as he wanted.

Wilson Stillwaters—half Miccosukee and pretty much *all* trouble—was totally in his element here. His tribe had been native to the Everglades long before any white man explored them—a fact he reminded Parker about often. "Where *is* Angelica? She's the one who begged me to find the perfect place to mount her trail cam."

Angelica Malnatti, better known as Jelly, had always been into shooting nature pictures wherever her family had been stationed. Mountains. Rivers. Anyplace without humans. But ever since her dad got transferred to the Everglades along with Parker's, she'd been practically obsessed with *wildlife* photography. Apparently she wasn't the only one. Parker had seen dozens of camouflaged cameras strapped to cypress trees in the Everglades and along the rivers leading into Chokoloskee Bay. Jelly wouldn't miss a chance to set up her camera in some remote spot. "She'll be here."

"Yeah, well if she's not here in two minutes, she'll have to swim." Wilson patted the control stick of the airboat. "*Typhoon* wants to whip up a tropical storm out there."

The name *Typhoon* was written vertically down each of the twin rudders mounted behind the propeller cage. It was the perfect name for the airboat. With a 350-cubic-inch Chevy engine mounted to the non-skid aluminum deck, the airboat could kick up more than just a little squall. Wind generated from the prop reached upwards of 150 miles per hour—rivaling that of a Category 5 hurricane. "Your uncle's airboat is gorgeous," Parker said. "You've gotta let me drive this thing."

Wilson jutted his chin toward the mangroves. "Here she comes. It's about time."

Sure enough, red braids bucking, Jelly pedaled like she was afraid they'd leave without her. With her dark-green Columbia shirt and cargo khakis, she totally looked like some kind of Everglades tour guide wannabe.

Jelly skidded to a stop and dropped her bike. Seconds later she hopped aboard. "Are you two finally ready?" In one smooth move, Jelly snatched Parker's cap and slapped it on her head as she passed.

Parker tried to nab it back, but she ducked out of the way. This hat-swiping thing was some new game of hers.

She tipped the visor of his hat and flashed Parker a proud smile. "What are we waiting for, Wilson? You promised me an Everglades run I'd never forget."

Wilson tested the rudders and slid the key into the ignition. "You're a real piece of work, Jelly." He fired up the engine. "Buckle up."

Which was impossible. *Typhoon* had no working seat belts. And Wilson wouldn't have used his anyway. Parker climbed onto the elevated double passenger seat just behind the driver's chair and sat next to Jelly. He dug a pair of foam earplugs from his pocket and twisted them into his ears.

Wilson laughed. "Miccosukees don't need ear protection."

"With the decibels airboats put out? You could damage your hearing, idiot."

"What?"

"Exactly." Parker backhanded Wilson's shoulder.

Wilson grinned and revved the engine. The throaty rumble of the 350 sent powerful vibrations through the airboat that could loosen fillings. And somehow it loosened up Parker at the same time. Calmed him. Maybe all that uneasiness he'd been feeling wasn't some kind of warning from his gut. Maybe it was just his own overactive imagination.

Wilson goosed the gas, and the airboat picked up speed as they entered the "sea of grass," as some locals called it. Wilson waggled the rudders, causing *Typhoon* to fishtail back and forth.

Jelly kicked the back of Wilson's seat. "We don't have seat belts, remember? If I fall off this thing, you're going to be soooo sorry."

Wilson laughed and swung the airboat from side to side again.

The next hour was pure heaven—especially since Parker got to drive most of that time. The grass rake bow skimmed right over spots where new patches of sawgrass seemed to be filling in the waterways. It was like the Everglades was taking back the lanes.

True to his word, Wilson found a spot in the middle of nowhere to strap Jelly's trail cam—which meant climbing out of the airboat into waist-deep water. Jelly was over the side without even the slightest hesitation. Somehow it didn't seem right that she went in alone. What if something snuck up on her while she was focused on mounting the camera?

"I'll give you a hand." Parker followed and helped her secure the camera to a cypress—just above the waterline. He scanned the surface nearby, looking for telltale bubbles.

"It has infrared," Jelly said. "If something moves within fifty feet of this sensor, I'll get pictures. Even in the dark."

Like he didn't know that.

"This spot is perfect." Jelly gave Wilson an approving nod. "The place is teeming with life."

"And *death*," Wilson said. "Never forget that."

Parker gave Jelly a boost back on deck and hoisted himself up a moment later.

"Don't get all morbid on me, Wilson." Jelly toweled off and draped the thing over Wilson's head.

"Hey." Wilson tossed the towel back at her. "This is about respecting the Glades. My people understand that."

The way he said "my people" always made Parker smile. With his blond hair—even long and wild as it was—he didn't look one bit Miccosukee. Maybe that's why he always had three or four micro-braids going—with bits of twine and beads worked in. Like he wanted to remind others of his native roots.

"People fish in the Glades," Wilson said. "Hunt in them. Fly over them—like they have the right. Like the place belongs to them. But nobody *owns* the Everglades—and she keeps score. When the time is right, she collects a toll."

"Ridiculous." Jelly laughed. "Like a trespassing tax?"

He gave a slow nod. "Paid in blood. Human lives."

"Don't get him started," Parker said. Wilson could go on for hours telling creepy stories about the Glades.

"If I didn't know better," Jelly said in that teasing way she was so good at, "I'd say Wilson believes there's some kind of curse on the Glades."

"My people say that's exactly what it is."

"It's *superstition,*" Jelly said, "plain and simple."

"Make fun all you want," Wilson said. "There are strange forces at work in the world. Things we don't understand."

"Boys are on *that* list—and you two are at the top. Are you going to start this thing back up—or do we have to row?"

Wilson acted like he never heard. "Guess how many people have died in the Glades."

"Here we go," Parker said. Wilson gave him this little speech the first time they'd met. They'd been friends ever since.

"Hundreds. Maybe thousands," Wilson said. He leaned forward. "Nobody really knows. Take airline crashes. 1972 . . . Eastern Flight 401—101 fatalities. 1996 . . . ValuJet Flight 592—all 110 aboard—gone. And then—"

"You need a shrink, Wilson," Jelly said. "You're not going to ruin this place for me with all your death-talk."

"Ruin it?" Wilson slung his arm over the back of the driver's seat and grinned. "The danger—knowing I cheat death every time I walk out of the Glades in one piece—that's what I love about this place."

"There you go again. You're obsessed with death."

"No," Wilson said. "I'm obsessed with *beating* death. Big difference."

"There," Jelly said. "You just admitted you're obsessed. Thank you for clearing that up."

Parker smiled. There was no way Wilson could be a match for Jelly when she got like this.

Wilson levered the choke, grabbed the key—but stopped short

of starting the engine. "Don't underestimate the Glades, Jelly. There's something absolutely evil about this place. A darkness. I've *felt* it."

And in that instant, that weird feeling was back. The sense that they shouldn't be there right now. Like the Glades were more restless than usual.

Parker eyed the water. Everything looked still. Quiet. Maybe *too* quiet. He couldn't shed the strangest feeling that the Glades were on the hunt—and about to collect another toll.

The sun kissed the horizon and hovered there like it didn't want to get any closer to the Everglades than it had to tonight.

Shake it off, Bucky. Whatever he was feeling, he was pretty sure it would disappear if they got moving again. "Getting late." The water looked black now, as if it had turned to oil. "We better get back."

Wilson nodded. Seconds later, he had *Typhoon* flying across the dark waters.

How Wilson knew his way back, Parker had no idea. Maybe he had some kind of Miccosukee GPS in his head. He pulled back the stick and put *Typhoon* into a sideslip. Parker leaned into the turn—and Jelly grabbed his arm and screamed. Spray showered all three of them and the airboat chattered to a stop.

"Yee-ha!" Wilson revved the engine and jockeyed the rudder stick back and forth—then tromped on the gas again.

The engine roared, and the propeller blast churned the water behind them into frantic ripples. Sawgrass whipped away from them in the prop wash.

Suddenly Wilson fishtailed to a stop and pointed. "Check it out."

An alligator—a big one—no more than thirty feet away, sitting low and motionless in the water. Pale orange sunlight glinted off the wet rows of armored scutes lining its back. In its own way, the gator was like an iceberg: more danger below the surface than above—and eyes just as cold.

A monster.

Wilson cut the engine and grabbed a bag of French bread from under his seat.

Parker stood. The sun was gone now—and it would get dark fast. As much as he'd like to stay in the Glades, something definitely didn't feel right. What was wrong with him? *God . . . are you trying to tell me something?*

Wilson twisted off a fist-sized hunk of bread and threw it halfway between them and the gator. "Got your phone, Jelly? Get ready for a great photo op."

The gator stared directly at them. It swept its serrated tail to one side, forming tiny whirlpools on the surface—and glided toward the airboat.

The beast was probably the biggest alligator Parker had seen—that wasn't stuffed and hanging in some Florida souvenir shop, anyway. Honestly, he'd wanted to see one this big—in the wild—since moving here. A rush of excitement swept over Parker, but it quickly gave way to a warning that rumbled like distant thunder somewhere deep in his head. He could almost hear his dad's voice. *Don't be stupid. You're pushing it. Be smart—and do the right thing. Like we always talk about.*

"Guys, I've got a weird feeling about being here." There. He said it. And the feeling grew stronger. "I hate to bust up this party, but we should be heading back." He looked to Jelly, hoping she'd pick up on whatever it was that he was feeling—and talk some sense into Wilson.

She gave Parker the pleading eyes thing—and already had her phone out. "Just a couple shots. I promise."

So much for her being the voice of reason.

Parker eyed the beast. Or was it eying him? "You know what my dad—and Jelly's—would say if they knew you were feeding gators?"

Wilson moved to the bow and coaxed the gator closer with another chunk of bread. "We Miccosukee make our own rules out here. Besides, they're park rangers. They *have* to say it isn't a good idea."

Jelly nodded. "And I wouldn't consider this *feeding*. It's just some scraps of bread. Hardly enough to feed a gator that big. We're just giving the thing a snack. An appetizer."

"And we're the main course," Parker said. "We don't want alligators approaching humans for food. We *are* food." And this guy looked big enough to eat all three of them.

Wilson laughed. "Now you sound like your dad."

Actually, to Parker, that was a compliment. His dad was big on doing the right things, even when others didn't . . . something Parker was working on himself.

Jelly was on her feet, making her way toward Wilson up front. It was like neither of them heard a thing Parker said. "Just a few pictures, then we'll leave. I promise."

Wilson ripped off another hunk of bread. He threw it five feet short of the gator.

The beast moved toward the bread without creating a ripple. Like it was in some kind of stealth mode.

Wilson eased over until he stood at the very edge of the airboat, imitating the sound of a baby gator just like a professional Miccosukee guide. "Euhh. Euhh. Euhh. Euhh."

Jelly stood right behind Wilson and glanced back at Parker. "A female will come to protect the young. A male to eat them."

A fact that Parker was well aware of. Jelly's dad had been stationed here only a few months longer than Parker's dad, but sometimes she still treated him like he was a total newbie.

The gator advanced. Crept closer. Parker estimated the distance between the nose and eyes. Eleven inches easily. So, the brute was an eleven-footer. Definitely bigger than any he'd seen in the few months he'd lived in the Chokoloskee and Everglades City area.

"Easy now. No fast movements," Wilson said. "Let's not scare it away."

The face of it was pure evil. Menacing teeth rimmed its mouth like it was coming to dinner—and brought its own utensils. "It doesn't look scared." Parker laughed. "Just hungry."

Wilson gripped the gator-tooth necklace around his neck. "He sees this—and believe me, he's scared. That's why he's moving so slow."

Did Wilson—or Jelly—stop to think that maybe the gator was being careful not to scare *its* prey away? "Yeah, or maybe he's stalking you."

Wilson laughed and tossed another clump of bread, but closer to the airboat this time. "Euhh. Euhh. Euhh. Euhh." The gator took the bait and it didn't stop. "That's it. Come to papa, you big galoot."

The alligator closed the distance and snapped up the bread without even the slightest pause.

Jelly stood there next to Wilson, grabbing pictures with her phone as the monster glided toward them. "Now I wish I still had my trail cam."

Parker rolled his pant leg above the survival knife strapped to his calf, sensing he needed to be ready. But what good would a knife be against a vicious carnivore like that gator?

"Look at the chompers on that thing," Wilson said.

Parker couldn't get past the size—and the terrifying look of it. Black. Powerful. Deadly.

"Move away from the edge, okay, Jelly?" The sides of the airboat weren't more than fifteen inches above the surface of the water—if that. Could the beast climb over the edge? "You too, Wilson."

Neither of them budged.

The gator clawed its way onto a small mound of sawgrass and roots next to the boat, allowing the monstrous size of the beast to be seen for the first time. Wilson grinned. "Got your phone, Bucky?"

Parker patted his pocket. "Yeah. Why?"

Wilson backed a couple of feet away from the edge. "Get pictures of me and Jelly with this beaut."

Right. And if Parker's dad ever saw the photo there'd be a lot of explaining to do. The gator crept forward and rested its chin on the top edge of the airboat—jaws open with that gator grin going on. The mouth, white and pink inside—and strangely clean looking. The teeth . . . absolutely wicked.

"Can that thing get in here?" Parker pictured it. Grabbing Wilson by the leg—

"Wouldn't *that* be interesting." Wilson tore off another hunk of bread and sidearmed it into the alligator's gaping mouth. A personal pizza–sized trapdoor of sorts opened in the back of the gator's throat for an instant . . . and the bread was gone. "If gators didn't have that watertight flap in the back of their throat, they'd drown. Did you know that?"

"Spare me the nature lesson," Parker said. "Just back away from that thing." Wilson was close. Too close.

"I'm going to bag me a gator this big one day." The French bread was half gone. Wilson took the stump and whacked the gator right on the snout. The gator didn't even react. It just stayed there with its jaws open like it was daring him to try it one more time.

Jelly gasped, but not like she was disgusted or anything. "Do that again. I'm switching to video."

"Their vision directly in front of their nose isn't so hot," Wilson said. He held the loaf off to one side. Immediately the gator swung its head toward it. Wilson jerked the bread away. "Pretty good off to the side, though."

Really good. And it looked like the gator was staring right at Parker now. The thing didn't blink. Creepy.

Parker wanted a weapon in his hands. Something a lot bigger than his survival knife. The aluminum gaffing hook on board looked ridiculously lightweight. He glanced around the airboat. Small tool box. First aid kit. A wooden paddle. It was probably too thin at the business end of it to do any good against a gator half that size. He picked it up anyway. He'd have liked it better if it were a Louisville Slugger.

There was something almost hypnotic about the gator. Parker knew they should leave, but part of him wanted to stay. Wanted to watch.

Jelly stepped closer to the edge of *Typhoon*—and the beast swung its head her way. She jumped back, stumbled over the dock line, and nearly slid backward off the other side of the airboat. Parker's hat flipped off her head into the dark water.

Parker grabbed her hand and pulled her to her feet.

She gave a weak smile. "That was fun."

"Uh-huh. Right." Parker used the paddle to scoop the hat out of the water and drop it on the deck. "Seen enough, Jelly?"

Jelly picked up his cap, smacked it against her thigh to knock off some of the water, and slapped it back on her head. "Just a few more pictures."

Whatever hypnotic spell the gator had over Parker was broken now. This gator was way too big to mess with. The unsettled feeling grew and crept over Parker. They didn't belong here. He checked his watch. "Let's go. If you're done tormenting the killing machine, that is."

"*Killing* machine?" Wilson waved the French bread from side to side in front of its nose. "It's nothing more than an overgrown lizard. With really big teeth."

"That *lizard* is at the top of the food chain here."

Wilson shook his head. "As long as we're in a boat, *we're* the top of the food chain. Get a picture of this."

"Seriously?"

"Then we'll go. I promise."

Parker gave Jelly a look—silently trying to talk some sense into her. What if the beast lunged into the boat and grabbed her?

"Be sure I'm in the shot," she said. "I've never seen one this huge."

Big help she was.

"Forget it. Let's go."

Jelly smiled the way she did when she was about to talk him into something he didn't want to do. "Pleeeease, Parker? For me?"

Something about the way she said it made him wonder if he was overreacting with all his jittery feelings. Maybe he was. Maybe he wasn't. It didn't really matter. Her mind was set on getting more photos. Trying to talk her out of it would eat more time than taking the stupid picture. Even though it didn't feel right to stay, maybe compromising was the best option.

"You're ridiculous, you know that?" Parker dropped the paddle on the deck and pulled the phone out of his pocket. "Let's just make this fast." He dropped onto one knee near the edge just in front of the propeller cage—a good seven feet from the gator. He swiped to the camera app and held the phone out over the water. He shot a burst of pictures, then checked the screen. "Got it. Now can we go?"

Wilson laughed. "Just shoot a quick video clip." He went back to swinging the loaf from one side of the alligator's head to the other, just out of reach of the monster's jaws. The monster's head swept from side to side a split second behind Wilson.

"He's figuring out your timing."

"Then you'd better film it fast so I can stop."

Jelly struck a pose next to Wilson. "Just ten seconds—then we're done. Promise."

"Okay, but you seriously better hope your dad never sees the footage. He'll put you on a leash, and your trail camera will never be strapped farther than your mailbox." Parker switched to video mode and held it out an arm's length from the boat—nice and low to the water for a dramatic angle. "My idiot friends are demonstrating just how incredibly reckless they can be—"

"Or how brainless alligators really are," Wilson said.

The gator snapped. Wilson jerked backward into Jelly, dropping the bread. The gator scarfed it up from the deck of the airboat. Parker kept filming.

"Whoa!" Wilson grinned. "*That* was fun." Suddenly the smile slid off his face. He stared at his arms for a moment, then rubbed down goose bumps.

The whole gooseflesh thing with Wilson—Parker had only seen that happen to him once before. Wilson had claimed his Miccosukee blood warned him of mortal danger. Which was totally bogus. More likely his years spent in the Glades sharpened his instincts. Wilson's subconscious picked up on some type of present danger.

"What is it?" Apparently Jelly noticed Wilson's reaction too.

Maybe Wilson was seeing the stupidity of what he was doing. Finally. Parker stretched out farther, still filming. "Admit it. This was stupid." He wanted Wilson's confession on the video.

Wilson looked up, scanning the surface of the Everglades like there was something else behind the goose bumps besides the gator in front of him.

"Bucky!" Eyes wide, Wilson pointed toward the water by Parker's phone.

A second gator, coming from behind the airboat—and Parker. Bigger. Massive black head. Not two feet away from Parker's arm—closing in.

Jelly screamed—and Parker's world spun into slow motion even as he pulled back. He saw every detail.

The gator lunging. Fast . . . so incredibly fast. Jaws opening. Swamp water streaming out. Yellow teeth closing over Parker's forearm.

He felt no pain. Just pressure—and incredible strength.

With a sideways snap of its head, the monster ripped Parker off the platform—and into the black waters of the Everglades.

CHAPTER 2

Everglades National Park
Saturday, June 13
8:37 p.m.

THE GATOR YANKED PARKER UNDER the surface with so much force that he felt his arm would rip off. It was a no-contest tug-of-war. The alligator went into the death roll, twisting Parker back to the surface and under again. *God, help!*

His shoulder grazed the bottom. It was that shallow. The monster's snout just inches away from Parker's face. The water too dark for a clear view, but he saw the pale smudge of his arm—with terrifyingly big teeth sunk deep. The bone in his forearm snapped, zinging a shudder through his shoulder.

The gator spun again with stunning power, churning the water.

Parker broke the surface—caught a comet of sky—but was under again before he could gulp air. He heard Dad's voice in his head, and immediately obeyed, clawing at the pouch of skin under the gator's jaw with his free hand. He grabbed the leathery hide and yanked as hard as he could.

Release. Release. God, make him let go.

Obviously the gator had other ideas.

CHAPTER 3

Everglades National Park
Saturday, June 13
8:37 p.m.

"DO SOMETHING, WILSON!" Angelica stood helplessly watching. "Do *something*!"

Parker was no more than a blur in the bloody froth as the alligator spun him in the death roll. She saw him for a millisecond; then he was gone again.

Fight or flight. Jelly was in neither zone. She stood there frozen. *This can't be happening. Can't.* She didn't dare go closer to the edge. The eleven-footer Wilson had been feeding was still there with its wicked grin.

Wilson grabbed the paddle and smacked it across the side of

its head so hard the paddle split. The gator dove underwater and out of sight. Would it go after Parker too?

"Bucky!" Wilson crouched at the edge, clutching the busted paddle—ready to pounce. But he seemed as helpless as Parker.

"Help him!" Angelica screamed. But what would she do if Wilson jumped in and the other gator got him?

Wilson looked terrified, which didn't help Angelica a bit. He scrambled to the back of the airboat—like a coach running the sidelines—just as the gator rolled Parker to the surface and back under again. "Fight, Bucky. Fight!"

But the thing outweighed him by what, five hundred pounds— at least. Parker didn't have a chance.

CHAPTER 4

LIGHT-DARK. LIGHT-DARK. The death roll kept him totally disoriented. Dizzy.

Keep fighting—or play dead. Dad's voice in his head again. *Alligators drown their prey, then stash the body underwater until the flesh softens up. They're easier to tear apart that way.*

This monster was too strong, and as long as Parker kept struggling, the gator would keep him tumbling.

Play dead. Play dead. God, help me!

His lungs were on fire, but Parker forced himself to go limp.

The beast seemed to sense it immediately. It took two more

complete turns before the thrashing stopped—and the gator released its grip.

Parker felt the bottom under his good hand and steadied himself against the frenzied spinning in his head. He counted off five quick seconds—hoping the gator would swim off to form a perimeter, keeping other alligators from its prize. Convulsing for air, he pushed off the bottom and broke the surface. Stood. Choking. Coughing. Gulping air. Water only up to his chest. No gator in sight—not on the surface anyway. His watch was gone, but his arm was still there. Airboat twelve feet away, and on a crazy-weird angle.

Wilson stood on the edge, the remains of a paddle in his hands like a harpoon. "Get in! Get *in*!"

Jelly motioned frantically, cheeks slick with tears.

Head still stuck in some kind of Tilt-A-Whirl syndrome, Parker sloshed and stumbled his way to the boat, expecting the wicked jaws to clamp down on him again.

"Hurry!" Wilson shouted. "The other one is close too." He slapped the water with the paddle—as if that would scare a 650-pound alligator away. "C'mon, Bucky!"

Parker clawed at the water with his good arm, the other hung limp at his side, trailing blood and torn flesh. It was impossible to walk straight—or was the boat moving?

He reached for the boat. Wilson tossed aside the paddle and dragged him halfway onto the deck. "Pull your feet in!"

Jelly gripped Parker's legs and tugged.

Parker rolled onto the deck. Coughed. Spit up swamp water. Coughed again. He eyed the edge of the airboat. Absolutely knew the beast could get in if it wanted to. "Get us," he choked the words out, "outta here." There was no way he should have gotten away from the gator. How had he escaped? Only God could have rescued him.

The dizziness eased slightly. Parker sat and tucked his feet in tight . . . far from the edge. "Go." The gator was watching. He knew it.

Wilson broke out the first aid kit. Tore through it. "Gotta slow that bleeding first." He pulled out an ace bandage.

Blood pooled on the airboat deck. Too much blood.

"Can you hold your arm out?"

Parker grabbed his mangled arm just above the elbow and held it out. Shredded flesh. Muscle. And the sickening white of exposed and shattered bone. But it wasn't *his* arm. It couldn't be. There was no pain. None.

"You'll be okay." Jelly took his bloody hand in both of hers. "Parker? You hear me? Parker, look at me."

But all he could see was his arm.

Wilson wrapped the bandage around and around. Blood seeped through nearly as fast as Wilson could get another layer looped around his forearm.

Wilson whipped off his T-shirt and wrapped it around the bandaging. "We gotta get you back." He helped Parker to his feet and pushed him into the seat. "Hold on. Can you do that?"

Parker nodded.

Wilson glanced at Parker's bloody arm, like he wasn't so sure.

"I'll help," Jelly said. She sat next to him, one arm around his shoulders, the other across him and gripping the armrest like a human seat belt.

The alligator surfaced. Stared Parker down with angry eyes. Probably wishing he'd held him under for another minute. Half that would have done the job.

"Go, Wilson." Parker had to get out of this Godforsaken corner of hell.

Typhoon roared to life. Wilson revved the engine. Threw the rudder stick full forward and stood on the gas. The airboat side-slid and Wilson steered it right at the alligator. Like he truly meant to take the thing out. The beast had that gator grin going on as it melted into the black waters again. Like this wasn't over yet.

Wilson drove like a lunatic. The grass rake gobbled up the water and the sawgrass in front of them. Jelly leaned into Parker, obviously doing her best to keep him in the seat.

Parker tried to grip the armrest with his bad hand, but he couldn't seem to make it work. He couldn't even close his fingers to make a fist. He pictured himself being thrown from the airboat on one of Wilson's wild turns.

Wilson looked over his shoulder. "Stay with me."

He had no intention of leaving. Not that Wilson's driving was making it easy.

Wilson glanced back again. "Talk to me. You're not looking so good."

He wasn't feeling so good either. "Cold." Which was weird. It had to be over ninety degrees. "Dizzy."

Wilson's eyes flicked down to Parker's arm. Parker followed his gaze to the blood drizzling off his fingertips and splattering to the deck. Tiny rivulets zigzagged their way to the edge of the airboat and over the side. He was leaving a blood trail for the gator to follow.

"Jelly," Wilson said, "more pressure on that wound!"

Parker was pretty sure she'd need more hands. His arm was losing blood in too many places, and if Jelly stopped holding him in the seat he was sure he'd be thrown to the deck—or water—on the next turn.

Wilson side-spun to a stop. Let *Typhoon* idle. She bucked as if in protest even as Wilson jumped off his seat.

Parker glanced back at their wake. Was sure he saw the alligator following—which would have been impossible, right? "Why . . . stopping?"

Wilson whipped the laces out of one of his shoes. "Tourniquet." He worked the lace around Parker's arm halfway between his elbow and shoulder. Tied it tight. Blood kept dripping.

"Gator . . . coming," Parker said. "Get us out." *Typhoon* rocked crazily, but the water's surface was as smooth as hot tar, and just as black. Actually it wasn't the airboat rocking—it was the sky. Weird.

Wilson pulled out his pocketknife. "If we don't slow the bleeding you won't make it to the dock."

Comforting thought.

Keeping the blade closed, Wilson worked the handle under the lace and twisted. The makeshift tourniquet bit in. *That* Parker felt. Wilson grabbed Parker's good hand and planted it on the knife. "Hold it there. Got it?"

Parker nodded. But his hand was shaking. No, make that his whole body.

"I can't hold him in place much longer," Jelly said. As if Parker wasn't helping—and she was doing all the work.

"Jus—go." His voice sounded slurred. What was going on?

Wilson looked at him like he thought Parker would keel over. He unclipped a lifejacket from the base of the seat. Whipped a nylon belt free from the loops. "Sit him on the deck."

They were talking *about* him—as if he wasn't there. *I'm okay.* He wanted to say it, but the words didn't come out. So strange.

Jelly helped Parker slide down with his back against the legs of the passenger seat bolted to the deck.

Wilson wrapped the nylon belt around Parker and then the seat legs. He clipped the belt and snugged it tight. "Ready to fly?"

Parker nodded toward his arm. Tried to smile. "Bus-ted wing."

Wilson swung back into the driver's seat. Throttled the 350 to a roar. Gained speed. He plowed through a patch of sawgrass. The airboat hardly slowed. He didn't bother following the natural lanes through the Everglades now. He barreled through, choosing the most direct course wherever he could.

Wilson had his phone out. Dialed it somehow. Talked frantically to someone. Who would he call? It's not like paramedics made runs into the Glades.

"It's bad," Wilson shouted over the airboat's engine. "I'll get him to Wooten's. He's lost a lot of blood."

Wooten's Airboat Tours—where Wilson's dad worked. Good spot. Lots of people. Right off the Tamiami Trail—the remote two-lane highway running east and west through the Glades. Great spot to meet the paramedics. Parker tried to keep the knife for the tourniquet twisted tight. But the strength seemed to drain from his good hand, and the pocketknife was wet. Slippery with his own blood.

Jelly pressed against him and gripped the leg of the chair with both hands. "Hang on."

"Your . . . job." Staying upright proved to be a challenge on even the slightest turn. Jelly was doing her best. But he outweighed her by what? Forty pounds? Blood flowed from the rivers of veins or arteries torn in his arm and spread out to form a red delta on the deck.

Wilson banked hard around a thick patch of grass surrounding a dead cypress tree.

This time Parker found himself sprawled on the deck, painted with his own blood. He lost his grip on Wilson's knife and felt the blood whoosh into his forearm like somebody had just released a blood pressure cuff. Blood pumped right back out his arm in countless places.

He was bleeding out.

Jelly threw herself on him like she thought he would roll over the side. "Wilson—we're losing him!"

Like—as in *dying*? Parker wanted to tell her that was ridiculous. But he couldn't speak.

"Almost there," Wilson said. "Hold on."

But there was nothing to grab. Even if there was, he felt so incredibly weak. He couldn't even lift his head. If not for the nylon belt tearing into his waist, likely he'd be over the side.

And the monster would get him for sure.

"You're going to be okay," Jelly said. "You're going to be okay." Her fingers stroked his hair.

Suddenly her face was inches from his. "Parker—where's the knife?" Jelly sounded frantic. "We need that tourniquet!"

Long gone. The roar of the motor seemed distant. Muffled. The engine vibrations traveled through the deck and right through his body. Or was he having a convulsion?

As far as he knew, he never passed out. Somehow Wilson found Wooten's Airboat Tours. Parker saw the docks as the airboat flew toward them. People there—thank God.

"Gator attack!" Even from fifty yards out Wilson was yelling for help. "He's lost massive blood."

Wilson roared in way too hot. He didn't let off the accelerator until he was almost on the docks. He jerked his foot off the gas. The airboat slowed too fast, forcing the bow to dip hard for an instant. As the bow rocked back up, the wake washed over the transom—and kept pouring in.

Too late Wilson must have realized his mistake. He punched the gas, but the back end of the boat was sinking as if a monster gator was dragging *Typhoon* down to its lair.

Parker slid against the legs of the seat as the bow rose and the stern settled on the shallow bottom. His weight shifted, the nylon belt dug into his flesh, and his whole body twisted around so he was facing the engine. Jelly was thrown over the side and into the backwash.

The tips of the airboat prop beat the water, sending up showers of spray before the motor gagged and died in an angry blast of steam. Now the wake roiled over him. For the second time, he was in the water. The nylon belt held him fast. Parker fumbled desperately for the buckle with his good hand.

Absolute terror. Water rising. The gator had followed them. Parker was sure of it. He'd finish the job.

Typhoon's stern hit bottom—the rudder tips just barely visible above the swamp water. The motor—powerless. Just like Parker.

Wilson was there, half crab-crawling, half swimming. Reaching for the belt trapping Parker. "C'mon. C'mon."

Jelly swam back to the side of the airboat.

Parker felt the clasp release—then weightless. Helpless.

Wilson grabbed him under his armpits. "We're outta here. We made it." Wilson dragged him free of the boat and towed him toward the dock, where others waited to pull him to safety. Jelly swam beside him. "Fight, Parker. Fight."

Fight? Did she see another alligator? Parker faced the Glades. He hiked his knees in close, ready to kick if a gator showed its ugly face. If he could even hit it with the way everything was spinning.

"Almost there," Wilson said. "Ten feet."

Seconds later strong hands lifted him out of the water and laid him on the dock. His head seemed heavy. So incredibly heavy. The boards felt warm under his cheek.

Wilson hoisted himself onto the dock and got close to Parker's face. "You're going to be fine."

Wilson's eyes flicked down to Parker's arm, then back. There was something in his look that Parker hadn't seen before . . . not in Wilson's eyes, anyway.

Fear.

Parker closed his eyes. Needed sleep. Just five minutes. His dad's voice played through his head. *Wilson just might be immortal. But his crazy stunts are going to get somebody else killed.* Of all the times for his dad to be right.

"Is he dead?" A stranger's voice. Sounding so distant.

"No," Wilson said. "Not yet."

CHAPTER 5

Wooten's Airboat Tours
Saturday, June 13
8:59 p.m.

ANGELICA WRAPPED BOTH HANDS around Parker's upper arm to make a human tourniquet.

"Let me do that." A man with a Wooten's staff shirt took over, his rough hands clamped down out over hers. "Okay." He nodded. "I got him. Pull free."

Her hands—slick with blood—slipped out easily. She scooted out of his way. Stared at Parker's mangled arm. Took his bloody hand in hers. "Don't leave us," she whispered. She bent down and kissed his hand. His blood . . . warm on her lips. His skin cold.

"Give us room," tourniquet-hands said.

Angelica stood on shaky legs and watched. Parker's eyes were closed. Mouth slightly open. Face pale as a gator's underbelly.

"Stay with me, boy," the man said.

Parker didn't answer.

Somebody else took Parker's pulse from his good arm. "I got nothin."

Wilson locked eyes with Angelica for a moment, then raked bloody hands through his hair. Stepped back. Stared like a zombie.

The guy working on Parker's pulse shook his head. "I think he punched out."

No. No. No. A siren wailed in the distance. Too much distance. Angelica looked at Wilson and saw it in his eyes. The paramedics were too late.

CHAPTER 6

ANGELICA GOT OFF HER KNEES and sat on the edge of her mattress. Moonlight ghosted through her windows. Normally she'd have her bedroom lights blazing if she was awake. But not tonight. The darkness suited her mood. Parker was in the Naples Community Hospital. In good hands—at least that's what everyone kept saying. He'd cheated death—three times. Or was it four? The alligator nearly killed him. He'd almost bled out on *Typhoon*. He'd been strapped to the sinking airboat and could have drowned. And his heart actually stopped at Wooten's dock. Oh, yeah. Definitely four times.

The paramedics couldn't find a vein for the IV. Kept saying

things about Parker being "too dry for a good stick" and that he had "blown veins"—while Angelica stood there crying her eyes out. They'd actually drilled a connector port into his leg to get the fluids directly into his bone—then slapped the defibrillator paddles on his bare chest and gave his heart a jump-start.

Somehow he'd wrestled free from death's grip. *Four times.* Wilson's talk about an Everglades curse crept into her mind. Maybe there was something to it. What if Parker was marked somehow? Selected. Like he was the millionth person to go into the Glades or something—and he was the designated toll.

"You saved him, God. You know it—and I know it." There was no other explanation as to why Parker was still alive.

She hugged herself . . . and never felt more alone—or stupid. She knew better than to feed alligators in the wild.

And the thing was, Parker had been so antsy to leave. She'd taken advantage of their friendship, knowing he'd have a hard time saying no to her.

Why did she do it? Parker loved the outdoors. And in every other place their families had been stationed together he'd never seemed too concerned about bear or cougar or any other predator roaming the wilds. Tonight—just before the attack—was the first time she could remember seeing him anxious to get back to civilization. Why did she trample over that?

Parker's faith in God was so much stronger than hers. It wasn't Wilson's talk of some Everglades curse that made him want to leave. He didn't believe in that kind of stuff. Did the Holy Spirit nudge him to get out? That was the only thing that made real sense. Even Wilson had a split-second warning just before the attack. He didn't have a supernatural gift—but the guy was super-aware of his surroundings when he was in the Glades. All his talk of cheating death—or maybe his superstitions—kept him in a high-alert state when it came to mortal danger. More on edge.

The real question? What was wrong with *her*? She was the only one who didn't see the danger coming. Wasn't she supposed to have some level of women's intuition? Why didn't she sense something? Or could it be she wasn't listening? She was so focused on getting the pictures she blew right past any warning signs she might have seen—and discounted Parker's growing uneasiness. She absolutely had to have those pictures, and Parker paid the price. She'd led him right into the alligator's jaws. Served him up on a platter for the beast.

You're an idiot, Angelica. Parker was her best friend. They'd grown up together. She never thought she'd see the day when he died—or be the cause of it. But it *was* her fault. Her decision had killed Parker—even if he was only dead for a couple of minutes.

One of the paramedics said Parker was incredibly lucky. But Angelica didn't believe in luck. Which was a good thing, because luck never held. It changed. And if this was all about luck, it was only a matter of time before Parker's turned and he was doomed.

She would never, *ever* put her friend in harm's way again. And she'd tell him tomorrow—if she could find a ride to the hospital. She'd never encourage him to go out into the Everglades again, either. In fact, she'd do everything in her power to keep him out of the Glades. Death did its best to steal Parker from her. She wasn't about to give the reaper another swipe at him.

Angelica looked out the window at the empty driveway. Heard the night sounds of the Everglades even through the glass. She slowly traced her lips with the tip of her tongue. Tasted Parker's blood—even though she'd wiped her mouth on her sleeve hours earlier. His life . . . on her lips. She wished she hadn't wiped a bit of it off.

The thing was, the Everglades had a taste of Parker's blood too. Literally. What if in some freakish, bizarre way there *was* a curse? What if the curse couldn't be satisfied with a taste? Which was ridiculous. Jelly had never been superstitious, and she wasn't going to start now. But what if there was something to the Miccosukee lore? What if Parker's blood had only awakened the Glades' appetite for more?

CHAPTER 7

Sunday, June 14
12:32 p.m.

ANGELICA WOULD *NEVER* ACCEPT a ride from Clayton Kingman again, no matter how desperate she was. How Maria could still be dating the guy was a total mystery, an absolute brain-bender. Even with her big sister sitting between them, the creep was way too close.

Maria's best friend, Rosie Santucci, offered to give the girls a ride to the hospital in Naples—but Clayton insisted on doing it himself. Part of his little control games.

Clayton's pickup had the extended cab with a second seat, but it was loaded with tarps, empty beer cans, a cooler—and who knew what all else. Angelica had actually hauled the cooler to the bed of the truck to make room for herself, but Clayton made her put it back.

"You'll sit up front with us." He just had to show her who was in charge—or he wanted to annoy her. Probably both. "And make sure there's nothing sharp in your back pockets before you slide in."

She stared at him. "Really?" Exactly what did he think she carried around, scissors or something?

The way he watched her climb up next to Maria could make a girl's skin crawl. "I wouldn't want you scratching the leather."

Scratching his eyes out was a whole lot more likely.

Clayton was twenty-one—but he drove all the way to Naples like a senior citizen. He knew how desperate Angelica was to see Parker, which was obviously why he'd stretched an easy forty-five minute drive into something well over an hour, including a stop for gas. He even took the time to clean bugs off the windshield that had probably been baking there for a month. The guy was a total creep.

Angelica unbuckled her seat belt the moment Clayton pulled into the hospital parking lot.

Clayton draped his arm around Maria's shoulder like there was no hurry at all. "Going to wait 'til I park to jump out, *Angel*?"

He was the only guy on earth who could make the name Angel sound disgusting somehow. "To you I'm Angelica," she said. "My mom is the only one who calls me Angel." She should have let it go, but Maria did way too much of that.

"Your mom is *back* . . . after all those months without a word?" He had that mock-sincerity thing going again. "When did *that* happen?" He leaned forward to make eye contact. "You should throw her a little welcome home party."

She stared out the windshield instead. *Don't answer him. Don't.*

Maria patted Clayton's thigh. "You know what she meant."

"But the way Angel—sorry—*Angelica* said it, I thought for a moment that your long-lost mommy had actually returned to the family she'd abandoned."

Out of Angelica's peripheral vision she could see his eyes, the intense way they bugged out when he was making a point. It was a family trait. She wasn't going to give him the satisfaction of looking at him. "Do you have to work at being so mean, Clayton?" Challenging him was always a mistake, but somebody had to do it. "Or does it come naturally?"

"Biting the hand that feeds you?" Clayton clucked his tongue. "Not smart, Angelica. Really stupid, in fact."

The only thing she was biting was her own tongue. What would Clayton do if she really told him what she thought of him? The real question was what Maria would do. Then again, Angelica already knew where her sister's loyalty leaned—and it scared the living daylights out of her.

"I think you owe me an apology, Angelica," Clayton said.

"For saying you're mean?" Why was it the moment she questioned something *he* said, she was expected to apologize?

He leaned forward to look around Maria, so that his eyes drilled directly into Angelica's. They looked dark. Rabid. "I guarantee you, Angelica. You've never seen me mean."

The threat in his tone unnerved her. She looked away. "I hope I never do."

"That's the first smart thing you've said this entire ride."

Maria forced a laugh. "She's sorry, Clay. I think she's a little emotional about almost losing Parker."

Was that the best Maria could do to stand up for her little sister? Angelica was sorry her sister was going out with Clayton—and sorry she accepted the ride from him—but not one bit sorry for calling him mean. "Look, I just want to get out of your truck and see—"

"Apology accepted."

His voice carried a smugness. Like he'd won a victory. But if she knew Clayton, this wasn't over. Not for him. He didn't simply want an apology. He wanted her to grovel. And he'd likely keep at her until she did.

Clayton drove slow enough down the rows of parked cars to annoy her, but too fast for her to jump out. For the moment, she was his prisoner—a little fact he seemed to be enjoying. He passed an empty parking space. Then a second.

"How about that space?" Maria must have sensed Angelica's frustration.

He drove right by it. "Just want to find something closer for our little Angelica here."

Our Angelica? Clayton possessed absolutely no part of her. Never would.

Clayton fingered Maria's hair, his hand brushing Angelica's shoulder as he did. Accident? *Right.* Angelica pressed herself against the passenger door.

He drove—no, make that *crawled* down the aisle. If her legs were long enough she'd stretch over and step on the gas herself.

Maria squeezed Angelica's knee like she understood. "Everything's going to be all right."

Why did people always say things like that when bad things happened? Did they really think those six little words would bring comfort? The truth was they had no idea what was going to happen. "Think he'll lose his arm?" She regretted asking Maria the moment the words came out.

Clayton snickered. "That'd be rich. The whole thing is ironic, don't you think? The park ranger's kid becomes gator-bait."

"Clayton." Maria said it like he was just a mischievous little boy.

But he wasn't a little boy. He was four years older than Maria. And he wasn't just mischievous. It ran way deeper than that. There was something twisted about him. He was a gravy-sucking pig.

What did Maria *see* in that guy anyway? For an instant, she pictured Clayton in the Everglades, an alligator ripping *his* arm off. Preferably the one around his sister's shoulder. Angelica smiled.

Clayton eased the truck into a handicapped parking slot.

"You need to have a *physical* disability to park here," Angelica said. "Emotional ones don't count."

"Ooohh," Clayton said. "You really don't know when to stop, do you?" Clayton reached across Maria and stroked the back of Angelica's head.

Angelica jerked forward and glared at him. Clayton was the one who didn't know when to stop. That smirk on Clayton's pretty face was one of the things Maria said she loved about him. Which proved just how different two sisters could be.

"Can't we get a ticket for parking here?" Maria said.

"Who uses handicapped spots at hospitals?" He cut the engine. "All the gimps are inside."

Angelica shouldered open the door. "Meet you in there, Maria." She took off running for the front entrance and didn't look back.

There were already several people waiting for the elevators. She took the stairs two at a time to the third floor instead.

She didn't break her stride until just outside Parker's room. She stopped abruptly, wishing for a moment that she'd waited for Maria. The door to room 324 was open. From this angle, she could just barely see Parker's dad, still in his park ranger uniform, leaning on his elbows in the chair next to the bed. Vaughn Buckman was the most decent man she'd ever known, and she probably loved him every bit as much as her own dad. Parker's dad was a man of action. Integrity. A solid follower of God, unlike her own dad. He wasn't a blood relative, but she'd known him as Uncle Vaughn her whole life. He rocked slowly. Eyes closed, hands clasped, and thumbs massaging his eye sockets like he was lost in prayer.

Knowing Parker's dad, he probably was. Angelica couldn't explain it, but that was part of the strength of the man.

Angelica took a couple of deep breaths and tucked some stray hairs behind her ears. Uncle Vaughn's eyes opened, almost like he'd sensed she was there. He smiled and motioned her in.

She tried to smile back, but it probably looked just as fake as it felt. Angelica stepped into the room, but stopped the moment she saw Parker's face. It was like seeing him lying on the dock all over again. Deathly pale. Eyes closed. And she'd done this to him.

She'd expected him to look better somehow. More alive. His arm was wrapped in enough gauze to outfit a mummy. At least he still had an arm to bandage.

Uncle Vaughn stood. "Angelica." He stepped around the bed and wrapped his arms around her.

She melted into him. "I'm so sorry."

"Nothing to be sorry about. It wasn't your fault. The way I hear it, you helped save his life."

First, she *put* him in the danger that nearly cost his life. *Then* she helped save his life. The tears came and wouldn't stop. "How is he?"

Uncle Vaughn took a deep breath and blew it out. "He's strong. He'll be okay."

More tears. Uncle Vaughn patted her back.

"His arm?"

"Messed up good. Crushed ulna. Torn veins. Arteries. Extensive nerve damage. Hundreds of stiches."

Angelica looked at the neat bandaging hiding the devastation underneath. Only the tips of his fingers were visible—but even they looked awful. Swollen stumps, stained nearly orange from the antiseptic. "But he'll get full use of it again, right?"

Uncle Vaughn hesitated . . . way too long. "Jury's still out on that one."

She looked at Parker. Tubes. Monitors. Two—no, *three* IV bags dripping life-giving solutions into him. "But they can fix that—I mean, eventually?"

Uncle Vaughn didn't exactly look hopeful. "Three surgeons worked on him half the night. They're doing what they can. Right now, they're just trying to save it."

She groaned. "What do you mean?"

"Infection."

Of course. Every one of the alligator's teeth ripping through his arm left a deadly trail of bacteria. Gator venom. "Oh, Uncle Vaughn." She reached for him again. Held him tight.

He gave her a squeeze. "You'll pray for him, won't you?"

"I haven't stopped." But she wasn't exactly a prayer warrior. That was Uncle Vaughn's department.

Uncle Vaughn nodded. "Good girl."

Parker stirred. Eyes fluttered.

Angelica stepped closer. "Parker? Hey, Parker, it's me."

A faint smile creased his face. "Jelly." His voice sounded thick. Hoarse—and as weak as he looked.

She took his cap off her head and set it on the tray next to his bed. "I came to return your Wooten's hat."

His eyes drifted closed for an instant. "About time."

Tell him, Angelica. Tell him you're sorry—and that you'll never pressure him to go into the Glades again.

Maria breezed through the open door at that moment, eyes full of concern. "Parker Buckman. You scared us half to death."

Parker licked dry lips. "Scared myself pretty good too."

Clayton shuffled in. "Hey, Gator-bait. Sleeping in?" The smirk still there.

What Angelica wouldn't give to see her sister deck him—or dump him.

"Gator-bait," Parker slurred. "Hoping that one doesn't stick."

Uncle Vaughn didn't look any happier about the nickname than Parker did.

Clayton stepped up to the foot of the bed. Hands tucked in his back pockets like this was all routine. "I've lived here my whole life, and no gator has ever tried to get a chunk of me."

"Which is hard to imagine," Angelica said, "knowing how much alligators like rotten meat."

Clayton smiled, but there was something in the look he shot her that triggered an icy chill down her back.

"You haven't lived here four months, and you get mauled?" Clayton shook his head. "Somebody needs to school you on living in the Everglades."

Was he making a dig at Parker's dad? And what did Clayton know about school? He was taking a "break" from school right now. Who drops out of community college?

"Only an idiot would hold his arm out over the water when alligators are around," he said.

Parker closed his eyes. Maybe he just couldn't stand seeing Clayton. If only it were that easy to make him disappear. Just close your eyes and poof—he's gone. "Helpful advice, Clayton. I'll remember that."

Uncle Vaughn reached into his pocket and pulled out some singles. "Do me a favor, would you, Clayton?" He handed off the money. "Find a vending machine and pick me up a couple candy bars. I really need some chocolate. Get one for yourself, too, for the trouble."

Clayton stared at Parker's dad a moment like he was trying to figure him out. He shifted his eyes to Maria. "Coming?"

She shook her head. "I think I'll stay."

He shrugged. "Whatever. Be back soon."

Uncle Vaughn waved him off. "Take your time."

Angelica smiled at Uncle Vaughn. *Genius move.*

The moment Clayton sauntered out of the room Parker's eyes opened. He looked up at Angelica. "Thanks for coming, Jelly."

Maria stepped closer. "Clayton drove us. Wouldn't take no for an answer." She smiled. "A real hero, that guy."

She was always doing that. Trying to make Clayton look good to everybody—especially her dad. It was nauseating. "Your hero made us chip in for gas."

Maria laughed. "Give him a break. He was almost on empty. And he left so quick to drive us that he forgot his wallet at home."

She actually looked like she believed that bunk.

Parker studied her for a moment. "You really like that moron?"

Maria blushed. "I do."

Angelica's stomach did a 360.

"Be careful," Parker said. "He's more messed up than my arm."

Maria shook her head. "He's a little rough around the edges, but most people just don't understand him like I do. Underneath that tough facade he's a real sweetie."

Parker looked up at her and squinted, like he'd looked directly into the sun. "What if the *sweetie* part is the facade?"

Maria laughed again. Tapped one of the IV bags. "What kind of drugs are they giving you, Parker?"

"Sodium Pentothal," Uncle Vaughn said.

"Isn't that . . . ?" Angelica looked at Parker's dad and smiled. *Truth serum.*

Maria leaned over and kissed Parker on the forehead. "Just get well."

Parker's cheeks showed the first bit of color since before the accident. Angelica felt hers burning too. For an instant, she willed him to brush the kiss off with his good arm.

"What was *that*?" Clayton stood in the doorway, holding a couple of Snickers bars. He had that bug-eyed thing going again.

"A little get-well kiss," Maria said—like she didn't even notice the expression on Clayton's face.

Actually, it looked like Clayton was glaring at Parker. But Parker's eyes were closed again.

Clayton slapped the candy bars down on the food tray. He turned and marched toward the door.

Maria looked confused. "Where are you going?"

"Need some fresh air."

He totally looked like he was playing the martyr card. Like she'd wounded him or something. Maybe he expected her to kiss *him* to make everything better. Disgusting.

He stopped in the doorway and turned back toward Maria. "Coming?"

Part of Angelica actually hoped Maria would join him—and she felt just a tinge of guilt about that. But how would she ever talk to Parker alone otherwise? And the things she had to tell him were best said without an audience.

"I think I'll stay a little longer," Maria said. "You mind?"

Clayton shook his head. "Not at all."

But that's not what his eyes said.

CHAPTER 8

WILSON HATED THE SMELL OF HOSPITALS. Every fifty feet there was one of those stupid hand-sanitizer stations—and one in each room, as far as he could tell. He was pretty sure hospitals only put them there so visitors could feel like they were doing something useful to protect the sick and dying. Like they were actively helping somehow. It probably didn't matter much one way or the other, but he slathered it on anyway—and kept his eyes locked on the doorway at the end of the hall. Room 324.

He tried to imagine what Parker's dad would say. Maybe he'd reach out to shake Wilson's hand—and crush it in a viselike grip. Maybe he should go into the room with his hands still dripping with the slimy disinfectant goop. It would be harder for Mr. Buckman to get a decent grip on him.

Should he have brought something? A plant? Balloons? Which

was absolutely ridiculous. But still, he wished he had something in his hands. Something to hold. Or maybe some kind of a peace offering . . . a way of saying he was sorry.

For everything.

"You didn't do anything wrong, Wilson. Not really." He actually said it aloud like he truly believed it.

Or wanted to.

"Just get it done." He headed for the doorway and didn't slow up. He reached for the alligator-tooth necklace around his neck, pulled it over his head, and balled it up in his fist. It was the perfect gift. All he had to do was slip it to Parker.

He squared his shoulders and strode into the room like he wasn't blaming himself for putting Parker there. He stopped three steps inside, right next to the hand-sanitizing station. Seeing Jelly and Maria was like a total gift. At least he didn't have to be alone with Mr. Buckman—who probably hated him right now.

"Wilson." Maria put her hands on her hips. She had that *what-were-you-thinking* tone.

What was he supposed to say?

Jelly rushed over and gave him a hug. Always the one to make someone feel like they weren't a total screw-up.

Mr. Buckman walked around the foot of the bed toward him. Wilson stiff-armed the sanitizer paddle, releasing a foamy dab of the slippery stuff just in case.

Parker's dad reached out and grabbed Wilson by the shoulders. Looked him right in the eyes.

Wilson couldn't bear to hold his gaze. He stared at the floor instead. "Sorry, Mr. Buckman. I messed up. Almost got Parker killed."

He gripped Wilson's shoulders tighter. "But you got him back . . . and for that I'll be forever grateful."

Wilson still couldn't look him in the eyes. Was he for real?

Maria marched over and poked Wilson in the chest. "I'm not so quick to forgive . . . *or* forget. You go out feeding alligators again and I'll feed you to one personally."

They all burst out laughing. Mr. Buckman. Maria. Parker. Even Jelly couldn't seem to help herself. Which totally melted the tension of the moment.

Wilson walked over to Parker's bed. "You look like a total mess."

Parker grinned. "Pretty much how I feel too."

"Your mom is gonna kill me, right?"

Parker gave a weak smile. "Maybe you better not be here when she gets in."

"Flying in from Boston even as we speak," Mr. Buckman said.

And she'd just gotten up there. "What about that news story she was doing?"

"She fixed it up with her editor. He got another freelancer to cover it."

Just one more thing that Wilson had messed up. He couldn't remember what the story was about, but getting the assignment was some kind of a big deal. Parker called it a career game-changer.

Wilson examined Parker's arm, but didn't touch it. After how bad the thing was mangled, he was kind of surprised it was still attached. "She'll never let me take you back out in the Glades." He tried to make it sound light. Maybe get another laugh.

"I won't either," Jelly said. She looked at Parker like she was expecting him to promise he'd never go back.

Parker didn't say a word, which was good in Wilson's book.

Actually the best thing Parker could do for himself would be to get back in the Everglades. Soon. Parker glanced at his dad like there was something he wanted to say, but he was looking for the green light.

Jelly stepped closer to Parker's bed. "I think we should make Parker swear never to go in the Everglades again." She turned to his dad—a dead-serious look on her face. "What do you think?"

Okay, she was going way overboard on this. There was no way Parker should make any kind of lame-o promise like that. And Wilson definitely didn't want her putting any ideas in Mr. Buckman's head. Parker would go back into the Everglades. Wilson would make sure of it. He opened his hand to give Bucky the gator-tooth necklace.

"I don't think," Parker's dad said, "we'll have to worry about Parker in the Glades anymore."

The way he said it made Wilson think he was missing something. Like there was more that Parker's dad wasn't saying. Maria and Jelly seemed to pick up on it too.

"What do you mean?" Jelly said.

Parker looked away.

"I put in for a transfer early this morning," Mr. Buckman said.

Wilson got that sinking feeling in his gut. He closed his fist around the necklace and drove it into his pocket. Maria squeezed her eyes shut.

"We'll be leaving Everglades National Park."

Jelly's lips parted slightly—like she couldn't believe what she'd just heard. "No . . ."

Clayton Kingman walked into the room. "You're moving?" He had this permanent smirk on his face. "Dude. Kind of a knee-jerk reaction, right?"

Mr. Buckman shot Clayton a look—like he wanted to jerk his knee right into Kingman's face. *That* was definitely something Wilson would pay money to see.

Kingman raised both hands and stood behind Maria.

The ticked-off look on Mr. Buckman's face disappeared as quickly as it had appeared. How did he do that?

"Where?" Maria's voice sounded flat.

Mr. Buckman shook his head. "I didn't give any preferences."

So he wasn't being picky with where they were willing to move—meaning the transfer would likely come quicker. Actually, Wilson kind of agreed with Kingman on that little point. This *was* a knee-jerk reaction.

Jelly slumped into the empty chair, like she knew exactly what all this meant—or maybe she saw it as her fault.

"You'll be missed." Kingman's tone wasn't hiding what he really must be feeling. The ranger who'd arrested him twice for hunting in the off-season was going to leave for good. Kingman would probably do backflips down the hallway.

Maria had this zombie look going on. "And *my* dad?"

Mr. Buckman hesitated. "That's not for me to say."

Suddenly Maria looked like she wanted to tear someone's head off. "He'll put in for a transfer too—I know it."

Wilson gave her space. He backed up to the doorway of the room, wishing he'd never come.

"That's what you two do . . . ever since the academy," Maria said.

Her eyes had this vicious look to them. Wilson had never seen her like this. Maybe Kingman was wearing off on her.

"One gets a new assignment, and the other transfers to the same station. Right? Grand Canyon. Rocky Mountains. Redwood.

Here. Where's it going to be this time?" Maria had fire in her eyes. "My mom got sick of it. That's why she left us—she couldn't take it anymore."

"That's not why she walked out." Parker's dad said it so quietly, Wilson almost missed it. "I think you know that." He reached for her.

Maria backed away—right into Kingman's arms. "I won't leave."

By the look on Kingman's face, he was just beginning to figure out what he might lose in the deal. Or rather, *who*. "Wait—your family would move too?"

"Let's go," Maria said. She pulled away from Kingman and marched to the doorway. She brushed past Wilson, then spun around and stopped. "Come *now*, Angelica, or find your own ride."

Jelly didn't move, and Maria disappeared into the hall.

"I'll drop you off," Mr. Buckman said.

Jelly reached for him, threw her arms around his neck, and sobbed into his shoulder. Wilson glanced down the hall, pretty sure nurses would come running—thinking someone had died. Kingman still stood there.

Kingman pointed at Parker, then at Wilson. "This is on you." It came out as more of a growl. "This is your fault. Both of you."

Kingman was half right, anyway.

He stormed into the hall, then stopped and motioned Wilson out to meet him.

Wilson hesitated—and glanced at Angelica and Bucky's dad, hoping one of them would tell him to stay put. Which felt kind of stupid. What was Kingman going to do, slug him right here in a hospital?

Maria was halfway to the elevators by the time Wilson stepped into the hall.

Kingman slung his arm around Wilson's shoulder and neck and steered him out of the line of sight from anybody in Bucky's room. He clamped down on Wilson's trapezius muscle with a grip that made his legs buckle for an instant. "The idea of Maria moving." Kingman leaned in close. "Honestly, that has me spitting mad." He didn't ease up on his grip. "You boys fix this. Got it? Or I'll fix you."

CHAPTER 9

Sunday, September 13
2:00 p.m.

SURGERY. HOSPITAL. REHAB. More surgery. Physical therapy. *Lots* of physical therapy. That was Parker's summer. He'd figured the transfer would have moved him out of the area long before school started, but that hadn't happened yet. Parker started his freshman year at Everglades City School just like Wilson and Jelly.

Typhoon had been pulled from the water and overhauled, and was tearing through the Glades again—although Parker hadn't gone back on the airboat once since the death roll.

And Mom was back in Boston on another writing assignment. This time she was going to be gone two or three weeks. It was just Parker and his dad, which meant they'd be eating a lot of quesadillas for dinner.

He'd done his best to avoid Clayton Kingman, but that had proved harder than Parker imagined. Everglades City was small, and the island town of Chokoloskee—where Parker, Jelly, and Wilson lived—was even smaller. Kingman never missed a chance to rub in the whole Gator-bait nickname. And with every month that passed, Kingman seemed more and more confident that the whole transfer thing would never happen. The good news? He wasn't threatening Wilson and Parker anymore.

One huge downside of the delayed transfer was going to Everglades City School. Clayton's dad was the principal. In all the other schools Parker had attended, the principals were decent. It was obvious they cared about their students. But Principal Kingman must have missed his true career calling. The guy would have made a better prison warden than a principal. He had security cameras all over the school and a bank of monitors in his office. He could pull them up on his phone, too. He'd warned the entire student body that there was no corner of the building he couldn't see. But honestly? He didn't need security cameras. Bradley B. Kingman was everywhere—watching everything. He didn't simply walk the halls. He patrolled.

Whenever Principal K looked at Parker, it seemed like he was trying to read his thoughts. Like the principal assumed he was up to no good, and it was his job to bust Parker before he could carry out his dastardly plans. No matter how hard Parker tried to do the right thing, Mr. Kingman watched him with a suspicious eye. Maybe it had something to do with Parker's dad being a ranger—and busting Clayton. Maybe not. But one thing was for sure. Everglades City School was Principal K's empire, and he made it his business to control every corner of it.

The Kingmans—both father and son—had done wonders for

Parker's prayer life, though. He prayed harder than ever for the weekends to come quick—and pass slow. He prayed for the transfer. Prayed for a ticket out of this place so his life could be normal. Good again.

Parker was pretty sure every area of life would be better once they moved. He'd be away from the Kingmans. If Dad's transfer was anywhere near Boston—like some of the rumors Dad had heard—Mom would likely be home more too. And he was certain that somehow his arm would recover faster if he lived somewhere else. All he had to do was get out of this place, and everything would be okay.

Parker sat on the front step of his porch waiting for Wilson and pressed the fingers from his bad arm into his other palm. Part of his therapy homework. The burn in his forearm started immediately. He gritted his teeth and kept pushing until his arm shook. He started the *one-one thousand* slow count to thirty. By fifteen he wanted to scream. Was dying for relief. Even at thirty he didn't ease up. *Five more seconds*. Just in case he'd been counting too fast.

By the time he spotted Wilson biking up the block, Parker was working on his hand grip with the rubber gripster ring. Wilson carried a wooden pole, maybe six feet long, like he was ready to joust. He skidded to a stop, tossed the closet pole on the ground, and swung off the bike.

"Still doing your exercises, I see."

Parker nodded. Anything to strengthen his gimpy arm. "A long way to go, though." If it was going to get better at all. Even three months after the mauling, he didn't have more than sixty percent of his function back—which wasn't good. "What's with the stick?"

Wilson grinned. "*Stick?* This is inch-and-a-quarter solid hard oak with a hand-rubbed wax finish for a better grip, my man. And it's part of your *new* therapy."

Just what he needed. More ways to torture his arm into cooperating. Parker eyed the rod. "Pole vaulting?"

Wilson snickered. "Way more fun. You're making a gator stick."

He'd seen guys in the Glades carrying one. Sort of like the gaffing hook he kept in his boat, but heavier—and stronger. Usually they were outfitted with some kind of spike on the end. "I'm not going near any alligators."

"Exactly." Wilson jabbed at an imaginary predator. "This will keep the gators from *you*."

"So will staying out of the Everglades."

"This is noggin therapy." Wilson tapped Parker's head. "I'm going to help you get your head straightened out."

Parker laughed. "Nothing's wrong with my head."

"Said the guy who still won't go near the Everglades. You can't avoid the Glades forever."

True, Parker had kept clear of the Everglades for the three months since the accident—which wasn't easy in a town practically surrounded by the swamp. As much as he'd loved the Glades before June 13, he pretty much hated them now. After what happened to his arm, nobody would call him crazy. Except maybe Wilson.

"This is for your own good," Wilson said. "You need to do this, Bucky."

All Parker had to do was hold out until Dad's transfer came in, which could be soon. Steering clear of the Glades didn't mean there was anything wrong with his head. Somehow over the course of days he spent in the hospital, the Everglades had become enemy territory. Parker was determined not to go back behind enemy lines. Ever. "What I *need* is to get out of this place." Out of southern Florida. Away from any state where alligators—or Kingmans—existed. "This isn't about fear, Wilson. This is about *escape*. Once I get away from here, everything will fall into place."

And he believed that. The total change of where he lived would solve all his problems—and give him a fresh start.

"You still having the bad dreams?"

Parker didn't answer. He wished he'd never told Wilson about them.

"You think they'll just magically go away after you move?"

Actually, he did. But then he'd never thought he'd still be having them now. Not every night, but definitely every week. He'd seen a therapist before being discharged from the hospital, but it didn't seem to make any more of a difference than his physical therapy did for his arm. He'd prayed about it too, but for some reason the nightmares hadn't stopped.

Wilson looked at him like he'd just read Parker's mind. "PTSD is something you've got to beat—not bury."

"Post-traumatic stress? Seriously?" Even the thought of PTSD scared the swamp water out of him. The gator left scars on his arm, but not in his head, right? "That's something soldiers get in battle situations. Not fourteen-year-olds."

"And you weren't in a battle for your life with that gator?"

"Totally. But that doesn't mean I've got PTSD—or that I'm burying anything," Parker said. "I just want out of Florida."

"Like *that* will make everything okay? *You* . . . are an idiot. Escape isn't the answer, my friend. There is no escape." Wilson thumped his head again. "How can you escape what's up here anyway? My people say—"

"Please—not another piece of Miccosukee wisdom." A change

of geography was all he needed. If he didn't live in a town under siege by the Everglades he'd get past this.

"The United States government tried to eliminate my people back in the eighteen hundreds."

Parker knew all about the local history.

"They could have run—like you want to do. And if they did, I'm sure they would have died out. But they didn't run. They hunkered down. Dug in. Held their ground. Faced the thing that threatened to undo them." He flexed his muscles. "It made them stronger."

It was an amazing story, really. The Miccosukees chose the least inhabitable place to live. They chose a place that was absolutely deadly for the soldiers pursuing them. The cost to the US government to take out one Miccosukee was staggering.

"My people were outmanned. Outgunned. Maybe they were out of their minds. But they were never conquered, Bucky. Never. Conquered."

It was true. Parker had seen the *Never Conquered* T-shirts so many local Miccosukees wore. They were probably the only group of Native Americans in the entire country who hadn't been wiped out or relocated. But Parker wasn't a Miccosukee. He didn't need to stay here. Didn't need to adapt or make the best of a bad situation. "I just need to get out of here, Wilson."

Wilson waved him off. "You have no idea what you need. C'mon, soldier." Wilson pulled a half-dozen nylon zip ties from his pocket. "Grab a blade from your room—we're mounting it to the end of this stick."

"Which blade are you talking about?" Parker had four machetes, two dive knives, a survival knife, and at least seven pocketknives in his bedroom.

"Something super strong. Your dad's old dive knife will be perfect." Wilson led the way to the workbench in the carport. "We have to hurry."

"What's the rush?"

"Noggin therapy starts," he checked his phone, "in about forty-five minutes."

Parker laughed. "Good luck with that." Since the accident, Wilson had crashed and burned every other time he'd tried to get Parker back in the Glades. But making the gator stick sounded like fun.

Parker hustled to his bedroom. The sign his grandpa had made him for his birthday was mounted above his headboard—and the stainless steel dive knife hung on the wall beside it. The brand name Dacor was stamped deep in the black molded handle. The vintage knife was from the early 1970s—and a total classic. He was pretty sure the company had disappeared long before he was born. The knife was one of the best gifts his dad had given him.

He pulled it halfway out of the plastic sheath. The blade was made from steel thick enough to use as a pry bar, with a serrated edge on the spine for sawing. The point curved upward slightly, with an edge as sharp as a surgeon's scalpel.

Parker glanced at the sign again. A single word, *INTEGRITTY*, was carved in clear pine. Spelled—or rather *mis*spelled—just like that. Grandpa had carved it for Parker's fourteenth birthday. The extra *T* was no typo—at least that's what Dad said when Parker got it. "You'll figure it out one of these days," Dad said. But it was still a mystery.

"Parker?" It sounded like Wilson poked his head in the front door. "Did you die in there or what? We gotta move."

Moments later the two of them stood at the workbench.

"Now," Wilson said as he held the handle up to one end of the gator stick, "we need to notch out the wood so we can snug the handle to the stick real tight." He grinned. "We don't want that blade shifting when you jab a gator—right?"

"Right." Parker circled his ear with one finger. "You're crazy if you think you're getting me into the Glades."

"We'll see."

Parker used a half-round file to shape the end of the stick to the contours of the handle while Wilson held the pole steady against the bench. Filing was awkward at first. His right arm didn't have the strength—or the steadiness of his left. Parker struggled to keep his filing smooth and even. If Wilson noticed, he didn't say anything.

"So, this noggin therapy . . . exactly how does it work?"

Wilson blew the sawdust away from where Parker filed. "Simple. We go to the Glades. Climb back on the horse."

But he hadn't taken a fall off a horse. He'd been mauled by a gator—and he didn't want to be within a mile of one ever again. "Not happening."

"Trust me."

Parker laughed. "Trust *you*?"

"You'll thank me when this is over."

"It's not even starting." Parker set the knife handle in the hollow he'd filed for it. Together they used pliers to snug the nylon ties tight, holding the knife firmly in place just like a bayonet on a rifle. They mummy-wrapped a length of parachute cord around it just to make sure it didn't budge.

Parker lifted the gator stick off the bench and tested the weight. It felt good in his hands. Balanced. He sighted down the length of it. Straight as a spear. He gripped it with both hands and jabbed at the air. "I love it."

Wilson admired the finished weapon. "What are you going to name it?"

Parker laughed. He hadn't seen that coming, but Wilson clearly wasn't joking.

"You name your boat. You name your bike. Your survival knife. You've got to name a sweet stick like this." Wilson ran his hand along the oak shaft. "How about *Conan*? Or *Terminator*?"

Naming the stick after a barbarian or a sci-fi antihero wasn't turning the crank for Parker. He wanted something a little quirkier—and definitely less serious. The stick wasn't going to be the survival weapon Wilson imagined. It was going to stand in the corner of his bedroom.

"C'mon," Wilson said. "We need a name for this thing."

An old song from the same era as his dad's knife looped in Parker's head. A ballad about some guy who'd lost his arm to a gator. Parker's grandpa sent a YouTube link shortly after the accident, probably trying to be funny. The song stuck in Parker's head, though, and played back at the craziest times. He smiled. "Amos Moses."

Wilson looked at Parker as if trying to tell if he was messing with him. "Weird. But so are you." He grinned. "Amos Moses it is. Better grab some mosquito spray. And a head net."

"I'm not going into the Everglades. I told you."

"Then you'll look like a total wimp. Our ride will be here any minute."

"Our *ride*?"

"Where we're going is too far to bike."

As if on cue, Clayton Kingman's black Chevy pickup rounded the corner and roared down the street toward them. Oversize tires with tread as deep as the ridges on a gator's back. "Tell me that isn't our ri—"

"Hey, I can't stand him either," Wilson said. "But I was at Jelly's telling her about the gator stick we were going to make—and trying to get her to understand why we had to get you back in the Glades. She was *not* happy, I'll tell you that. I think if her dad were home, she'd have marched right over and told him to drop me off in the middle of the Glades and make me swim home."

"Now *that* sounds like a good idea," Parker said.

Wilson waved his comment off. "Anyway, Kingman was there with Maria, and he backed me up. Said you'd be a wimp the rest of your life if you didn't go."

"Oh, yeah. I'm sure he'd love to see me go back in the Glades," Parker said.

"He was all over the idea. Next thing I know, Maria sort of volunteered him to drive us. I felt cornered, you know?"

"He threatened you in the hospital—did you forget that?" Parker couldn't believe this. "He hates us."

"Honestly," Wilson said, "that was months ago. I think Kingman forgot all about it. That was only if Maria moved, anyway. And she hasn't."

Even from a half block away it was obvious that both girls were in the truck with Clayton. "There's no way I'm getting into that pickup."

"He actually looked happy about driving us," Wilson said. "And you really think he'd try to hurt us with Maria there?"

Not physically, but the guy had other ways of hurting everyone around him. Putting them down. No, *beating* them down with his words.

"Look." Wilson sounded just a little desperate now. "You're always talking about doing the right thing. Well this is it. If you won't do it for you, think about Jelly and Maria."

"What does this have to do with—?"

"I'll explain later," Wilson said. "Just don't back out."

"Back *out*?" Parker glared at Wilson. "I was never *in*."

Elbow hanging out the driver's window, Kingman pulled into the driveway way too fast. He hit the hooks and slid to a stop on the gravel, not five feet from where Parker and Wilson stood. If Parker had jumped out of the way or looked scared, Kingman would have won his little game. Kingman locked eyes with Parker—like he knew how hard Parker fought to stand still.

Kingman blasted the horn, and Parker instinctively jumped. Kingman leaned back against the headrest with that "gotcha, boy" look in his eyes.

Maria sat up front with the jerk. She was actually leaning against him. *Sick.* Jelly sat in the second seat of the double cab.

Kingman leaned out his open window. "C'mon, Gator-bait. You're burning daylight."

Parker hesitated. His eyes met Maria's. She angled her head sideways slightly, like she was disappointed in him or something. Did she really think he'd be revved up to do this?

Kingman laughed. "Told you the gimp wouldn't do it. Poor little fraidy-cat ranger's kid."

Parker could have turned and walked away. Which was exactly what he should've done. But he stood there unable to move. He caught Jelly's eyes from the back seat. She looked nervous, but he couldn't read exactly why. She shook her head slightly. Okay, she was trying to tell him not to do something. Don't wimp out—or don't get in the truck?

Honestly? He didn't like either option. Either he'd be labeled a coward, or he'd be pressured into playing the fool and going where he didn't want to go. Terrific.

There was only one way to shut Kingman's stinkin' mouth, though. Parker marched over and dropped Amos Moses in the bed of the truck. "I have to get a long-sleeved shirt." The mosquitoes would drain him if he only wore his T-shirt.

"Make it the orange one," Wilson said.

"Just make it fast." Kingman revved the engine. "I don't have all day."

Parker ran into the house—and wished he could run right out the back door and keep going. But he was trapped, wasn't he?

He pulled his orange UV-blocking shirt over his head. Why did Wilson tell him to wear this one? He grabbed his day pack and tossed in the face-netting and mosquito spray. He'd need a weapon. He reached under his bed for his Gerber LMF II Infantry model survival knife. He'd named it Jimbo—after the legendary maker of the Bowie knife, Jim Bowie. It still gave him a rush every time he strapped it on. With its partially serrated stainless steel blade the thing could cut through anything. And with the sharpener actually built into the sheath, he kept the thing razor sharp. It was ready for action every time he pulled it out. He strapped Jimbo to his calf and rolled his pants back over it. He could only imagine the stupid comments Kingman would make if he saw he'd brought it.

He wished Mom wasn't in Boston. She could have come up with some excuse to keep him home. He whipped off a quick note to his dad and left it on the kitchen table. It wasn't likely he'd stop home in the middle of his shift, but he didn't want his dad worrying if he didn't see Parker around. His dad gave him a lot of leash, and Parker appreciated it. Not telling Dad what he was up to was a great way to lose that privilege.

A minute later he was back at the truck. He tossed the pack in the bed alongside Amos Moses.

Wilson met him at the bed. "Sorry, bro. This isn't exactly how I pictured this going down."

How could he have expected any different? "I'm going to kill you when this is over."

Wilson grinned. "I think Jelly will help."

Parker followed Wilson into the extended cab.

Jelly was already buckled in. She leaned forward to look past Wilson. "Sorry," she mouthed.

Which was the weird thing. Since the accident she seemed to be just as determined to keep Parker away from the Glades as he was himself. But here she was, going along for the ride.

Kingman spun his tires in reverse, the sound of gravel and crushed shells pelting the wheel wells.

Parker could feel the sweat trickling down his scalp. He clenched and unclenched his weaker fist. Stretched his forearm.

Wilson leaned close. "I did this for your own good—you know that, right?"

"Absolutely. And if Amos Moses 'accidently' sticks your bee-hind when we get out of this truck, know I'm doing it for your good too."

Wilson laughed.

"Exactly where are we going?"

Kingman looked at him in the rearview mirror. "Best place in southern Florida to get a real Everglades experience." He glanced out the front windshield for an instant, and then was back—like he didn't want to miss Parker's face when he dropped the bomb on him. "Gator Hook Trail."

Parker's stomach twisted like it would have crawled out of the truck if it could. He'd never ventured down that trail—and for good reason. During this season, Gator Hook was a wet trail—as in, it led right out *into* the Everglades. "No way."

Kingman laughed like he enjoyed making Parker squirm. "Meow."

Parker stared out the side window as Kingman sped over the causeway, through Everglades City, and finally east onto Tamiami Trail, the two-lane highway heading through some of the densest wilds of the Glades.

Dad led small, elite tours down Gator Hook Trail when he'd first been assigned to this station. Three fully armed and experienced rangers went with every group, just to be safe. One led, another stayed midway in the column of hikers, and one took shotgun. Literally—one ranger carried a twelve-gauge pump-action. Parker could smell the Glades on Dad's clothes when he'd come home. Sometimes his pants would be soaked to his waist. He'd wanted to take Parker on the trek, but it had never worked out. And after the accident, there were no more offers.

"Gotta make a pit stop," Kingman said. He pulled into Wooten's Airboat Tours—one of the biggest tourist attractions in the area. Wilson's dad took visitors out into the Glades on huge airboats that could easily carry fifteen passengers. "Air barges," Wilson called them.

Kingman parked right up front in the handicapped section, where there was a clear view of the docks and tourists loading and unloading for airboat rides. "I'll only be here a minute."

As if that little explanation made it okay to park there.

Wilson slouched back in his seat the moment Kingman trotted out of sight. "Why couldn't he do that before he picked us up? If my dad sees me riding with Kingman? He'll have my hide."

And Parker's dad wouldn't exactly be thrilled to hear where he was headed—or that he was getting a ride with Kingman, either. Dad was a people person. He found something to like about almost everybody. But Kingman was "bad blood," he'd said. And not just because he gave the rangers such a hard time. Parker sensed there was something more that his dad wasn't saying.

"I'm not sure how I'll explain this to my dad either," Parker said.

Wilson gave him a sideways glance. "You'll be back long before his shift is over. Why even tell him?"

Parker thought of the sign over his bed. "It's the right thing to do." His grandpa was a man of integrity—and so was his dad. Parker intended to be one too. But doing the right thing wasn't always easy. For a moment he wondered if he should get out of the truck and abort this whole thing. He could phone his dad to pick him up.

Suddenly Kingman hustled up and swung behind the wheel. He pulled back out on Tamiami Trail, tires squealing.

By the time they passed the Skunk Ape Research Headquarters, Parker was wishing he'd never gotten in the pickup—no matter how bad it made him look to Maria or Jelly.

Wilson leaned forward against the seat belt. "You've spent a lot of time in the Glades, Clayton. Ever seen a skunk ape?"

There was a picture of one in the gift shop of the research building. Grainy. Distant. But it definitely looked like a sasquatch: the legendary bigfoot—or a skunk ape, as they called them here.

The rearview mirror framed Kingman's eyes like a mask. But the driver was looking at Parker, not Wilson. "No skunk ape. But I've seen some spooky things in the Glades. *Crazy* spooky. Things that would make guys like Gator-bait here pee in their pants." He glanced out the windshield, then back to the mirror—looking directly at Parker again.

Those eyes were as scary as anything Parker might see in the Everglades. *Charles Manson eyes*, his dad called them. Whatever that meant.

Kingman slowed to turn off the Tamiami onto Loop Road. How did Parker get himself into this? Clayton tromped on the gas. The pickup bounced and lurched across a series of potholes. The monster tires kicked up a smokescreen of dust behind them. Amos Moses banged around in the bed like even it knew this was a bad idea and wanted out.

Parker had been down this gravel road with Dad. Once. Surrounded by water, the twenty-six-mile route cut through a small section of no-man's-land in the Everglades known as Big Cypress National Preserve. Loop Road eventually caught up to the Tamiami Trail again, but there was plenty of weird stuff before it did. Some homes at the far end of Loop Road—or the people who lived there—were definitely dialed in to the strange side of the emotional spectrum. They made it clear with signs—and other ways—that they didn't want visitors. Nobody would ever catch Parker knocking on their door.

Kingman eased off the gas and pulled over to a couple of tables under a shelter roof. "Gator Hook Trail," he said. A cloud of dust passed over the truck and drifted into the jungle-like brush at the trailhead.

They piled out of the truck, and the mosquitoes swarmed them immediately. Parker pulled the netting over his cap, slipped his pack over one shoulder, and grabbed Amos Moses from the bed.

Kingman stood watching, a stupid smirk on his face. He nodded toward the gator stick. "Nice shepherd staff, Bo-Peep. I don't think you'll find any sheep where you're going." He pointed toward a warning sign bolted to one of the shelter support posts. Bears, alligators, panthers, and venomous snakes were pictured. No sasquatch. And definitely no sheep.

"Are you really going to do this?" Maria had a doubtful look on her face.

"Of course he's not," Kingman said. "Call us when he chickens out." He waggled his phone. "Meantime I'm going to take Maria on a little drive down Loop Road and back." He pulled her close. *Sick*. What on earth did she see in that jerk?

Maria and Kingman climbed into the truck and backed away. Parker turned his back to Loop Road. He didn't want to give that sleazeball the pleasure of thinking he was admiring his truck.

The start of Gator Hook Trail was clearly marked, and Wilson led the way. Jelly fell in behind Parker. The trail sloped downward slightly, then narrowed as the brush closed in from both sides. Parker alternated scanning the overhanging branches and the sides of the path for snakes.

Wilson's footprints in the black mud weren't the only ones visible. But how long had it been since anyone had ventured out here—and did everyone make it back?

The brush and overhanging trees gave way to a huge expanse of water—with the trail leading right into it. Short grasses and clumps of sawgrass rose above the surface, thick enough in some areas to give the illusion that there were patches of dry ground. But there weren't. Cypress trees formed a line in the offshore distance like there was an island out there. Another illusion. There wouldn't be a foot of dry ground for miles and miles and miles. The cypress thrived in the water.

Wilson stopped. "The trail goes back something like two and

a half miles. Ends in a cypress forest. You'll see markers every once in a while—like that one." He pointed to a small yellow circle of spray paint on the trunk of a spindly tree. "You won't get lost. Trust me. And put this on." Wilson took off his gator-tooth necklace and handed it to Parker. "This has always kept me safe."

Parker stared at him. He didn't need Wilson's necklace to keep him safe. But having Wilson himself around could come in handy. "You're not going in?"

He shook his head. "What good would that do you? This is a head game you gotta play alone. This is mental."

"You're mental if you think I'm walking out into the Everglades by myself." Parker fought back a sense of fight or flight welling up inside him.

"Parker's right," Jelly said. "I thought *we* were going with him. I never agreed to this."

Jelly and Wilson went at it nose to nose. Parker didn't try to stop them. Not that he expected them to work out his problems. He needed to do that himself—and right now.

Parker quietly stepped back from his friends. The thing was, Wilson honestly thought this was what Parker needed. He could be right, but was Parker willing to bet his life on it? One thing was for sure: If he did sense trouble, Wilson wouldn't let him fend for himself. He'd be by Parker's side. And hadn't Dad taken groups of hikers on the Gator Hook Trail "wet tour" dozens of times when he hadn't seen *any* alligators up close? What if this *was* the best way to end the nightmares?

He looked out over the still waters of the Everglades. Endless. Instinctively he looked for alligators. Now he got why Wilson wanted him to wear the orange shirt. It would be easier to find him if he didn't come back. This was insane. "God," he whispered, "what should I do?"

"What if something happens?" Jelly was practically shouting now.

"Something *will* happen." Wilson wasn't exactly using his inside voice either. "He's going to get his courage back."

Get his courage back? Couldn't Wilson see Parker was just using his head—and that his determination not to go into the Glades had nothing to do with being afraid?

"He's got plenty of courage," Jelly said. "It's just buried under a mound of fear right now. And for good reason."

Buried under a mound of fear? Nice. She thought he was scared too. The fact that she thought he had a good reason to be afraid didn't help much. He'd survived a death roll from the biggest gator he'd ever seen—and fought his way back to the airboat. He'd struggled to free himself when the angel of death had him in a full nelson. Pushed himself every stinkin' day to do the physical therapy despite the pain. Yet Wilson and Jelly had him labeled as a coward, just because he kept his distance from the place that nearly killed him.

Is that the way it would always be? If this was what his best friends thought of him, what did everyone else think? Which was one more reason he had to get out of this place. Make a fresh start somewhere. In a place where people wouldn't see the labels people plastered on him here.

Jelly and Wilson kept at it. Arguing back and forth about Parker as if he wasn't even there.

Parker tuned them out. Stood at the water's edge. An egret stood on its stilt-like legs, poking around with its banana beak, searching for food just twenty yards away. It didn't look one bit worried about predators. *What's wrong with me?*

This *was* an issue of courage, wasn't it? Or rather, the lack of it. Wilson was right. Parker *was* afraid. And he was right about another thing too. He wasn't just afraid when he was in the Everglades. The fear was part of him. Inside. He felt it at night. In his room—safe from the swampy Everglades. And wherever Dad got transferred, would that fear get boxed up somehow and follow Parker in the moving van? Would it catch up with him no matter where he went?

He prayed to God it wouldn't. And at the same time he knew the fear had to be conquered. Here. In the Everglades, right where it started. Could taking Gator Hook Trail free him from the nightmares? Could it free him from the labels others stuck on him?

Parker stared out over the seemingly endless expanse. Maybe going in alone would help, but honestly? Could he even do it?

"If Parker climbs in Kingman's truck with dry pants, he'll know he didn't wade into the Glades," Wilson said. "Then Maria will lose more than that twenty-dollar bet."

Wait—Kingman put money on Parker chickening out? Is that what Wilson wanted to tell him before they left?

"He'll rub her nose in it every chance he gets—yours too."

Kingman definitely would. Maria trusted that Parker would take the trail—even though Jelly seemed to hope he wouldn't. Deep down they both believed he'd do the right thing. And a man of integrity does the right thing—even when he's scared.

How could he let them down? He wouldn't be simply wearing labels after that. They'd be tattoos. Something he'd never outrun.

He *had* to go in—without Wilson and Jelly. But he wouldn't be alone, right? Didn't Jesus say he'd never leave one of his followers?

He took a deep breath. Let it out. Slipped Wilson's gator-tooth necklace over his head. Not that he put any faith in the thing, but it did feel good around his neck. There was only one place to put his faith. He knew that.

"Okay, Jesus," he whispered. "I really wish I could walk on the water like you. But I'll settle for you walking *in* the water with me now."

He gripped Amos Moses—and stepped into the warm waters of the Florida Everglades.

CHAPTER 10

"I NEVER AGREED TO THIS," ANGELICA SAID. "I thought we were all going in *together*." She should have stuck to her guns. She'd been all about keeping him out of the Glades. How did she let Wilson talk her into this?

Wilson smiled, but he wasn't even looking at her.

She followed his gaze and saw Parker—already a good thirty feet from shore and in water up to his shins.

No.

"Wait, Parker—you don't have to do this."

He didn't look back. "I think I do."

Angelica took a step toward him, but Wilson grabbed her arm and spun her around. "What are you doing?"

"Going with." Or she'd stop him. Convince him to come back to shore.

"And when your sister's boyfriend sees *your* pants wet, what's he going to say?"

"I really don't care."

"He'll totally discount the fact that Parker went in," Wilson said. "He'll say Parker only went in because someone went with him."

Jelly groaned. Wilson was probably right, which infuriated her more. Clayton was such a sleaze. "I don't care what Clayton Kingman thinks."

"Maybe Parker does."

She totally disagreed. Parker despised Kingman. Why would he care what the guy thought of him?

Parker was taking it slow. Deliberate. But he'd doubled his distance from them already. He turned back for an instant. "Exactly how far am I supposed to go?"

"Follow the trail markers. I was here early this morning and tied my hat to the trunk of a cypress. You can't miss it. It's about a mile out."

"A mile out—into the Everglades?" Jelly hauled off and slugged Wilson on the arm—hard. "Are you out of your Miccosukee mind?"

Wilson ignored her. "Bring back the hat, and you've passed your therapy session for today."

Parker gave a single nod. He had that determined look on his face. He was putting up a tough front, but he was scared. Only someone certifiably insane wouldn't be.

Like Wilson.

"And for extra credit, walk a little farther until you see a cypress with a massive strangler vine around the trunk. Bring me a picture and I'll buy you pizza."

Parker waved him off, scanning the surface of the water as he did. Without a word, he started wading through the water again.

Wilson pulled out his phone, set it on the video mode, and took a quick shot. "Just in case Kingman doesn't believe he did it."

"And if something happens to him," Jelly said, "I'll turn it in as evidence against you as an accessory to murder."

Wilson laughed. "You're ridiculous, you know that? He'll be fine."

No, if *Wilson* was out there alone, *Wilson* would be fine. The guy was Teflon when it came to danger. But Parker? The Everglades had marked him. Claimed him. Somehow he'd wrestled free from its death grip, but now he was walking right into its clutches. He may not be so lucky this time. "What about the curse you talked about. The toll, remember?"

"I thought you didn't believe that stuff."

"I don't." But that didn't stop the sense that she was on the edge of the airboat again. Helpless. Watching. Expecting a gator to drag Parker under at any moment. She shielded her eyes against the sun. In her head she knew the curse was ridiculous. But in her heart? Somehow she had to get her head and heart working together.

Parker had the sheath off the blade strapped to Amos Moses. Even from this distance she could see Parker's shoulders were hiked up. Tense. Did he see something?

If she knew Parker, he was praying at this very moment. She definitely didn't have the level of faith in God that Parker did. But walking into the Everglades was stupid. And faith or no faith, did anyone have the right to expect God to bail them out when they weren't using the good sense He gave them?

"You have any trouble," Wilson shouted, "just give a whistle, and I'll be out there—pronto."

Parker raised one hand but didn't turn to look back this time. He kept his eyes on the water in front of him.

Parker definitely had a loud whistle, but still, the idea of relying solely on a whistle wasn't making Angelica feel any better. "What if we don't hear him?"

"Sound carries across the water. I could hear his whistle from two miles out—maybe more. Unless you don't shut up, of course."

Slogging a mile back into the Everglades? "But what if we don't get out there in time?"

"I'll get there."

"Really? And what can you do if he's attacked? You weren't exactly jumping off *Typhoon* into the water to help him when he got mauled."

Wilson clenched his jaw but didn't say a word. But she was pretty sure her words packed a lot bigger wallop than her punch did.

Parker wasn't supposed to go back in the Everglades. He was tempting fate again.

No, not fate.

He was thumbing his nose at the Everglades themselves. Giving them another chance at the one who'd been chosen by the Glades to pay the ultimate toll—but had lived to tell about it. She didn't believe Wilson's Miccosukee superstitions, yet couldn't totally discount them either. Which bothered her. She just needed more faith. There was no such thing as a place being cursed, right?

Then again, there were stories of places that were cursed in the Bible. Hadn't Parker told her that once? Jericho—the famous fortress city whose walls collapsed when the Israelites marched around it seven times and shouted. After the city was destroyed, Joshua pronounced a curse on the site. Whoever would rebuild that city's foundation and set the city gates in place would do it at the cost of his firstborn *and* his youngest son. Angelica didn't understand it all, but years later—when Jericho was rebuilt—it happened just as Joshua said it would. Only God could truly curse a place. Could He have put some kind of a curse on the Everglades as well?

Honestly, she didn't know what to think. But to completely throw aside all caution was gambling with Parker's life, right? That was one thing she could be sure of. Anyone walking into the Everglades alone was on a collision course with disaster—toll or no toll.

Parker approached a stand of scrub trees maybe fifty yards from shore. The spot where the trail took a turn. He hesitated. For an instant, he looked back and waved Amos Moses at them. The blade caught the sunlight. It flashed and winked at her like it was part of some inside joke. Or was Amos Moses sending a signal—a distress call?

Parker turned and walked deeper into the Everglades before she could raise her hand to wave back. Seconds later he disappeared completely from view.

CHAPTER 11

FIND THE HAT. FIND THE HAT. Parker scanned the trees ahead for any sign of it. The water was over his knees now, but it was clear—when he wasn't picking up glare from the sun. If he couldn't see the bottom, he'd have turned back by now. Still, he kept the blunt end of Amos Moses ahead of him in the water, doing a side-to-side sweep of the bottom. Alligators could stay under for who knew how long . . . waiting. For what? Some idiot like him to walk into them.

The stainless steel blade of the gator stick was just above his head. If anything attacked from behind, he'd raise the blunt end of the stick and thrust behind him. He doubted the dive knife on the other end could penetrate the gator's armored hide, but it would keep the gator from getting his teeth in him.

Hopefully.

He spotted the next yellow spray paint circle. Good. He was still on track.

Parker glanced behind him, halfway hoping Wilson and Jelly would be there. Waving him down. Refusing to let him do this alone. Trying to catch up.

No such luck.

Which was for the better, right? Kingman would never let up on him if he knew Parker didn't go in alone.

The truth was, he didn't care what Kingman thought. It was what *Maria* thought of Parker that mattered. But right now, it seemed that whatever Kingman thought mattered an awful lot to her.

What Jelly—and Wilson—thought about him mattered a whole lot right now too. Probably more than it should. And maybe if they stopped labeling him as a coward, he could stop doing it himself.

The bottom looked like mud, but it was just a thin layer of sandy muck over solid limestone. Which meant his shoes weren't sinking into it like he thought they would. That was something anyway.

Twice he stepped into a solution hole—basically a pit or giant pockmark in the limestone base. They were filled with the muck, so there was no way to see it before he stepped in it. His foot would drop down a few extra inches before he hit rock. That split second before he touched bottom was totally unnerving. But he'd step right out of the hole again, and everything would be okay.

What would Dad say if he knew he was out here? Parker would have to tell him. Anything less would be dishonest, right? But Dad would definitely question Parker's judgment on all this. Disappointing Dad was about the last thing Parker wanted to do.

He'd rather not have to mention a word about Gator Hook Trail. But if he could pick and choose when to be a person of integrity, he wouldn't be a person of integrity at all. The more Parker thought about it, the more he was sure that Dad would understand why he had to walk the trail—alone.

But Mom would have a cow. Ever since the accident, she was just as anxious to move as Dad. There were days he'd come home from school and find her studying lists of US National Park posts, praying for God to lead in His perfect way.

Keep your head focused on what you're doing, Parker.

How far was he from shore? Not far enough to turn around and go back yet. And too far for Wilson to get there in time if he truly needed help. A blue heron flew overhead like there was nothing to worry about. From up there maybe. But down here?

He studied the surface of the water for an alligator head. For its eyes. Looked for telltale bubbles that might betray where an alligator lurked.

Nothing.

But that didn't mean they weren't around. Alligators were everywhere. Gator Hook Trail was a place of predator and prey.

And he was the prey.

He developed a rhythm. Sweeping the path with Amos Moses. Stepping ahead, each step carefully placed. Not so fast as to slosh the water. That would only attract gators. But not too slow where he'd be out here any longer than he had to.

He spotted the next yellow circle. How many had he seen so far? Six? Seven? The Glades stretched out in front of him in a wide-open section. Mostly short grasses poking through the water. He could see for probably two or three miles to his left and right. Ahead thick clumps of brush and trees reached out of the swamp like zombies coming out of a watery grave. Would the water trail lead through those? Farther ahead he could see the towering cypress. A whole forest of them growing out of the black waters.

If he were on dry land this would simply be a field. An open meadow on the edge of a jungle-like forest. He'd be in no more danger than he would in his own backyard.

But he wasn't on dry land. He was in the Everglades. The air was heavy. Not a breath of wind rippled the water's surface. He pressed on.

Halfway through the still expanse he stopped. He just stood there. Out in the open he felt safer. He planted the blunt end of Amos Moses on the bottom and rested it against his shoulder. Slowly he released his grip and reached for his phone. He took a panoramic shot—but even as he did it he wasn't sure why.

Maybe to prove he was really out there. Alone. Or maybe it was something more.

But if he didn't find the hat, at least he could show how far he'd gone.

He stood perfectly still. As if he could somehow blend with nature here. Maybe then he'd not be noticed by any wildlife that would see him as an intruder—or a meal. He willed himself to relax. Not let down his guard, but to take a breath. If Jelly were here she'd be telling him to take in the beauty.

Parker scanned the horizon in every direction as far as he could without moving his feet. It was gorgeous—in a way that nature always is. *Sometimes the most amazing places in God's creation are also the most dangerous.* Dad had told him that how many times?

"Jesus, thanks for keeping me safe so far. Keep it going, okay?"

Tiny fish—like minnows—surrounded him. Pecked at his cargo pants. He shook his leg slightly. The fish scattered, but in seconds they were back. Slamming into him. Bolder now. What was up with that?

"You're an intruder, Parker. You don't belong here." Time to move. Get this done. Get out.

He found the next trail marker sprayed on the trunk of a tree poking out of the water, surrounded by scrubby bushes and short grass. He made his way toward it, sweeping the water ahead of him with Amos Moses.

That moment of calm—or whatever it was he'd felt a minute ago—was gone. A sense of dread crept in like the water slowly reaching higher up his pant legs.

The Glades were rampant with nasty reptiles, and the trail wound through sections that seemed like perfect places for them to wait.

For a sucker like him.

How long had he been out here? It seemed like an hour. Still, he hadn't seen one alligator. That was strange. "Thank you, God." But he had a growing sense that they were watching.

Parker's phone vibrated in his pocket. Probably Jelly wondering if he was okay. Maybe he'd let her sweat a little. Truth was, he needed to stay on high alert—and definitely didn't need the distraction. He needed to watch. Listen. And keep both hands on Amos Moses.

He waded through and around patches of grass and brush big enough to hide the most dreaded evils of the Everglades. Gators. Pythons. Venomous snakes. He caught a break when the trail opened up for maybe thirty yards before being choked by the next screen of high weeds and heavy brush.

And then he saw the hat—tied to the trunk of a marker tree, just like Wilson said. He stood for a moment and stared at it, sensing there was something else there. Something he couldn't see. He had a sense that evil was closing in . . . and tightening like a noose around him. He got the definite feeling that he'd proven everything he needed to prove. Was it his own fears messing with his head, or was God telling him to turn around and leave the instant he got that hat?

He'd prayed for God's protection plenty of times since leaving shore—and didn't feel one bit of shame about it. And he wasn't about to stop now.

"C'mon, Parker. Grab the hat and get out. Grab the hat and get out." He took a couple of quick breaths and moved toward the orange Wooten's Airboat Tours cap.

He scanned quicker now. Left. Right. Behind him. Then back at his target. Maybe it was the way the sun hit the water, but it looked black now—and it rose nearly to his waist. Plenty deep for a gator to come at Parker without him seeing it until too late. He should have never come out here.

By the time he got to the tree his heart was thumping around in his chest like an animal trapped in a cage. He didn't bother unknotting the rope. Parker yanked the cap free and stared at it for a moment. Wooten's slogan ran through his head. *On an airboat, nobody can hear you scream.* And if a gator pulled him under, nobody would hear him scream out here, either. He stuffed the cap under his belt, noticing his hand shaking even as he did.

Euhh. Euhh. Euhh. Euhh.

Parker's stomach knotted. The cries of baby gators. And they were close. If the babies were around, mama would be nearby too.

There was no way he was going for the "extra credit" picture of the strangler vine. He had the unexplainable feeling that if he traveled any farther down Gator Hook Trail, he'd never get back to shore. Something was waiting for him just ahead. He knew it. Something bad was definitely going to happen if he stayed on this path. Even when both arms were strong, he was helpless to fight off the alligator. What did he think he'd be able to do if he ran across a gator this time?

C'mon, Parker. Keep it together.

He backed away from the tree. Scanning. Scanning. Always scanning.

And then he saw it. The unmistakable nose and eyes of a gator. No more than thirty yards up the trail. Maybe a nine-footer. Young. Fast. Aggressive. And likely hungry.

"Okay, easy now, Parker. You've got what you came for. Get out before that thing gets what *it's* coming for." He backed a few more steps away from the marker tree, keeping his eyes on the gator.

But there was no way he was going to walk backward all the way to shore.

He turned and sloshed back down the trail he'd just come from. The splashing made noise. Plenty of it. But he'd already been spotted. What difference did it make now?

A shoulder check proved the beast was still there, but the gator's back was exposed now, showing its full size. The serrated edge of its tail swept side to side lazily, like stalking Parker required no real effort on his part. Or maybe the thing was wagging its tail, sure he'd just found his dinner.

Parker tried to step up the pace, but his pants caused such drag he didn't feel he was going faster at all for the extra effort. He'd need to conserve his strength. If this came down to a fight, he'd need every bit of energy he had.

Through the thick brush and weeds again. Around the bend. He looked back.

The gator had cut the distance between them in half.

"Okay, God . . . you see that thing, right? I'd really appreciate it if you'd tell it to leave."

Parker pulled Amos Moses out of the water now. Sweeping the trail ahead was only slowing him down. He gripped it with both hands, like a spear, and pushed forward harder.

He made it to the vast open section. The swamp-meadow. But it didn't look the same. The beauty was gone. It mocked him now. The trees marking shore and the trailhead seemed impossibly far away.

The gator was still trailing him. And gaining. Was it just curious? Or hungry?

Parker hiked his knees higher, almost galloping. But he'd never be able to outrun the gator—not in water this deep. And wouldn't his frantic moves make the gator bolder?

He needed something to throw at the beast. Something to slow it down. A stick of dynamite would be perfect. All he could hope for was that the gator waited a little longer to attack. Long enough for Parker to get away.

He gave another shoulder check.

Oh yeah. The thing was definitely moving in on him. Its tail swinging rhythmically, like it was enjoying the hunt and didn't need to push hard to catch him. At this rate the gator would be on him long before he got close to shore. Parker didn't want the thing blindsiding him. If it got to within twenty feet he'd turn and face it with the business end of Amos Moses.

He worked himself into a high-stepping trot as he made his way toward the trailhead, glancing behind him every couple of steps now.

Suddenly a second gator surfaced fifty feet away—dead ahead.

Bigger than the one behind him. Between him and shore—and coming his way.

Parker stopped immediately. How did this happen? He was back in the water. Between two alligators. Something that wouldn't have happened if he'd stayed out of the Everglades, like he'd promised himself. He'd been an idiot . . . and now he was trapped.

CHAPTER 12

THE SUN'S REFLECTION OFF THE WATER practically burned holes into Angelica's retinas. At least it felt that way. Angelica shielded her eyes with both hands and kept staring out into the Everglades. Looking for any sign of his return. She should have gone with Parker. What was taking him so long?

"Do you think he's okay? Why wouldn't he pick up his phone?"

"He's fine—and probably trying really hard to ignore you," Wilson said. "I, for one, can't blame him. I'd pay twenty bucks for a little peace and quiet right now."

Was he really that sure? Did Wilson have some Miccosukee sense that Parker was fine? Angelica wanted to believe that. Needed to. But there was no such thing. She tore her eyes from the trail to look Wilson's way, hoping some of his confidence might rub off on her. But Wilson didn't look nearly as convinced as she'd expected. He scooped his knife out of its sheath. Bounced it in the palm of his hand.

Obviously even Mr. Invincible sensed something was wrong. As far from shore as Parker was, the water was deep enough for a gator to grab his leg without him seeing it coming. What if it pulled him under faster than he could signal for help?

"How long has it been?" She tried to sound casual. Like she hadn't already asked him twice in the last ten minutes.

"I think I'd pay *forty* bucks for that peace and quiet." Wilson paced along the shoreline but kept staring toward the bend in the trail where they'd last seen him. "Sixty-three minutes, give or take." He gripped the knife. Switched hands. Regripped.

There was no way Wilson believed everything was fine. "Maybe," Angelica said, "we should go in."

He didn't answer.

"How long did the trip take you this morning—when you tied your hat to that tree?" If it took him less than an hour they *had* to go in.

"Apples and oranges," Wilson said.

"What's *that* supposed to mean?"

Wilson hesitated. "Comparing the times won't do a bit of good. So let's forget it, okay?"

She did *not* like the sound of that. "Wilson—are you saying you're that much faster, or is there something you're *not* telling me?"

He gave a loud sigh. "My dad took me early this morning. Before he went to work. I used a kayak."

Angelica whirled around and glared at him. "You *paddled* out there? You sent *Parker* out into the Glades on foot—but you didn't even get your socks wet? I thought you'd walked the trail yourself to make sure it was safe."

"There wasn't time." Wilson shrugged. "But I kinda wish I did, now. I really have no idea how long it would take him to get there and back—on foot—in the water. It depends on how deep it gets."

"Do you even *know* how deep the water is out there?"

Wilson shook his head. "I've never seen it more than waist deep. Chest deep at the most."

"If I had that gator stick," Angelica said, "I'd whack you over the head with it and give *you* a little 'noggin therapy' right now." She took a deep breath. "I'm going in. Stay if you want, but I can't stand this any longer." There was no way she'd venture out there alone, but Wilson didn't need to know that. Maybe if she actually stepped off the shoreline, Wilson would join her. But they had to do something. "I think he's in trouble."

CHAPTER 13

"DEAR GOD . . . I promise you . . . if you get me out of this one I'll . . ."

He'd what? Never go in the Everglades again? Hadn't he just broken that promise to himself? Besides, he wasn't so sure he was in any position to bargain with God.

"Jesus, I know your Word says you'll never leave me, but I'm feeling really alone right now." That day on the airboat, he'd known the right thing to do. But he'd compromised and taken the photos. And today, he'd known he shouldn't get in Kingman's truck. But he compromised, and now look where he was at. If he was so serious about being a person of integrity—or doing the right thing—why did he keep compromising? It had to stop. And he would.

"God, I don't deserve to be bailed out again by you . . . but I'd really appreciate it." Was there a guardian angel assigned to Parker? If so, he was going to be busy in the next few minutes.

Parker stood sideways in the path, gauging the distance between him and the alligators. The one in front of him barricaded his way of escape—at least if he stuck to the path marked by the yellow paint. And would there be any point to swing wide around it? It would take him longer to get to shore—and give the alligators more time to do their deed. And if he did try a roundabout route, how many more gators would he encounter? How would he fight them off? And if he didn't stick to the trail, how would Wilson even find him?

Wilson. Maybe he could come from shore and scare away the one blocking the path to safety. There was no time to make a phone call, and he sure-as-shootin' wasn't going to let go of Amos Moses to dig his phone out of his pocket anyway.

He couldn't just stand here and wait for Wilson—or for the gators to get to him, though.

Handle the worst first. His dad's voice in his head. That worked for homework or jobs that needed to get done. He was pretty sure Dad never tried that approach on alligators.

He whirled toward the bigger gator . . . the one blocking his escape to shore. He'd whistle—and hope Wilson would come running. But Parker couldn't wait for him. When he got close enough, he'd charge the alligator. What other choice did he have?

Every step toward the gator would be a step closer to shore. "God, help me." He wiped his hands on his cargo pants and regripped Amos Moses. He whistled. Shrill. Sharp. And totally desperate.

CHAPTER 14

FOR AN INSTANT, Angelica and Wilson looked at each other, as if wanting to make sure they really heard Parker's whistle.

Immediately Wilson was in the water, sprinting toward the bend in the trail.

Angelica lit out after him.

"Stay back," Wilson shouted. "Phone for help if I'm not back in ten minutes."

She splashed through the shallow water. "You're not leaving me behind."

But he was widening the gap between them—fast. In almost any other situation she'd ask Wilson to slow up for her, but the thought of Parker out there alone kept her from asking. She pictured him—the way the alligator had thrashed him around that awful day in June. Now the Everglades were collecting on an old debt. Exacting their toll. The curse *was* real. "Run, Wilson—run!"

Angelica lost sight of Wilson for a moment when he whipped around the sawgrass and brush where the trail angled off. The water was over her knees when she got to the same spot.

The instant she cleared the bend she saw Parker—maybe half a football field out—and running their way. She heard him too. Shouting—no, *roaring* with some kind of primal war cry. He held Amos Moses out in front of him like he intended to shish kebob someone—or something. An alligator glided toward him . . . apparently undaunted.

No!

The thing was big. Ten feet?

Holding the gator stick with both hands, Parker lowered the blade to water level like he intended to harpoon the beast. He looked like a madman and the bravest person she'd ever known, all at the same time.

Arms pumping, his own blade flashing, Wilson bounded toward him. "Stick him, Parker! Run him through!"

Amos Moses carved a neat line across the surface. With a fresh roar Parker cocked both arms back and thrust at the gator.

He torpedoed it with enough force to make the gator writhe—even though the blade appeared to glance off without piercing the reptile's armor. It seemed Parker lost his grip—and his balance. He fell headlong onto the thrashing gator.

"Parker!" Angelica stumbled forward but regained her balance instantly. "Parker!" That's when she saw the second gator coming up behind Parker. The thing dove, its wicked tail snapping before it disappeared below the surface. "Behind you!"

Parker was on his feet again—but without the gator stick.

Somehow he'd pulled his survival knife from the sheath on his calf. Angelica was pretty sure the ten-foot alligator hadn't expected its prey to attack like he did. Feet wide, crouching like an animal ready to spring, Parker squared off with the confused beast. "Come on. Come on! You want me? Come on!"

Mouth wide and teeth gleaming, the alligator swung wide of Parker and disappeared under the dark waters.

Wilson sloshed to Parker's side, his own knife drawn to guard his flank. Seconds later Angelica joined them.

Parker whirled left. Then right. "Where is he? Where is he?"

Wilson shook his head. "You hit him good, man."

Parker looked Angelica's way—and apparently saw her for the first time. "Jelly—it's too dangerous out here!"

She threw her arms around Parker. "I thought you were going to die."

He pulled her close with his good arm. He still had the knife in his other hand. She pressed up against him and felt his heart hammering in his chest with a savage fierceness.

"We have to"—Parker gulped in air—"get out of here. Another one was trailing me." He released his grip on her and looked back at the trail leading off into the Everglades.

"Holy buckets, Parker," Wilson said. "That. Was. Amazing. Totally killer."

Jelly glared at him. "I'm about ready to kill *you*."

Wilson grinned.

Constantly scanning the surface of the water, Parker reached for the floating end of the gator stick. "Seriously. We gotta go." Knife in one hand, Amos Moses in the other, he nodded toward shore and led the way.

Jelly snatched his red Wooten's hat, slapped it on her head, and fell in behind him. He didn't even try to take it back—which was smart of him. She wasn't going to give it up just yet. Wilson took shotgun and walked backward, knife at the ready—just in case.

She watched the surface, left and right, looking for any sign of the rogue gator. She stayed as close to Parker as she dared without tripping him up.

By the time they rounded the bend Wilson had fallen slightly behind. Just a few feet, but enough to fuel Jelly's uneasiness. "Keep up, Wilson. *Please*."

He hopped in place for a moment, then hustled to catch up. "I am totally juiced."

Obviously true. Any more adrenaline and it would be seeping out his pores. He actually looked disappointed the gator hadn't attacked again.

Parker looked jumpy, and he didn't sheathe his knife until the water dropped to mid-shins. "Okay, Jimbo. Amos Moses will take it from here." He kept a white-knuckled grip on the gator stick.

"Did you get to the cypress with the strangler vine?"

Parker gave him the evil eye. "Ask me again and you'll feel a strangler vine around your throat."

Wilson laughed. "You didn't make it to my hat, either?"

Parker pulled the cap out from his belt and slapped it on his head. "It's mine now."

"Fair enough." Wilson smiled. "You earned it."

"Oh." Parker reached for the gator-tooth necklace around his neck. "You can have this back."

"You keep it, Bucky. You earned that, too."

The three of them stepped on shore seconds later. If it wasn't so muddy, Angelica might have knelt down and kissed the ground.

Wilson took the lead on the single-file path and chattered on.

And on. And *on* about his noggin therapy and how well it had worked and how Parker had conquered his fears and how much fun they could have on the airboat again.

Parker didn't say anything, not until they were nearly back to the gravel road. "If I never go back in the Glades again, it'll be just fine with me."

Which was a relief to hear, but somehow he looked different. Angelica studied his face. The fear she'd seen so clearly on the drive was gone. And he was smiling.

Maybe Wilson's crazy therapy worked. Maybe Parker had conquered his fear of the Glades. But Wilson's little plan backfired somehow, too. Whatever fear of the Everglades that had haunted Parker seemed to have transferred to her—and no amount of noggin therapy was going to change that. Not fear for herself. It was for Parker. It wasn't one bit logical, but in her heart of hearts, she feared the curse was real—and Parker had escaped death one more time.

The truth was, she *wanted* Parker to be afraid of the Glades, didn't she? It was selfish of her, but Parker's fear had kept him safe ever since the attack. If his iron resolve to avoid the Everglades really was gone, he'd actually be in more danger. He'd take chances again.

Even in this heat she felt goose bumps rising on her arms. She furiously rubbed them down—as if that would change anything. A raw dread welled up inside her. That same feeling she had on June 13 after the ambulance took Parker away. When she waited for word if he was going to make it. She was in a different kind of waiting room this time, but still wondering if he would survive. Somehow he was still marked by the Everglades. Singled out. Yes, he'd escaped today. But she knew just as certainly that his survival streak couldn't hold.

Wouldn't.

Angelica dropped back a good ten feet or so while the guys led the way through the jungle-like brush. Wilson jabbered on about how he should patent his noggin therapy.

Parker was flying high. She definitely hadn't seen him this confident since before the accident. He slugged Wilson in the arm—and Wilson tagged him back. Both of them laughed like it was the greatest thing.

What was it with guys?

The canopy over the trail thickened and blocked out the sky. That didn't dim her thinking a bit, and before they got back out in the sunlight she made a promise to herself. She would do everything in her power to keep Parker out of the Everglades. Not that she hadn't tried over these last three months, but now she'd double her efforts. The transfer would be coming. As much as she'd hate to see him leave, she felt like there was some kind of cosmic clock running. If Parker didn't get out of this place before the time ran out, he never would.

She shook off the dark thoughts and followed Wilson and Parker through the last of the brush and into the open. Clayton was there, holding Maria's forearms down at her side—and he was all in her face. "I'm not arguing with you," Clayton said. "You're the one arguing."

The instant he noticed them coming, he let go of her and backed away.

Maria stood there rubbing down her arms, then wiping tears from her cheeks like she didn't want Angelica to see them.

It seemed like they were constantly fighting lately—and Clayton always won, one way or another. It was always Maria who ended up doing the apologizing.

What did you bully her about this time? Angelica glared at him. Let her eyes say what she didn't dare. He smiled back. She totally wanted to smack that smug grin off his face.

"Here comes Bo-Peep," Clayton said. "Still have your shepherd's staff, I see."

Parker didn't answer. Amos Moses in hand, he stopped at the passenger door of the truck. He angled his head slightly as if trying to piece together why Maria was crying. "You okay?"

"She's fine." Clayton couldn't say two words without coming off arrogant. Condescending. "Right, sweets?"

Maria nodded and gave the fakest smile Angelica had ever seen.

"Looks like someone totally peed his pants." Clayton pointed at Parker. "Don't even think of getting in my truck unless you're sitting on a towel."

Parker stared at him for a moment . . . holding Amos Moses like he was thinking of using it to stick Clayton like that ten-foot gator.

If only it were that easy to chase Clayton away.

"I didn't bring a towel," Parker said. "I didn't know we were heading to a wet trail."

"I didn't know we were heading to a *wet* trail," Clayton mimicked. "I figured your mama made you wear a diaper anytime you got near the Glades. I had no idea you'd wet through like that."

Angelica wanted to stuff a diaper in his big fat mouth.

"There's a couple tarps in the bed." Clayton jerked his thumb toward the back of the pickup. "Pull one into the cab and sit on it."

Parker looked at Maria once more, then walked to the bed without a word.

"And I'm going to need a little gas money from you kiddies," Clayton said.

He was just looking for a fight, wasn't he? Someday, somebody would give him one too. Angelica hoped she'd be there to see it—and to give a gigantic hug to whoever beat Clayton to a pulp.

Wilson brushed past Clayton and climbed into the truck, but Clayton didn't say a thing about his pants being wet. Or about Angelica's. For some reason, Parker was the only one in Clayton's twisted sights today.

Angelica glanced at Clayton—still outside the truck and watching Parker pull the tarp from the bed. "So what did you two fight about *this* time?"

"It was my fault," Maria said. "I had no right to talk to him like I did."

What? "He had no right to pin your arms down like *he* did—or to get so angry at you." She glanced over her shoulder. Parker stood behind the truck, shaking dirt off the tarp. Clayton pulled open the driver's door.

"Drop it," Maria whispered. "It's over."

"What's over?" Clayton looked from Maria to Angelica and back.

They were over—as far as Angelica was concerned.

"Nothing," Maria said. "We're fine."

Why did she cave like that?

Jelly looked at her sister's smeared mascara. This relationship with Clayton had gone on long enough. Her stomach turned. She glared at Clayton. In that instant, she made herself another promise. She was going to do everything in her power to bust the two of them up. For Maria's own good. She should have done that long before this, but Maria had always talked her out of it.

She'd keep that blood-sucking leech away from her sister. And she knew exactly how she was going to do it—even if that meant snitching.

CHAPTER 15

PARKER STARED OUT THE SIDE WINDOW and did his best to tune out Maria and Kingman's stupid conversation. His adrenaline rush seemed to have drained out of him the moment he'd belted himself in Kingman's truck. Regret took its place. As much as he was relieved to be done with Gator Hook Trail, he'd done it all wrong, hadn't he? He should have told his dad where he was going—right up front. Gotten his permission. And the truth was, he knew he was making a bad choice at the time, but he kept going. He'd been an idiot.

On Gator Hook Trail he'd made a decision to stop compromising—hadn't he? And if he was serious about that, he'd need to fess up to his dad about what he'd done. The thought soured his stomach.

Before passing Wooten's on the drive back, Parker gave himself a deadline. He'd tell his dad tonight. It was the right thing to do. He hated the thought of how disappointed his dad would be, but maybe it would help him work harder at doing the right thing from the get-go next time.

A dog ran onto the oncoming lane of Tamiami Trail like the thing was being chased. A Jeep Wrangler clipped it. The driver didn't even tap the brakes. There wasn't time. The dog tumbled directly into the path of Kingman's pickup—and the Wrangler kept going.

Kingman swerved to the shoulder and braked so hard that Parker's belt dug into his chest.

"Oh my gosh!" Maria gripped the dash. "Clayton—he's hurt."

The dog struggled to get on its feet.

"Clayton," Maria said, "you have to do something."

Kingman killed the engine and elbowed open the door. "Give me a hand, Gator-bait. The rest of you stay in the truck. We don't want to spook the pup into running and getting hurt worse."

The last thing Parker wanted to do was follow Kingman. But the way Kingman likely saw it, he was doing Parker a big favor by giving him a ride—and now he owed him. There was no way he could refuse Kingman. Besides, how weird would he look to Maria and Jelly if he refused to help a wounded puppy? He unclipped his belt and ran to catch up with Kingman, which wasn't easy with his sopping-wet clothes.

Kingman motioned for him to slow down. "You're going to scare him, idiot."

It was a golden retriever—with a collar and leash dangling from it. The thing looked young, no more than a year old. It stood on three legs, with its hind leg hiked up at an awkward angle.

"Easy, pup." Kingman advanced slowly. "I'm just here to help."

Parker never pictured him as a dog lover, but he actually looked like he cared. Weird.

"I had a golden," Kingman said. "My mom got it for my eighth birthday. Named him King."

No real surprise on the name choice.

"But he barked, you know? My dad hated the yipping." Kingman knelt down and patted his thighs to coax the wounded puppy closer. The retriever's ears went flat against his head. "I tried to keep him quiet. God knows I tried. Kept him in my room at night. Even smuggled a box of Cheerios out of the kitchen. King was always barking at something he'd hear outside in the night, so I'd give him some snacks right away, you know, to get him quiet."

"So you trained him to stop barking?"

Kingman didn't answer. Just kind of stared at the puppy. "My dad got home real late one night. King barked and barked. Man, I got a fistful of Cheerios—put it right in front of King's nose. Begged him to take them. But he wouldn't listen. King was on a mission to prove what a good watchdog he was or something."

For just a second Parker saw Kingman—and what he might have looked like as a desperate kid trying to keep his puppy quiet. "So King didn't stop barking?"

Kingman shook his head. "My dad stormed into the room. *There's only one king in this house—and nobody barks at the king.'* Those were his exact words. Said anybody who couldn't keep a dog from yapping had no right to own a pet. I promised him I'd do better. King would never bark again. My dad laughed and clipped the leash to King's collar anyway."

Parker couldn't believe Kingman was telling him all this. "So what happened?"

"He took King for a ride in the car. I waited up—with the

Cheerios." Kingman shook his head. "But King wasn't with him when Dad got back. Never saw him again. I never ate Cheerios again either."

Parker didn't even know what to say. He'd been seeing Kingman as a total scumbag. This didn't change his opinion, but now maybe he had a little intel as to why.

"Come here, puppy." Kingman patted his pockets, like maybe he was wishing he had some Cheerios. He reached for the retriever's collar. The dog nipped Kingman good.

Kingman jerked back and sucked the blood off his own hand. And in that instant, his whole face changed. Got harder somehow.

He reached for the dog again, but this time the retriever backed away, a low growl rumbling up from deep inside it. "Don't want to be friends? Okay . . . have it your way. My old man was right. I got no right to have a pet." Kingman glared at Parker. "Gator-bait, win that dog's trust—right now."

Thankfully, the Tamiami Trail was quiet today. There wasn't a car or truck in sight. Parker eased around Kingman, walking slow. "Easy now. Nobody's going to hurt you." He reached out a hand, and the dog hobbled toward him—giving Kingman a wide berth. The dog sniffed Parker's hand and rested its head against Parker's leg. A tag dangling from the collar read *Snak-pak*. "Hey, Snak-pak. I'm not going to hurt you. We're just going to get you some help." The dog's tail wagged a couple of times, then drooped back down. "There's a phone number on the tag."

Kingman hesitated for a moment—like he was struggling with a decision. He whipped out his phone. "Read me the number."

Seconds later Kingman had the owner on the phone and set up a rendezvous. By the time he disconnected, he was smiling like Parker had never seen him smile before. "Get this. The guy bought

Snak-pak for their sixth-grade son, who loves it to pieces. The kid was sick when he thought the dog was gone. It's going to be some reunion when they get Snak-pak home."

Parker never pictured Kingman doing something that decent. Was this the side of him that Maria saw? "You did the right thing."

Kingman's smile faded. "Now you sound like my old man—always telling me what was the right thing to do, like he was Mr. Perfect. But he's nothing but a hypocritical poser. A pompous, pet-hating pig." He spit on the side of the road.

The guy could change moods quicker than the Jeep had clipped Snak-pak.

"You'd better not repeat what I told you," Kingman said, "not one word about my puppy as a kid—or so help me you'll wish you hadn't."

Parker avoided Kingman's eyes. He reached both arms under the dog's chest and belly. "Easy now, Snak-pak." The moment he lifted, the dog squirmed a bit. "Trust me, okay?"

"You hear me, Gator-bait?"

Parker nodded—still focusing on the wounded puppy. "I got you, Snak-pak. We're not going to let anything bad happen to you."

"You remember what I just told you," Kingman said, "or you won't be so lucky."

CHAPTER 16

PARKER'S DAD HAD BEEN WORKING extra shifts with Uncle Sammy—like he usually did when Mom was out of town. He still wasn't home by the time Parker flopped into bed. He sent a text to his dad, telling him he needed to talk when he got off shift, no matter how late. Parker didn't want to take the chance that he'd change his mind. He'd stared at the INTEGRITTY sign on the wall—waiting to hear Dad's F-150 pull up the driveway. The moment he did, Parker left his room and told his dad everything. Wilson's noggin therapy idea. Riding in Kingman's truck. Gator Hook Trail—and getting trapped between the gators. And he told Dad about his decision to show more integrity . . . to work harder at doing the right thing.

Dad had taken it all as well as a parent possibly could. Not that he didn't get frustrated that Parker hadn't gotten permission first—and that he'd taken such risks. And Dad definitely laid down the law in more than one area. But deep down Parker knew his dad was proud of him. For facing his fears on Gator Hook Trail, sure. But mostly for his renewed commitment to do the right things.

Despite all the bad choices, Dad said Parker had reached a whole new level on his "trust meter" because he'd fessed up and told him what he'd done—even though Dad may have never known otherwise. *That* meant the world to Parker. Parker couldn't imagine anything that would cut him deeper than disappointing his dad, which cemented his decision to stop compromising all the more.

On the way to school Monday, he told Jelly and Wilson that he'd spilled to his dad the night before.

Wilson couldn't believe it. "Your crazy need to always do the right thing is going to get us in trouble someday, Bucky." Those were his exact words.

And by how quiet Jelly had been, Parker was pretty sure she agreed with Wilson—at least a little. But it was the right thing to do, and he had no regrets. On Gator Hook Trail he'd made the decision that he had to stop compromising, and he intended to stick with his plan.

On Tuesday, Dad picked him up from school just before lunch for the monthly doctor appointment. The orthopedic surgeon's office was all the way out in Naples, and the break from classes was welcome.

But on the ride back to school, there were other things on Parker's mind. "You think my arm is ever going to be right again?"

Dad was quiet for a moment. "I'm just glad you still have it."

Not the answer he was looking for. "I can't wait to get out of this place." Sure, the trek down Gator Hook Trail seemed to dissolve some of his fears of the Glades, but it didn't change his restlessness to leave. He wanted out—more than ever. Everything about life would be better if he could get out of this place. Even his arm would heal better, right?

Dad slowed as he entered the Everglades City town limits. "If you could choose a place—any post—where would you hope we get transferred?"

He wasn't going to get picky. "Anyplace but here." Honestly, sometimes it felt like he'd just die if he didn't get out soon.

Dad nodded and stared out the windshield of his F-150 like he was in a different world. Or wanted to be. "I'll drop you at school. I'd hoped to get you back in time for part of last period, but it's not looking so good now."

Parker grinned. "I won't complain." The doctor had an absolute gift of twisting and pulling Parker's arm until he winced in pain. That was enough torture for one day. He didn't have any desire to check in with Principal Kingman for a pass to his last class. He stretched his hand open, then slowly balled it into a fist. His arm felt a whole lot worse after the doctor got done with him.

"Doctor Marvin was happy to hear how you're keeping up with your therapy."

Parker would be an idiot not to exercise. "But my arm isn't getting any better. It's been the same for what . . . three weeks?" Asking the doctor about it wasn't exactly encouraging. Doctor Leo Marvin acted like he deserved a medal for how the gimpy arm functioned. Like he'd never expected it to do this good in the first place.

"Give it time. Sometimes progress is so slow it's hard for us to see it at all." Dad pulled the pickup into the turnaround in front of the school and braked to a stop. "I'm proud of you, Parker. I ever tell you that?"

Parker smiled. "All the time." He was fortunate that way—and he knew it.

"See you tonight. After my shift—but it may be late again."

Parker searched his dad's face. "Problems?"

"High school kids from Miami and beyond are doing Watson's Run solo—at night—and in kayaks," he said. "Almost one a week. The more we warn the schools, the more kids try it. Definitely have to come up with a new strategy before someone really gets hurt."

Watson's Run. Named after "Bloody" Ed Watson, local resident and infamous serial killer from back in the early 1900s. The hot-tempered murderer ended up getting ambushed and killed by a mob—just outside Smallwood's Store in Chokoloskee, minutes from Parker's house.

Watson's Run was a water trail that snaked up the Lopez River out of Chokoloskee Bay, through Sunday Bay, Oyster Bay, and Huston Bay before following the Chatham River down to the old Watson place. The route was wild and totally uninhabited. Snakes. Gators. And enough twists and turns to mix up even a seasoned guide. In the dark, the chances of taking a wrong artery were extremely high. "That's pure insanity."

Who would want to chance that route, or be at Watson's place at night? The way Parker heard it, Watson's land had a really bad vibe. Some sensed pure evil in the area. According to local history, some fifty skeletons were found on his land alone—and who knows how many bodies he dumped in the Gulf or in the Glades.

"We just picked up another high-school senior last night," Dad said. "And a good thing we did."

"What happened?" If he could keep his dad talking, maybe he wouldn't have to go back to class after all.

Dad laughed. "Stalling?"

Busted. "Maybe a little."

"Well, I've got to get back to work. Ask me tonight. I'll tell you this much. It was close. If kids don't stop, one of these days someone is going to get killed." Dad hit the auto unlock button and checked the time. "You've got what, maybe five minutes before class ends?"

Parker nodded.

"Don't bother going inside. You'll still be in the office signing in when the bell rings. Want me to drive you around back to your bike?"

"I'll walk around the building. I'm going to wait for Jelly anyway." Parker slid out of the truck and watched his dad pull out. He hustled around the school and unlocked his bike. He beelined it for the fishing boats moored along the waterway that bordered the back of the school property. Since he had to wait, he'd much rather do so by the boats than the bike rack.

Wilson had a detention to ride out after his last class, so he wouldn't be joining them. If it wasn't for the fact that Jelly wanted to talk to him so badly after school, Parker probably would have grabbed his bike and headed for the *Boy's Bomb*. A ride in his skiff was just what he needed. Instead, he sat on a short stack of stone crab traps where he had a good view of the back doors to Everglades City School. He sent Jelly a quick text to tell her he'd meet her outside, and sat back to wait.

He spread open the fingers of his sixty-percent hand. Balled his hand into a fist. Rotated it slowly. Examined it like it wasn't even his own. There were more scars from his elbow down than he could count with the fingers on both hands. Purple scars. Raised. Freakish. The straight ones from the surgeon's knife. The jagged from the alligator's jaws. A Frankenstein arm.

The kind of arm that got him lots of points and stares from kids. Parents looked too, but in a different way. As if they feared something like that could happen to their own kids. Their reactions were almost always the same. They'd bend down and talk to their kid, explaining the dangers of the Everglades or alligators no doubt. If they'd just treat Parker like a human being he'd be happy to tell their kids all about the dangers. Parents glanced at Parker while they talked, like they were afraid he'd actually come close. As if his scars would scar them in some way.

Older kids were pretty cool with his scars. They did the *I don't even see them* act. Even Jelly never mentioned them—although he caught her glancing at them often enough.

She never talked about the transfer either. Except once when she confirmed her dad was planning to leave too. As soon as Parker's dad got his new assignment, Jelly's dad would put in for a transfer to the same post. Both their dads had been together since, like, forever. And Jelly's dad said it was about time he followed after Parker's dad for a change instead of the other way around.

Parker hoped it was true. And Uncle Sammy likely had another reason for wanting to get out of Dodge. To get Maria away from Clayton Kingman.

The trouble was, Maria Malnatti was still crazy about Kingman. Teachers-running-down-the-halls-with-scissors crazy. Follow-Kingman-to-the-ends-of-the-earth crazy. Which was pretty much where Everglades City was, the way Parker saw it.

Yeah, Sam Malnatti was as anxious to get out of Everglades City as Parker's dad was. Maybe more. In the meantime, Uncle Sammy was doing everything he could to bust Maria and Kingman up. That's what Jelly told him, anyway.

Despite Wilson's best efforts—and schemes—over the last couple of days, Parker had successfully steered clear of the Everglades since Gator Hook Trail. He took the skiff out yesterday, but only into Chokoloskee Bay and around the Thousand Islands. He hadn't even ventured up the Lopez River. There were way too many gators there. The rush of Gator Hook had worn off, along with the feeling of Superman invincibility that followed. Parker was in his right mind again. Thinking clearly. And he never wanted to see another alligator up close in his life.

A set of double doors swung open and Clayton Kingman's dad stepped out of Everglades City School. Principal Kingman stood there for a moment, hands on hips, like he was a king surveying his empire. Prematurely white hair. Face so clean-shaven that it looked waxed and buffed. Thick-necked and thick-waisted, the principal was shaped roughly like a six-foot sweet potato. But there was nothing sweet about him. How the guy kept his shirt tucked in so tight was a mystery. It was like he stapled his shirttails to his legs or something.

Principal K snapped his wrist up to check his watch, making no move to go back inside.

Terrific. What was he doing in the *back* of the school? Normally he posted himself at the front so he could boss the bus drivers around. He hooked a walkie-talkie in the holster at his side. Parker sat perfectly still. He did *not* need the principal to see him outside—before school was officially over.

The bell announcing the end of last period rang, and within thirty seconds kids poured out the doors.

Principal K stood right in the middle of the flow. He didn't make any effort to get out of the way. Kids swerved around him like none of them wanted to get near him. He kept giving orders. "Walk. Slow down." Clearly Principal K didn't understand that his authority ended the instant that final bell rang. That's the way Parker saw it, anyway.

But the kids obeyed. They slowed their pace. Parker was pretty sure it had nothing to do with respect. Kingman ruled his kingdom with a different tool. Fear. What would it be like to be raised by a dad like that? No wonder Clayton Kingman was such a headcase.

Parker watched for Jelly, and he picked her out the instant she sidestepped around Kingman.

Parker counted off ten seconds to let her get some distance from Principal Kingman, then gave a short whistle and stood.

She zeroed in on him, waved, and hurried his way.

Principal K spotted him too—and followed.

CHAPTER 17

ANGELICA COULD *FEEL* Principal Kingman following her. What on earth did he want this time?

"*Miss* Malnatti."

Mr. Kingman had a gift of using a formal tone to talk down to people. Even at this distance, she could see Parker's face cloud. She stopped and turned to face the principal.

Mr. Kingman was all sweet-tea smiles. "I see Mr. Buckman appears to be waiting for you. Your friend didn't make it to last period, did he?"

He knew very well Parker didn't. Nobody left or returned to the school without stopping at the office. *His* office. How could her sister go out with this man's son? Did Maria have to check in with him every time Clayton took her out for a date?

"*Miss* Malnatti." More gums. More teeth. "It was an easy question."

Why was he pressing her to snitch?

"Did Mr. Buckman return to class?" He held up a finger. "The truth, Miss Malnatti. The truth."

Just the way he said the word *truth* reminded her way too much of Clayton.

"Did. Buckman. Return. To class?" He raised his eyebrows.

"No, sir. But he texted—like two minutes ago. He just got back from the doctor. It was probably too close to the bell, and he just decided to—"

Mr. Kingman held up one hand. "I'm not interested in your theories. But I am curious as to what devilry Mr. Buckman was up to this time."

"Devilry?"

"Mischief. Trouble." Mr. Kingman talked down to her like she was a third-grader. "Some sort of activity performed with the help of the devil."

"I know what devilry means." She just couldn't believe he used that term when speaking about Parker.

Mr. Kingman sighed in that loud way he did when he wanted someone to know they were testing his patience. "Let's just go to the source and see if we can get this whole mess straightened out."

Mess? Seriously? If he was so eager to clean up messes, why didn't he do something about his son?

Mr. Kingman headed directly for Parker—who was already heading for them, like he knew it was pointless to avoid this. Angelica hurried to keep up.

"Mr. Buckman," Principal Kingman said. "Miss Malnatti tells me you didn't return to class after your appointment, yet here you were, waiting for classes to end."

Parker's eyes darted toward her.

She gave him the most apologetic look she could, hoping he'd read the truth in her eyes. *I didn't throw you under the bus, Parker. Honest.*

"I just got back from the doctor." Parker raised his bad arm slightly. "Didn't see the point of going back to class for less than five minutes."

Mr. Kingman gave a dry chuckle. "Didn't see the *point*? My, my. I see we must curb you of your mendacious ways."

He loved throwing big words around—acting surprised that whoever he was talking to had no idea what it meant, and then explaining the meaning in the most condescending way.

Principal Kingman let out a long sigh. "Mendacious has to do with being dishonest—which you most certainly were, Mr. Buckman. Five minutes or fifty, the point of going back to class is honesty. Integrity. Responsibility. Respect. Now I realize those may not be the most celebrated virtues up north where you came from, but they're held in the highest regard down here." He pointed to a star-shaped tie tack pinning his red necktie in place. Brass with diamonds. "This is the Star of Integrity. I got it—no, *earned* it— from my father."

Not again. How many times had Angelica heard him drone on about the Star of Integrity? He'd managed to build a whole assembly out of the topic. But he was lecturing the wrong person. Parker had the strongest sense of integrity of anyone she'd ever known—besides his dad. Parker didn't need some cheesy piece of jewelry. Principal K just *talked* about integrity. Parker and his dad lived it.

Mr. Kingman straightened the star so the tip pointed directly at his double chin. "Integrity is a little thing you'd do well to develop yourself, Mr. Buckman."

Parker's face got really red. "Thank you for the inspiration, sir."

To Angelica's relief, he said it without even a hint of sarcasm. She did *not* want Parker to say anything that would earn him a detention—and with Mr. Kingman, it wouldn't take much. The keys to surviving in an empire led by a dictator like Mr. Kingman were simple: Don't cross him. Don't contradict him. Don't disrespect him in any way. And stay off his radar—which was the hardest thing of all.

Mr. Kingman's walkie-talkie squawked. He drew the unit from its holster like he'd rehearsed the move. A lot. He tilted his head slightly to listen. "Seems we have some minor altercation by the buses." He holstered the walkie-talkie. "Tell you what, Mr. Buckman. You come to my office first thing tomorrow morning and we'll have a little chat, hmmm?"

Parker nodded.

Mr. Kingman raised his eyebrows like he was expecting something more.

"Yes, sir."

Mr. Kingman smiled. "Well," he tapped his walkie-talkie. "Duty calls." He spun on his heel and walked at a man-on-a-mission pace for the school.

Parker let out a breath of air. "That was fun."

Jelly snagged Parker's cap off his head and slapped it on hers. "I'm soooo sorry. I never—"

"I know you didn't," Parker said. "That's just the way he is."

"In all the places we've lived, I've never met a principal I didn't like. But Principal Kingman is in a class all his own."

"Easy, there, Jelly. Keep talking like that and you'll never earn a Star of Integrity either.

Angelica laughed. "He's got an ego the size of the Everglades."

"His son isn't much different."

Clayton. She hated the thought of him dating her sister. "Actually, that's who I wanted to talk to you about."

Parker gave her a curious look.

"Let's talk on the way to the skiff."

He hesitated. "What did he do?"

She shrugged and avoided his eyes. The real question was how much she dared tell him.

CHAPTER 18

PARKER SWUNG INTO THE CIRCLE K for snacks. Normally Jelly wouldn't buy a thing—just poach some of his food. But Jelly still had half her PB and J sandwich left. The fact that she hadn't even finished her lunch was another clue. Something was really eating at her. Parker pedaled alongside Jelly through town and past the visitor center. She didn't give him so much as a hint as to what was going on with Kingman. What was she waiting for?

Growing circles of sweat soaked through his T-shirt. Even the wind he created from pedaling wasn't enough to keep his legs dry, thanks to the heat radiating off the asphalt.

They hit the three-mile bridge out to Chokoloskee before Jelly got past the small talk.

"Maria and Clayton broke up."

Parker let out a whoop. "Seriously? When?"

"Last night."

She didn't exactly look happy, which made no sense.

"So why aren't you doing cartwheels?"

Jelly stared at the road like she hadn't heard the question. "It was messy."

He wanted to ask her what she meant by that, but he knew her well enough to sit tight and wait for it. She liked to process out loud, and he'd probably get more information if he didn't bombard her with questions.

"And it isn't over."

Parker glanced at her.

"My dad *thinks* it is. But it definitely isn't." Jelly looked at him—and hit a pothole. She lost control for an instant, but pulled it together enough to keep from spilling.

Parker swerved around her and circled back to where she'd stopped.

"My tire," she said. "Great."

It was flat, and they were barely halfway across the bridge. He dropped his bike on the shoulder and inspected Jelly's front tire. "This thing is shot."

Jelly raised her face to the sky and growled. "Not one more thing."

A faded blue and white Chevy pickup slowed alongside them. It looked like early seventies. There wasn't a single quarter panel without dents and scratches. A total beater—and towing a twenty-foot Carolina Skiff that was in a lot better shape than the truck.

The driver stopped right in the lane. He looked like someone out of one of those swamp-dweller shows. Ragged black beard halfway down his chest. Face as pale as a bar of soap—like he only came out at night. "Wanna ride?"

Jelly took a step back. "It's just a flat. I can walk. Thank you, though."

In the months he'd lived here, Parker had never seen this guy before. But that's the way it was with some locals. They lived on the fringes of the Everglades—and of society.

"Toss the bike in the bed." The stranger motioned. Nails long, and as black underneath as his beard. "Hop in."

She flashed Parker a desperate look.

"We're okay." Parker stepped in front of Jelly. The bench seat was loaded with crumpled fast food bags, empty cups with tops and straws, and oily-looking rags. "Thanks anyway."

"I weren't offering *you* a ride. Nothing wrong with your bike. The girl's the one what done got the flat."

He locked eyes with Parker for a moment, just boring into him with a freaky intensity.

The man leaned forward to look around Parker. "If you change your mind, darlin', just give a wave and a holler." He pointed at his rearview mirror. "I'll be watchin'."

He pulled forward slowly, like he really expected her to motion him back.

The trailer bounced past as the pickup gained speed. The Yamaha 115 outboard mounted to the transom looked brand-new.

"*Night Crawler.*" Parker read the name on the back of the boat. "Just the kind of guy you want to get a ride from."

"Now you're giving me second thoughts." Jelly smiled. "And I was just about to flag him down."

"Really? Well, let me help you." Parker raised one hand high. "I'm sure he's still watching."

She dropped her bike, lunged at his arm, and dragged it down.

"If he turns around, I'm taking your bike—and *you're* riding with the creep."

Parker couldn't think of any situation where he'd be desperate enough to get a ride from the guy. "The truth is, I think there's a lot of creepy people just like him living down here."

"You're exaggerating. I'll admit there's some scary people living down here." Jelly picked up her bike and started walking it toward Chokoloskee. "But almost everyone I've met seems decent. Just as normal as we are."

Parker walked his bike next to her. "So you're saying you're normal?"

She veered her bike into his path to cut him off. "Watch it, Parker. You can be replaced."

"You'll have to do it soon enough." He regretted the comment the moment he said it.

Jelly's smile faded. "Any word on the transfer?"

He shook his head. "Nothing official. But my dad's supposed to hear something any day now."

She nodded, but kept her eyes on the pavement.

"I feel like this . . . *place* . . . is some kind of prison. I just have to get away from here," Parker said. "I have to escape—and I just know life will be better after I do."

She was quiet. Way too quiet.

"Seriously, Jelly. Don't you ever dream of getting out of this place?"

Jelly looked up at him. "Every blistering day. I used to love it here. At least I thought I did. But after the accident, everything changed."

He'd suspected something like that. But she'd never actually admitted that before. "Once we find out where my dad gets assigned, how long before your dad gets transferred there?"

Jelly shrugged. "My dad said that could take months."

Which was the huge downside of the move. But she'd get there, and then everything would be fine. Time to change the topic. "Tell me about the breakup. What made Maria finally see the light?"

"She didn't. My dad gave her kind of an ultimatum."

Parker groaned. "Don't tell me she still thinks she's in love with the maniac."

Jelly nodded. "She says she's going to marry him."

He couldn't have been more stunned if Jelly had taken the ride from the swamp guy. "What? No way."

Jelly held up one hand like she was taking a solemn oath. "She told me. And if you tell anyone, you're dead."

"She's *seventeen*. A senior in high school." Even though he rarely saw her there. "Is it even legal to get married that young?"

Jelly shook her head. "But she'll be eighteen in February."

Maria was fun and nice, and always used to make time for Parker—before she started with Kingman. Parker was pretty sure Maria could get any guy. "Why would she settle for a clod like Clayton Kingman?"

"He can be a charmer. At least he was at first." She stared out over the water as she walked. "He complimented her a lot in the beginning—and coming from a college guy, that meant a lot."

"He's a college *dropout*."

"But older," Jelly said. "That was the key. And he flattered her, if you ask me. She used to go on and on about how good he was at listening and encouraging her."

"That does *not* sound like the Clayton Kingman we know," Parker said.

"My theory? It was all strategic on his part. Kingman did it just to gain Maria's trust—and she confided in him more and more.

Hopes. Dreams. Fears. Her weaknesses. Times she messed up. He'd ask her so many questions. Seemed so caring. Eventually he got her to tell him really private things. I mean, she told him everything. *Every*thing. All the stuff she used to tell me, I guess. I think he used it against her. He used her secrets to keep her in line."

"And she thinks a guy who does that actually loves her?"

"He loves *himself*," Jelly said. "Oh sure, he'd buy her gifts all the time. Make her think she was special to him. He got her to lower her guard a million ways. But I'm absolutely convinced he was just grooming her so he could control her or manipulate her to do whatever it was he wanted. Like she was his pet to train."

Suddenly he could see it. The strategy behind what Kingman was doing, anyway. "It's like teaching a puppy to obey." *Good doggy.* Rewarding with treats and compliments. *Bad doggy.* Keeping a tight leash. Yanking them back in line. Shaming them. "Eventually a well-trained puppy follows the trainer around everywhere—"

"Right," Jelly said. "And they do exactly what their trainers tell them to do."

And with a guy like Kingman being the trainer . . . with his own agenda? That did *not* sound good.

"It was like he broke down her defenses," she said. "He'd rip her up about something, saying she was a lousy girlfriend—or sister—or daughter. Saying she was stupid. She'd be all depressed and busted up about it, and then the guy would flatter her in some way. Stroke her ego. Suddenly she was flying high again."

Good puppy. Bad puppy. "And Kingman had her eating out of his hand." He pictured Kingman with a box of Cheerios.

"It's like he's got a hold on her somehow." Jelly tapped her forehead. "Almost like it's some kind of mind control. He's brainwashed her. She's a totally different person."

"There's a spooky thought." Maybe Kingman wasn't controlling Maria's mind, but he'd sure messed with it.

"I told my dad how Maria said she was going to marry the jerk," Jelly said. "That clinched it. That was enough for my dad to bust them up for good. And there's even more that he doesn't know."

"Like what?"

She shook her head. "Don't even ask. I promised I wouldn't tell."

It wasn't like her to keep secrets. Not from him, anyway. Whatever it was, it had to be big. Parker resisted the urge to ask for more details, even though the questions were piling up in his head.

They walked in silence for a few minutes. His shoes felt like they were on fire by the time they reached the Chokoloskee end of the bridge.

As they passed the marina he spotted the blue and white pickup by the launch ramp. The bearded man was removing the straps holding his boat to the trailer. "There's the *Night Crawler*," Parker said.

Jelly glanced toward the ramp. "Are you referring to the boat or the guy driving the pickup?"

Parker laughed, but stopped when the guy turned and looked right at them. "What's he doing?"

"Making me really nervous," Jelly said.

The man just stood there staring. Clawed at his beard—making no attempt to hide the fact that he was watching them. "*Mr. Crawley* is staring at you," Parker said. "Like I'm not even here."

"I wish *I* wasn't."

The guy hadn't moved. Just stood there. Watching. Parker waved his hand in a big arc. *We see you, creep. You sicko.*

"Stop!" Jelly grabbed his arm and pulled it down. "He's going to think I want a ride."

Parker laughed and waved with his other arm.

Which cracked Jelly up. "Idiot."

The guy was still watching. And if he thought they were laughing at him, well, Parker didn't care. Chances were really high Parker wouldn't see him again before he moved.

The laugh seemed to do Jelly good. Even after she stopped laughing, she was still smiling. She pulled the rest of her sandwich out of her pack and took a bite. An appetite had to be a good sign.

"PB and J, PB and J." Parker gave her a sideways look. It was the only kind of sandwich she ever seemed to have for lunch anymore. "Don't you ever get tired of it?"

"Never," she said. "And I never will. I wish you weren't leaving."

"I can't get out of here fast enough," Parker said. "I just wish our dads would get transferred at the same time."

"Maybe I can go with you." She glanced at him. "Think your parents would mind me moving in with you guys until my dad gets the new assignment? I could take your room, and you could sleep on the couch."

Parker laughed—but part of him wasn't so sure that she was joking. "Back to Maria and Kingman. At least they're broken up. So that's a good start for Maria getting free from him, right?"

"I wish it were that simple." She hesitated. "There's something I want to tell you . . . but I'm not supposed to."

He'd be lying if he said he wasn't interested in hearing. "Hey, if your dad told you not to talk about it, I don't want you getting in trouble or anything."

She shook her head. "My dad doesn't know. It's stuff Maria told me."

Jelly stopped as if wishing she hadn't just said that. And suddenly Parker wasn't sure he wanted to know more than he already did. What if she told him something that really shouldn't be kept a secret from her dad? Something he needed to know so he could protect her. Wouldn't Parker be obligated to tell her dad? Wouldn't that be the right thing to do? Maybe it was best Jelly didn't say more. But the truth was, Parker wanted to understand what was going on.

She glanced over her shoulder once.

Who did she think would've overheard her out here? "How about we get out on the water and you can tell me all about it. If you want to, that is. And if you don't want to talk, at least you'll get your mind off of it."

She looked like she was weighing something out. "I think that's exactly what I need."

There was something about the way she said it. Whatever she was hiding, it was really bothering her.

"He scares me, Parker. I don't think I dare say more than that. Not yet." She stared out over the water. "There's no light inside Clayton Kingman, Parker. Only darkness."

"Are you afraid for you—or Maria?"

"Both."

A chill flashed through Parker. Is that how it was every time Kingman was at Jelly's house to see Maria? Was Jelly secretly afraid? "But you said it yourself. They're busted up. What can Kingman do now? There's no reason to be afraid of him anymore, right?"

Jelly shook her head. "I'm still scared of him, Parker. More than ever."

CHAPTER 19

ANGELICA WATCHED PARKER TWIST the plug into place on the transom of the *Boy's Bomb*, then helped drag the skiff off the beach just beyond Smallwood's Store. Both climbed aboard without a word. He'd been quiet ever since she told him she was truly afraid of Clayton.

Parker primed the gas and adjusted the choke. Jelly looked toward Smallwood's Store. The old wood building was built on stilts like it didn't want to touch the beach below it. Like it knew that somehow the sand was tainted with blood—and wanted no part of it.

And there *was* blood in the sand. Ed Watson's blood. Somewhere within a hundred feet of where the *Bomb* normally sat on the beach, that murderer had been murdered a long time ago. The area had a dark history of attracting rough characters—and Parker was right . . . it still did.

The motor caught and sputtered to life. Parker worked the throttle and choke until it idled smoothly and a steady stream of water shot out the side of the outboard. He threw it in reverse and backed away from shore.

He opened the throttle and headed southwest. But he kept looking at her. Like he expected her to burst into tears or something equally ridiculous. When he rounded one of the nameless islands he cut the motor and let the *Boy's Bomb* drift.

"I have to tell you more," Jelly said. "But I can't tell you everything." She had to be careful. If Parker believed that the right thing to do was to tell her dad, he'd do it. Or he'd do *something* to fix this—and make things worse.

"Nobody can hear us out here, Jelly."

He leaned back. Looked relaxed. It was the *Boy's Bomb*—and being out in the bay where there were no gators. It had that effect on him. Her too. But for Angelica it wasn't so much about being out on the water. It was more about being off the island. And maybe it was the size of the boat—or the teal color? Or maybe it was the way Parker loved the thing. But being out in the boat always made her feel safe. She opened up. Told how Maria and Clayton had been arguing more. How Clayton was more vicious. Cruel. But instead of pulling away, Maria seemed drawn to him all the more. That's what really worried Angelica.

To his credit, Parker listened—without peppering her with questions.

Angelica told how she talked to Maria about it—but how Maria had defended Clayton. And how Maria even made her promise not to tell her dad.

Angelica explained that she didn't want to snitch, but how she'd played a game of twenty questions with her dad until he'd learned enough to force the breakup.

When her dad told Maria she couldn't see Clayton anymore, she'd run out of the room and called Clayton. The guy was over minutes later—and had the nerve to argue with her dad.

"Clayton had a smirk on his face the whole time. You know what he said?"

Parker shook his head.

"Maria is mine. She's going to marry me, and there's nothing you can do about it, old man."

"How'd your dad handle *that*?"

"He threatened Clayton right back. Got all in his face and told him to stay away from his daughter. Said he'd get a restraining order out on him. Told Clayton if he stepped one foot on our property he'd fill him with buckshot." And he said a lot more, too. Even with the sun beating down on her she shuddered. "He doesn't have the same standards as your dad, Parker. If it really came down to protecting one of his girls? I think he'd do it, too."

Parker nodded. "How's Maria?"

"Furious."

"After the way her boyfriend talked to her dad? She should be."

Angelica squinted into the sun. "I wish. According to Maria, it's my dad who is totally out of line."

Parker shook his head in disbelief. "So, after all that Clayton said, Maria still wants to date that animal?"

"If she was eighteen right now, she'd marry him." *Stop, Angelica. You've said enough. Don't tell him another word.*

Parker winced. "That is so sick. It's like you said. Maria's been brainwashed. As long as she stays away from Kingman she'll straighten out and see him for the monster he really is."

Kingman being a monster? Parker got that part right. But he didn't understand Maria at all. He didn't know how messed up her thinking was right now—or what she might do. "A day away from him isn't going to cure her. Neither is a week."

"But it will help. As long as your dad keeps them apart, her mind will clear and she'll see the kind of guy he is," Parker said. "Do you think Kingman will stay away from her?"

Angelica knew the answer to that. But Maria had made her promise not to tell—complete with a very nasty threat if Angelica spilled the beans this time. As much as she wanted to tell him more, she couldn't. "Clayton Kingman is dangerous, Parker. Really, really dangerous. Don't underestimate him."

Parker seemed to be searching her eyes for what she wasn't saying. "*How* dangerous?"

"He's a predator in his own way—and really good at it."

Parker shook his head. "He's bad, but I'm not sure I'd call him a predator."

"That's my point," Angelica said. "You can't figure this guy out. You don't think like he does. You're too nice a guy. Too trusting. His mind is sick, Parker. When he gets angry—" She had to stop. Say no more.

"When he gets angry . . ." Parker let the words hang there.

She would tell him just this little bit more—and that was it. "I get the feeling he's got no conscience. That there is something absolutely evil about him just clawing to get out."

"And if it does?"

"There's nothing he won't do." She locked eyes with him, trying to say with that look what she didn't dare say aloud. "People will get hurt. Bad." Her dad—and eventually Maria. Anybody who got in his way.

"Do you think he's capable of—"

"Don't even say it, Parker. I can't say more. Not another word."

Parker looked at her like he knew she was serious. "It's going to be okay."

Angelica wanted to smile back. Nod. Agree with him. But she couldn't—because right now things didn't look like they were going to be okay. The worst was yet to come—she could feel it. And right now, she was afraid to imagine how bad that might be.

CHAPTER 20

BY THE TIME PARKER NOSED THE *BOY'S BOMB* onto the tiny beach by Smallwood's Store, Jelly had gone quiet. Like she was off in her own world somewhere, imagining worst-case scenarios. Typical Jelly.

Even though she'd said plenty about Kingman, he had the gnawing feeling that she was holding back. Something important. But he couldn't imagine anything worse than what she'd just told him.

Jelly vaulted over the side into the ankle-deep water, dock line in hand. The thing with Jelly was that everything she said was calculated. She was way more careful than he was that way.

He ran through the conversation in his mind. She wouldn't answer his question about Kingman staying away from Maria. Maybe he had to look at this a different way. "You think your sister will stay away from him?"

"My dad laid the law down on that one."

Parker lashed the bow line around the base of a cypress tree. But she didn't really answer his question, did she?

"What do *you* think?" He watched her body language. "Will she stay away?"

She hugged herself. "I pray to God she will."

Again, not really a direct answer. "Jelly . . . do you know something you're not telling me?"

"I know I'd better be home by dinner or my dad will come looking for me."

Parker smiled. She *did* know something . . . but she didn't want to feel like a snitch. "Want to play twenty questions?"

She looked at him. Long enough for him to know his instincts were right. "No more questions, Parker. I gotta go."

"I'll walk you."

"I'm a big girl."

"That's what Mr. Night Crawler thought too." Parker hustled to the back of the skiff and pulled the transom plug and dropped it in the storage compartment under his seat. If a storm rolled in, he didn't want to come back to a boat half filled with water.

She hugged herself again and nodded. "But no more questions."

Parker raised both hands. "Not one." By not giving him a straight answer she'd already told him what he needed to know, right?

"Sorry . . . I hope that didn't sound bad. I just need to think."

Oh yeah. She was holding back. "We don't have to talk at all, Jelly." Which was good, really. It would give him time to make some plans to keep Kingman and Maria apart until Jelly's older sister got her head screwed on straight.

They walked side by side. They'd barely passed Smallwood's Store before a plan popped into his head.

The little plot was crazy simple, but it wasn't the type of thing Parker would even try to pull off by himself. It made no sense to ask Jelly to be a player. With whatever secret she was hiding from her dad—and from him—she was already in a tough enough spot. She might even try to put the kibosh on the whole thing. At this point, the less she knew, the better.

But Parker knew exactly who'd love to be part of the scheme.

Parker picked up the pace. As soon as Jelly was safe at home Parker was going to make a quick phone call. There wasn't much time to pull this together. But he couldn't wait until tomorrow to put his plan into motion. What if Maria and Kingman tried to meet before then?

Ready or not, he would start tonight.

CHAPTER 21

TWO HOURS AFTER DINNER Parker was up in his room, getting ready. He strapped Jimbo to his calf and covered it with his pant leg. Not that he figured he'd need it, but he liked the feel of having a survival knife cinched to his leg. Besides, it made the whole plan seem a bit more dangerous—and that just added to the excitement.

The more he tried not to look at the INTEGRITTY sign, the more he couldn't look anywhere else. Dad was on shift. Mom was away on an assignment. There was nobody home to ask him where he was going, what he was doing, and how long he'd be gone. Nobody to make him question if he was doing the right thing. But if he really wanted to be a person of integrity, he needed to ask *himself* the tough questions.

This new plan of his . . . was he doing the right thing?

Fact: It was all about keeping Kingman from Maria. That was a good thing.

Fact: Jelly wanted to keep her sister away from the guy—so did her dad. But Parker wasn't so sure either of them could do that. So anything Parker did to help ensure they'd stay apart was definitely a good thing.

Next question: Was he doing a good thing—but in a bad way? He played out the plan in his head. Like he was watching a movie of the whole thing. Everything went perfectly. Nobody got hurt. He wasn't going to damage anything permanently. He wasn't doing anything more than delaying Kingman long enough to keep him from seeing Maria tonight.

But what if something went wrong? There were a million ways it could, but the beauty of the plan was its simplicity. The chances of anything going wrong were low. And if something did start going south, they could always abort, right?

Final question: What would Dad say if he knew? One thing for sure—if Parker didn't talk to his dad before he did this, he'd figure Parker was home. If he let his dad think that, Parker would be dishonest.

He wrestled with it for a few moments. If he was serious about integrity, he couldn't choose when he'd be honest, right? But did he really want to risk Dad pulling the plug on this? He'd been honest with Dad about the whole Gator Hook Trail fiasco—after the fact—and he'd taken it really well. Appreciated his honesty, and all that. But what would it do to Dad's "trust meter" if Parker didn't tell him about this until after he'd done the deed? He'd be making the same mistake. Wouldn't that be pushing it? He'd break trust for sure.

"Ugh," he growled. "Sometimes I hate trying to be this person of integrity." He whipped off a quick text to his dad before he changed his mind.

Planning to run out tonight. Uncle Sammy busted Maria and Kingman up. I think Kingman plans to sneak out to see her. Wilson and I are going to make sure that doesn't happen.

Dad texted back seconds later.

Pump the brakes, Parker. Not sure I like the sound of that.

Parker just had to reassure him.

We won't be seen. We won't get near him. We won't destroy anything. We won't be out late. We won't get hurt.

A moment later a new text came back.

Sorry, need details.

Parker laid out his plan quickly—and explained why he felt he needed to do this. There was a long pause before Dad's response. And it wasn't a text. Dad phoned—and listened while Parker gave the best sales pitch ever. But Dad finally gave him the okay, with a short list of conditions.

Honestly? Parker was shocked that his dad had agreed. Maybe his dad picked up on that somehow.

"Look, Parker," he said. "Clayton is bad blood. He's dangerous. And he's hurting Maria—and my best friend's family. I'm not going to stand by and let that happen, and neither is Uncle Sammy. Not without a little resistance."

Parker's pulse practically doubled.

"This is war for Uncle Sammy. And for me and you, this is *spiritual* warfare. We trust God to work things out for good all the way around . . . but that doesn't mean we sit on our hands."

He reminded Parker of the Bible account of Jonathan—King Saul's son—who along with his armor bearer attacked an entire garrison of Philistines. God had been moving Jonathan to do something . . . and a huge victory came as a result.

"So be careful. Stay under the radar. Don't be talked into doing something you don't feel is right—not by Wilson or Angelica or anyone else. You keep asking God what He wants you to do, and don't deviate from that. And pull the plug if things don't feel right, son. Maybe God is moving in your heart to take some action here. I can tell you He's been moving in mine."

Parker wanted to ask him what he meant by that. But at this moment he was flying high. He'd done the right thing—talked to his dad—and his dad didn't say no. "Thanks for the green light, Dad."

"Call it a yellow light," Dad said. "A yellow *flashing* light. Proceed with caution."

And that was the thing with Dad lately. He'd been giving Parker more leash—because he'd proved himself trustworthy. Not that he got everything right, but he was honest with his dad. There was no way Parker wanted to mess that up.

"Call me when you get home," Dad said. "And don't disappoint me."

He had no intention of letting Dad down.

He biked across the bridge from Chokoloskee to Everglades City and met Wilson three blocks from Kingman's place. They rode to the stand of mangroves bordering the Kingman house and ditched their bikes out of sight.

Wilson grinned. "I love this stuff."

The truth was, Parker did too.

"You sure you're okay with this?" Wilson had that mischievous spark in his eyes. "We're doing a *bad* thing, Bucky."

Was this a dig at his Christianity? Probably. "We're going to stop a bad thing from happening. That's how I'm looking at this."

"I like how you think." Wilson gave him the side-eye. "What do you figure your dad would say if he ever finds out?"

Parker hesitated. "Already talked to him about it."

Wilson stared at him. "You're crazy—you know that?"

There was no way he'd get Wilson to understand how important being a person of integrity was to Parker. To follow in the footsteps of his dad. His grandpa. How important it was to him as a Christian. He shrugged. "It was the right—"

"Thing to do," Wilson said. "Yeah, I've heard you say that a time or two."

The Kingman house was more of a palace, in Parker's opinion. He'd seen it before—but not up close. Obviously some principals made good money. The house was massive, especially since it was only the two of them living there. The way Parker heard it, Kingman's mom had slipped away one night a couple of years earlier. From what Parker had seen of Clayton and his dad, nobody would blame her.

The palace was set way back from the road without another house within shouting distance. Apparently the principal liked his privacy.

A crushed shell driveway wound its way through a deep stand of mangroves. The trees formed a thick natural barrier, blocking the house from sight. It was the perfect place to ditch their bikes. Parker propped his against a tree—pointing toward the road in case a quick getaway was needed. Wilson did the same.

Without a word they made their way through the mangroves and jungle growth to a clearing. Between the mangroves and the palace, there was enough Florida thatch lawn to hold a baseball diamond. Or nearly an entire football field. Honestly, there had to be nearly seventy-five yards between the house and the trees.

The house backed up to a lake. Small enough not to have a name. But big enough to have alligators. Even from here Parker could smell the swampy water. Foul. The scent of decay. Death.

The night sky was dark enough to give them good cover, but they stuck to the deepest shadows anyway. The lights were blazing in the Kingman house. Clayton's pickup was there, hopped up on its oversize tires. Kingman's eighteen-foot Boston Whaler skiff—complete with a 115 Yamaha outboard—sat on a trailer hitched to Clayton's truck. The word was, it was a high-school graduation gift from Kingman's dad. The name *King of the Glades* was painted along the side of the hull near the stern in a typestyle that looked like it belonged on a Harley-Davidson T-shirt. A gator skull was painted below it with glowing eyes and huge, dagger-like teeth.

Principal K's Lexus was parked right in front of Kingman's rig. Lights on the corners of the eaves lit up the entire drive.

"A lot of good it did to wait until after dark," Wilson said. "It's bright as day on their driveway."

"Perfect," Parker said. "We won't need flashlights."

Wilson clapped him on the back. "I really do like how you think sometimes. Got the toothpicks?"

"In my pocket." Parker eyeballed the spare under the bed of Kingman's truck. "As long as we let the air out of two of his tires, it should keep him home tonight."

Wilson nodded.

They'd keep the truck between them and the house, but they didn't need to take any unneeded chances. Parker scanned the windows along the front of the house to be sure nobody was looking out. That's when he saw the surveillance system mounted high on the corners of the house—aiming right at the driveway. "Security cameras."

Wilson nodded. "I noticed." He tucked most of his hair in his baseball cap and pulled it low over his eyes. "They'll never recognize us." For just an instant his eyes flicked to Parker's arm.

Instantly Parker tracked with him. "The scars. A dead giveaway."

Wilson pulled his long-sleeved fishing shirt over his head. "Switch."

Seconds later Wilson was wearing Parker's black T-shirt. "We've got to move fast. If they have some kind of monitor inside, they'll spot us right away," Parker said.

Wilson nodded. "Ready when you are."

Parker took a deep breath—and pushed back the part of him that kept asking if this was such a great idea after all. Right at this moment? The plan didn't seem quite as simple and foolproof as he'd figured earlier. He'd never thought about Principal Kingman having security cams, which was a dumb mistake. But this was about helping Jelly do something she couldn't do for herself. It was about doing something for Uncle Sammy. It was about keeping Maria out of danger, since she wasn't smart enough to do it for herself. And honestly? It was definitely about a little payback to Clayton Kingman.

Parker tightened the adjusting strap on the back of his cap, wishing it were a ski mask instead. Grabbed a handful of toothpicks from his pocket. "Let's do it."

CHAPTER 22

PARKER SPRINTED FOR THE PICKUP, staying low. Wilson ran a half step behind him. They both dropped down behind Kingman's truck and hunkered close to the right rear tire. Parker had the valve stem cap off in three quick turns. Easy enough to do lefty. Holding the toothpick and forcing it into the valve to hold it open? Not so easy with his left. He switched the toothpick to his gimpy right hand.

"C'mon, Parker," Wilson said.

The toothpicks dropped. Parker tried picking one up, but he might as well have tried to pick up a single hair. Would his hand *ever* be able to do the things he used to do without even thinking?

"Gimme one of those." Wilson snatched up a toothpick and scooted to the front tire.

Parker was still trying to get a grip on a toothpick when he heard the hiss from up front. At least Wilson was getting somewhere.

Wilson scrambled back beside him, grinning. "Ever hear a more beautiful sound?"

The sound of their bikes churning up gravel on their way out of here would definitely top it.

"Let me do that." Wilson jammed a toothpick into the black stem, forcing the valve open.

How long would it take before the tire would be flat? Five minutes? Ten? There was no way they'd be sticking around to find out. Parker glanced toward the house. Still no signs of life. Perfect.

Wilson was watching too. "Should we do the other side?" He had that look in his eyes like he was having too much fun to quit yet.

"Overkill," Parker said. "Two tires flat. One spare. He's just as grounded as if we got all four." He eyed the Lexus. But what was to stop Clayton from borrowing his dad's car? "If we want to keep him off the street, we've got to fix the Lexus, too."

Wilson's eyes lit up. "I'm telling you, I love how you think."

Parker stayed low and ran to Principal Kingman's ride. He twisted off the valve cap of the back tire and managed to pry the toothpick in place. Barely. Maybe it was because they were that much closer to the house, but the hiss sounded louder. Parker cupped his hand over the valve stem and peeked at the house through the Lexus windows.

"If he figures out it was us, he'll make us pay," Wilson said. "Daily detentions 'til Christmas."

"That's why we're not going to get caught," Parker said. But with every second that hissed by, the odds were rolling the wrong way.

Wilson moved to the front of the Lexus and jammed the tooth-pick in place like a pro—if there were such a thing as professional tire-flatteners. Suddenly Parker's tire stopped hissing. His tooth-pick sat on the driveway. For a moment Parker tried forcing it back into the valve stem, but the pick was getting soft now. Parker slid up his pant leg and yanked Jimbo from its sheath. He poked the pointy tip into the valve stem. The air blew out with more force than ever.

Parker checked the pickup. The tires were definitely looking splashy on the passenger side of the truck. Another couple of min-utes and the truck would be resting on its rims.

"What's wrong with this thing?" Wilson fumbled with the toothpick on the front tire. The air wasn't flowing out with much force at all. Not like the other ones. He pulled out a new tooth-pick and tried forcing it into the valve with the other pick still there. It wasn't helping. Wilson grabbed the tire at the ten and two positions like he was gripping a steering wheel. "C'mon you lousy stinkin' tire. Deflate for me." He gave the wheel a shake, his shoulder thumping the fender in the process.

Instantly the horn sounded in a rhythmic blast.

Wilson froze—eyes wide. "Ooops!"

Honk.

Of course the principal would have an alarm. Why hadn't Parker thought of that earlier? He peered over the fender at the house. No movement.

Honk.

Wilson crouched like he was ready to bolt. "We gonna run for it—or what?"

Honk.

Parker stalled. The Lexus tires weren't nearly flat enough. "Not until this thing is flatter." He pushed the knife tip harder against the release in the valve stem.

Honk.

Wilson scooted next to him. "Gimme the blade. We gotta speed things up." He grabbed the knife with both hands and thrust it deep into the sidewall of the tire. Air whooshed out.

Honk.

Parker couldn't believe it. "Are you *crazy*?"

Wilson scurried to the front tire of the Lexus and did the same. Air gushed out the instant he tugged his knife free. The back tire was already on its rim. The front tire would be in just a few seconds.

Honk.

Parker glanced back. Kingman's truck was listing to one side noticeably now. The rear tire flat as an alligator's tail. The front tire close enough. Parker darted to Wilson, snatched his knife back and slid it into its sheath. "Time to go."

Honk.

The front door of the house flew open. "Uh-oh," Wilson said.

Honk.

Instantly Parker and Wilson were on their feet and running— no, *flying* like a couple of bats out of a very dark cave.

Honk.

"Hey—HEY!" It was Principal K himself. "Get back here, punks!"

Parker didn't look back, but sprinted for the shadows with Wilson at his side.

"STOP!" Principal K let out a string of obscenities that Parker had never heard tied together quite like that before.

"I said STOP!"

Like that was going to happen.

Wilson took a slight lead. "If you get caught, I'm not stopping."

"If I can't outrun the principal, I deserve to get caught."

Wilson laughed, and Parker closed the gap between them.

"Give it up!" Principal K sounded winded—and not as close.

Parker didn't slow a bit, but made a beeline for the mangroves, Wilson right beside him.

"I've got security cameras," Principal K shouted. "Surrender now, and I won't press charges."

Right. If he figured out who they were, he'd press charges no matter what. And if Principal K was so sure the security cameras would reveal their identity, there was no way he'd be chasing them so hard right now.

Parker chanced a shoulder glance the moment they were in the mangroves. The principal was easily fifty yards behind them—but he wasn't running anymore. He stood there, bent forward, hands on knees, sucking wind. Exactly what Parker wanted to do. But he didn't let up, and neither did Wilson.

They ran into the deep shadows. Close enough to see that their bikes were right where they left them. Only then did they stop to catch their breath.

"Holy buckets, Parker." Wilson gulped air. "I will *never* give you a hard time about bringing your survival knife—to anything."

Parker drove his fist into his side to relieve the cramp and laughed. "What happened to our plan? We were only supposed to let the air out of the tires."

Wilson grinned. "That *was* letting the air out of tires . . . Miccosukee style. We had to improvise, right?"

Two expensive tires . . . destroyed. How was he going to explain that to his dad? From the cover of the trees, they watched what was going on at the Kingman palace.

Clayton was outside now, stomping around his truck like he wanted to rip someone's head off. The principal hobbled back to his driveway and got in a shouting match with his son—each blaming the other for not catching the vandals. It was like watching a verbal prizefight. Both of them champions of control and manipulation, squaring off against each other.

Parker could just barely make out Wilson's smile in the darkness. "Now *that*," Wilson said, "was fun."

Parker agreed. "As good as getting shot at by poachers?"

Wilson grinned. "Better. Think he recognized us?"

"Not a chance," Parker said. "He'd have called us back by name."

"What about the security cameras?"

Parker studied the Kingman house. "We stayed on the shadow side of the pickup and the Lexus. We had hats. Dark clothes. There's no way he'll ID us." He sincerely hoped that was true.

Clayton Kingman did a quick walk around his truck, bent over to inspect the tires, then swung open the passenger door and leaned inside. When he turned back toward the mangroves, he was holding a shotgun. The thing was outfitted with a pistol grip—no shoulder stock. He cocked the pump action to chamber a round.

"I know you're out there," he shouted. "And I'm going to find you. And when I do—"

Principal K stepped in front of his son as if to hide the shotgun from view. Like he knew exactly the kind of thing Kingman might do—and wasn't about to let that happen.

Kingman shoved his dad to the side.

Wilson took a step back toward the bikes. "Do you believe this? What kind of headcase pulls out a gun because of a flat tire?"

Parker watched from the shadows of the mangroves. Stunned. He still couldn't believe Kingman shoved his dad like that.

Principal K was back—and shouting. "Put. That. Gun. Away. Do it now, boy."

Kingman hesitated for just an instant, then ejected the cartridge and caught it in midair. He tossed the shotgun inside the truck. But just as quickly he pushed past his dad and ranted at the tree line again. "I have a message for you." He held the shotgun cartridge high. "When I find you, I'm going to give you a little taste of Everglades justice."

Principal K reached for his son's mouth like he was going to clamp his hand over it. "That's quite enough—"

Kingman shoved him for the second time, and this time Principal K went down on his backside, hard.

"What is *wrong* with him?" Wilson shook his head. "They're just tires—and the Lexus got the worst of it."

"This goes a lot deeper than the tires," Parker said. It was about a puppy—and the dad who took it away.

"I knew the dude was bad," Wilson said. "But he's way beyond that. The guy is totally psycho."

"If Kingman would attack his own dad like that," Parker whispered, "imagine what he'd do to us."

"He'd have to catch us first." Wilson backed toward the bikes. "Uh-oh. Check out the principal."

Principal K was on his mobile phone. Talking loud. Waving one hand as he did, and pointing in their direction. "Calling the police?"

Wilson nodded. "Time to fly, Bucky."

Parker would've loved a set of wings at that moment.

A siren sounded in the distance. The police could be quick when there was nothing else going on.

"I *will* find you." Kingman stood there staring at the tree line, then turned back toward his truck.

It was time to go. Actually, hopelessly past time. They grabbed their bikes and ran them out to the road before mounting them.

Wilson let out a long breath of air and clapped Parker on the back. "We did it."

"I think the victory dance may have to wait," Parker said. "We've still got to make it home without the police spotting us."

Avoiding the police in a little town like Everglades City would be tricky. Parker knew that. There would only be one police car out at night—which was a plus. But after Principal K told the cop what happened, that one cop could canvas a town this size incredibly fast. The streets were straight, the homes and buildings low, and the ground as flat as Principal K's tires. A cop could see for blocks in any direction—and palm trees didn't offer the kind of cover they'd need. Two guys on bikes would be spotted fast.

They hadn't gone three blocks before they had to duck in the shadows while the police car raced past on its way to the Kingmans'. "Ready for the ultimate game of hide-and-seek?"

"Totally." Wilson pulled out onto the street again. "Question is—do we hide, or beat it back to the island?"

If they didn't get out of Everglades City now, who knew how long they might get pinned down. "Let's make a run for it."

Wilson agreed. "We've got to get across the bridge—fast."

More like a low causeway, really. A two-lane road to the island, three miles long. Low guard rails—where there were rails. Rocks leading down to the water on either side of the low bridge. Some areas of brush on either side, but also wide-open places with no cover at all. Which meant absolutely no place to escape—or hide— if the cop was smart enough to widen his search to Chokoloskee while they were still crossing. They'd be caught for sure.

Adrenalin was a high-octane fuel, and Parker's tank was full. He never felt more alive—or juiced. Sure, Kingman made some ugly threats, but how would he deliver on them? He would *never* find out who nailed their tires. Parker wasn't going to tell a soul, and Wilson wouldn't either. "Still having fun?"

Wilson flashed him a grin. "Best night I've had in weeks. How long do you plan to keep Clayton and Maria apart?"

Parker didn't have to give that much thought. "As long as it takes."

"You really think a couple of flat tires will stop him?"

Parker laughed. "It will tonight."

"And what's your plan for tomorrow night, Einstein?"

Parker had no idea. "We'll think of something." For now, he just wanted to get to Chokoloskee.

"If it's anything like your plan tonight," Wilson said, "I'm in."

CHAPTER 23

ANGELICA HATED THAT SHE'D RESORTED to spying, but how else was she going to know what was really going on in her sister's head? She leaned in close to the bathroom vent and heard every word—at least on Maria's side of the phone conversation.

"Clayton, you've told me—like three times already. Four tires flat. Two kids got away. The police are looking for them right now."

Angelica wished she could hear what Clayton was saying.

"You just told me it was two *kids*. It's probably just students pranking your dad. What makes you think *my* dad is behind it?"

What? The guy didn't miss a chance to put a wedge between Maria and Dad. *Jerk.* There's no way Dad flattened Clayton's tires.

"I didn't say I didn't believe the tires are flat." Maria's voice . . . too apologetic. Too weak. "I just don't think my dad had anything—"

152

And of course the jerk doesn't even let her finish. Angelica wanted to march into her room and rip the phone out of her hands. Disconnect the call. What was wrong with Maria?

"I'm not doubting your instincts."

Animal instincts were more like it.

"I'm sorry. Honest, I truly am. I should have never questioned—"

You're sorry? Because you expressed your opinion? "C'mon, Maria," Angelica whispered. "Why are you apologizing to him? *You* didn't flatten his tires. And Dad didn't flatten the tires either."

And somehow—in that moment—Angelica knew exactly who was behind the vandalism—or the *devilry*, as Mr. Kingman would have put it. She smiled. *Thank you, Parker and Wilson. You're my heroes.*

Suddenly Angelica was keenly aware of the quiet. She raised up on her tiptoes and leaned closer to the vent. Not a word. Not a sound. Did Maria suspect Angelica was listening? Had she moved to the other side of her bedroom? Angelica eyed the bathroom door, half expecting her sister to barge in and catch her standing on the toilet, ear to the vent.

"Mmmm-hmmm."

Maria's voice. Okay. She was still there. Angelica tried to relax.

"I understand. With the tires flat, there's definitely no chance of us meeting tonight. But we'll find another time and place. I promise."

Now Angelica really wished she could hear the other end of the conversation.

"I'm so sorry this happened," Maria said. "I love you too. You know that, right?"

Sick. Angelica's stomach swirled. She'd heard enough. She stepped off the toilet and turned on the sink faucet. She rested her elbows on the counter and scooped the water in her hands. Let it flow through her fingers.

The way Angelica saw things, Maria had fallen under the toxic narcissist's spell. And he was definitely obsessed with her—in the worst way. Angelica's theory? He loved himself so much that he thought Maria should too.

Clayton had the nerve to phone Maria, even after Dad had made it really clear Clayton was to stay away. Didn't he know Dad would check Maria's phone? Sure he did. Clayton was flaunting the control he had over Maria. But he was making a big mistake too.

"You don't know my dad," Angelica whispered. "You really think he can't stop you?" If Dad found out Clayton hadn't backed off, he definitely wouldn't wring his hands helplessly. Dad would do anything to protect his girls—which was a good feeling. But it scared her too, because unless Uncle Vaughn stopped him, Dad might do something that could land him in jail.

But maybe her dad wouldn't have to do anything. Parker was already working to keep Clayton away from Maria, wasn't he? And he'd obviously roped Wilson into helping him. Flattening tires? Totally primitive. And maybe brilliant at the same time. It kept Maria from seeing Clayton until the tires were fixed. But did Parker really know the kind of guy they were messing with?

Angelica watched the water circle the drain and disappear. If only it were that easy to rid themselves of Clayton. Just whoosh him down a drain somewhere.

But it wasn't only Clayton who bothered her at this moment. It was the fact that Maria still said she loved him—and wanted to be with him.

Love was blind. She'd heard Dad say that before, hadn't she?

But in Maria's case love was deaf and dumb, too. It was the only way to explain why she stayed with him. Couldn't she see how controlling he was? How mean? Oh yeah, love was definitely messing with Maria's head.

Angelica turned off the faucet and stood there just staring into the mirror. Maybe Clayton was right. Maybe there was nothing Dad could do to stop the jerk—without ending up in jail. But that didn't mean Angelica had to sit back and do nothing. She'd get her sister to wake up and see Clayton for the beast he really was.

Right. And exactly how was she going to do that?

Between Maria's infatuation and Clayton's obsession, Angelica knew there was no way she'd be able to keep the two of them apart.

But they hadn't seen each other tonight, thanks to those flat tires. She owed Parker and Wilson a big thanks on the ride to school tomorrow. They'd done it for her. She was sure of that. And she was sure of one other thing as well. They'd come up with more plans to keep Clayton away from Maria . . . and Angelica wanted in.

CHAPTER 24

PARKER LACED HIS HANDS BEHIND HIS HEAD and stared at the darkened ceiling above his bed. They'd made it home. But the scene at Kingman's kept replaying. Kingman pulling out a shotgun. The rage. How hard would it be for Kingman to find out who wrecked the tires?

Kingman had always given off a spooky vibe. But the way he went off on his dad? The guy was capable of anything if he was angry enough. If Kingman *ever* figured out Parker was behind the tire stunt, he'd beat the tar out of him.

Or worse.

Which was one more reason they'd have to be really, really careful that Kingman—or his dear dad, Principal K—didn't find out. Parker's stomach squirmed at the thought of his meeting with the principal in the morning. What if he asked him a point-blank question about the tires?

God . . . the plan was so simple . . . just letting air out of the tires. No real damage would be done. How did it get so tangled? I feel I have to do my part to help keep Maria and Kingman apart . . . but I made a real mess here. Help me do the right thing. Show me what that is.

But if he wanted to make this right, he'd have to pay for the two wrecked tires, wouldn't he? Sure, Wilson was the one who knifed them, but Parker was the one who came up with the plan to flatten the tires in the first place. Maybe he could save up for the tires and send an anonymous note with the cash. He'd ask Dad what he thought.

Parker's gimpy arm was already asleep—and tingling like the thing was plugged in. Too bad *he* couldn't drop off to sleep as easily as his arm. He shifted and pulled his gimpy arm out from under his head with his good hand. He twisted his fist into his forearm and palm to dull the prickles.

They'd tried to hammer out a plan for tomorrow—without success. Every idea they came up with had bigger holes than Wilson had punched in Principal K's tires. How long would they have to keep Clayton and Maria apart before her head cleared and she stayed away from him all on her own? They couldn't pull something off every night, could they?

He reached for the black tactical flashlight on the lampstand by his bed and thumbed it on. The 2,000 lumen LED lit up his room. He slid the zoom to narrow the beam and tracked the perimeter of the room along the ceiling. The beam picked up the INTEGRITTY sign on the wall over his head, and Parker held it there.

"What was the deal with that spelling, Grandpa?" There was a

Bible verse written on the back side of the plaque. Something from Psalms. But it didn't give a clue as to why Grandpa had deliberately misspelled the word.

Gritty. Would that be as in sandy or grimy or something? Was he trying to say that being a person of integrity meant getting your hands dirty sometimes? Well, Parker had certainly done that tonight.

A knock on his bedroom door made him bolt upright—fists clenched. Okay, so he was a little jumpy.

Dad poked his head in, silhouetted by the hall light. He was still wearing his ranger uniform. "I saw the light. So you're awake?" He whispered it, barely loud enough to hear.

Which was crazy. Mom was still out of town. Dad and Parker were the only ones home, and obviously both of them were awake. "Yeah. You don't have to whisper."

Dad was always trying to fill in for Mom whenever she was away. Even though he was tired, he tried to make the time to talk. "Got your text that you got home okay. You said the results were a mixed bag?"

Parker glanced at the sign once more and gave him the quick rundown—and his idea for an anonymous payment for the tires.

"That sounds like the right thing to do," Dad said. "And anonymous is a must. You've confessed to me—and to God—and that's enough. I really don't want to risk Clayton finding out it was you. Not after the way you described him."

"Even Wilson said it was like he was possessed."

Dad's eyes narrowed a bit, and he gave a single nod. "We need to take this before the throne." Dad bowed his head and talked to God. He asked for wisdom. For protection. And for Maria's freedom.

They both were quiet for a few moments after he finished. The seriousness of it all swept over Parker again.

"We'll talk more about this," Dad said. "But for now, you've got to understand I can't allow you to be anywhere near Kingman. Got it?"

"I want to stay as far away as I can," Parker said. Which was absolutely true, but it was definitely going to make it trickier to keep Kingman away from Maria.

"Uncle Sammy called. He'll be here in a few minutes. Didn't want you wondering if you saw his headlights when he pulls up."

Which was strange. "Kinda late, isn't it?"

"He needed to run by his house after the shift to check on the girls, but wanted to drop by here afterward to talk."

Dread found a foothold in his stomach. The two of them generally worked together for their entire shift. What did Uncle Sammy need to talk about that he couldn't bring up at the ranger station? "Something wrong?"

"He's really concerned about Maria." Even in the dim light Parker could see his dad's jaw clench and unclench. "He needs to unload. I'm not going to say a word about you seeing Clayton push his dad around, or Sammy will never sleep tonight. But I'll tell him tomorrow. He needs to know how volatile and unstable Clayton is, but that's going to ratchet his fears up quite a bit too."

But something about Dad changed even as he said it. Parker didn't get the idea that his dad was only going to be a listening ear. He'd dropped into ranger mode. As a park ranger, he wasn't just a nature guide. He was an expert on human nature, too. He had the instincts of a cop—just like Uncle Sammy. *This is war.* Hadn't his dad said something like that?

"Maria is still gaga over Kingman," Parker said.

"She sure is."

Headlights swept across the room through the bedroom window. The headlights blinked off. "Take care of Uncle Sammy, Dad."

The door of Uncle Sammy's pickup slammed shut. "Okay. Sleep good." He stepped out into the hall and closed the door behind him.

Parker turned off his flashlight. He swung his legs over the side of his bed and tiptoed to the open window. He could see Uncle Sammy leaning against the grill of his pickup, one boot hooked on the bumper. Parker stayed in the shadows and watched as Dad crunched across the crushed shell driveway and extended his hand. Uncle Sammy gripped it and pulled Dad into a hug, which wasn't like him at all. Weird.

"That sorry piece of toxic waste messed with her head," Uncle Sammy said.

"But you busted them up," Dad said. "She'll come back around. Maria's smart. She'll—"

"I've never seen her like this." Uncle Sammy stared at the sky. "Not ever. It's worse than I thought."

Parker stepped closer to the window. Strained to hear. Either Dad didn't answer, or he spoke too quietly for Parker to pick it up.

"She's going to do something," Uncle Sammy said. "I feel it."

"Like what?"

"No idea." Uncle Sammy picked up a handful of gravel. "She's gotten reckless. Like she doesn't care about anything—or doesn't want me to think she does."

How could she have changed so much?

"Okay," Dad said. "She's acting up a bit. Don't you think she's just busting your chops for breaking them up?"

"Definitely," Uncle Sammy said. "But you know how she is when she gets something in her head."

"Like her dad."

"Exactly what has me worried." Uncle Sammy sidearmed a rock toward the black jungle bordering their lot.

"How can I help?"

That was just like his dad. Always ready to do something. Like he knew Uncle Sammy needed more than just someone to listen. Parker pressed closer to the screen.

"I've got a real bad feeling about this." Uncle Sammy shook his head. "Honestly? I'm scared."

Words he'd never heard come from Uncle Sammy's mouth before. Not ever.

"Understandable," Dad said.

He looked at the silhouettes of the two men he respected most in the world. Dad was looking down, toeing the crushed shells and gravel. Uncle Sammy stared into the blackest part of the brush. Hands on hips.

"You're taking this to the next level . . . the thing we talked about." Dad said it like it was a fact. Not a question.

What *exactly* was the next level?

Uncle Sammy nodded. "I can't ask you to be part of this."

Part of *what*?

"Too late for that," Dad said. "I told you before. If it comes to this . . . I'm in."

Neither of them said a word. Like they both knew there was no backing out. Like they had a little plan of their own to keep Clayton and Maria apart.

"If this goes down as planned, we're heroes," Uncle Sammy said. "And Maria is free from whatever hold Kingman has on her.

But there are some risks, too." Uncle Sammy stood there, still staring out into the black like he was imagining the worst. "Even the most careful plans can go wrong."

After tonight, Parker couldn't argue with that.

"The wrong person sees this—or tries to step in—and this could go really bad," Uncle Sammy said. "The police could get involved. We've got to go in with our eyes open."

Uncle Sammy's words hit Parker with the force of thunder. And lightning. What on earth did he mean by that? Obviously, they were planning on something way beyond flattening tires.

"This is war, brother. We've got to do something," Dad said. "And don't think I won't be praying."

Uncle Sammy didn't say anything for a long moment. "She's going to hate me. At first anyway. But it will get better, right?"

Dad put his arm around Uncle Sammy's shoulder. "I'm sure of it."

"Okay, get everything set up," Uncle Sammy said. "But we don't fire the starting pistol yet. We do the deed only if we're sure there's no other way."

The *deed*?

"I don't think we can wait long," Dad said.

Uncle Sammy nodded. "I'll do anything to protect her from that animal." He pulled a thick envelope from his back pocket. "They'll be needing this."

The whole scene was like something out of a movie. The envelope—what else could it be? It had to be cash, and a lot of it. They were hiring someone—but to do exactly what? Not that Parker didn't think Kingman deserved the worst Dad and Uncle Sammy could throw at him—but at what risk?

Dad took the bundle. "They'll need a timetable. Even if it's tentative."

"Saturday night," Uncle Sammy said. "I won't wait longer than that."

Four days.

Uncle Sammy shifted his weight. "She'll thank me for this someday, right?"

Dad didn't answer right away. "Someday."

"Good enough." Uncle Sammy climbed back into the pickup.

Parker ducked away from the window an instant before the headlights beamed through it. He plastered his back against the wall and tried to calm his own breathing. Uncle Sammy backed out of the driveway, the shell fragments crunching under the all-terrain tires.

Dad must have stayed outside a full two minutes after the truck was out of earshot. The screen door opened. Dad stepped inside. A minute later Parker heard Dad's office door close.

It looked like Dad wasn't going to be getting much sleep tonight. Parker sat on the edge of his bed and stared at the floor. Dad wouldn't be the only one.

CHAPTER 25

THE WAY PARKER SAW IT, Jelly must have gotten a whole lot more sleep than he did. She was actually grinning when she rode up on her bike. She planted both feet on the ground and looked from Parker to Wilson and back.

"You two definitely dance to the beat of a different drummer—or however the saying goes," Jelly said. "I wanted to stop Maria from seeing Clayton, but couldn't come up with a way to do that. You two did. I came to thank you and . . ."

Wilson looked skeptical. "Go on."

"I want to know if you're a couple of one-hit wonders, or if you've got more songs on your playlist to keep Clayton and Maria apart."

Parker motioned for her to keep her voice down. "You're asking if we have a plan for tonight?"

Angelica nodded. "And I'm here to tell you that the three of us can make beautiful music together. I want to help. I want in."

For an instant, Parker wondered how she'd figured out they were behind it. Would it be as easy for Kingman to find out? He hoped not. But the fact that Jelly wanted to join them was a good thing. Moments later they were on their bikes and heading for school.

Jelly fell in behind him. "So, what's your plan for tonight?"

Parker had no idea. "We're kind of making this up as we go." But they'd have to think of something.

"Right now Bucky's got some other things to think about." Wilson grinned. "This is Wednesday. You've still got to get through your little meeting with the principal this morning."

"Don't remind me." But it wasn't the meeting with Principal K that consumed Parker's thoughts on the ride across the bridge to Everglades City. Not that he wasn't dreading it. It was just that right at this moment he couldn't get his mind off Maria. The nicest girl he'd ever known—a one-in-a-thousand—tangled up with the biggest jerk of a guy living south of the Tamiami Trail. Or north of it, for that matter.

And now Parker's dad—and Maria's—were going to do something that could get them in a swampload of trouble if something went wrong. He thought of how things had worked out last night with the tires. Even the simplest plans can take unexpected turns. Maybe if Parker stepped things up a little—to keep Kingman and Maria apart—Dad wouldn't have to risk everything by launching his plan with Uncle Sammy.

Wilson rode in the lead position. "I'm going to go way out on a limb here. You told your dad we improvised our plan last night—and slashed those tires."

Funny the way Wilson said *we*. Parker didn't answer.

"I knew it," Wilson said. "I wouldn't tell my dad in a million years. You're *such* a boy scout, you know?"

It was the right thing to do. "I've got no regrets. No secrets. And that feels good."

"I'll bet," Jelly said.

"Boyscout Bucky." Wilson shook his head and smiled at the stupid little nickname. "So did your dad ground you?"

"I was honest with him," Parker said. There was no need to tell Wilson about paying for the tires. "He hasn't pulled in the leash." Which was amazing, really.

"I need a dad like that," Wilson said. "Either he's really smart— or he's totally clueless."

Parker didn't need to point out the obvious. At that moment he wanted to tell him about what he'd seen—and overheard—last night. Jelly too. But something made him hold back, and he wasn't sure why.

Jelly pulled up beside him, standing on the pedals to keep up. "Worried?"

He shrugged. It wasn't exactly the kind of thing a guy wanted to admit to a girl, even if it was only Jelly.

"It'll be okay," she said.

He glanced over at her. How could she possibly know that? He wished he had her confidence. Then again, if she knew that her dad was planning something that sounded really risky, maybe she'd be a little less positive herself. "How long do we need to keep them apart? I mean, before she starts seeing how lucky she is to be free from him?"

Jelly gave him a confused look. "Maria and Clayton?"

"Weren't we just talking about them?"

She angled her head slightly and gave him one of those looks like she sometimes did when she was trying to figure him out. "I was talking about your meeting with the principal."

"Oh." Parker nodded. "Right. Actually I've been trying not to think about that meeting. So, how long before Maria gets her 20/20 back?"

"If she saw what we saw last night," Wilson said, "she'd be over him already."

Jelly didn't answer. Not like she was ignoring him. More like she'd zoned out.

"Jelly?"

"She thinks she's in *love*. You two are ridiculous, you know that? You think a girl can stop loving a guy just like that?" She snapped her fingers. "It's going to take more than a couple days for her to get over him—even if Clayton *is* a total creep."

Wilson raised his eyebrows in mock offense. "Gee, Jelly, we're all on the same side here, remember?"

Jelly didn't seem to appreciate that comment. But she kept her mouth shut—and suddenly the whole ride got awkward.

Parker pictured the envelope Uncle Sammy handed Dad last night. How much money was there—and what was it supposed to buy? Obviously, whatever it was, they wanted to keep it secret. So secret that Uncle Sammy didn't hand off the money at work. Parker would have to tell Jelly about this, but maybe he wouldn't bring Wilson in the loop just yet. The more people who knew— the greater the chances were that Dad and Uncle Sammy would get caught. But doing what?

Parker needed Jelly's take on the mysterious conversation. But it would have to wait until they were alone—and Jelly wasn't so edgy. "So how are we going to keep Kingman and Maria apart while your dad is on shift tonight?"

Jelly shook her head. "No idea. I've begged and pleaded with her. Nothing I say is going to change her mind."

They rode into the outskirts of Everglades City together, leaving Chokoloskee and the bridge behind them. Last year Maria used to bike with them to school. Now that she was a senior, all that changed. Scratch that. It was Kingman who changed her. He picked her up and drove her to school and back home again—until the breakup. Now Rosie was giving her a ride.

"The tire flattening was genius," Jelly said. "Simple. Uncomplicated. Totally effective."

Wilson jerked his thumb toward Parker. "That was all Bucky."

"Except for the Miccosukee tire-knifing part," Parker said.

"So come up with another plan before school is over today," Jelly said. "I'm counting on you guys." She looked directly at Parker.

Great.

"Knifing the tires again won't work," Wilson said. "If I were Kingman, I'd have the truck booby-trapped somehow. He'll be ready for anybody messing with the truck again."

"Agreed." Parker had no intention of getting near Kingman's truck.

"We've both got paintball guns," Wilson said. "We could hide in the brush. If Kingman leaves the house and heads to the truck . . . blam, blam, blam, blam—ka-chow. We let him have it."

"Until Kingman pulls out his pump-action," Parker said. "I'm not sure paintball guns are going to be our best shot," Parker said.

"Our best *shot*. I get it." Wilson grinned.

They zigzagged their way to Storter Avenue and rode along

the waterfront until Everglades City School came into view. They all slowed as if nobody wanted to be the first to ride onto school grounds.

"We'll keep thinking," Parker said.

"I've still got a stash of bottle rockets from the Fourth," Wilson said. "And a killer Roman candle. Maybe we rain a little fire on him. Keep him pinned down somewhere."

This time Jelly laughed. "Tell me you don't do your best thinking in the morning. Please."

"What?" Wilson looked at her, then back at Parker. "I'm serious."

"Exactly what I was afraid of," Jelly said.

Now Parker worked to hold back a smile. "We don't have to rush into a plan. We've got all day to perfect it."

Wilson nodded and gave Jelly a slightly disgusted look. He pulled ahead and hopped off his bike at the rack.

"Promise me you won't go with Wilson's plan—whatever it is," Jelly said. Whatever burr was under Jelly's saddle seemed to be gone now.

"We need to talk," Parker said just loud enough for Jelly to hear. "Without Wilson."

Jelly opened her mouth slightly like she wanted to ask a question. But to her credit she closed it without a word, her lips forming a tight line. She gave a single nod like she understood.

"After school."

She nodded again. "Do you ever get the feeling this is going to get a lot messier before it gets better?"

He swung off his bike and pictured Uncle Sammy handing Dad the envelope. "You have no idea."

CHAPTER 26

ANGELICA LOCKED HER BIKE TO PARKER'S. Keeping Maria and Clayton apart; was Parker doing all this for her—Angelica—or was it because he still had some kind of crazy boyhood crush on Maria? He wouldn't be the first one to fall in love with his babysitter as a kid. But he'd outgrown that years ago, right? He wouldn't be that stupid, would he? She pictured Parker's expression when Maria walked into his hospital room. When she kissed his forehead. The truth was, guys did dumb things all the time. Parker was living proof of that. As far as Angelica was concerned, Parker was Exhibit A that God existed. Only God could have kept him alive after all the crazy things he'd done and gone through.

Her mind drifted to the curse Wilson talked about. On the one hand, believing the Miccosukee superstition was ridiculous, and she knew it. But deep down she wasn't ready to totally discount it. There was that little gnawing issue of that story of Jericho. A definite geographic area that was cursed—for real. Isn't that part of why she'd volunteered to help the guys keep Clayton from Maria? Sure, it was about saving her sister from that gravy-sucking pig, but there was another motive there too, wasn't there? It was about staying close to Parker before he left, to help make sure he got out in one piece.

"See you boys later," she said. "I've got to stop by my locker."

Wilson waved—and was off.

Parker locked eyes with her. "Remember, we have to talk—after school."

"Give me a hint," she said. "What's so important that—"

"Not here." He looked over his shoulder once. "And I've got to get my game face on for the meeting with Mr. Kingman." He turned and was gone.

She made her way to her locker and stood there staring into it. Her life was a mess. She was doing her best to hold everything together, but no matter what she did, Maria was slipping away. And Parker was taking greater risks. Now Parker had some mysterious information to share. Whatever was on his mind, it definitely seemed to have him spooked.

Angelica slammed her locker. "Heaven help me," she whispered. She had an uneasy feeling she was going to need all the help she could get.

CHAPTER 27

PARKER CRUISED THROUGH THE DAY like he was golden or something. Mr. Kingman didn't seem to have a single suspicion that Parker was the tire-assassin. He just railed on about the horrors of skipping the last five minutes of school after the doctor appointment the day before. Then he slapped him with a detention. Big deal. He never told Principal K that Dad had given him permission. Knowing the principal, he'd get Dad in here to learn about the Star of Integrity—and somehow he'd get Dad serving a detention too.

The hardest thing about the little meeting was trying to avoid looking at Principal K's eyes—without being too obvious. Parker was sure the principal would see something—a tinge of guilt, maybe—and then he'd grill him about the tires. Parker kept his focus on Principal K's nose instead. The principal's schnoz angled off to one side . . . something Parker had never noticed before. But now that he did, it struck him as really, really funny for some reason. He drove one knuckle into his thigh to keep from laughing.

Parker spent the first half of his detention whipping through his homework, the second half trying to come up with a plan to keep Maria and Kingman apart. By the time he left school he was no closer to a solution than he'd been on the ride this morning.

Jelly was waiting by the bikes. Sitting on the asphalt cross-legged—and writing furiously in a notebook. Apparently, she was trying to get her homework done too.

She smiled when she saw him. "How's the delinquent?"

"Ready to get out of here." He unlocked his bike. "Why were you sitting on the pavement instead of the grass?"

"Fire ants."

Like it was the most normal answer in the world. "And why is it you love this place so much?"

"*Used* to love this place." She packed her books in her pack. "Not so much anymore."

Parker smiled. "So you've had enough of the bugs and alligators and pythons and—"

"That isn't it. I still love the wilds here—and the danger of everything living in the Glades."

He nearly made a joke about Mr. Night Crawler—the guy they'd dubbed Creepy Crawley—but caught himself when he saw how dead serious she looked. "So what is it?"

She hesitated, like she was choosing her words carefully. "There is something wrong with this place. Something out of balance. And it's robbing me of the people I love most in this world."

Okay, that was heavy.

"My mom left us five months after we arrived. Just up and walked out. And Maria? I've lost her, Parker."

"She'll come around," Parker said. "I promise you that."

"I wish I had your confidence," Jelly said. "There's something evil about the place. And whatever it is, it won't be satisfied taking my mom and my sister. It will keep taking and taking." She looked at him for a long moment, and then off toward the stacks of stone crab traps. "Everyone I truly care about."

Maybe she was more right than she knew. What if whatever her dad had planned went wrong—and got him in trouble somehow?

Jelly let out a deep breath and smiled. "Well, I never planned to say all that. You ready to go?"

Parker scanned the area. "Where's Wilson?"

She straddled her bike. "His dad called. Told him to get his tail home. Pronto."

"What was that all about?"

"Wilson had no idea. He said to call him after dinner. But honestly? It isn't looking so good for his help tonight."

"He said *that*?"

"He didn't have to. I could hear his dad's voice—and he wasn't on speakerphone."

Parker mounted his bike. "So no Roman candles tonight."

Jelly giggled, then turned serious. "Now tell me what you couldn't tell me this morning."

By the time they were halfway across the bridge to Chokoloskee, he'd filled her in on what he'd seen and overheard the night before.

Jelly shook her head like the whole thing was insane. "This whole place is cursed. What do you think they're planning to do?"

Parker didn't even want to share his theory, as if saying it out loud would make it somehow more likely to happen. "I was hoping you had some ideas."

Jelly rode in silence for a minute. "There's a payment involved—so our dads aren't in this alone."

Parker gave her a sideways glance. "I could have said that much."

"And," Jelly said, "whatever they're paying to have done could end up with some kind of disaster."

"If things don't go just right," Parker said.

"You think it's something illegal?"

That was the crazy thing. His dad upheld the law. And so did Jelly's. That was part of their job as rangers. "I just can't see that." But he couldn't think of a thing that was legal that required mysterious payments, either. Maybe the lines of what was legal and what wasn't got blurred a bit in times of war.

They passed the ramp at the Fishing Hole Marina. Parker instinctively looked for the *Night Crawler* where he'd seen the trailer before. Which was ridiculous. Of course, Creepy Crawley and his boat were gone.

"Here's my theory," Jelly said. "They're hiring somebody to threaten Clayton good. To put a real scare into him."

"Do you see that working?"

"Maybe they're paying someone to rough him up." Jelly made a fist and held it up. "Bang, zoom . . . to the moon and all that, you know?"

"Which would be illegal from the start—and I can't see my dad doing that." But how desperate would Dad need to be to do something like that? No, it just didn't fit. "Besides, why would they need a massive bundle of money just for someone to knock Kingman around? I'll bet people would line up and *pay* for the chance to rough him up." Parker coasted to a stop and put a leg down. "Whatever they're planning, it's got to be pretty drastic, right?"

Jelly braked and stared at him. "You think my dad would put a hit on Clayton?"

"*Our* dads. They're in it together, remember? My dad would never do that—and he wouldn't let yours do that either."

Jelly shook her head. "I don't know, Parker. You're not a dad— and neither am I. But good dads would give their lives to protect their kids, don't you think?"

"Stop," Parker said. "Don't go there."

"I'm just saying . . . my dad would die for me—or Maria. And your dad would die to protect you." Jelly shrugged. "Is it so hard to believe that they'd kill?"

"Yes, it is."

"Soldiers learn to kill just to protect those they love." Jelly sat on her bike, deep in thought. "And we call them heroes. My dad is a hero too. So is yours. What if they're going to hire some lowlife to get rid of a scumbag?"

"That can't be it." His dad was the most godly man he know. "Hiring a hit man would go against everything he believes. Everything he taught me."

They rode down Smallwood Drive in silence for a couple of blocks.

"Or," Jelly said, "what if the money is to *buy* something illegal?"

Was she crazy? Where was she going with this?

"Hear me out. They buy illegal drugs—lots and lots of them. Enough to supply an army of druggies for a month. Plant them in Clayton's truck. Call in an anonymous tip—and he gets busted for dealing. That would keep him off the street—and away from Maria."

He hadn't even thought of that. "You've got a criminal mind, you know that? Where does that come from?"

"Has to be the company I keep." She smiled back. "Maybe you're wearing off on me, delinquent."

The idea was crazy. Bold. But it could work. The thing was, it still didn't sound like something a man of integrity would do. But if he were desperate enough? "I don't know what to think anymore."

"You said they were going to get things lined up, but not actually put their plan into action yet, right?"

Parker nodded. "That's what they said."

"Which means we need to come up with a plan of our own so they don't have to use theirs."

Easier said than done.

"Any ideas yet?" She looked at him like this whole thing was riding on him.

"Working on it." He'd brainstormed with Wilson between nearly every period today. And he still had no plan. "Go home. Keep your eyes on her. Let's touch base after dinner."

She gave him a suspicious look. "What are you going to do?"

"Go out in the *Bomb*. Tool around the bay a bit."

She nodded like she understood. Like she knew he did his best thinking when he was out in his boat. On the water.

Jelly didn't say another word until she had to turn off for home. "You'll come up with something," she said. "I'm praying you do."

Praying. He'd do a little of that while out in the boat too. It was about time he tapped into that source—because Parker was fresh out of ideas.

CHAPTER 28

PARKER WAS ALREADY LATE for dinner by the time he beached the *Boy's Bomb*. But with his mom still in Boston working the freelance job, regular mealtimes were a little rare anyway. He raised the outboard, lashed the bow line to a cypress, and mounted his bike on the fly to head home.

But his time out on the water had cleared his head. Wilson might have said it was the fresh salty air, but Parker knew it was the fact that he'd taken the time to actually talk to the God of the universe. He'd gone to the throne, as his dad liked to say. An idea came to mind before he'd headed back to the beach.

Up until that moment, every idea he'd had was about how *Parker* could keep them apart. He'd been thinking about the whole thing wrong. What if he turned this around so that Kingman and Maria actually *wanted* to stay away from each other?

His new plan was crazy. Out of the box to the point where it made the tire-flattening event look totally amateur. Everything would have to go just right if his new plan was going to work. There'd be zero margin for mistakes—and he needed to get started pronto. He pedaled past Smallwood's Store and headed for home like he was being chased by a swarm of angry wasps. Pulling this thing off would be a perfect ending to a really decent day—if he didn't get stung somehow.

Dad's truck wasn't on the driveway, but Parker found a note on the kitchen table.

Mac and cheese in the fridge. Running errands. Will be home late.

Parker pictured the bundle of cash. Imagined Dad off on some remote spit of land jutting into the Everglades somewhere, paying somebody to do *something*. No matter how hard he tried to conjure up the image, he couldn't make it seem real. He couldn't imagine Dad working on a scheme to plant drugs on Kingman—or hiring someone to put the fear of God into him. It wasn't possible. He'd never known his dad to deliberately do something illegal, especially something that would hurt someone else. There had to be some other plan, but for the life of him, Parker couldn't figure out what it was. "Dad . . . what are you up to?"

Whatever Dad and Uncle Sammy had planned, likely they were pushing the limits—or if something went wrong, maybe even crossing some kind of invisible boundary that shouldn't be crossed, right?

Which was why Parker had to get out in front of this. Keep Kingman and Maria apart before his dad did something that would change his life—and Parker's—forever. Honestly, the sooner they *all* escaped this place, the better life would be.

Parker slid his dinner into the microwave and hit the timer. He closed his eyes, reviewed the details of his crazy plan, and drew in the delicious smell of the mac and cheese. His stomach turned and rumbled as the plate went round and round.

His phone buzzed with a text message before he'd finished half the meal. Jelly.

She's meeting him tonight and won't listen to me. If I tell my dad, she'll know—and she'll do something really stupid. I know it. You've got to do something. Got a plan yet?

He texted back.

Keep her busy. On my way. Will explain plan when I get there. Meet outside.

He put the plate back in the fridge, left a quick note for his dad, and tore out the door. The plan was out there, all right. Way out . . . as in orbit. But sometimes the smartest solution was the craziest one. And this one was absolutely insane.

CHAPTER 29

ALL ANGELICA HAD TO DO was stall her sister long enough for Parker to arrive. He said he had a plan—and it had to be better than slashing tires. Actually, she didn't care what Parker had in mind. As long as it worked.

Maria stepped back into the room. Freshly-applied lipstick. The deep red one she always wore on dates. *Killer Kisser* . . . Clayton's favorite. She picked up her phone. Scrolled through it.

If only her dad wasn't working so many hours. If he were here, Maria wouldn't be wearing the lipstick right now.

"We need to talk," Angelica said.

Maria didn't look up from her phone. "So you can report to Dad?"

Her words stung. "Do you even *hear* yourself anymore? This isn't you."

Maria held her hands up and looked at them. First the palms. Then the backs. "Pretty sure this is still me."

"See? What's with the sarcasm? What happened to my big sister?"

Maria sat and scrolled through her phone again like she didn't hear a word. Angelica stared at her. This was the sister who was there for her when Mom left. How could one guy change her so much?

"Do you remember how you felt when Mom walked out on us?"

Maria's head snapped up. "Do *not* compare me to Mom. Ever."

There was no comparison. Maria had been more of a mom to her than her real mom ever was. But now Maria was leaving. Pulling away from her—for a guy who was increasingly abusive. It wasn't supposed to be like this. "I need you."

"I'm not your mom."

Angelica didn't know if she gasped aloud—or just inside. But Maria's words hit her like a punch to the gut. "No, you're not Mom. But right now you remind me a lot of her."

"Do not *say* that."

"Mom abandoned me. Us. For some guy who didn't care one bit about what would happen to our family," Angelica said. "How is that not *exactly* what you're doing now?"

If the accusation hit home, Maria never showed it. "Can we just drop this? I don't want to fight."

"Then why do you want to be back with *him* so much? All you ever did before the breakup was fight."

For an instant Angelica saw the softness of the old Maria in her sister's eyes.

The doorbell rang, and the new Maria was back. Clayton's Maria—whoever she was.

Maria looked out the window. "It's only Parker."

Angelica went for the door. "Give me a minute to stall him off. I still want to talk."

Maria didn't answer, but she didn't argue either. That was something. She hunkered over her phone, texting madly. Angelica didn't need two guesses to figure out who Maria was talking to.

Parker stepped away from the door and off the porch. He bent over his bike like he was inspecting the chain. "Jelly," he spoke to the bike instead of looking at her—like he was afraid Maria was watching and didn't want to arouse any suspicions.

"I need you to buy me two minutes with her phone," Parker whispered. "Can you do that?"

"What are you going to do?"

"Text Kingman."

"With her own phone?" Angelica smiled. "Interesting. But you won't find Clayton on the contact list. She took his name off after the breakup—in case my dad checked her phone."

Parker kept his back to her, lifted the rear wheel off the ground, and turned the cranks a couple of times. "Then how are they communicating?"

"Look under the name *Kayla*. It's actually Clayton's number."

He stood and brushed his hands on his cargo shorts. "When did her mind get so devious?"

For an instant, Angelica thought he was joking. But the look on his face said otherwise. "When she began dating a devil."

"Let's do this," he said. "Two minutes. What's her passcode?"

"Just remember Christmas Eve. 1224." Angelica led the way back inside. Maria was still there—scrolling through her phone.

She looked up—past Angelica—and smiled. "Hey, Parker. What are you up to?"

He shrugged. "Trying to save the world from monsters."

Jelly could *not* believe he just said that.

Maria laughed and set her phone on the end table. "There's no such thing as monsters, Parker Buckman."

"Yeah, when I was a kid, that's what my favorite babysitter always said when I had bad dreams—and I had some doozies," Parker said. "I remember one nightmare that woke me from a dead sleep—some kind of monster with razor sharp teeth—and I must have screamed bloody murder or something."

"You scared me half to death," Maria said. "I sat on the edge of your bed and smoothed your hair and sang to you until you calmed down."

Parker shrugged like what Maria had done was no big deal. Like it didn't mean that much to him at the time—or now. But he was trying just a little too hard to be casual about the whole conversation, it seemed to Angelica.

"That's when you told me monsters didn't exist," Parker said. "Remember?"

"And you believed me."

"Until this." Parker raised his maimed arm a bit. "Now I know monsters are real."

Maria looked sympathetic. "I guess you learned the truth the hard way."

"And I'm still learning." Something flared in Parker's eyes. Anger? "Not all monsters have claws and crawl on all fours. The worst kind walk on two legs."

Angelica knew exactly where he was going with this, and likely Maria did too. She had to stop him before he said something about Clayton. She raised both hands. "Before you start giving all of us bad dreams, I need to talk to my sister for a couple minutes. Alone."

Parker took a step back, toward the door. "Want me to wait outside?"

Angelica was impressed. There wasn't even a trace of his real motive showing. "No, stay here. We'll just go in the other room." She headed for Maria's room and motioned her sister to follow. "C'mon."

Maria scooped up her phone.

Angelica stopped and planted her hands on her hips. "Really?" She pointed at the phone. "Can't you just leave it alone for two minutes?" She held her breath.

Maria's ears reddened at the edges. She hesitated and looked over her shoulder at Parker instead. She never used to be that suspicious before dating Clayton.

Parker pointed toward the kitchen. "You ladies mind if I hunt for some cookies and milk? Fighting monsters can really work up a guy's appetite."

Okay, get the guy an Oscar.

Maria laughed and seemed to relax. "Just loaded the cookie jar with Oreos."

"Double Stuf?"

Maria nodded. "What other kind is there?"

Parker hustled for the kitchen. Maria's thumbs flew over the screen. She studied it for another moment, then dropped it on the couch and brushed past Angelica. "Two minutes."

She just erased the exchange with Kayla. Angelica was sure of it. She was taking no chances. She followed Maria into the bedroom and closed the door behind her.

Maria sat straight-backed on the edge of her bed. "If you make one more crack about me being like Mom the conversation is over."

Angelica swung the desk chair between Maria and the door. Not that she could stop her if Maria tried to bolt, but she could slow her down. She straddled the chair backward, and leaned against the backrest. "Mom left us for a guy. He was a jerk. I was only saying—"

Maria stood. "I warned you."

"Sorry." Angelica held up both hands. "Not another word about her. I promise."

Maria hesitated, then sat.

"Let's say that Rosie started going out with a guy," Angelica said. "And—"

"I would be happy for her," Maria said. "Rosie Santucci is my best friend—so we support each other."

Angelica ignored the dig about being besties. "But imagine you knew some things about this guy that terrified you, and you were absolutely sure he was going to hurt her. Wouldn't you warn her?"

"Rosie's a big girl," Maria said. "I'd trust her to make good choices."

"But let's say you knew she was in danger with this guy. And every time you tried to warn her, she just shut you down. Pulled away. Wouldn't you keep trying?"

Maria shook her head. "If I truly *was* a good friend I'd support her."

Her sister wasn't making this easy. "What if Rosie is too close to the situation? What if she isn't seeing clearly?"

"In other words, I think I can see things better than my friend? Sounds arrogant to me."

Angelica leaned in. "Not at all. But sometimes the outside view is the more clear one, right? Let's say you've heard Rosie argue with her boyfriend. And you're convinced that boyfriend will hurt her someday."

"He'd never hurt her."

"Maybe not as long as he believed she loved him. But what if that changed? What if Rosie saw something—but didn't know how to get away?"

Maria looked at Angelica for a long moment. Her eyes softened. "Rosie would call me. If she believed she needed my help getting away from him, I know she'd get word to me somehow. Are you hearing me?"

Maria paused long enough to let that sink in. "If I say I really love my friend, I need to trust she'll let me know if she needs help, don't you think?"

"Okay," Angelica said. "Let's pretend you've seen a scary side to the boyfriend. A side that terrified you. You saw a cruel streak and a rage inside him that Rosie just couldn't see. By the time Rosie realizes she needs help, it may be too late. Have you thought of that? Why can't Rosie just trust *your* judgment for once—trust that you know this guy to be dangerous?"

"Rosie knows he won't hurt her. Period."

"But I've seen the bruises." The words slipped out before Angelica realized her mistake.

Maria's eyes hardened, and she looked like she was ready to stand again. "Are you still telling me a story about Rosie? Because it sounds like we've just entered a new chapter here. And if that's the case, I think our little story time is done."

Angelica took a deep breath. "I'm sorry. It's just . . . how do you stop someone you love from making the mistake of their life if they won't even let you talk?"

Maria sat there. She might as well have been wearing a mask, because whatever she was feeling wasn't showing on her face. What if Maria wasn't feeling anything at all? Could Clayton have caused Maria to be that hardened?

Angelica shuddered. She was not going to cry. Was not. She blinked back tears. Clearly the conversation was over. And if she pushed too hard now she'd lose her voice to Maria completely. There was no talking her out of this. Not until she saw Clayton for who he really was—or he got tired of her and left her for good. Had it been two minutes yet? "Talk to me about something. Anything." She blotted her eyes on her sleeve. "I need to pull it together before I go back out there." Which was true. She didn't want Parker to pick up on the hopeless feeling that swept through her.

But more importantly she needed to stall. She had to give Parker the time he needed, and pray his plan to keep Clayton and Maria apart tonight was more effective than her own attempt had just been.

CHAPTER 30

THE INSTANT THE BEDROOM DOOR CLOSED, Parker was back in the living room. He practically pounced on the phone. There was no "Kayla" in recent messages—but the name popped up as soon as he started typing it in. He stretched the fingers on his bad hand. Tried to work out the numbness, and pecked out a message.

They're on to our plan.

He sent it off and kept going. That's the way Maria always texted Jelly. Short rapid-fire messages.

We have to abort. Tonight is out.

He paused. Turned off the ringer an instant before a text fired back. Change location?

Parker smiled. "Hel-lo, Kayla."

No. I'll still go. But I'll be followed. He tapped Send and kept typing.

Promise me you'll stay home. If you don't show, they'll think you stood me up. Send.

I'll play that I'm furious. Send.

I may text, ask what happened. Send.

Because I'm going to leave my phone where my dad can check it. Send.

Write something nasty back. How it's over—and you never want to see me again. Send.

Kayla, aka Kingman, was back seconds later. Think he'll buy it?

Parker shook the prickling numbness out of his hand and texted back.

I'll sell it. Believe me. Send.

Don't contact me after that. Give me three days. They have to be convinced it's really over. Send.

I may keep texting you, begging you to text back. I may say I don't understand—but DO NOT answer the texts. Promise me. My dad is a phone-Nazi. He'll be checking. Send.

I promise—but I'm not afraid of your dad.

"You should be afraid of Uncle Sammy," Parker whispered. We'll meet Saturday night. Send.

He glanced toward the bedroom door. Still closed—but the girls were awfully quiet. "Just a little longer, Jelly."

Maria's phone vibrated. Where?

Would three days be enough time for Maria to come to her senses? If he could send Kingman on a wild goose chase he'd buy another day.

Loop Road. Park at the Gator Hook trailhead just after sunset. 8pm. I'll get Rosie to drop me. Send.

Kingman responded almost immediately. Good choice.

Parker kept texting. I'll get there as quick as I can. I may have to lose my sister. My dad is covering a second shift that night, so if I'm late don't worry. Send.

Parker's hands were shaking. Actually, it was just his gimpy hand.

Kingman was back. You're brilliant. And beautiful. I want you more than ever. I'll be there.

Parker gripped the phone. Wanted to crush it.

When my dad is sure it's over—I'll get all the leash we need. OK? Send.

Parker fired off another one. See you at Gator Hook—Saturday. Send.

The phone vibrated. Godzilla couldn't keep me away.

Sick. How perfect that the monster himself would mention another one.

Parker's internal clock screamed he was over the two minutes he'd asked Jelly for.

Gotta run. Send.

Maria's phone vibrated instantly. This will work.

"Oh, yeah," Parker whispered. "Working pretty good so far." Now if Kingman would just stop texting back.

Erasing now—don't reply. Send.

Parker arrowed back a screen and deleted the entire exchange with "Kayla"—and heard the bedroom door open.

He flicked the ringer back on and placed Maria's phone exactly where he'd found it on the couch. He made a beeline for the kitchen on tiptoe—and prayed Maria wouldn't see him running.

CHAPTER 31

ANGELICA STALLED AT THE THRESHOLD—her hand on the knob—hoping Parker had heard her open the door. Praying she'd given him enough time. She turned to face Maria. "I love you, you know. Everything I'm doing—or will do—is because I love you."

Maria reached and drew Angelica in close. "I know, Baby. I know. I love you too."

Just not enough. Angelica knew her sister was no closer to leaving Clayton than she'd been at the start of their conversation.

"Parker's going to wonder what's going on." Maria nodded toward the hallway. "Ready?"

Angelica took a deep breath and blew it out. If she stalled now, Maria would get suspicious. She swung the door open wide and strolled down the hall ahead of Maria.

Instinctively Angelica glanced at Maria's phone on the couch. Had Parker pulled off his little plan?

Maria scooped up the phone and scrolled through it. Relief flashed across her face for an instant. She slid the phone in her back pocket and looked toward the empty kitchen doorway. "Hey Parker, did you find everything you were looking for?"

He stepped out of the kitchen, the cookie jar tucked under one arm like it was a football. Parker worked an Oreo to one side of his mouth and gave them a lopsided grin. "Mission accomplished."

Yes. Hope surged inside Angelica. *Yes, yes, yes.*

Parker set the cookie jar down. "And now I'm going for a bike ride. You girls want to join me?"

"You two go." Maria waved them off. "I've got things to do anyway."

Not anymore. Angelica was dying to say it. But Maria would find out soon enough.

CHAPTER 32

PARKER PEDALED ALONGSIDE JELLY, grinning. There was no way to describe the feeling welling up inside him. It reminded him of when he'd seen the *Boy's Bomb* for the first time. Used—but in great shape. The teal color gleaming under coats of wax. He'd taken the boat for a test drive before they actually bought the skiff. Total freedom. Euphoria. Dad stood on shore watching while Parker opened the forty-horse Merc up—and skimmed across the water. He made a bunch of ridiculously sharp turns at full throttle—just to see what it could do—and didn't slow up for the waves. He got a faceful of spray more than once, and the whole thing turned out to be one of those life-doesn't-get-better-than-this moments.

And this ride with Jelly—right now—was another one. Pedaling hard. Wind blowing back his hair and rushing in his ears. He kept looking at Jelly, and every time she just shook her head, grinning back.

They headed for Smallwood's Store—almost instinctively. He needed to get out in the boat. Feel some spray.

"Okay, give me the whole thing again," she said. "Every text."

Parker went over the sequence of messages as best as he could remember them.

"You. Are. A. Genius!" Jelly shouted into the wind as they pedaled right down the center stripe.

Parker felt like he could pedal to the doctor's office in Naples. And back.

"The plan was simple," Jelly said. "Perfect. And you coming out of the kitchen with your face stuffed with cookies totally obliterated any suspicion."

Kingman was head and shoulders taller than Parker, and outweighed him by at least seventy-five pounds. Parker had taken on that ugly giant—and won. "From one to ten—ten being boiling mad—how hot would Kingman be if he found out it was me texting him?"

Jelly's smile vaporized. "What *if* he finds out?"

"How would he?"

"But what if he did?" She looked dead serious.

Weird. One second she was laughing, riding high, and couldn't stop talking about what they'd just pulled off. And now?

"You're taking a risk," she said. "You know that, right?"

Parker shrugged. "We both are."

"But I'm her sister. Why are *you* doing it?"

"Kingman's a jerk. Maria's way too good for him. We're protecting her, right?" He glanced at Jelly. Clearly, she was waiting—like he wasn't giving her the answer she'd hoped to get. "And we're trying to keep our dads from doing something really risky, remember?"

She nodded. "Anything else?"

"If we don't keep them apart, he'll hurt Maria. You said it your-self, right?"

She kept pedaling. "So that's it? You're doing all this to protect Maria . . . and help our dads?"

How many more reasons did she need? "Yeah, I guess."

Jelly pulled ahead—and actually looked annoyed. Parker gave her some space. Seriously, what difference did it make *why* he was doing this? He was helping, and that was all that mattered, right?

She coasted until he pulled up alongside her again. "What if our dads already made the payout? They'll be taking some kind of crazy risk for nothing if your little plan actually keeps Maria and Clayton apart."

That was not a happy thought. What was making her so nega-tive all of a sudden?

"There's no way of knowing," Jelly said.

Actually, there was a way. Something Parker could do anyway—and he'd check it tonight.

They neared Smallwood's Store, and Jelly slowed her pace. "Your dad. Mine. You. Wilson. Everybody is risking so much, just because Maria is being stupid."

"Actually I had fun pancaking those tires. Believe me, Wilson did too. And the texts? I'm still flying high."

"Yeah, and your head is in the clouds," Jelly said. "What do you think Clayton would do if he figured out it was you behind that stuff?"

Kingman was a back-shooter. He was slimy that way. "He'd try to catch me off guard. When I wasn't expecting it."

"The guy is filled with demon-rage, Parker. I've seen it—in his eyes, anyway. You've seen it too. And what if that rage comes out of its cage?"

Kingman threatened his own dad with a shotgun. The way Parker saw it, he was scary-close to pulling that trigger. "It could get ugly, I guess." Which was an understatement.

She propped her bike against the cypress and sat on the edge of the *Boy's Bomb*. "He'll kill you."

Parker's gut twisted—like his body was telling him Jelly's words were true. He glanced at the cypress trees, half expecting Kingman to appear. "I'll be okay." But he made himself a promise, too. Unless he was going to school, he'd never go out without his Jimbo strapped to his leg. Then again, did he really think he'd pull a survival knife on Kingman, even if things got really crazy? "He's not going to find out I was behind the texts—or the tires."

She shook her head. "Don't be stupid. Unless we keep them apart, they'll compare notes. They'll talk about the day—and the exact time those texts went out. Maria will realize you were the only one alone with her phone, and she'll tell Clayton. I know it. We should never have messed with them. I shouldn't have let you use her phone."

What was it with her? One minute she thought he was brilliant, and now she was worried he'd made a really dumb mistake. Suddenly it felt like it was getting too late to go for a ride in the boat. He'd head home. Maybe Dad was back by now.

"We just stick to our plan." Parker flashed a smile. Okay, maybe he forced it a bit. "All we have to do is keep them apart, right?"

"But what if we *can't* keep Clayton away from Maria?" She stared out at Chokoloskee Bay beyond Smallwood's. "After what you've just done . . . we need a Plan B."

Parker looked at her. "Plan B?"

She nodded. "How to keep Clayton away from *you*."

CHAPTER 33

ANGELICA HEARD MARIA'S MUFFLED SOBS through the bedroom wall long after she'd gone to bed. She probably didn't think anyone could hear. Maybe she didn't care if they did. But it did prove one thing. Parker's plan had worked. He'd kept Clayton away from Maria for another day. Obviously, Maria figured that Clayton stood her up.

If only he really did.

If Maria had the least suspicion about what Parker had masterminded with the texts, Angelica would have known by now. Hopefully Maria wouldn't ever figure it out.

Should she go to her sister's room? See if Maria had a change of heart? But Angelica knew better.

Dad had to hear her crying, but he didn't go to her room to try to fix things. He wasn't exactly on Maria's hero list right now. But more than ever he was at the top of Angelica's. Dad had done the right thing by breaking them up. The hard thing. He'd protected Maria, even though he had to guess she'd hate him for it.

She pictured Parker's face when she'd questioned him about his motives. Confused? Hurt? "I'm doing this for you, Jelly." That's all she really wanted to hear. But she didn't even get a mention. Parker was doing it to protect his dad—and Angelica's. She didn't doubt him on that. But deep down it was all about Maria. Even *he* couldn't see the obvious. He still had a shadow of his stupid old "babysitter crush" feelings for Maria. When Maria and Parker were talking about him with the bad dreams? He looked pitiful. Whipped.

Parker could be so stinking naïve. And not just about matters of the heart. He still wasn't fully grasping the danger he'd be in when the truth of what he'd done surfaced.

"What a mess you've made of everything, Maria."

For just an instant, a crazy thought crossed her mind. That somehow Angelica would make an even *worse* mess before this was all over.

CHAPTER 34

PARKER DIDN'T KNOW EXACTLY what time it was, but it felt late—and he still couldn't get to sleep. He forced himself not to look at the time, because that would only make it worse.

Dad had gone to bed at least a half hour ago. Was he having as much trouble sleeping as Parker was? Whatever Dad and Uncle Sammy had planned, it could get dangerous if something went wrong. That was for sure. But what they *didn't* know . . . was that they didn't need to do a thing. Not yet. If the texts worked as well as Parker and Jelly thought they would, maybe their dads would never need to do *whatever* they were planning.

The simplest thing—and definitely the most honest—would be to tell his dad what they'd done. Then Dad could put his own plan on hold until he could see how the texting scheme panned out. They'd join forces in a sense.

Unless he hadn't made the payout. If Operation Payola hadn't started, there was no need to tell Dad anything yet. It wasn't that Parker feared getting in trouble. Would Dad be upset about the bogus texts he'd sent Kingman from Maria's phone? He was pretty sure Dad would be okay with that. Keeping Kingman from Maria was a war, and he'd just fed the enemy some bad intel, that was all.

The thing that really gnawed at him? He'd have to tell his dad he'd hid in the shadows and eavesdropped on his conversation with Uncle Sammy. Wouldn't his dad be disappointed in him? Maybe he could stall that conversation off just a little longer.

So that just left the big question. Had Dad already set the plan in motion?

After Dad took the money from Uncle Sammy last night, he'd gone into his office and closed the door before slipping off to bed. Unless he took the money with him to work today, likely the money was stashed in the office somewhere—which meant he hadn't put his plan into action yet.

There was only one way Parker would know if he could delay his confession. He had to see if the money was still there.

Parker tucked his pillow under one arm, grabbed the LED flashlight from beside his bed, and tiptoed out of his room. Mom and Dad's door was shut. No light coming from under the door. If Mom wasn't still in Boston, there was a chance they'd still be talking. But with her gone, he'd be dead to the world. There was no way he'd hear Parker in the office—if he was careful.

Okay, Parker. Get going. Let's do this. He crept down the hall, through the kitchen, and into his dad's office. He closed the door without making a sound and placed his pillow at the bottom of the door. He dropped onto his hands and knees and made sure the pillow covered the entire space between the bottom of the door and the floor. Satisfied, he stood and flicked on the flashlight.

The room was only what, six feet wide? Maybe eight feet long. Dad kept his office as neat as his uniform. Bookcase, desk, chair, and a second chair for when Mom or Uncle Sammy joined Dad there. How long would it take to search it?

He started at the bookcase, trying to avoid looking directly at the alligator skull sitting on top of it. He focused on the shelves of books instead, just to be sure the books were pressed all the way back. He checked behind the bookcase, and under it too. No bundle of cash.

Parker moved to the desk. Sat in Dad's chair for a moment. The cork bulletin board mounted to the wall in front of him had a few neatly clipped articles tacked in one corner. Every one of them was written by Mom. Dad had drawn a heart around her name on the byline.

Parker missed her. Not that he'd admit that to anyone. But she'd been gone a lot on assignment lately. That was another problem with living in a podunk town at the bottom of the Everglades. A person who wanted to make a living freelance writing for papers and magazines couldn't do all their work from home. Sometimes they had to go where the stories were. And clearly there was nothing happening in this corner of the world. Nothing anybody wanted to read about anyway.

A stack of manila folders sat on the corner of the desk. None of them thick enough to hide a stash of cash. Framed pictures lined the back of the desk—and Parker checked behind every one of them. No bundle of Benjamins.

His desktop was organized, with an odd collection of items

that held a special meaning to Dad. An old silver dollar. A cue ball. A hunk of supposed kryptonite. But no wad of cash.

The desk was unlocked. Parker slid open each drawer without a sound. Checked to make sure the payout wasn't taped to the bottom of one.

"C'mon, Dad," he whispered. "Where'd you hide the money? Tell me you didn't actually transfer it to some drug mogul— or Guido the thumb-buster." But in his heart he knew his dad wouldn't be part of something like that. There was no way.

He checked the time. How long had he been in here? It was crazy, but he felt like a burglar in his own house. He crawled under the desk—but there was no envelope duct-taped there either.

After another five minutes, he had to face the facts. There was no money here. He leaned back in Dad's chair and did a sweep of the room with the flashlight. Door. Extra chair. Bookcase. He stopped and stared at the alligator skull on the top of the bookcase. The jaws were propped open with a small dowel rod—giving it the appearance of an all-too-familiar, menacing grin.

Uncle Sammy showed up with the skull just two weeks after the mauling. Parker had never asked, but he was pretty sure that it wasn't some random rogue gator that the rangers euthanized. Alligators could be territorial. Parker was sure Dad and Uncle Sammy had hunted the gator down who had nearly killed him— and they'd taken its head. It wasn't a trophy as much as it was an act of vengeance.

Parker stood, keeping his flashlight on the pockmarked skull. The empty eye sockets were black, yet the beast seemed to be looking right at him. Would Dad have hidden the money there, knowing Parker would steer clear of it? Grabbing the extra chair, he swung it around in front of the bookcase and used it as a stool.

The chair didn't give him enough height to get a visual inside the beast's jaws. He reached—then hesitated. *C'mon, Parker. It's just a skull.* The numbness in his arm seemed to get worse. Penetrated deeper somehow. Spread up to his shoulder.

Carefully, he slid his hand through the gaping jaws, past the stick propping them open, and onto the top of the bookcase behind it. His fingers brushed against a package. A bundle—just the right size. *Bingo.*

"Clever, Dad." This was definitely the cash, right? Dad wasn't hiding a stash of coupons up there. Parker knew he'd kick himself later if he didn't make one hundred percent sure.

He slowly lifted the bundle, angling it slightly to avoid knocking out the prop stick holding open the jaws. The instant he saw it, he recognized it as the same package Uncle Sammy had given Dad.

Parker glanced at the office door. Held his breath to listen for any movement in the house. Then he quietly slid the rubber bands off the bundle and opened the envelope.

Parker shined his flashlight inside—and stopped. There was a *whole* lot of cash inside. More than he'd ever seen at one time, that was for sure.

Dad, what are you getting yourself into?

Benjamin Franklin stared into the beam of the flashlight and didn't even squint. He had that slight smile on his face like he knew exactly what the payment was intended for—and he wasn't telling.

Maybe if Parker knew how much money was in the envelope he'd get a clue as to what Dad intended to do. He took the bundle back to Dad's desk and sat.

A warning sounded in his head. Telling him to put the money

back and get out of there. What if Dad walked in? But it wouldn't take more than a couple of minutes to count a stack of hundreds, right?

He slid the money out of the envelope and saw the scrap of paper when he did. No name. Just a phone number. Parker set the paper on the desk and whisked through the stack of money, counting as fast as he could.

Seventy-three hundred dollars. Which was an odd number. Maybe it was seventy-five hundred and he'd miscounted. Whatever. He was close enough. But what on earth was Dad going to do with all that money? He could buy a decent used skiff for less. He could buy enough guns to fill an arsenal, with plenty of ammo to boot.

If the money was about buying drugs and planting them in Clayton's truck, didn't seventy-three hundred seem like total overkill? Wouldn't a thousand bucks be enough to get Clayton arrested—and away from Maria for a long, long time?

Parker's heart beat out its own warning now. Or maybe it was the fact that he knew this was way too much money for the drug idea. It seemed like the right amount of money to hire some brute named Guido to do a little job, though. But that couldn't be right. Not *his* dad. There had to be another answer that had nothing to do with illegal drugs or shady hit men.

Dad, what are you doing with this?

But the important thing was, the money was still here. Parker didn't have to wake Dad up to tell him what he'd been up to. Not yet. And as long as the money stayed put, Dad wasn't putting himself in any danger.

What are you planning, Dad? And how can I keep you from doing it?

Parker could hide the money someplace else. Lock it inside a desk drawer and lose the key. But what if Dad checked the gator's throat in the morning, just to be sure the money was safe? If the money was gone, Parker would be the first one he'd question. Maybe the right thing to do was to just tell Dad he'd purposely listened in on the conversation with Uncle Sammy.

Parker restacked the money, put it in the envelope, and picked up the scrap of paper. The phone number was the key. If Parker dialed it, maybe he'd find out exactly what Dad planned to do. Then Parker could come up with a plan to stop him.

He rummaged in the drawer for scratch paper and jotted down the number. The last four digits were 4033. He stared at it for a moment and smiled.

Parker didn't have to hide the money in a different spot. All he had to do was make sure Dad never connected up with the contact person. And that would be easy. Parker grabbed a black pen to match the ink on the scrap of paper. He shook his hand and flexed his fingers. Then he turned the two threes into eights.

You are a genius, Parker! He slipped the paper back in with the money, stretched the rubber bands around it, and stood on the chair.

He placed the bundle deep into the throat of the alligator skull—and felt his phone vibrate. He jerked his hand away from the alligator, knocking out the support dowel in the process. Gravity did the rest. The jaws snapped shut around his scarred forearm.

"Ahhhhh!" How loud had he just said that? He lifted the jaw open with his good hand, eased his arm out, and set the prop back in place. Prickles shot up and down his arm in waves. He stood there, rubbing his forearm down, staring into the black eye sockets of the monster. Wilson would say it was a sign. That it was some kind of warning that Parker was still under that Miccosukee curse of the Everglades. Which was ridiculous.

Get out of here, Parker. You've been in Dad's office way too long.

Parker swung the chair in place and scanned the room to be sure everything was just as he found it.

His phone vibrated again.

Jelly.

Whatever was on her mind at this hour would have to wait a few minutes. Right now, he had to get out of here. He flicked off his flashlight, grabbed the pillow from the floor, and tiptoed back out into the darkened hallway.

He'd found the cash—and by changing the phone number, he just might have saved his Dad and Uncle Sammy from making a mistake. He crawled onto his bed and flopped on his back. He pulled out his phone, but hesitated before checking Jelly's text. He pictured the alligator skull—the way it had chomped down on his arm. *The* arm. Freak coincidence? Or *was* it a sign? An omen? Was God warning him to steer clear of this whole thing? Sometimes God used mysterious ways to keep people on the right paths . . . or off wrong ones.

He kicked back. Hiked up his knees. Pulled out his phone and read Jelly's text.

You awake?

Parker smiled and texted back. He couldn't wait to tell her about finding the money. But not tonight. He'd wait until he could see her face. And that wasn't the type of thing he'd chance texting about anyway.

Had an awful blowup with Maria.

Not good. He texted back. Is she okay?

Parker tried to picture the two of them arguing, but it just didn't fit. They were close. Always had been—especially after their mom walked out. Never in a million years would he have figured a bozo like Kingman could get between them. Poor Jelly . . . this thing was putting her through the wringer.

He stared at the screen. Why hadn't she responded?

`Jelly?`

Nothing. For what seemed like a full minute. Maybe she was talking to Maria again.

`No. She's not okay. She's been messed up ever since she started with Clayton. Thanks for asking how I am.`

Great. `Sorry. How are you?`

`Nice try. But a little late.`

Oh, C'mon, Jelly. `Really. How are you?`

`Forget it. Go back to sleep.`

He waited to see if she'd break down and send something anyway. She could be stubborn, but he was pretty determined too. `Tell me about the fight.`

He waited a full minute this time.

`Is she on to us?`

Still nothing. But she was following the texts. He was sure of that. There was no way she turned off her phone. Okay, maybe he'd toss her a carrot. Draw her out. `Found out something about the other situation. Really great news, actually.`

The little dots appeared at the bottom of the screen. "Got you, Jelly. I knew you couldn't resist."

`Good for you.`

He stared at the screen. "What is going on with you?" `Look, I'm sorry, okay?`

`Yeah. It sounds like it.`

What was her problem? `Let's talk. Can I call?` He could

tell her about finding the money. So what if he didn't see her face. Maybe that would get her out of the funk she was in.

He watched the screen. She was taking her sweet time answering.

Not tonight.

He read it over again in some kind of stunned disbelief. She'd never turned down a call. Ever. Yeah, it's kinda late. Let's hang out tomorrow morning. Talk then.

Maybe.

Maybe? What was wrong with her? Obviously, she wasn't in a good place, and he couldn't pull her out of it with texting. He had to back away before he made things worse—if that were possible.

Okay. I hope you get some good sleep. Hopefully she'd wake up on the right side of the bed, too.

This is Angelica you texted. I think you must have sent that last message to me by mistake.

What? He reread what he'd just sent. Who else would I text that to?

Maria. She's the only one you really care about, right?

Terrific. Now she was resorting to exaggeration—and making shock statements. "You're being a drama queen, Jelly. But I'm not taking the bait." Don't be stupid.

Just the opposite. I'm finally wising up.

"Girls are insane." Parker wished he'd never answered her text. How did this get so messed up? "You know what? I'm not going to play your games." He tossed the phone on the nightstand next to his bed.

What did Jelly want from him? Wasn't he trying to help her save *her* sister? How could she think Parker didn't care about Jelly herself? Maybe he'd talk to her tomorrow.

Or maybe he wouldn't. Maybe he'd wait until she called him.

He rolled onto one side and settled in. Balled up the extra pillow and tucked it under his arm like a football. What he really needed to do was forget about the conversation with Jelly. Forget about Maria. Forget everything and just get some sleep. He'd sort things out in the morning.

But telling a guy with nearly perfect recall to forget was like telling an alligator to let go of an arm once the beast had locked onto it. It wasn't likely to happen.

Parker pictured the skull in the office again, with the jaws closed on his arm. Maybe it was some sort of warning. Maybe not. But deep inside he got the feeling that no matter how hard he tried to avoid it, this whole thing was going to come back and bite him somehow.

CHAPTER 35

PARKER DIDN'T TEXT JELLY THURSDAY—or Friday. He avoided her at school the best he could. His strategy was simple. Ignore her—and she'd break the ice. She'd come around eventually, telling him how ridiculous she'd been. The problem was, his strategy wasn't working.

Saturday morning Parker biked to the *Boy's Bomb* ten minutes after Dad left for work. He needed to clear his head. The weirdness with Jelly bothered him a whole lot more than Maria's problems right now. She hadn't said a single word to him since the texts Wednesday night.

Fine. He was done. She'd contact him when she was ready. He didn't need the drama.

The problem was, he really *wanted* to talk to her. If nothing else, just to hear how well the texts to "Kayla" had worked. He wasn't ready to march in a victory parade just yet, but still, his crazy plan of keeping Maria away from Kingman seemed to be working so perfectly it was almost spooky.

But really, the genius plan only dealt with half of the problem. Sure, he'd kept Maria and Kingman apart, but what about the part about her seeing him for who he really was?

He locked his bike to a support beam under Smallwood's Store and walked the rest of the way to the boat. If all went well, tonight Kingman would slither his way to Gator Hook Trail thinking he'd meet Maria there. What would Kingman do when Maria didn't show? Would he give up on her for good? Or would he figure out that this had all been a scheme to keep them apart? If Maria caught wind of that, she and Jelly would likely have a regular WWE SmackDown. And what would Parker do next? How could he keep Kingman away from Maria again?

Parker stowed his backpack in the boat.

Wilson showed up minutes later. He locked his bike and hustled over. "Just the two of us?"

Parker shrugged. "You tell me. Jelly hasn't said a word to me in almost three days."

Wilson looked back at the road leading to Smallwood's. "I thought I had her talked into it. Maybe I read her wrong."

"Join the club."

Wilson laughed and kicked off his shoes. "What she needs is a peanut butter and jelly sandwich. That always makes her feel better."

It would take a whole lot more than that. Parker untied the bow line from the cypress tree, screwed the transom plug in place, and together they dragged the boat into shallow water.

Minutes later they were tooling into Chokoloskee Bay. Parker glanced back more than once, hoping Jelly would be on shore, waving them down. Wilson sat in the front with his back to the bow and his arms slung over the sides, catching spray.

"So what's the latest from Jelly?" Parker tried to make it sound casual. Like he didn't really care.

"Good news, bad news." Wilson sat up. "As far as Jelly knows, your little scheme worked. Maria and Kingman haven't been together. Not once."

Just as he'd hoped. "And the bad?"

Wilson looked off at the islands dotting the bay. "Maria is acting totally bizarro."

Parker looked at him. "Bizarro?"

Wilson shrugged. "Taking chances. Doing crazy things."

"Like?"

"Like the real Maria has been abducted by aliens, and the girl living in their house is just a Maria look-alike. Wednesday night she opened up her dad's truck on the bridge like it was a drag strip. Raced one way, then turned around and raced back. Kept doing it until the cops showed up. They clocked her at 105. Jelly snapped a picture of the ticket and showed me the image."

"A hundred and five miles per hour? Maria?"

"Thursday Maria snuck out of the house sometime after midnight—but not to see Kingman. She hitched a ride to the Rod and Reel Club and tried to buy alcohol. At *seventeen*. A cop drove her home—and told her dad."

"Seriously?" Nobody in her family drank. Not Uncle Sammy. Not Maria's mom.

"I say Maria is paying her dad back for busting them up."

That theory actually made sense. "She's liable to kill herself in the process."

Wilson draped one hand over the side of the boat, catching spray. "I think she's got a death wish, man."

"Suicide? No way. Maria isn't that stupid." At least she never used to be.

"Offing herself would be the ultimate way to hurt her dad, though, don't you think?"

"She's too smart for that."

"Smart?" Wilson snorted. "She was dating Kingman, remember? And last night she put a brick through the glass door at the Subway. She reached in, unlocked the door, and actually went inside. Does that sound smart to you?"

Wilson left the question hanging there. But at this point Parker was still trying to picture Maria busting the window.

"She made herself a sandwich." Wilson laughed. "The cops found her sitting at a table chowing on a foot-long Italian like nothing was wrong. She didn't even try to get away. This time they took her to the station and her dad had to post bail."

Parker stared at him. "Unreal. She's totally off the map." He wasn't sure what bothered him more: Maria's insane stunts, or the fact that Jelly hadn't broken radio silence to talk to him about it. Actually he did know. What had gotten into Jelly?

Wilson dragged one hand in the water. "I like her creativity. I mean, hey, I'm kind of looking forward to what she's going to do tonight—unless she goes and gets herself killed."

Parker had no idea how Wilson could be so casual about the whole thing. "At least she's not with Kingman. With any luck she'll wise up and stay away."

Wilson splashed a handful of water at Parker. "I told you, she's stupid. And if you ask me, she's more head over heels about the wacko than ever. She's becoming a total nutcase herself."

When Maria used to babysit years earlier, she was the closest thing to perfect that Parker had ever known. Her laugh. Her
smile. The way she'd look at him when he talked to her. She *got*
him. He had never known a girl could be so fascinating. And mag-
netic. Something drew him to her. He couldn't explain it then, and
wouldn't now. She was nothing short of an angel. Now she was acting like she was possessed. How could Kingman mess with her head
that much? Or maybe he'd had the wrong picture of Maria all along.

Parker eased back on the throttle and cut the engine. The wind
was light in the bay. Smallwood's Store and the landing were long
out of sight, but Parker knew exactly where they were. He grabbed
his lunch and tossed Wilson the other bag. "At least Kingman will
be busy tonight—waiting for her at Gator Hook Trail. By the time
he figures out she's not coming, it will be too late for them to meet
some other way."

"How are we going to keep them apart *after* tonight?" Wilson
eyed him.

"If she's so in love with the moron," Parker said, "how much
can we really do?" He hated to admit it, but facts were facts. Maria
seemed determined to be with Kingman, and would likely keep
doing risky things until she got her way.

Wilson nodded. "Maybe you're right. Maybe it's time to let this
go." He scanned the bay for a long moment. "You haven't looked
at a chart once. You know your way back?"

Parker gave the area a quick scan. Funny how he noticed the
little unique features of so many of the islands—and could remember how they fit on the chart like a jigsaw puzzle. "Yeah, I know
the way."

"That memory of yours is freaky," Wilson said. He settled
back. "But it comes in pretty handy out here."

Actually, today he wished his memory wasn't quite so sharp. Then maybe he could forget that Jelly wasn't talking to him—and that Maria was in love with a guy as dangerous as Kingman. Maybe he could stop worrying about the fact that Dad and Uncle Sammy had something planned that could go bad—if Parker's number-changing strategy failed somehow. And maybe if Parker had a little temporary amnesia, he wouldn't be so uneasy about Kingman figuring out who was behind the tires and texts. If his memory was a little sketchy, he wouldn't be thinking about Kingman—and how a sick guy like him would get his payback. Actually, Parker's super memory wasn't doing him a bit of good today. Right now, what he'd really like to do? Forget.

CHAPTER 36

PARKER DIDN'T PULL THE DRAIN PLUG from the transom of the *Boy's Bomb* after they got back and hauled the skiff up onto the beach. Normally he would, but leaving the plug in place was his little way of making sure he'd have to come back to the boat later. Hopefully he'd take it for another ride while he was at it. Maybe Jelly would be over whatever was bothering her by that time and she'd come with.

It seemed like forever since he'd heard her laugh. A ride in the boat would do her good. It would definitely do him some good to be with her, too.

He biked back to the house after Wilson left. Dad's pickup was gone. Parker grabbed a step stool from the kitchen for a little extra height, and gave the throat of the alligator skull a visual check.

The bundle was still there.

Good. Since Maria hadn't been seeing Kingman in the last few days, maybe Dad and Uncle Sammy were holding off from setting their plan in motion. What if whatever they had planned would put Dad's transfer at risk?

Parker hustled to the kitchen and snacked on a pack of frozen Twinkies, a handful of homemade chocolate chip cookies, and a chocolate shake. Actually, it was just chocolate milk that he'd shaken good before filling his glass. He slurped off the foamy bubbles on top.

He scrolled through the texts between him and Jelly again. The ones from Wednesday—when things all fell apart. She claimed she was "wising up" in her last text. And she'd been acting stupid ever since.

He read them again. And then he saw it. What if she *wasn't* being a drama queen? What if she really believed what she'd said?

"She honestly believes I care more about Maria than I care about her?" Hearing his own voice made him even more sure that was exactly why Jelly was so mad.

How could she think that? He reread the texts. Thought back on when she asked him why he was doing what he was doing. What had he answered her? Something about Kingman being a jerk—and how he needed to keep Kingman away from Maria. And he definitely said he wanted to help Maria. But did he say anything about the one thing that was *really* driving him? That Jelly was hurting—and he knew it—and he wanted to help *her*?

That definitely was what he'd been thinking, but it wasn't obvious in the texts he'd sent. But she should just know he was doing it for her, right? She was his best friend.

But he'd never actually *said* she was the driving force, had he? So maybe she was mad—because she was hurt.

The more he thought about it, the more he saw how this thing was one big misunderstanding. He'd been thinking Jelly was acting stupid? Yeah, and it only took Parker three days to figure out how he'd messed up. Who was the stupid one now?

He just wanted the old Jelly back. At three o'clock he sat on the front step to his house and sent her a text.

Going out in the Bomb later. Wanna ride?

He waited. Just watched the screen. Nothing.

"This is ridiculous. What are you doing, Parker? Give her some space." Maybe she was busy. Maybe she still thought he was a jerk. Maybe he needed to give her a reason to even *want* to answer his texts.

He pecked out a quick text—then spent the next five minutes reading and rereading it.

Hey, I'm really sorry about my dumbness Wednesday. I see it now.

When he was absolutely sure the text couldn't make things any worse, he sent it—and waited.

Five minutes later she replied. Thanks. Can't talk now. Will text when I can.

"Okay." He smiled. At least it didn't sound like she was mad anymore. The chances of going out in the *Bomb* were looking good after all. He grabbed his bike and headed to the landing. He'd walk the shoreline until she texted back.

He was sitting on the dock at Smallwood's Store when his phone chirped just after four-thirty.

Jelly.

He swiped open her text and glanced over at the *Boy's Bomb*, half expecting she would be there.

Maria knows everything. Stay away from Clayton.

He stared at the text and fired back one of his own.

He knows too?

No. She promised she wouldn't tell him.

Which was amazing. How did you manage that?

Had to make her some promises back.

Parker didn't like the sound of that. Like clean her room or something?

Or something.

He stared out over Chokoloskee Bay. Was she deliberately being evasive? You're sure Kingman doesn't know?

Pretty sure. But don't take any chances.

If Clayton didn't know about the texts being bogus, then he'd be expecting to meet Maria at nine tonight. Is she going to meet him at Gator Hook Trail?

She's messed up. I'm scared. Can't say more.

Parker stood. Started pacing the weathered planks of the pier. Why didn't she answer his question? Let's go out in the Bomb. You'll feel better.

No. Want to stay here. See if I can talk her out of it.

She almost never turned down time in the *Boy's Bomb*—when she wasn't hopping mad at him. Talk her out of what exactly?

I can't say.

Parker's stomach churned. You don't know what she's going to do, or you know but can't say?

Second one.

"Gee, Jelly . . . what's going on?" Why not?

I told you. I promised.

Okay, so they formed some kind of uneasy alliance not to rat each other out. He dialed her phone.

She picked up on the first ring. "I can't talk." It definitely sounded like she'd been crying, but her voice wasn't shaky. In fact, she sounded determined. When she got that way, there was no chance she'd budge. Still, if she didn't want to talk, why answer the phone? Maybe what she was really saying was that she couldn't just offer him information, but deep down she was hoping he'd figure it out. "All right. You can't just open up and tell me what's going on, right?"

"Right."

Okay, this was the tricky part. "How about we play twenty questions?"

Jelly didn't answer, but Parker could hear her breathing on the other end.

"Hey, if I ask something you absolutely can't answer, we stop, okay?"

She didn't say a word.

Okay, she was game—barely. He'd have to step carefully or she'd kibosh the whole thing. Start with easy stuff. Questions he already knew the answer to. Things that wouldn't put the promise she'd made at risk. "So you had a talk with your sister."

"Yes."

"She's done some crazy things this week, and you found out what she's planning next, right?"

"Yes."

So far so good. "Something stupid?"

"Yes."

"Worse than anything she's done so far?"

A pause. "Yes."

The sun was slowly backing away from shore. From Chokoloskee Bay. From Parker. "When is she going to do this?"

Jelly didn't answer.

But it wasn't a yes or no question, either. "Is she going to do this soon?"

"Yes."

"Tonight?"

Silence. Had he pushed too hard?

"I don't want to play anymore," Jelly said.

"No, no, no. I'll drop the question." The answer was obvious by her reaction anyway.

Careful now, Parker. Back off a bit. Sunlight flashed off the surface of the bay—like a signal light on a ship with a desperate message. "You said she knows everything. So she knows about the tires, and the texts to Kingman—that it was me?"

"Uh-huh."

Parker groaned. Part of him wanted to know how Maria had put it all together. He could find that out later. Right now, he had to stay focused. "But Maria's not going to tell Kingman?"

"No."

Of course. Maria didn't have to tell Kingman a thing. There was nothing to stop her from meeting up with him tonight. She knew exactly where Kingman would be at nine o'clock. It would be like Parker had actually set up the time and place for a rendezvous.

Maybe Jelly couldn't do anything, but Parker could still stop this. All he had to do was leak the information to his dad, or Uncle Sammy. It was time to circle back around to the question she'd dodged with the texts. "So, she's going to meet him at Gator Hook Trail?"

"No."

What? Jelly had never lied to him. Not that Parker knew of, anyway. But this made no sense. "You're saying Maria knows Kingman is going to be there, but she's *not* going to meet him? Not?"

"Correct."

He had to make sure he was getting this right. "She's going to stand him up?"

"Yes."

"And you're not ecstatic?"

"No."

"Because it sounds like great news to me. I'm thinking it proves she's having second thoughts. Am I right?"

"No."

Okay. Think, Parker. He stared out past the *Boy's Bomb*. Following the frenzied shoreline as it circled the bay. He stopped at the mouth of the Lopez River. Maria was going to do something insane tonight instead of meeting Kingman. Which made some sense—in a twisted way. Maybe she figured that pulling another reckless stunt would make her dad let her date Kingman again—for her own safety. Not that dating Kingman would be any less dangerous. "So she's going to do something really stupid, and you're going to stop her."

"I can't." She said it without hesitation. And with force. Like she was impatient with him. Like he should be figuring this out sooner.

This was crazy. "If you aren't going to stop her, then tell me about her plan. Wilson and I will stop her." Better yet, he'd bring his dad in on the new intel. He'd find a way to stop her. Hopefully some way that didn't call for a $7,300 payola and some super risky plan to make it happen.

"You haven't been listening. I *can't*."

Parker looked out over Chokoloskee Bay. For one brief second he wanted to chuck his phone as far from shore as he could. "Jelly . . . you *do* remember the whole point of all we've been doing is to protect Maria, right? Wilson and I are doing our best—but you've got to help us out a little." Okay, he probably could have gone all day without saying that, but come *on*. She was being totally ridiculous about this.

"Boys can be so stupid, you know that?"

Boys could? Parker held his tongue, but it wasn't easy. "Just tell me already so us *stupid* boys can protect *your* stupid sister, okay?"

A long pause. Uncomfortably long. "We're past protecting Maria. If you haven't figured that out, you're dumber than I thought. I gotta go."

"No, wait—please." Twenty questions was over. Obviously. But for all the answers he got, Parker was more confused than ever. "You know what Maria's going to do. Tonight. And you won't tell me so we can protect her. What am I missing?"

Jelly gave an exasperated sigh. "I break my promise to her—and she breaks hers to me. You figure it out. And I've said too much already."

Jelly disconnected before Parker could even say goodbye. He stood there on the dock, staring out over the bay.

His mind whirled. Maria promised not to tell Kingman about what Parker had done—as long as Jelly kept Maria's secret about her plans tonight. That's what she said, right?

And hadn't Jelly warned Parker about what Kingman would do to him if he ever found out about the tires—and the texts?

"Jelly was right . . . how stupid can I be?"

The promise Jelly made . . . it wasn't about protecting Maria.

"Jelly made the promise to protect me."

CHAPTER 37

ANGELICA BURIED HER HEAD in her pillow and cried the moment she hung up on Parker. She hadn't broken her promise to Maria. But now she was pretty sure Parker would figure out why. She shouldn't have played the stupid twenty questions with him in the first place.

But there was nothing she could do about it now. About any of it.

And she sure wasn't going out for a ride in the *Boy's Bomb* with him. She'd break down and tell him everything for sure. He was in this too deep already. Clayton would eventually find out what Parker had done. He was relentless that way. He'd badger Maria until she spilled. And even Maria wouldn't be able to stop him from some cruel payback. Clayton's blend of swamp justice.

Would Clayton really kill Parker? Everything in her gut said he would—and nobody would find his body.

The only chance Parker had was if Maria had a total heart change—saw Clayton for who he was—and didn't go through with her plans for tonight. In a totally weird way, Parker's fate was tied to Maria's.

Angelica checked the time. Five o'clock. Which meant she had exactly three hours to find a way to get Maria to change her mind.

CHAPTER 38

HOW DO YOU STOP SOMEONE from sneaking off and doing something stupid, when you don't have any idea what they're planning to do? Parker thought about that for a minute. The answer was obvious. Don't let her out of your sight.

He checked the time on his phone, and the battery life. He grabbed his trail pack and dumped everything out of it, then refilled it with whatever he could think of that he might need.

Flashlight. Extra batteries. Quick charge stick for the phone. Hoodie. Mosquito spray. Survival knife. Water bottle. Binoculars.

What else?

He was probably forgetting something, but if he didn't act fast he might be too late. He zipped the bag, slung it over one shoulder, and dialed Wilson.

He answered on the second ring. "Gonna try talking me into knifing tires with you?"

"I had more of a stakeout mission in mind."

"I'm in. Where?"

"Maria's. She's going to try something, and our job is to keep her from doing something stupid. I'll bike by your house in three minutes."

Wilson laughed. "I love it. I'll be on the driveway."

Sure enough. Parker was still a half block from Wilson's when he saw his friend straddle his bike with a pack of his own strapped on his back. Wilson stood on the pedals and rode out to meet Parker so he never had to slow down.

Parker filled Wilson in on the ride to Maria's. By now the whole idea of Jelly "protecting" Parker had him totally annoyed. She would risk Maria's safety to protect him? He was pretty sure it had something to do with his gimpy arm. She didn't think he *could* take care of himself, so she was stepping in like some overprotective mom. Oh yeah, Parker definitely hated that she felt the need to be his Mulan or something. No thanks. Parker could take care of himself.

They stashed their bikes behind a wall of blue crab traps stacked across the street from Maria's home.

"Let's do our surveillance from here," Parker said. They could see through the traps decent enough, and the vantage point gave them a clear view of the house. If Maria tried to leave, they'd see her. And they'd be close enough to do something about it.

"So run this by me again," Wilson said. "We see her sneaking out, we follow. That's it? I mean, if she's on foot . . . great. But what if she has a ride? How are we going to keep up with a car if we're riding bikes?"

Parker didn't need Wilson to tell him the plan had some massive logic gaps. But at least they'd be doing something. Maybe they could just block the driveway with their bikes. "You have a better idea?"

Wilson smiled, reached in his backpack, and pulled out his paintball marker. He screwed the barrel in place and just held it out for a second, like he expected Parker to give him a medal.

"Seriously?"

"We can't keep up with a car, so our job is to keep her from getting in one, right?" Wilson pulled the compressed air cylinder from his pack and screwed it onto the gun. "You gotta use your head, Boyscout Bucky."

"Using a paintball gun to stop her . . . *that's* using your head?"

Wilson attached the ammo hopper, pulled out a plastic bag of paintballs, and scooped handfuls in. "I have 250 rounds. We ought to be able to keep her holed up in the house with that. Unless she calls the police or something."

Parker kind of liked the idea, but seriously? "You're crazy."

"No, you're crazy for not bringing yours. But if we run low on ammo you can keep her pinned down while I bike home for more."

"You can't just sit here and peg her with paintballs."

Wilson eyed Maria's house. "I've nailed you from just as far."

"No, I mean, we *shouldn't* do this."

Wilson stared at him. "She's going to do something stupid. We've got to stop her. You said it yourself."

"So, we *do* something stupid to *stop* something stupid?"

Wilson grinned. "I knew you'd come around."

The thing was, Wilson's plan actually made sense. And now that Maria knew Parker was behind the tires and texts, what difference did it make that she knew he was stepping up his game?

He fired off a text to his dad.

Camping out by Uncle Sammy's. Making sure Maria doesn't sneak out. Will catch you up later—but I think she is planning something crazy tonight.

A minute later Dad responded.

Uncle Sammy and I are keeping an eye on the king. Sounds like we've got some teamwork going.

Okay . . . so that was good. Between Dad and Uncle Sammy— and Wilson and himself—they had this covered, right?

Wilson took a practice shot toward Maria's house. They were well within range. "I pelt her a time or ten. Not in the face. Just mess her up a little. If the sting doesn't stop her, the paint will. She won't meet anybody looking like a Picasso. She'll have to go back inside and change. When she comes out—I'll do it again. Eventually she'll run out of clean clothes. She'll have to stay home and do laundry."

Parker laughed. Okay, it was a crazy idea. But crazy had been working for them so far.

"C'mon, Bucky. All we have to do is delay her so she can't go out and do something she'll regret for the rest of her life, right?"

Absolutely true. Maybe Parker was overthinking this. "How many changes of clothes do you think she has?"

Wilson snorted. "We could be doing this all night."

CHAPTER 39

THE ONE THING PARKER FORGOT? Food. By six-thirty his stomach was giving him all the reminders he needed. "I'm starving."

"We gotta get something to eat." Wilson rolled a couple of paintballs in his hand like a pair of dice. "I'm almost hungry enough to try one of these."

Parker shifted to work out the stiffness in his legs. "You could bike home and grab us something. You'd be back in ten minutes."

"And miss the chance to add some color to Maria's outfit?" Wilson shook his head. "Maybe you could phone Jelly. Ask her to bring us a couple of the PB and J sandwiches she loves so much. And maybe a pack of Twinkies or something."

"Right." Parker nodded. "Hey Jelly, we're waiting to ambush your sister. Can you bring us some snacks?"

Wilson laughed. "I see no problem with that." He raised his

head above the crab trap. "What if Maria's not in there? Then we're guarding an empty house, when we could be raiding your fridge."

"We just saw her ten minutes ago."

"They *have* a back door."

"That leads to a backyard—which leads to nowhere." Parker picked up the binoculars and trained them on the windows again.

"You look like some kind of stalker, you know that, Bucky? Spying through the windows."

"Thanks, you jerk." What if she did slip out the back? Could they have missed her?

"Funny how life has a way of going in circles," Wilson said. "She used to be your sitter, but it looks like you're babysitting *her* now."

Parker grinned. "We should be getting paid for this."

"Seeing the look on her face when I peg her with this," Wilson patted his paintball gun, "is all the pay I need."

A red pickup rounded the corner and headed for Jelly's house. Rust rimmed every wheel well. The bed didn't sit quite straight—like the supports underneath were half eaten away too.

"Incoming," Wilson whispered. "Chevy Silverado."

"Rosie Santucci's truck." Parker tucked the binoculars in his pack. "Maybe Jelly called Rosie, hoping she could talk some sense into her."

"Don't count on it," Wilson said. "If Maria isn't listening to her dad or her sister, I doubt her best friend will turn her around either."

Parker rubbed down his bum arm. The sun cowered low in the sky, reflecting off the windshield. "Can you tell if it's really her driving?"

"Too much glare," Wilson said. "I wouldn't put it past Kingman to use her truck."

The driver backed the Chevy into the drive.

"If it's him, I open fire, right?"

Why give Clayton a chance to get near Maria? Parker nodded.

Wilson smiled. "This is shaping up to be a really great day."
He raised the paintball marker to shoulder height. Steadied it on
a short stack of crab traps.

Parker gauged the distance between them and the truck. "We'll
have a good lead on him if we have to run for it."

Wilson took aim. "I'll slow him down a little first."

The cab door swung open, and Rosie stepped out. Instantly,
Parker relaxed his shoulders. He hadn't even realized how tense
they were.

Wilson lowered the paintball marker, clearly disappointed.

The front door opened and Maria flew out of her house to
meet her. Perfectly faded jeans. Oversize L.L.Bean fishing shirt
with the sleeves rolled up and buttoned in place with those strappy
things. Small backpack over one shoulder. She looked really happy.
Like the old Maria.

"Well look who came out to play." Wilson sighted down the
barrel. "Nice of her to wear a bright orange shirt." He closed one
eye. "I love an easy target."

"Hold on. Let's see what's going on first."

Maria held Rosie in a long hug the way some girls do. She
tossed her pack in the bed of the pickup. Then they walked around
the side of the house arm in arm, both of them chattering and
smiling like they hadn't seen each other in years. "Wish we could
hear what they're saying."

They disappeared behind the house—but seconds later were
back, each carrying one end of Maria's single-seat kayak. Maria
held her paddle in the other hand. They were still chattering—and
moving fast.

"Kayaking now? It'll be dark soon," Wilson said, "and the truck bed is empty. If they're going out in the bay, where's *Rosie's* kayak?"

Parker sensed some kind of warning alarm ringing in his head. "She's dropping Maria someplace." Kayaking alone—at night with no lights? Definitely a bonehead move. "Jelly said Maria was going to do something really stupid—and she was going to try to talk her out of it."

"I guess Jelly failed." Wilson took aim. "Take 'em out?"

"Definitely." Parker wished he'd brought his own paintball gear. "Don't hit her face."

Wilson squeezed off a shot. Probably more for gauging distance and aim than anything. The shot went wide. The girls didn't seem to notice.

"Got you now," Wilson adjusted and fired off a burst of rounds.

Instantly Maria jerked and screamed. Blue splotches exploded on her shoulder, stomach, jeans. She dropped the kayak and curled up behind it. It was positioned sideways, like a red wall across the driveway.

Wilson nailed Rosie twice before she found cover behind the kayak. He peppered the side of the kayak with a long burst. "Raise your head," he whispered. "I dare you."

Parker grabbed a handful of paintballs and topped off the hopper. "Keep them pinned down."

"Oh, yeah." Wilson grinned.

"Why didn't I bring my paintball gun?" Parker said. "She's giving us easy shots."

Rosie crawled closer to Maria. She kept her head low, but not her rear.

"Christmas comes early." Wilson took steady aim. Squeezed the trigger. With a scream, Rosie dropped out of sight.

"Yes!" Parker clapped him on the back. "Let's make sure they keep their heads low too."

Wilson sprayed the side of the kayak with blue paint. "They aren't going anywhere."

"Not unless they're trying out for the Blue Man Group."

Wilson laughed. "Exactly."

The front door opened and Jelly bounded out—heading straight for the kayak. "I didn't tell him. I didn't tell anybody!"

"What's she doing?" Whose side was she on?

She stopped just behind the kayak—standing right out there in the open. "I promise you—I didn't snitch."

Maria said something to Jelly, her body rising above the protection of the kayak as she did.

"Thank you, Angelica." Wilson sighted in and squeezed off two quick shots.

Maria screamed and dropped behind the kayak.

"Stop it!" Jelly scanned the stacks of crab traps, looking their way. "I know it's you. Stop!" She stepped in front of the kayak and spread her arms out wide, making herself a human shield.

What was up with her?

"She's crazy," Wilson growled. "She's going to mess up everything."

Maria and Rosie stayed low, but pushed the kayak toward the truck. Jelly kept just ahead of them—blocking an easy shot. In her efforts to protect Parker, she was actually helping Maria escape? He couldn't live with that. "Ping her."

Wilson hesitated and glanced at Parker. "Jelly?"

Parker grabbed the gun from Wilson. "We have no choice." He took quick aim and squeezed off a shot.

Jelly screamed and clutched her arm—but didn't move. The kayak kept inching toward the truck.

Parker couldn't believe it. "Don't make me do this, Jelly."

"Take her out," Wilson said. "Or give me back the gun."

Parker went into rapid-fire mode. Jelly shrieked and lurched as the paintballs pelted her legs, stomach.

"It's a new dance," Wilson said. "We'll call it the Herky Jerky."

Jelly doubled over and took one on the top of her head. She clutched her noggin and dropped to her knees.

"Oops." Parker stopped, but kept the sights on her. "Load me—just in case."

Jelly stood and took another step even as Wilson scooped handfuls of paintballs into the hopper. "What is she thinking?"

Parker pegged her knee. Thigh. But she didn't drop behind the kayak for cover. "Stubborn, isn't she?"

"I love that about her," Wilson said. "Finish her off."

"Gladly." Parker took careful aim. He squeezed the trigger—and hit the back of Jelly's hand.

Shrieking, Jelly dropped to her knees again and shook her hand. She cradled it, and rocked back and forth.

"So many bones—so little padding," Wilson said. "Nothing worse than a shot to the hand—except maybe one to the face. That still out of bounds?"

Jelly stood—spread her arms again—and marched for the truck.

"C'mon, Jelly," Parker growled. "Back off."

"She's insane," Wilson said. "We're trying to help her, right? If I had a sister, I wouldn't just stand there and let myself get shot for her—no matter how much I loved her."

It wasn't love for Maria that was making her take the hits, and Parker knew it. The truth of it fried him. "Stop it, Jelly." He pulled on the trigger again and again. "Stop."

Jelly howled, stumbled backward, and fell over the kayak. She stood immediately, tears streaming down her cheeks. She looked right at the crab traps. "Why are you doing this?"

Parker lowered the gun. He couldn't bear to see her get hit. But he couldn't live with the thought of Jelly doing this to protect *him* either. "I don't need your protection," he shouted. "Your sister does. So let us do what we need to do."

"Just let her go," Jelly shouted. "You don't know what you're doing—and you're going to mess everything up."

"*We're* messing things up?" Wilson snatched up the gun. "My turn." He sprayed the side of the kayak again. Jelly didn't dive for cover. "You asked for it, Jelly."

Wilson let her have it. "I almost feel bad hitting her. Almost."

Jelly staggered backward, then turned and hobbled for the front door. "Finally." Wilson painted her back to help her along the way. Jelly disappeared inside.

"One down," Wilson said. "I should slap on a new cartridge soon. Just to be sure we have maximum force. Gotta make every shot count. And if the shot doesn't raise a welt, it doesn't count."

Parker scanned the area just to be sure nobody was watching. Somebody making a helpful call to the police was the last thing they needed.

The girls pushed the kayak toward the bed of the pickup—still sideways—careful to stay low.

Wilson took aim. "They're not giving me a shot." He kept the rounds flying anyway. He burst more paintballs off the kayak and the ground around it, but the kayak didn't stop.

In fact, they were moving the kayak faster now, closing the distance between them and the back of the pickup truck. "We gotta stop them." Parker wondered if Rosie left the keys in the ignition. He could run over there, grab the keys—

The girls stood—picking up the kayak as they did—and hefted it along with the paddle into the bed of the pickup. The girls stayed behind the tailgate. Perfectly protected.

"Shoot 'em," Parker said.

"I got no shot."

The pickup worked as a shield now.

"Not good," Wilson said.

"Don't try to hit both of them." Parker scooped more paintballs into the hopper. "Focus all your fire on Rosie. Maria isn't going anywhere without a driver."

Suddenly Rosie rounded the back of the pickup, heading for the driver's door. Maria ran for the other side at the same time.

Wilson let Rosie have it. She screamed and twitched her way to the door, yanked it open, and scrambled inside. Maria slammed the passenger door closed.

The engine roared to life.

"Paint the windshield," Parker shouted.

Wilson half stood, half crouched, and went wild with the semi-automatic, splattering paint against the windshield, blocking their view the best he could.

The wipers and washers came on, smearing the paint—but clearing it enough to see. Tires spinning, Rosie fishtailed out of the driveway, across the street onto the neighbor's lawn, then made a jerky correction back onto the road. The kayak and paddle slid from one side of the bed to the other. For an instant, it looked like it might topple out. But it settled in as the pickup roared out of range.

"I can't believe it." Wilson lowered his paintball gun. "Now what?"

Parker was already standing, slinging his pack over his shoulder. "We go after them."

CHAPTER 40

THEY'D NEVER CATCH THE PICKUP, but maybe Parker could get to wherever Maria was launching before she paddled off. Talk to her—like he should have days ago. Tell her how sick Kingman really was, and the danger she was in for sticking with him. "Only two likely places to put in this side of Everglades City. Let's divide and conquer."

Wilson unscrewed the barrel from the paintball marker and stuffed it in his pack. "I'll hit the marina. I can watch the bridge from there too."

If she crossed the bridge and left Chokoloskee, they'd never catch her. "I'll check Smallwood's."

Jelly flew out the front door—still covered with paint and storming their way. "What's wrong with you two?"

"I didn't know the Blue Angels were in town," Wilson said.

Definitely blue—but the expression on her face wasn't angelic. Angry tears streaked her face. "She thinks I broke our deal. She'll tell Kingman—and he'll be out for blood."

Parker's blood, to be specific. "I don't *need* your protection." Okay, Parker said it with too much force, but she was stepping way over the line here. How could he live with the thought that Jelly let Maria do something stupid—because she was protecting him? He helped cram the last of the supplies in Wilson's pack.

"Let's go, Bucky." Wilson slung the backpack over his shoulders. "Before Jelly slows us down."

Wilson was right. And the pickup was already out of sight. Parker stood on the pedals. Pushed hard—with Wilson right beside him.

Jelly ran to cut them off, but they swung wide around her.

"It's over," Jelly shouted from behind them.

Their friendship or the chance to stop Maria? Parker wasn't sure. He kept pedaling.

Minutes later Wilson peeled off and headed for the marina. "Good luck."

Parker prayed aloud and pushed hard, the wind roaring in his ears. No sign of the red pickup—until he neared Smallwood's. The Chevy pulled out of the entrance and back onto the road just as Parker got there. No kayak in the bed. No Maria in the cab.

If Rosie figured Parker was part of the paintball ambush she might have run him off the road, but she flew right by without even swerving. With all the paint on the windshield, she probably didn't see him.

His legs felt like concrete. *Almost there. Almost there.*

A blue and white pickup was parked in front of Smallwood's

with a boat on a trailer behind it. He recognized the boat immediately. *Night Crawler.*

A man stood in the shadows of the wood beams under
Smallwood's Store. For an instant, his face glowed orange as he lit
his cigarette. Creepy Crawley himself.

Parker didn't like the idea of talking to the man, but maybe
he saw what direction Maria paddled. Then he'd hop in the *Boy's
Bomb*, give chase, and talk some sense into her. He'd be honest.
Put it all out there. She'd listen. He was sure of it. She'd always
been such a good listener.

Parker headed right for Crawley. They guy didn't move. Just stood
there, eyeing him suspiciously. Even as Parker slowed he spotted
Maria. Wearing the backpack, she was already in the kayak no more
than twenty yards offshore beyond where the *Boy's Bomb* was beached.
She had a cap on her head, with an LED headlamp strapped to it—
but turned off. Going out in the bay alone, at this hour? It was way
beyond risky. He veered off and pedaled for the beach.

Her paddle was slung across the cockpit. Even from here he
could see the blue paint. She held her phone up, taking a selfie.

Seriously?

"Maria!" He dumped his bike by the *Boy's Bomb* and hustled
across the crushed shell beach to the water's edge. "Wait!"

She stowed the phone and picked up the paddle. "Go home,
Parker." No smile.

"You're not my babysitter anymore—in case you didn't notice."
He kicked off his shoes and waded into the water.

She dipped one end of the paddle into the water and pushed
back a few feet. "You're begging for trouble. I'm warning you." Her
voice . . . stone cold.

"*Warning* me?" He couldn't believe those words came out of

her mouth. He hesitated. He'd never catch her like this anyway. A kayak could skim across the water a whole lot quicker than he could get to her. But he'd overtake her easily with the *Boy's Bomb* if he had to. "This is me you're talking to."

She scooped handfuls of water onto the kayak, rinsing off the blue paint. "What do you *want* from me?"

"To listen."

She looked toward where the sun had ducked below the horizon. "Too late for listening."

"You could have your pick of any guy. Why a clod like Kingman?"

She angled her head slightly. "You don't get it, do you?"

"Get what? That he's got a cruel streak as long as the Chokoloskee bridge? That he's a controlling, manipulating, narcissistic snake? Or are you talking about—"

"I love him, Parker." She scrubbed at the paint on her sleeves. "I honestly love Clayton. I'm *so* tired of my dad, my sister, you, and everyone else telling me who I can and can't love."

It sounded like she pulled the line from some sappy chick flick.

"I *want* a guy who will fight for me. Every girl does. It's romantic. Heroic."

How could she not see this? "He's dangerous, Maria. *Scary* dangerous."

"More than you know," Maria said. "Which is why you should back off. He'll hurt anyone who tries to get between us. Even a nice kid like you."

"Kid?" Is that how she still saw him? He was only three years younger—and at least that many inches taller than her.

She scanned behind him, as if she was afraid someone else may show up to stop her. "Who did you phone? My dad? Your dad?"

Parker shook his head. "Nobody. There wasn't time."

"Good. And keep it that way," she said. "Consider yourself warned. I won't protect you forever."

What was it with girls protecting him? "You're the one who needs protection." Parker brushed his pocket, making sure the keys for the *Boy's Bomb* were there. If he had to give chase, all he'd have to do is drag the skiff into the water and start her up. She didn't have a chance. But if he stalled a bit more, maybe Wilson would join him. "Kingman is a maniac. A monster. He'll hurt you." He couldn't believe he actually said all that. To *her*.

She laughed. Like Parker was some kind of joke. Naïve. "You don't know him like I do. Nobody does."

"And what does that tell you, Maria? You really think your dad, and Jelly, and me, and every other sane person I know are wrong?"

"I don't see him the way you do at all."

"Love is blind."

She shook her head. "Not my love."

"Oh my goodness, Maria—do you hear yourself? You're in denial. Kingman is going to burn you. Everybody has been risking their neck to pull you out of that fire—but you want to jump right back in."

Her face clouded over. "You're the one who's jumping into a fire. Don't say I didn't warn you. But like you said, I'm not your babysitter anymore. Guess you're going to have to learn the hard way." She paddled backward a few strokes like she was antsy to get going.

The sky-glow from where the sun dipped below the horizon had weakened massively. Darkness crept in from all sides—cautious and slow, as if making sure the sun was really gone. "So what's this kayaking at night all about . . . what are you going to do?"

"Prove a point." She sounded defiant. "Everybody should have left us alone."

Her kayaking in the bay—at night—was one more reckless stunt. "So you'll keep doing idiot things until your dad lets you date Kingman again?"

"Something like that."

"But how can you settle for that guy? I just don't get it. You're perfect." The words slipped out somehow—but it was too late to take them back.

The sound of bike tires on the crushed shell lane directly behind him made him turn for an instant.

Jelly. Blue paint and all. She rode right past Crawley—who had moved in way closer. He stood there leaning against a cypress—and probably heard everything. He flicked his cigarette to the beach and ground it with his foot. He flashed an oily grin and nodded his head like he wasn't hiding the fact that he'd been eavesdropping—and had no intention of stopping.

Jelly gave Parker a sad look. "That *perfect* girl has made up her mind. Just let her go."

He focused back on Maria. "So you don't get your way, and you just paddle off into the night? Who's acting like a kid now?"

She didn't answer, but glided backward faster. Parker stood there for a second, watching in disbelief. He'd untie the boat, drag it into the water, and in five minutes she'd have an escort—whether she wanted one or not. He'd keep her safe—wherever she was going. Or he'd capsize her and force her to shore. She'd be plenty mad, but Uncle Sammy would sure be happy. That had to be the right thing to do. And as soon as he got the boat started, he'd call Dad. Let him know what was going on.

There was no sense in hiding what he was doing. There was

nothing she could do to stop him. As long as Jelly didn't get in his way.

He hustled to the cypress, untied the line, threw it into the bow.

"What are you doing?" Jelly said. She dropped her bike. "You have to let her go—or you know Clayton is going to hurt you, right?"

"Would everybody stop worrying about me? Nothing's going to happen." He hoped he sounded a whole lot more confident than he felt. Parker leaned into the bow. The boat slid into the shallows and he vaulted over the side.

"Parker," Maria shouted. She was another thirty yards deeper into the bay. "When you see Rosie, you might ask her for your gas tank back."

He whirled to check. Sure enough, the quick-connect hose lay on the deck of his boat like a dead snake. The five-gallon gas tank was gone. A sinking feeling came over him. She'd outsmarted him.

"Bye, Parker." Maria scooped the water and arced into a smooth turn. She paddled away from shore at a fast clip.

She was going—just like that. Nothing he'd said made a bit of difference. He stood there in the *Boy's Bomb* . . . stunned. She'd been one step ahead of him the entire time. It was like she'd totally anticipated his moves.

"Does she have a plan, or is she just going to paddle out there like a kid having a tantrum until daddy gives in?" He turned to face Jelly.

Fresh tears were streaming down her cheeks. They mixed with the blue paint that had run from her hair.

"Oh, Maria has a plan all right," she whispered.

"But you're not going to say what it is."

Jelly's lips formed a tight, thin line like she'd glued them shut. She shook her head.

The sound of an engine starting drew his attention. Crawley's pickup kicked up gravel and roared off toward the marina, pulling his boat behind. Good. Parker didn't like the idea of the creep hanging around so close to Jelly anyway.

Parker scanned the darkening water. Spotted Maria nearly a hundred yards from shore. How long would she stay out there to make her point? And how far from shore would she go?

He stood and stepped to the stern. Planted both hands on the outboard motor and leaned out over the water a bit. As if that would give him a better view.

He had to call Dad, even though Jelly would likely try to stop him. Dad would get Uncle Sammy. They'd get out there and pick Maria up. "You sure Maria didn't tell Kingman that meeting at Gator Hook Trail is bogus?"

"She said Clayton was still going there—like the text told him to."

What if Maria had lied to Jelly? What if she'd tipped Kingman off, and he wasn't on his way to Gator Hook Trail after all? What if he was meeting Maria in the bay? What better way to punish her dad for breaking them up than to meet Kingman anyway?

Parker rummaged in his pack and whipped out his binoculars. He made a quick scan of the bay. No sign of Kingman in another boat.

Maria suddenly veered like she was making a course correction. What was she up to? Instead of heading farther into the bay, she headed right toward the black mouth of the Lopez River.

He spun and stared at Jelly. Dread dropped anchor in his gut . . . and he knew exactly what Maria had planned. "She's doing Watson's Run."

CHAPTER 41

ANGELICA HATED THE WAY PARKER looked at her. Like she'd betrayed him or something. But he just didn't understand.

"You *knew* she was doing Watson's Run?"

She nodded.

"We missed our chance to stop her. What was the point of letting Maria blackmail you into keeping her secret?" Parker pointed out into the bay. "I figured it all out anyway."

"You don't know the half of it," she said. Maria had plans for tonight. Tomorrow. And the day after that.

"I think I know enough," Parker said. "Maria threatened to tell Kingman—and you actually believed her. You're afraid he'll hurt me."

"*Hurt* you? You really think that's all he'd do?" Clayton would feed him to the alligators. She knew it in her heart. "We've been over this."

Parker looked toward the Lopez River and back. "Do you know how insane it is to do Watson's Run at night? Alone?"

What was she supposed to say? Of course it was dangerous. "That's why Maria is doing it. I tried talking her out of it. God knows, I really tried."

Parker hopped out of the boat and dragged it back onto the beach. Angelica hustled over to help.

"Forget it, Jelly. I got this."

She stepped back. "Don't be angry with me. Please."

"I'm not." Parker stormed to the back of the boat and pulled the drain plug from the transom. He threw it into the compartment below the driver's seat. Then just as abruptly, he fished the plug out and screwed it back in the transom.

She couldn't believe it. He was planning to go back out—wasn't he? He'd get the gas can and go searching for her—in the dark? Of course he would. That's *exactly* the kind of idiotic plan he'd put together. He was always trying to do the "right" thing. But without all the facts, he had no idea how wrong that move would be.

Parker coiled the stern line and hung it from the cleat, but he still didn't look at her.

"C'mon, Parker. Don't do this." She needed him. Couldn't he see that? She felt trapped—and needed her best friend more than ever. "Talk to me."

"Says the girl who kept me in the dark." He took a grip on the bow line with his good arm and leaned back to scooch the boat higher on the beach.

She stepped up to help.

"I'm not an invalid, you know." He lashed the bow line around the cypress, fumbling the first attempt because of his gimpy arm. "I don't need you protecting me. I can take care of myself."

No. He couldn't—and it had nothing to do with his injured arm. Vile beasts like Clayton didn't fight fair. "*You* can take care of yourself? That's what has me worried. I'd feel a whole lot better if you'd said you were trusting God to take care of you. You're the one with the strong faith, supposedly. But you haven't even mentioned God once. You're doing this on your own. You aren't listening to me. I sure hope you start listening to *Him*."

Parker tore into his backpack and pulled out his phone.

"What are you going to do?"

"Call my dad. See if they can get a ranger to find her on the Lopez before she gets too far." He punched in the numbers and held it to his ear.

"You make it sound like this is my fault," Angelica said. "She's been *planning* this for days. Somehow she discovered the bogus texts. I just found out this afternoon."

Parker didn't answer. "Dad, it's me. Call me when you get this. Maria's in trouble." He pocketed the phone and stared out over the water.

"We could have stopped her," he said. "Wilson and I—we had them pinned down. But you *helped* them get away."

"I had no choice."

"There's always a choice." Parker dialed the phone again. "C'mon, Dad. Pick up."

"Did you hear what I said before? Maria's been *planning* this. This isn't some random, spur-of-the-moment thing. She had me cornered—and we didn't have a chance to come up with some countermove."

He didn't look convinced.

"She's in love with him."

Did he wince? It was slight, but she was sure she saw it.

"Yeah, so she says. But loving a guy like that? It makes no sense." He peered into the darkness in the direction of Lopez River. Lifted the binoculars and focused in. "She's gone."

Tears burned in her eyes. "She's been gone ever since she started dating Clayton," Angelica whispered.

Parker looked at her and paused—like he wanted to ask her something. He hotfooted it for his bike instead.

"What are you going to do?"

"Meet Wilson. Find my dad." He straddled his bike. "And get my gas tank back." He took off without even a wave goodbye.

That was it? No . . . *How are you doing with all this, Jelly? Are you scared? What is it you're not telling me?*

"Parker, wait. Please." *Ask me to play twenty questions—right now.* She would spill. She would. She wanted to. And it wouldn't take much pressure. All he had to do was ask the right questions—and show the right heart.

He didn't even look back. Obviously, all Parker could think about was Maria. He passed Smallwood's, pedaling hard.

"Parker," she whispered, "please stop." Her eyes burned—and Parker blurred. Hot tears wet her cheeks. Again. An emptiness enveloped her. A supreme sense of loss.

She should be feeling something more, right? But there was only a disconnected numbness. Parker was bent on doing something heroic, no doubt. He was going to find that gas tank and go looking for Maria. The real kicker? He hadn't even invited Angelica to help.

She sat on the edge of the *Boy's Bomb* and watched. Willed him to circle back and try to patch things up. Or at least look back. Even once.

Parker was totally focused—but not on Angelica. He rounded

the bend by Smallwood's and disappeared into the shadows. This place . . . the Everglades . . . had taken from her again.

First her mom.

Then Maria.

And now Parker was gone too.

CHAPTER 42

PARKER TORE INTO THE MARINA and gave the parking lot and waterfront a quick scan. He spotted Wilson by the launch ramp and let out a sharp whistle.

Wilson waved and hustled over. "Nothing going on here. Creepy Crawley put in just a few minutes ago like he was on a mission, but no sign of Maria."

Parker skidded to a stop. "She's doing Watson's Run." He gulped in air. "Alone."

Wilson looked stunned. "She's insane. Even *I* wouldn't try that at night."

Parker gave him the thirty-second update, and dialed his dad again. When the voicemail kicked in, he disconnected and tried Uncle Sammy—which was another swing and a miss. "Where *is* everybody?" Every minute that passed gave Maria a bigger lead.

Wilson mounted his bike. "What now?"

Parker raked his hands through his hair. "We get my gas tank back."

Wilson gave him a sideways look. "You planning to go in after her?"

Somebody had to.

Wilson nodded like he read Parker's thoughts. "Want company?"

"I thought you said you'd never do Watson's Run at night."

Wilson grinned. "I meant alone."

CHAPTER 43

PARKER SPOTTED ROSIE'S RED CHEVY on her driveway from a block away. They'd made good time, but were still way behind. He had to admit, swiping his gas tank was brilliant.

The tank belonged to Parker. He didn't need to sneak up like he was doing something wrong. "We ride up and see if the tank is in the bed—and if not, we ring the bell."

"I say we flatten her tires while we're at it," Wilson said. "Send her a message—the Miccosukee way. Got your knife?"

Parker glanced over. Wilson was serious. "I don't have a beef with Rosie. She was just helping her friend."

"She *stole* from you, Bucky. So, she busted one of the ten big ones, right?"

It was a funny way to refer to the Ten Commandments. "And I'm pretty sure I'd be breaking one if I tried to get even with her."

They banked into Rosie's drive, dropped their bikes, and ran to the pickup. The gas tank was there—like she'd expected him to come after it.

"Bingo." Parker climbed into the bed and hefted the five-gallon tank over the tailgate to Wilson, using his good arm to do the heavy lifting. "We'll have to empty some of this, or it'll take forever to get back." There was no way he could ride his bike and balance the loaded gas can.

"I'm on it," Wilson said. "Try your dad again."

Dad answered on the third ring. "What's up, Parker?" His voice sounded strained.

"I've been trying to get you and Uncle Sammy."

"I've had the ringer off. Sorry. But Sammy's here with me. What do you need?"

"It's Maria. We were watching her house but she gave us the slip—and she's going to do something stupid—"

"Well, she won't be seeing Clayton—that's for sure," Dad said. "We've got a visual on Clayton right now. If she comes to meet him, we'll intercept her."

What if Kingman was in Chokoloskee Bay? What if Maria told him the text was bogus and he was going to meet her just inside the mouth of the Lopez? Maybe she wasn't going to do Watson's Run alone after all. "Where are you?"

Another pause. "Gator Hook Trail."

"And he's there?" So, Maria definitely *didn't* tell Clayton about the bogus rendezvous text. "You're sure it's him?"

Dad chuckled. "Oh yeah. He's been here for nearly an hour. Pacing like he's expecting her any minute—and we're here to make sure that doesn't happen. We got an anonymous tip that he was going to be at the trailhead—and it was a good one."

It wasn't hard to figure that Maria was somehow behind the

"tip" that pretty well guaranteed her dad couldn't stop her. Did she have Rosie make the call? One way or another, Maria had planned everything out. "She's not going to Gator Hook Trail. She's doing Watson's Run."

Dad hesitated. "You're sure." The urgency in his dad's voice was unmistakable.

"I saw her leave—I tried to stop her—"

"When did she put in?"

"Twenty-five minutes ago. Maybe thirty. From Smallwood's."

Dad groaned. "Sammy, we gotta go back. Floor it."

Even over the phone he could hear the engine roar. "What can I do, Dad? Tell me what to do."

"Nothing you *can* do." His voice was louder now, practically shouting over the sound of the wind. "You did plenty getting us this intel. Keep your phone on you. Be safe. We got this. Thanks, son." He disconnected.

There had to be something he could do. Dad and Uncle Sammy were too far out. By the time they drove back and got on the water, she'd have a crazy long lead on them. Too long.

Parker should have felt better. Hey, the grown-ups had this. They'd think of something, right? But he still felt like garbage.

"I emptied it so we can ride." Wilson held up the gas can. "But I know where we can get more after we get closer to the boat. Now we can make time—and catch up to Maria."

But too much time had been lost. And Maria had things too well planned. That mass of dread in Parker's gut felt heavier. They might get to the mouth of the Lopez fast, but once they started up the river they wouldn't be going any faster than a kayak would. They'd never catch up to her. They wouldn't even get close.

CHAPTER 44

Fishing Hole Marina, Chokoloskee
Saturday, September 19
9:16 p.m.

"THIS WAS YOUR PLAN?" Parker straddled his bike at the fringes of the marina, his feet on the ground. "Boosting gas?"

Wilson climbed into a Carolina Skiff sitting on a trailer parked in the shadows. "If the owner of this boat found you stranded in the bay with an empty tank, you think he'd offer you some gas? He'd give it to you gladly." He reached over and grabbed the empty tank from Parker's hands. "So this isn't stealing. And we won't take more than a couple gallons anyway. You can fill the guy's tank tomorrow if you want."

"It's stealing—and there's nothing right with that." He dug in his pocket.

"What do you need?"

"Cash. I'm not going to take the gas without leaving him money." He fished out a five-dollar bill. It wouldn't be enough. "Do you have a pen? I've got to at least leave a note."

"Seriously, Bucky?" Wilson's tone sounded more disgusted than anything. "While you're playing Mr. Perfect here, Maria is getting away. You okay with that?"

Parker wasn't okay with any of it. But Wilson was right about one thing. They just had to get out there. Find Maria. Fast. "Let's go." He slipped the money under the edge of the outboard's gas tank with enough of it hanging out for the owner to spot it. He wouldn't want the guy going into the bay thinking he had more gas than he did. "But I'll be back tonight to make this right."

"Yeah, yeah. We're wasting time here, boy scout." Wilson swung onto his bike, grabbing the *Boy's Bomb* gas tank as he did. He kicked off, and built up speed. Even with the tank being mostly empty, Wilson had a hard time steering straight.

Minutes later Wilson stopped and handed the tank back to Parker. "Can you ride the rest of the way with this?"

Parker tested the weight. "Definitely. Let's get out of here."

Within fifteen minutes Parker had the less than half-full tank reconnected in the *Boy's Bomb*. Jelly was gone—which was just as well. They didn't need her slowing them down. Together Parker and Wilson dragged the boat into the shallow water and hoisted themselves inside.

Parker primed the gas line with the squeeze bulb and the outboard fired up immediately. Parker revved it a couple of times and adjusted the choke until the engine sounded smooth and strong. He backed away from shore and spun the boat around. The moon was bright and nearly full, but still the distant shoreline was one black mass—like a massive gator low in the water. He opened the throttle and steered in the rough direction of the Lopez River.

He handed his phone off to Wilson. "Text my dad. Tell him what we're doing—and that we'll turn back if he catches up to us before we find Maria."

Wilson gave him a look like he thought Parker was crazy. His thumbs flew over the screen and he pushed send. "Okay. You've notified the troop leader—just like a good boy scout should."

Parker only throttled back when they got too close to shore to risk going faster. Wilson pulled out the portable searchlight from under the seat and swept the shoreline until they found the mouth of the Lopez. Parker steered right for it, and dropped his speed even more.

Even as he entered the Lopez, he could feel the change. It wasn't just that the overhanging trees blocked out the stars. The air felt thicker. The shadows blacker.

Wilson held the light in the dead center of the river. The Lopez twisted and turned like the river itself was a giant python, leading them to its lair.

Parker spun the wheel, doing his best to keep the boat away from the banks—and away from anything that might drop down on them from branches above. He half expected Maria to appear at any moment—relieved to see them. She'd realize how stupid she'd been. And she'd listen as he and Wilson talked some sense into her. But the surface of the water was deathly still. Not a ripple from a kayak as far as he could see.

The searchlight picked up the fiery orange glow reflecting back from pairs of alligator eyes. Lots of them. Watching. Waiting. And Maria was somewhere ahead in the darkness, with who knew how many gators. "We aren't alone."

"Wicked peepers on those beasts," Wilson said.

Like embers from the pit of hell.

Suddenly water pooled around Parker's ankles. He dropped the gearshift into neutral. "Give me some light back here. We've got water."

And it was coming in fast.

"You forgot the plug, idiot."

Sure enough, now that they'd slowed down, water was rushing in through the drain hole at the bottom of the transom like somebody had attached a garden hose.

Parker stood. "I put the plug back in when I left to find you—and the gas tank—so I'd be ready. I'm sure of it." He dropped to his knees and swept his hands through the water in the stern—now a good five inches deep and getting deeper by the second. "I must not have screwed it in tight enough." He'd been making one mistake after another.

Wilson stood over him, shining the light in the sloshing water. "Where's your spare?"

Parker pointed to the compartment under the seat. "Plastic container. Blue lid. I've got a couple spares in there." Wilson swung the light away, plunging the stern into dark shadows while he rummaged through the storage bin.

"Found the container," Wilson said. "But there's nothing here, Bucky."

"Impossible." Parker scrambled to the seat and double-checked. "I always keep spares." But Wilson was right. No plugs.

"Got anything we can jam in the hole?"

"Your finger."

Wilson hesitated for an instant, then dove for the back and plugged it with his palm. "If you think I'm sticking my finger through that hole so a gator can gnaw it off, you're crazy. Find something else."

Parker found a rag under the seat and forced one corner of it into the hole. It wasn't perfect, but it made a decent temporary fix.

Both of them stared at the makeshift plug. Only when it held for a full minute did Parker dare look around to assess their situation. Going into alligator-infested waters with minimal gas and only a rag to keep them from sinking? Not happening. Their search for Maria was over less than thirty minutes after they'd left Smallwood's. He swung the searchlight for one last look upstream—hoping to see the red kayak. He let out a piercing whistle. Shouted her name. Listened.

Nothing—except the creepy sounds of the jungle surrounding them. It would be up to his dad to find Maria now . . . and Uncle Sammy. "We've got to go back."

Wilson nodded. "What is it with you and the Everglades?"

Parker rubbed down the numbness in his arm. "The place is toxic." He was no believer in the Miccosukee curse. But he couldn't deny that bad things kept happening to him here.

Wilson swept his light around the jungle-like banks as if expecting something to lunge at them. "You gotta wonder if this place is out to get you somehow, right?"

Like it wasn't going to let him escape before it did. "All the time."

CHAPTER 45

ANGELICA SAT ON THE EDGE of her bed in nearly complete darkness, staring at the dimmed screen of her phone. Maria was out in the dark somewhere. It hardly seemed right for Angelica to have more light than this.

Maria posted images, just like she said she would. Every hour or so, beginning with the one when she launched. Her sister's plan seemed to be working perfectly. Word spread fast in a town this size. Everybody knew she'd paddled up the Lopez alone. Dad was crazy-worried, just like Maria hoped he'd be. She'd wanted to punish him. And she'd done a bang-up job of it. He was out there searching for her with Parker's dad. But Maria had too much of a lead to be at risk of being overtaken. The Lopez was a great equalizer. With all the twists and shallows, a skiff with an outboard was a lot more clumsy than a kayak.

Angelica had kept her end of the bargain. And apparently Maria stuck to her plan. Her sister had worked out everything to the last detail. Angelica reached in her pocket and pulled out three transom plugs and set them on the nightstand by her bed. Too bad Maria didn't have a plan for how Angelica was supposed to deal with the aftershocks. And the guilt.

CHAPTER 46

AFTER SECURING THE BOAT on the beach by Smallwood's Store, Parker and Wilson biked home and parted ways. Parker texted his dad with a quick update of his own failed attempt to catch Maria. He hated to send it. Hated to admit how helpless it made him feel. But he wanted his dad completely focused on finding Maria, not worrying if Parker was safe.

Parker went to his room, wrote out a quick note to the owner of the boat where they'd gotten the gas, and dug up another five dollars in singles and change.

The last thing he wanted to do was bike back to the marina, but what if the boater left early in the morning to fish or something? He'd head out thinking he had more gas than he did—and could end up stranded. And he'd told Wilson he'd be back tonight to do this—so there was the little issue of keeping his word, too. If he delayed doing the right thing now, what would keep him from coming up with another excuse in the morning? A quick glance at Grandpa's sign confirmed what he already knew. It's rarely right to stall off fixing a wrong.

Besides, with Dad and Uncle Sammy in hot pursuit of Maria, it wasn't like Parker would be able to sleep. Not until he heard they'd picked her up.

He pedaled to the marina, but didn't push hard. There was no point. He found the boat, left the note and extra cash, and climbed back over the side.

"Unreal, Bucky."

Parker's heart nearly exploded in his chest—even though he recognized Wilson's voice immediately.

"This is unbelievable. Lunacy. Nobody in their right mind would do this." Wilson stepped out of the shadows. "You're even more of a boy scout than a Boy Scout, you know that?"

Parker tried to steady his breathing. "What are *you* doing here? You scared me half to death."

"Just had to see how deep this integrity thing goes with you."

"So, I guess you got your answer."

"Oh yeah." Wilson shook his head. "You're totally obsessed with this cockamamy doing-the-right-thing stuff. You need help, man." Wilson grinned. "I was too revved-up to sleep anyway. Sorry I spooked you."

Parker grinned back and slugged Wilson in the arm. "No you're not."

Wilson laughed. "You're right. I'm not. Can we go home now?"

Parker appreciated the company on the ride home. But a loneliness settled in the moment he stepped into his dark house. Sure, he was the only one home. But that wasn't it. This was more of an emptiness. Like he'd lost something important—and nothing was ever going to be the same.

CHAPTER 47

EXACTLY WHEN PARKER ACTUALLY drifted off to sleep, he had no idea. The last he remembered, he was staring at the ceiling above his bed, praying and waiting for Dad to come home—or text with an update.

The early morning sun was doing its best to peel the paint off his bedroom wall at the moment. He squinted and sat up fast. The whole ordeal had to be over by now. Maria probably got picked up hours ago. Why hadn't his dad let him know?

His phone ended up under his pillow somehow. He grabbed it and checked for messages. Only one—from Jelly.

Check Maria's Instagram.

He pulled up Maria's account and sure enough . . . there were a *bunch* of posts. He whipped back to the first picture she'd posted—the selfie she'd taken when she launched from the beach at Smallwood's Store. The one he'd seen her shooting as he rode up. In the post she announced to the world that she was doing Watson's Run. She looked like the Maria he'd always known. Like she was going on an adventure and totally looking forward to it.

She'd posted another picture just thirty minutes later, shortly after she'd entered the Lopez River. Probably about the time Parker and Wilson were biking from Rosie's house with the gas tank. The following couple of pictures she'd posted were similar. Smiling. Looking almost defiant. Like she was proving a point. One was posted at 10:35. The other at 11:00.

He scrolled to her next photo—posted just after midnight. Another selfie. Another caption. Maria in the cockpit of her kayak—but no smile this time. The water surrounding her was oily black, and she looked so completely alone. Except for one thing. The glow from the eyes of the alligators trailing her wake. The light from her flash reflected off them perfectly. Had she known? *I may have taken a wrong artery. I'm hopelessly turned around. Wish it was morning. At least I've got company. LOL!* She definitely wasn't laughing in the photo. Parker studied her eyes. They were different.

There was only one more post. The selfie wasn't posed like the others. Blurred and slightly angled, it looked like it had been taken on the fly. Wet hair in her face. *Have to keep moving . . . gators. One's a monster—and aggressive. I'm thinking Watson's Run was a bad idea.*

"Dear God," Parker whispered. "Tell me they found her okay." He glanced out the window. No pickup.

Which probably meant Dad and Uncle Sammy had caught up to Maria, right? They'd brought her back to the marina or the ranger station and were having a heart-to-heart with her. That's why Maria's posts stopped. That had to be it.

Parker checked his phone. No missed calls or messages. He rubbed down the goose bumps on his arms.

He punched in Dad's number, but the thing went to voicemail immediately. *Great.*

He swung out of bed and ran down to Dad's office. Everything was just as it had been when Parker got in last night.

So Dad hadn't stopped home yet.

"C'mon, Dad," Parker whispered. "Tell me you're not still out searching." He stepped closer to the nautical chart tacked to Dad's wall and quickly located the opening of the Lopez River. Parker studied it. Pictured the point where he and Wilson had been forced to turn back.

He turned and faced the alligator skull. Was the beast grinning?

For an instant, he remembered the cash. He boosted himself onto his Dad's desk and stood. He stared down the empty throat and froze. Seventy-three hundred dollars. Gone.

Had Dad paid someone to keep Maria and Kingman apart? It was wasted money. Maria's latest stunt kept them apart just as effectively as Parker's texts had.

Parker's phone rang. He hopped to the floor and whipped the phone out of his pocket. *Dad.*

"Parker." Dad hesitated. Cleared his throat.

Parker's stomach churned. "Dad? You found her, right? She's okay?"

He cleared his throat again. "We found her kayak."

Was the room spinning, just a bit? "What?" Parker grabbed the edge of Dad's desk to steady himself. "What about Maria?"

"Still looking." His voice had that official park ranger sound.

But it was forced. "I just didn't want you hearing from someone else. We're meeting at the marina to refuel. Mobilizing more SAR teams to broaden the search."

More search and rescue teams? For an instant Parker wished this was like any other Sunday morning. They'd go to church and— Parker shook off his thoughts. "I want to help."

Dad was quiet. "Meet me at the marina. We'll talk about it then."

That didn't sound promising. "Where'd you find her kayak? On shore, right?" Maybe she'd gotten spooked, pulled her kayak up the bank, and made a shelter. But there really wasn't much shore along the Lopez River at all with how high the water had risen. Maybe she climbed a tree. "Dad? The kayak—where was it?"

"In Sunday Bay. Not far from where the Lopez opens up into it."

Dad's words hit like a gut punch. He checked the chart. Found Sunday Bay. "Just floating there . . . empty?"

"Just meet me at the marina."

"Dad. Tell me."

A long pause. "Upside down. Half submerged. Gotta go. Just get here." He disconnected.

Parker slumped down into Dad's chair and stared into space.

The gator skull stared back—its smile stretching ever-so-slightly wider.

"Jesus," Parker started his prayer—but had no idea what to say next. "Jesus, help us." Maria had kayaked right into the mouth of the Lopez, and kept paddling down the twists and turns of the river's throat. And sometime after midnight, the river had swallowed Maria Malnatti whole.

CHAPTER 48

PARKER DASHED A TEXT OFF to Wilson and pedaled for the marina. Wilson swooped in alongside him on the way, and they both kicked on the afterburners.

The marina was buzzing. Locals, mostly. Word had spread fast, and every guy with a boat small enough to handle the shallows of the Lopez River was heading out to search.

Several rangers stood by the docks, talking to Parker's dad. Parker dumped his bike and ran to him.

Shirt untucked, uniform wet up to his chest, Dad looked like he'd been out searching all night. He smiled when he saw Parker. It was one of those sorry smiles people greeted each other with at funeral homes.

Dad held up a finger to the other two rangers. "Give us a minute." He put his arm around Parker's shoulders and steered him away from the others. Wilson followed.

"Search and rescue is out in full force. Has been since sunrise." He avoided Parker's eyes.

"Any other signs of her? You checked the shore all around where you found her kayak?"

"Her paddle. Half of it anyway."

"Half?" Wilson stepped closer. "Broken—or *bitten* in two?"

Dad hesitated. "I really can't tell with any certainty."

Parker groaned. "Where'd you find it?"

"Stuck in the reeds. Maybe thirty yards from the kayak."

Had an alligator attacked? Did Maria try to beat it away with her paddle? What if the monster clamped down on it—and jerked it from her hands with enough force to make her lose her balance and roll the kayak?

"We righted the kayak and searched the area. I locked in the coordinates and took a few pictures." Dad pulled out his phone. "We found nothing more."

"Can I see the photos?"

Dad gave him a questioning look.

"I just have to see." It made no sense, but he had to see if there was something they missed. And there was another reason, wasn't there?

Dad scrolled back, settled on a photo, and handed Parker the phone.

The kayak was near shore. Upside down. With the bow a little lower than the stern. No paddle in sight. The shore was dense with black willows, cypress, and sedge grass everywhere in between. Spanish moss hung in ghost-like clumps from low branches.

Wilson shouldered in to view the screen. "Looks like a million other places on the Lopez. Good thing you took the coordinates. You'd never find this place again without them."

But no two places look exactly alike. The spot was unique. Parker just had to absorb it all. Like the cypress with the massive strangler vine wrapped around it. And another cypress, set back from the shoreline by what, maybe twenty feet? Barely distinguishable in the photo, but the way the trunk twisted in one spot reminded Parker of a giant licorice stick. And the vine wrapped around it partway up the trunk almost perfectly horizontal—like a strap. Oh, yeah. Parker could find this spot. He let his brain burn every tiny detail into some kind of neurological high-res scan. He was going to find this spot—and he needed to recognize it when he got there.

The kayak seemed to be resting against a mostly submerged log. True, there could be millions of submerged logs similar to that. But at that angle? With two cypress knees peeking out of the surface like a pair of gator eyes? There was only one spot that looked exactly like that in the entire Everglades. He closed his eyes—but still saw every detail. Okay . . . the picture was definitely locked in his memory.

"You searched the area really well, right?" It was a stupid question, but he had to ask.

Dad nodded. "We scanned the water. Waded through it. Yeah, we checked it good."

Waded through it—like they were looking for her body? "How about back—away from the river?"

"Back there?" Dad pointed at the dense growth in the picture. "We waded back in there too. We shouted for her. Saw nothing. Heard nothing."

"But what if she was trying to get away from the river?"

"There was no dry ground, Parker. The entire area was underwater."

Dad's phone chimed in Parker's hand. Dad reached for it, and reluctantly Parker handed it back. He'd hoped to scroll through any other pictures his dad took and lock those in the memory vault too.

Dad checked the text. Answered back. It didn't look like the news was great.

"How can we help, Dad?" But he already had an idea of how he wanted to help, didn't he?

Dad looked at him for a long moment. "We've got plenty of people searching."

"The *Bomb* can handle the Lopez. We've done it before." Not all the way to Sunday Bay, though.

Dad looked like he was thinking it over. But Parker knew Dad didn't want him anywhere near that area. The protector instinct was hardwired into him. And he'd put in for the transfer just to get Parker out before something worse happened, right? Dad put himself in danger every time he ventured into the Everglades, but it didn't seem to bother him. It was his job, and his faith in God was strong. But he wasn't quite so relaxed when it came to Parker.

"Look, if it makes you feel any better," Wilson said, "I'll go with him."

Parker was pretty sure that wouldn't make Dad feel any better.

"For now, let's not glom up the river with too many boats. I think I'd feel best knowing you were on land."

Parker groaned inside. Dad wanted to keep him safe. He got that. But Dad was protecting a little too much right now. Everybody was. "Dad. Please. It's daylight—and there will be other boats around. I can't sit back while everyone else is out searching." Did his dad have any idea how horrible he'd feel if he couldn't help in the rescue effort?

Dad ran both hands through his hair. "Parker."

"I'll be careful."

Dad looked at him for a long moment. "If I were your age . . . look, I get it." He stared out at the bay for several long moments. "But—"

"I've got to, Dad. Please." Parker gave every reason he could think of to convince his dad. Gave him everything he had—without giving his dad a chance to speak. "Dad, let me do this."

Dad squeezed his eyes shut. Wrestling with his own thoughts—or maybe praying.

Parker resisted the urge to charge back in and beg some more. He glanced at Wilson, who looked like he was holding his breath.

"Okay," Dad said. "I'm going to let you go in, but here's the way it's going down. If you have a problem with any one of these ground rules, you can just stay here. Got it?"

Parker would agree to just about anything right now.

"You stay in the boat. Under no condition do you get out—you got that?"

"Absolutely."

"You don't go toolin' around in the *Boy's Bomb* alone. Understood?"

Wilson raised his hand. "I'll be with him all the way."

Dad nodded. "You bring food. Water. Your survival knife. Machete. Even that gator stick you made. You go in with a full tank of gas—and a three-gallon spare. And the spare prop and tools."

"Done."

"And you keep your phone on, bring a recharge stick, and you text me every thirty minutes—without fail."

Parker would text every five minutes if that's what it took.

"You're back before dark. On shore. Got it?"

He gave his dad a hug. "Thanks, Dad."

"You've been honest with me," Dad said. "That earns you trust. Don't disappoint me, son."

Parker wouldn't dream of it. He squeezed his dad hard.

"Very cool, Mr. Buckman," Wilson said. "I'll get him back safe."

Hopefully without Parker needing a tourniquet this time.

"You won't regret this, Dad."

Dad stepped back from Parker and smiled. "I already do. So you better get going before I change my mind." He waggled his phone. "If I get an update, I'll call you, pronto. You two keep your phones close."

That was a given. And not just to get updates from his dad. What if Maria fought off some rogue gator out there? Or what if there was someone stalking her like she'd feared? Maybe she ditched the kayak and got inside the tree line where a poacher's skiff couldn't go. Maybe she was still on foot somewhere in the shallow water. Maybe she was having a hard time picking up a signal. But when she did, she'd call somebody. She'd tell them where she was so they could get her out of there. It made perfect sense. In that terrain—and at night—she probably hadn't sloshed her way more than a half mile from the kayak. The area where the kayak was found had to be searched again. That's all there was to it.

Even if the spot looked like a million others to Wilson, Parker was going to find it. Dad and Uncle Sammy may have searched the area good, but now Parker was going to do a little checking there himself.

CHAPTER 49

ANGELICA SLUMPED AT THE KITCHEN TABLE. She felt like a zombie, and was pretty sure she looked like one too. She'd cried herself out hours ago. The past night had to be the worst night of Angelica's life. And she was pretty sure this wasn't going to be the last one.

She was tired of asking herself if she did the right thing. Of course she didn't. But she wasn't exactly given a choice.

Angelica dragged herself to her feet and trudged out of the house. Dad wanted her at the marina and needed her to bring him a fresh shirt. He'd be joining in the search again soon, and he wanted to see her before he left. She wasn't so sure she wanted to see him.

Likely Dad figured that Angelica knew all about Maria's plan. Parker's call to his dad last night would have made that an easy guess. Dad would never understand why she didn't tip him off soon enough to actually stop Maria. How would she face him?

CHAPTER 50

PARKER WAS ALREADY CALCULATING how many minutes it would take to gas up and gear up the *Boy's Bomb*. Too many. But before they left the marina, there was one more thing he had to do.

"I need to see Maria's kayak." It made no sense, but there was a tiny part of him that had to be sure it was hers. What if someone else was doing Watson's Run last night—and they just happened to have a red kayak? It was ridiculous, but he had to be certain, right?

Wilson nodded and took off at a fast jog to the pier where Dad and Uncle Sammy's ranger skiff sat tied.

A red kayak sat lopsided on the dock. There was no question it was Maria's. The traces of blue paint inside the lip of the cockpit were enough to confirm that. Parker pored over every inch of it with Wilson. They turned it over, checked the bottom, then set it upright again. No claw marks. Just normal scratches any kayak would have that got a lot of use.

"The hull is good," Wilson said. "So she just tipped somehow?"

Maria could handle a kayak as good as anybody Parker knew. The only way she'd flip was if someone—or some*thing*—tipped her. Either scenario would have been imaginable from her last texts.

"Parker." Wilson pointed to a nylon mesh bag attached to the inside of the cockpit.

A mosquito net was jammed in the bag. Nothing unusual about that. "What?"

His face looked dead serious. "Look closer."

Parker had no idea how Wilson saw it, but there *was* something else. Parker unzipped the bag, dug behind the netting, and pulled out a waterproof case—with Maria's phone inside.

The thing was still on—but the battery was dangerously low. Parker held it for a moment, piecing together what this meant.

But he knew.

If Maria was trying to get away from someone, or *something* . . . she'd have grabbed her phone. Unless there wasn't time. Or—

Wilson whistled quietly. "Do you think a gator got her?"

"No." Parker blurted it out. Truth was, he didn't know anything. He rubbed down the buzzing in his gimpy arm.

But now that they had her phone, one thing was for sure. If Maria was back in the jungles along the Lopez River . . . she had no way of telling anyone she was alive.

CHAPTER 51

NEWS OF MARIA'S PHONE swept through the marina like a tidal wave, drowning every floundering shred of hope as it did. Parker hated that they'd been the ones who found her phone. Hated bringing it to Maria's dad. Seeing the expression on his face.

Parker saw Jelly the minute she rode up on her bike.

She flew into her dad's arms, and the two of them stood there clutching each other like they were afraid the other was going to be ripped away.

"She knew Maria was doing Watson's Run—but didn't tell her dad," Wilson said. "Can you imagine how lousy she must feel now?"

Parker felt pretty lousy himself. Especially since the *reason* she kept her mouth shut was to protect Parker from Kingman. Whatever frustrations he'd felt with Jelly the night before totally melted away. She was his friend. She was hurting. And she needed his help. As much as he was chafing to join the search, he hated to go without saying something to her. But he had to give her some time with her dad first.

"Do you believe this?" Wilson scanned the scene. "Any of this?"

Uncle Sammy was still holding Jelly. Dad was with them now, too. "They act like Maria is . . ." He couldn't finish the thought.

Wilson glanced at Parker. "You've got to admit, the odds of finding Maria in one piece are—" He clamped his hand over his mouth. "Poor choice of words."

Parker didn't want to go there. But he couldn't help it. He pictured Maria in the black waters—her arm in the jaws of an alligator, and the gator kept rolling her over and over and over—

Parker headed for the marina parts department. "I'm going to get a new transom plug for the boat."

Wilson stepped up alongside him. Minutes later they were back with the right plug.

Parker's dad was off to one side deep in conversation with a couple of other rangers. Jelly was still hanging on her dad, but her eyes met Parker's. She looked tortured. Parker stepped toward her.

"Bucky," Wilson nudged him. "Looks like his Majesty is going to grace us with his presence."

Clayton Kingman roared up in his pickup, towing his Whaler behind him . . . *King of the Glades*. He swung around and backed into position above the ramp. He jumped out, released the cinch straps and bow line winch hook, hustled back to the pickup, and backed his royal boat into the water.

Again, he burst out of the cab, holding a pump-action twelve-gauge shotgun this time. Flat coating—army green. Pistol grip. The one they'd seen the night of the tire fiasco.

"Nice cannon," Wilson said. "A poacher's weapon of choice."

"For sure." But having a shotgun like that along was smart, right? For most guys going into the Glades—either on an airboat or a skiff—a shotgun was as essential as a spare gas tank. It made a whole lot of sense to have a weapon aboard that had a chance of actually stopping a gator—even if you weren't hunting them. It would be a whale of a lot more effective than a gator stick.

Uncle Sammy pulled free from Jelly and stormed toward the launch. Parker and Wilson followed.

Clayton sloshed through the water and propped the shotgun in the boat. He grabbed the bow line and pulled *King of the Glades* to the dock. Seconds later he parked the truck and ran for the boat.

Uncle Sammy was on Kingman before he got back to the pier. "What do you think *you're* doing?"

Kingman almost pushed past him—but Uncle Sammy spun him around.

"I said, what are you doing here?"

Kingman didn't look one bit intimidated. "Searching for my girl."

"Not the thing to say to her dad, idiot," Parker whispered. He inched closer.

"This I want to see," Wilson said. "Maria's dad will twist him into a pretzel."

"I hope so."

Uncle Sammy grabbed Kingman's arm. "Get. Out."

Kingman windmilled his arm free. "Back off."

Uncle Sammy gave Kingman a chest-shove. "She never would have done something like this before she met you."

"Don't pin this on me." Kingman shoved him back. "This was *your* fault, old man. You know it. And I know it."

Uncle Sammy grabbed a handful of Kingman's T-shirt and smashed his fist into Kingman's face.

Kingman doubled over, but only for an instant.

"Hey, hey!" Parker's dad ran for the dock now—along with two other rangers. Jelly followed close behind.

Kingman lunged at Uncle Sammy like all the pent-up frustrations of the breakup, the tires, and the bogus texts boiled out of him.

Uncle Sammy staggered backward—and Kingman kept coming. He took a wild swing at Uncle Sammy's face, but the ranger dodged the blow.

Uncle Sammy had his legs under him again. He motioned Kingman closer. "C'mon, tough guy. Try that again."

Parker's dad was there. Between them. Arms outstretched to keep them apart. "Enough."

Parker intercepted Jelly and held her back. Fists clenched, she tried to get past him like she wanted a piece of Kingman, too. Parker wrapped his arms around her—putting her in a human straightjacket. "Whoa, whoa, whoa, they don't need you in the middle of this."

"This is all on you, old man." Kingman's eye was already swelling. "If you weren't so paranoid about us going out, Maria never would have done something so stupid. She'd have been with me last night. And *I'd* have gotten her home safe."

"Safe? Nothing about you is safe!" Uncle Sammy lunged for Kingman.

Dad blocked his path. Two other rangers helped Dad hold Uncle Sammy back.

Uncle Sammy stretched to look past them. "You changed her."

"She *wanted* change." Kingman pointed at Uncle Sammy. "Mostly she wanted to get away from you."

"That's enough!" Dad gave Kingman the side-eye while still struggling to hold Uncle Sammy from pushing past. "Shut your ugly mug, dirtbag."

Parker stared at his dad. He agreed with him—wanted to give him a medal or something—but Dad never talked like that. Not ever. How is it that Kingman could bring even him to do something he would never consider normally? Maybe it was Kingman's special gift. The ability to bring out the worst in everyone.

The slightest smile creased Kingman's face. Like he knew he could do more damage with his words than he ever could with his fists. He stabbed a finger at Uncle Sammy. "She only put up with *you* because she had *me*. The day she turned eighteen we were going to get married."

Would Maria really be that stupid, to marry a guy like him? Jelly seemed to wilt in his arms—like she knew it was true. Parker relaxed his grip.

"*That* wasn't going to happen," Uncle Sammy said.

"Yeah, you busted us up." Kingman took a step toward Uncle Sammy. "And obviously this was her way of lashing back. She couldn't wait to get away from you—did you know that? You're a lousy dad—and a worse ranger. No wonder Maria's mom left you."

Uncle Sammy seemed to deflate. Like all the fight drained out of him. Jelly slipped free from Parker and ran into her dad's arms.

Dad left Uncle Sammy to the other rangers and got in Kingman's face. "Put a sock in it boy—or I will."

Uncle Sammy just stood there, looking incredibly tired . . . and lost. Jelly leaned in close and whispered something in his ear.

Kingman raised both hands in surrender. "I'm done. You

rangers can stand around and jaw all day. *I'm* going to look for my girl."

Uncle Sammy came back to life—and Dad blocked his path to Kingman again.

Kingman backed toward his skiff. Face red. "I'm going to find her. And when I do, we're going to get back together. Get used to the idea, old man."

Wilson leaned toward Parker. "If what happened on the Lopez was a gator attack, it got the wrong person."

Uncle Sammy struggled against Dad's restraint. "If you get near my daughter again, I swear I'll—"

"Do nothing." Kingman glared at him. "Because that's who you are. Mr. Ranger-Do-Nothing." He turned and stalked to his Whaler.

"What did Maria ever see in him?" Wilson said.

Parker shook his head. He had no idea. But if it was true that the full-court press to keep Maria away from Kingman actually drove her to pull the crazy kayak stunt, Kingman didn't just have a beef with Uncle Sammy. Parker was a big part of that, too.

"Time to go," Parker said. Kingman was right about one thing. They were wasting time here. "We'll bike home. I need to pack some supplies. Then to Smallwood's Store to get the *Boy's Bomb*. We'll gas up—and head up the Lopez."

"What about Jelly?"

She was still clinging to Uncle Sammy. The idea of talking to her seemed almost pointless. What would he say? Right now the best thing for everyone was to find Maria.

"I think she'll want to stay close to her dad." Parker backed away.

Wilson kept pace. "You do know you're talking about going back in the Everglades. With snakes. And alligators."

"You getting cold feet?"

Wilson laughed. "Just making sure you don't. And what about the Everglades toll? You feel spooked at all—like there's a target on your back?"

"What?"

"I'm just saying—that curse is real. And if you feel marked . . ."

"The only thing I feel," Parker said, "is that we've got to find her."

Wilson gave him a long look. "Or die trying."

CHAPTER 52

THE INSTANT ANGELICA SAW PARKER ride off with Wilson she knew what he was going to do. *Parker, what are you thinking?*

But he wasn't thinking. Just like most guys, he was reacting. Going off to play the hero. But Parker didn't belong in the Everglades. She wasn't ready to admit there was some kind of *curse* on him, but how many times could one guy brush with death and not become a statistic? And Clayton was out there searching—and about as stable as a bottle of nitroglycerine. What if Parker met up with Clayton in the middle of nowhere?

Clayton was scary, even on a good day. But in his state of mind? He was more dangerous than any gator Parker might come up against. Out in the Glades, Clayton could do anything he wanted—and who would know?

The transfer could come in any time now. Why couldn't Maria have waited to do this until after Parker moved?

The moment Jelly's dad and Uncle Vaughn joined the other rangers to talk strategy or next steps—or whatever rangers talked about in search and rescue mode—she pulled out her phone and texted Parker. No sense beating around the bush. Just hit him directly.

`I know where you're going. Please don't.`

She watched the screen. It must have been two whole minutes before he answered. His reply was just as honest.

`I'm so sorry about all this, Jelly. Sorry for how I treated you, too. But I have to try.`

Which she already knew.

`I can't have you risking your life. You're not going to find her.`

Nobody was going to find Maria. In her heart, Angelica knew that was true. She'd known it from the moment Maria told her the details of her plan.

`We'll find her. I promised my dad I'll be back before dark. I'll text you.`

She looked around at rangers and locals scurrying around the marina. Loading skiffs. Studying charts. Each person trying desperately to get in the search—or back in it. This is what came from keeping secrets. Pain. Fear. Chaos. Unimaginable grief. And crushing regrets.

But she had to keep Maria's secrets. What choice did she have?

Angelica had to face the facts. The time to tell her dad about Maria's plans was long past. Snitching now wouldn't change what had happened to Maria. Her mind replayed the conversation in her bedroom Wednesday. While Parker was messing with Maria's phone. Looking back, Maria was a rocket on the launchpad at that moment. The countdown had started—and nothing Jelly said could stop it.

Now it was too late to protect her, and there was no way she could change that fact. But guarding the secrets a little longer could make all the difference in the world for Parker. She could still protect him from Clayton, even if Parker didn't believe he needed protecting.

Clayton Kingman would kill Parker if he knew what he'd done. She was absolutely sure of it. He'd kill Wilson, too, if they were together. Fill them both full of buckshot and hide them where they'd never be found. Angelica shuddered, as if her whole body couldn't agree more.

Her phone dinged again, reminding her she hadn't answered Parker.

She texted back.

`Play it safe. Don't get yourself hurt.`

She couldn't bear the thought.

`Thanks. Text me if they find her before we do.`

Parker still didn't get it. One look at the face of almost any ranger said they didn't expect Maria to be returning alive and well in one of the rescue boats. Not after finding her phone in the kayak.

But Angelica didn't need to look at any ranger's face to know that. And now Angelica was left with a dark secret that burned a hole in her soul. A secret that—if she dared tell—could change everything. But she had to keep it. It was the one thing that she was sure of. Keeping the secret was the only thing keeping Parker alive.

No, Maria definitely wouldn't be riding back on one of the rescue boats. The search efforts were pointless.

Maria was gone.

The truth? Maria was gone long before she disappeared in Sunday Bay.

CHAPTER 53

THE DAY DRAGGED. Angelica wanted to sleep. Her body was screaming for it. But sleep was out of the question. In a weird way she was punishing herself, and she knew it. She didn't deserve the luxury of sleep. Her dad and Uncle Vaughn had raced back to the Lopez River in their outboard hours ago. With everyone in search and rescue mode, how could she possibly sleep now?

Angelica camped out at the docks and waited. Boats came back and fueled up—and went right back out again.

Couldn't Angelica have stopped all this from happening? She could have told her dad what Maria had planned, and taken her chances on the fallout from her sister and Clayton. Couldn't her dad and Uncle Vaughn have protected Parker from Clayton's payback? Why hadn't she trusted *them* to protect Parker? Or trusted God Himself? She'd felt Parker's safety was up to her, and still did. She'd made a monumental mess of everything. Angelica hid things from her dad, and now he'd been crushed— all because of her.

She held the key, but even now . . . seeing the agony . . . she couldn't bring herself to tell what she knew. That secret was the key that could release her dad from the prison he was in—but it would open another door, too. A cage that held a monster. One key. Two doors. To unlock one would open both, and she couldn't live with that. She'd have to keep that secret until Parker left Everglades City for good.

There was no way out of this. Angelica just wanted to disappear. To not exist. To escape into some kind of oblivion.

A single shoe and an orange shirt sleeve were found just after three o'clock. The sleeve, shredded just above the elbow, with dark stains shadowing the frayed edges. Was it mud—or blood? Dad raced back to the marina—and identified both as Maria's.

He swept his arms around Angelica and held her tight. "We'll find your sister, sweetie. I promise."

He was stuffing his own despair to be the dad. To be there for Angelica. She buried her face in his cotton shirt. Inhaled the strength of this man who would move heaven and earth for his girls. But this time he was making a promise he couldn't keep.

"Dad's got to stick with this." He pulled away and held her out at arm's length. "You going to be okay?"

She nodded. "You do what you need to do, Dad. Stay safe— and don't worry about me." She wasn't worthy.

He hugged her again. "That's my girl. My good, strong girl."

But she didn't feel strong. And she was definitely, positively not at all good. Truth was, she was a horrible girl for holding back the secret that would change everything.

The news of the phone had been bad, but hearing about Maria's sleeve hit the searchers like a torpedo at the waterline.

The search and rescue mission took an unofficial change. It was now a search and *recovery* mission. It was like rangers had the toe-tag ready for the morgue—and just needed a body to tie it to. Rangers would be looking for scraps of clothing now. Her other shoe.

Closure.

Which was something Angelica was pretty sure she'd never get. Not as long as she lived.

Rangers refueling at the marina inspected the sleeve and shoe before heading back to Sunday Bay. Even Clayton roared back in *King of the Glades* to see the evidence for himself—and find out exactly where they'd been found. He pulled up to the dock sloppy fast. He shoved the throttle in reverse so hard that the engine screamed, but the Whaler still hit a post hard, leaving a giant scuff on the boat's rub-rail.

Before heading back to search he made a point of pulling Angelica aside.

"Maria told me everything." He swung an arm around her shoulder and pulled her close. "I know what Gator-bait did. And his half-breed friend, Cochise." His breath was hot on her neck. "She made me swear not to touch them—because of that deal she had with you. So you be strong. Keep your end of the bargain. Or I'm going to find them out there in the Glades one day. That's a promise, Angel."

How much did he know? Obviously enough. She watched Clayton get back in *King of the Glades* and hightail it toward the mouth of the Lopez River. She stood on the dock in a kind of stunned shock. Maria's betrayal was even more far-reaching than Angelica had imagined. *How could you tell him, Maria?*

"I hate you, Clayton Kingman," Angelica whispered. Before

Clayton, Maria always did what was best for Angelica and her dad. For the family—especially after Mom went AWOL. But Clayton changed all that. He was like black mold. A mind-toxin. He poisoned her. Changed her thinking. Somehow he'd so effectively groomed Maria that even her decision-making process got bent. Twisted.

Clayton was a predatory monster. A beast. A deceiver. A manipulator. A narcissist with a cruel streak coursing through him as big as the Everglades itself. And he was a master at what he did. Clayton had charmed and bullied Maria in just the right doses to keep her coming back to him—more dependent on him each time. He had turned her into nothing more than a marionette—and he controlled her strings. When faced with a decision, Maria chose what was best for the puppet master every time. Paddling up the Lopez alone was a brainless move, but Maria wasn't totally to blame. Clayton was. She watched his boat grow smaller. "I absolutely despise you, Clayton Kingman." With every cell in her body.

Angelica braced herself against one of the dock posts, the reality of the whole thing sweeping over her again. Her older sister had always been so smart. She was the sensible one, Dad always said. The one who made such good choices.

Until Clayton.

And her decisions had spiraled downward ever since. This was where bad choices led. Angelica sat on the edge of the dock and hugged herself. "Maria . . . what were you thinking?"

But she hadn't been thinking. She was following her heart—and had rationalized away all the warnings. Ignored the red flags.

And now Parker was following his heart, too. Yellow flags. Red flags. Nothing was going to slow him down. They were all green flags to him, waving him on . . . and on and on . . . deeper into danger.

CHAPTER 54

THE NEXT FEW DAYS WERE SHEER AGONY for Angelica. Worse than anything she had ever known in her entire life. Parker and Wilson searched the Lopez River on Sunday, but they never made it to Sunday Bay. With their late start, they couldn't make it there and back before sunset. The way she heard it, as much as Parker hated to turn back, he was totally dialed in to following his dad's guidelines. Of all the guys she'd met . . . in all the places she'd lived . . . she'd never met anyone with half the dedication to doing the right things as Parker had.

Going to school was another one of those rock-solid rules Parker's dad laid on him. He'd wanted to go out searching Monday morning early, but Uncle Vaughn insisted that would have to wait until after classes were done for the day.

There wasn't enough daylight for the boys to make it all the way to Sunday Bay and back after school, so going out on the river was pointless as far as Angelica was concerned. She was pretty sure Uncle Vaughn knew that too. But Parker and Wilson went out anyway.

By Tuesday night, even Clayton had given up the search and trailered his boat out of the water. After a nearly sixty-hour search effort—that anyone would call a superhuman feat of endurance—he left the area in a daze.

"She's gone," he'd said to a ranger who'd helped him dock his Whaler. "She's gone. I've got to get out of this place." Rumors surfaced that he'd headed for the Keys. Angelica hoped he'd keep going. Cuba would be nice. South America even better. The South Pole was probably too much to hope for.

One other enormous change happened Tuesday. The transfer came in for Parker's dad. A ranger had been seriously hurt in the Boston area, so they needed a replacement—pronto. With Boston being the very place Parker's mom had been freelancing, it was a perfect fit. Uncle Vaughn jumped at the chance. A moving truck was going to be at their home Saturday.

Wednesday, Parker's mom got back in town. She'd taken a few days off from her freelance project to help pack things up at home for the move. Hopefully she would need Parker's help—and put an end to his search efforts.

The speed of the move shocked everyone. Who ever heard of a transfer needing to happen that fast—even with the rangers? It was the one ray of hope in Angelica's week. All she'd have to do is keep Parker out of the Glades Thursday and Friday. Two more days—and then she could breathe easy, even though the thought of Parker leaving was suffocating in its own way.

Wednesday Parker told Wilson about the mysterious bundle of

money. There was no point to keeping the secret anymore. Wilson absolutely believed that they were putting a hit on Clayton—a theory Angelica had already abandoned.

Angelica had a new theory what the money was intended for. Boarding school. She had no idea if $7,300 was enough to pay for a semester—or a year—or if it included a fee for somebody to physically take Maria to some school. But her dad had actually floated the idea of Maria finishing her senior year at Black Forest Academy, a private school somewhere in Germany. That was over a month ago, and Maria had absolutely hated the idea. Dad had never brought it up again. Would he have been planning some way to get her there anyway? Angelica wished her dad's plan had worked, but once Maria paddled away from the beach, none of that mattered anymore.

Her dad and Uncle Vaughn had stopped searching in the daylight. Now they were only going out at night—and didn't show up again until after dawn. It made no sense. They had the thing upside-down somehow. But sleep deprivation could mess with anybody's head, right?

Did Angelica's mom know about Maria disappearing? Parker's mom had written an article about the tragedy. Had Mom read it? If she did, it wasn't enough to bring her home—wherever she was now. Apparently, when Mom walked out she never looked back. When Maria insisted on doing Watson's Run, she'd acted a whole lot more like Mom than she'd been willing to admit. That's how Angelica saw it, anyway.

After school Wednesday, Angelica finally told the boys about Clayton's threat Sunday night when he'd pulled her aside at the dock. How he knew about what they'd done—and how he seemed itching for payback. She didn't say a word about the secret she was keeping. That wasn't the point. She just had to warn them to be extra careful. "Stay clear of him, okay?" That's all she asked. Naturally they brushed it off in that stupid way that guys do.

"He actually called me Cochise?" Wilson looked genuinely happy about that. "Wrong tribe, but an amazing warrior. It's a compliment. I think it says that deep down Kingman is afraid of me, right?"

"Kingman isn't afraid of anyone," Angelica said.

Wilson laughed. "Well maybe he should be."

The way Angelica saw it, Wilson and Parker were the ones who could use a little more healthy fear. Clayton was far worse than anything they'd find crawling in the Everglades.

Actually, Parker needed a better grip on reality all around. Even at this point, four full days after Maria disappeared, he still believed she was alive, lost back in the wilds somewhere. Even Wilson thought Parker was delusional.

"ValuJet Flight 592," Wilson said. "Eastern Flight 401. Mob kills. Ed Watson. Like I've said, the Everglades is a place of death. You need a reality check, Bucky."

As much as Angelica hated hearing Wilson's logic, she kept her mouth shut. Maybe Wilson could get Parker to give up the useless search.

"That's what happened to Maria, Bucky. The Glades claimed another life."

Parker glared at him. "They find a shoe and you think she's dead?"

"You're forgetting the bloody sleeve. You think that ripped off because she was scratching mosquito bites?"

"There's been no *body* found," Parker said. "And until we find *that*, I say she's still alive. I feel it in my heart."

"My *Miccosukee* heart—" Wilson thumped his chest—"says it's the toll."

There was no point to searching anymore. Everybody seemed to know that—and Angelica most of all. Nobody could change what had happened to Maria. And they weren't going to put anything to rest by discovering the "truth" about what really went down after her last Instagram post.

Angelica was in the boat nearly every time the boys went out now. Not that she was actively searching, but at least she felt like she was doing something to keep the guys safe. It was better than waiting—and wondering—on shore.

Parker and Wilson turned back early from their run on the Lopez Wednesday. Parker had been quiet. Like, *really* quiet. When he finally did talk, Parker mentioned he'd come up with a new theory of what happened to Maria. He wouldn't say what it was, just that maybe they'd been looking at this thing all wrong. He said he needed to process it a little—and it was obvious his wheels were turning. Angelica's stomach did a couple of rollovers itself just imagining what he might be thinking. She helped the boys pull the *Bomb* onto the beach after Parker raised the motor.

"Let's meet back here after dinner," Parker said. "If I still think the idea makes sense, I'll float it past you then."

Whatever he was thinking, it must have been a scary thought, with the way his face looked. No matter how hard she tried to get him thinking about the move to Boston, she could see his new theory was gnawing at him inside. That did nothing to make Angelica feel better.

The thing of it was, Angelica was the only living soul in Everglades City, Chokoloskee, or the entire Everglades National Park who truly knew what happened Saturday night.

And she still wasn't going to tell anybody.

CHAPTER 55

IT WAS TIME FOR PARKER TO FLOAT his new theory past Wilson and Jelly. They met at the *Boy's Bomb* after dinner. The idea was to go for a ride in Chokoloskee Bay before sunset and talk about taking a whole different approach to the search for Maria. Talk them into it was more like it.

Jelly was dragging her feet, clearly in no hurry to climb into the boat. It seemed like she knew the second they were out on the water she'd be in a conversation she didn't want to have.

Parker leaned on the outboard motor. Maybe he didn't need to be out on the water to hit them with his idea. "We have to try something different."

"Yeah. Like quitting," Jelly said. "Honestly, I don't think I can go up the Lopez one more time."

"Part of me still wants to get all the way up to Sunday Bay," Parker said. "But I'm not sure there's a point to it anymore."

"Amen," Jelly said. "Finally you're ready to stop this madness."

Sometimes Parker could *not* figure her out. How could she just give up on her sister that easily? "I'm not ready to *quit*. But we need to go somewhere the other searchers *aren't* going."

"There are no more searchers," Jelly said. "And they've checked every inch of that river."

Parker shrugged. "There's one place nobody has tried."

Wilson untied the boat from the cypress. "Talk to me."

Jelly gave him a look that he couldn't read. She sat on the edge of the *Boy's Bomb* with her feet in the sand. She looked lost. Like she didn't want to go out in the boat, and didn't want to stay on the beach. Maybe she was feeling the need to escape the area for good just like Parker. But how could he leave without some answers?

Parker grabbed the outboard motor with two hands, like their pastor grabbed the podium when he was about to say to say something important or shocking. "What if Crawley grabbed her? He saw her paddle off toward the river Saturday night—and Wilson . . . you said he launched within minutes of her."

"Creepy Crawley," Wilson said. He seemed to be thinking about that one. "He lit out of that marina like a man possessed."

"So he just *happened* to be in the area," Jelly said. "And then sees my sister and decided to go after her? Just like that? Even though both you and I saw him listening? He'd have to know he'd be a suspect. Sounds like a real stretch."

"He's sick," Parker said. "You saw how he treated you on the causeway. He saw an opportunity, and he took it."

"I think he could be our guy," Wilson said. "That's my two cents."

"Which is exactly what your opinion is worth." Jelly stood abruptly and marched off toward Smallwood's Store.

Wilson jerked his thumb toward Jelly. "Where's she going?"

"Anywhere to get away from this conversation," Parker said. "She just wants this to be over. But how could this ever be over unless we get answers?" Still, if Jelly needed space, Parker had to give it to her. He turned his back to the store so it wouldn't look like he was watching her.

Parker and Wilson sat there looking out over the water for what seemed like minutes. A skiff cut a straight line across the bay. The white foam wake spread behind it, like the boat was opening some giant zipper on the surface of the water.

"So we have two theories now," Wilson said. "One. Maria got tipped and eaten by a monster gator. Theory two. She got murdered by Crawley—*then* got dumped in the river. Either way, I think gators are part of—"

"Thanks for that visual." Parker stared at the scars on his arm. "And do *not* say that around Jelly."

"Fine," Wilson said. "But let's face it. One way or another, Maria's gone."

Parker thought about that for a minute. "But what if Crawley didn't kill her? What if he kidnapped her?"

Wilson looked at him like he was crazy. "There was no ransom note. And what about the ripped sleeve?"

"He could have planted the sleeve to throw everyone off the trail. And there's no ransom because he wasn't looking for money. He wanted *her*."

"Like he's keeping her prisoner?" Jelly's voice.

Both Parker and Wilson whirled around. When did she get back—and how much had she heard?

"That's disgusting." Jelly's chin trembled when she spoke—like she was going to lose it. Yet there was a fire in her eyes, so maybe she was shaking with anger. "And your theory is so out there, Parker—it's beyond a stretch."

There was no sense arguing with her.

"Hold on," Wilson said. "I've heard stories of girls—"

"Stop, Wilson!" Jelly took a step back, hands plastered over her ears. "Can't you ever just know when to *stop*?"

Wilson raised both hands. "Just trying to help."

"You really want to help? Really?" Jelly got all in his face. "Then drop the whole thing. I don't want that ride in the bay anymore," Jelly said. "You two go out without me."

Like that was really going to happen. The ride in the bay was over. Parker walked around to Jelly's side of the boat. "Look, do you really believe Maria is . . . you know . . . dead? I mean deep down." They were sisters, right? If Maria was alive, shouldn't Jelly have some sort of sense that she was?

She wouldn't look him in the eyes. "I can't talk about this anymore. I just can't get away from it—but I need to. I can't stomach it anymore."

Okay, Parker got it. This was incredibly hard for her. But how could he leave the state Saturday without exhausting every option? He'd be living over a thousand miles away, wondering if Maria was Creepy Crawley's prisoner. "I just thought maybe we can poke around his place a little. Just check it out."

Wilson perked up at that suggestion. "I'm up for that."

"You're both out of your mind if you go within a mile of wherever that pervert lives." Jelly hugged herself. "One way or another Maria's gone and she's not coming back. Let's just leave it at that."

But what if Crawley hauled her off to his lair with some

demented plan to keep her? Parker shook his head. "Leave it at that?"

"Go to the police with your theories if you want," Jelly said. "Let them deal with him."

"They'd have to get court orders," Parker said, "and that would take time—something we don't have."

"I want to go home. The search for Maria is over," Jelly whispered. "Why can't you just accept that?"

The search was over? Not the way Parker saw it. This new Crawley angle just gave him a new place to look.

CHAPTER 56

NOBODY DID MUCH TALKING as they pedaled away from Smallwood's Store. Which was fine by Wilson. He was tired of trying to think through all this stuff. It really wasn't all that complicated. In a way, Wilson felt bad for Bucky. Clearly he thought there was still hope of finding Maria. But she had likely become part of the food chain within hours of paddling into the Everglades. Sometimes the obvious answer was the right one.

The fact that Bucky really thought Maria could be alive was bizarre. Even though he hadn't lived in the area for even a year yet, Bucky knew way better than most just how deadly the Glades could be.

If Wilson had been with Maria when her kayak capsized in Sunday Bay, she'd have been fine. He knew how to survive, and he'd have gotten her out of the Glades safely with or without a kayak. The Everglades were deadly, but Wilson would have been okay. He knew the ancient laws of the Everglades. He knew which boundaries he could cross—and which were sacred. Maria couldn't possibly have survived—because she'd been alone. Maria had no more chance of surviving this long in the Everglades than a snowman would.

The idea of Crawley creeping on her was an interesting twist. But it was pretty much a shot in the dark. Not that Crawley wasn't a loony bird—and there were a handful of guys just like him in the area. Wilson would rather come face-to-face with a fourteen-foot gator than with some of the locals. But there were just too many holes in Parker's theory. Like, exactly how did Crawley get Maria into his boat?

But checking out Crawley would be an adventure. Wilson was pretty sure the guy lived in the remote areas on the fringes of the Everglades. It would be crazy risky—and a total rush.

"Parker," Angelica said. "Promise me you won't go looking for Crawley's place."

Bucky didn't answer.

"Wilson? Promise me."

"If he's going—I promise I won't let him go alone," Wilson said. "That's the honest truth."

"You two don't get it," Jelly said. She growled once and pedaled harder—like she was trying to work out some of her frustrations on the bike.

Jelly was the one who didn't get it. She didn't understand guys. Period. As long as Maria was missing, Bucky would do whatever it took to find some answers. And as long as Bucky kept looking, Wilson would stick with him. It was as simple as that.

There was an upside to Bucky thinking Maria was alive. He

was running out of time to find her. Which meant he'd be desperate. He'd go deeper into the Glades. Further out of his comfort zone—which would bring him smack-dab into Wilson's.

Bucky was leaving, and Wilson would lose his adventure partner. If Bucky really had to leave the Everglades, he might as well do something over the top. Something he'd never forget. He needed to go out with a bang.

Checking out Crawley might be the wildest adventure they'd had yet. Wilson would do some quick research—find out where the crazy lived. Then he and Bucky would do some recon together. So what if Wilson didn't think Crawley had anything to do with Maria's fate? If Bucky thought Crawley was involved, Wilson would definitely be open to checking the guy out.

A plan began to form in Wilson's head, one that would test even his own limits. Wilson smiled.

"Listen, guys." Jelly clamped on the brakes and fishtailed to a stop.

Wilson swerved to miss colliding—and clipped Bucky instead. They managed to avoid going down, and stopped just beyond Jelly. "Are you trying to kill us?"

"Actually," she said, "I'm trying to keep you *alive*. Trust me on this: Crawley is a dead end. Just leave him alone. He didn't attack my sister. He didn't kidnap my sister."

"And how would you know that?"

Jelly hesitated. "Call it a hyper sense of women's intuition. Whatever happened to Maria, she did it to herself, okay?"

"Easy, Jelly," Wilson said. "We're trying to help."

"You want to help?" Jelly looked from Wilson to Bucky—and back. "You *really* want to help? Then how about helping me get my mind off Maria for a couple days. Let's just hang out together."

Bucky stared at the ground. Wilson didn't need to be a psychic to know what he was thinking.

"I am asking you both—as friends—to let this go," Jelly said.

Wilson shrugged and looked at Bucky. Jelly eyeballed him too—like both of them knew this was really Bucky's call.

Bucky toed the ground. "You're hurting. I get that. Something terrible happened to Maria. But nothing is going to happen to me."

"That is such a guy thing to say," Jelly said. "You think you can just Superman your way through this?"

Bucky's eyes darted to his scarred arm and back. "No, but I don't have the fear like I did before. I know God's got this. And He's got me."

Wilson had definitely seen the changes in Bucky.

"The Everglades curse," Jelly said. "The toll. You're forgetting about that."

"I thought you didn't believe in that stuff," Wilson said.

"I don't"—she tapped her head—"up here. But something in my heart says there are strange things in this universe that we don't understand. And this is one of them. What about Jericho—are you forgetting that?"

"This isn't Jericho, Jelly," Parker said. "There's no curse here."

"I want to believe that, Parker. Honest I do." She hesitated. "Back when we lived in Colorado, you told me about the Garden of Eden and the serpent—remember that?"

Parker nodded.

"What did God do to all snakes because the one had deceived Eve?"

"This isn't the Garden of—"

"Say it, Parker. What did God do?"

Parker hesitated for just a moment. "He cursed snakes."

Now *this* was getting interesting to Wilson. "Seriously? How did I not know that?"

"It's true. Snakes have been cursed by God since the beginning." Jelly looked from Parker to Wilson and back. "Well, the Everglades are crawling with snakes. Rattlers. Cottonmouths. Pythons. Coral snakes. Even anacondas. If snakes are cursed creatures—and this place is loaded with snakes—is it so hard to believe the place could be even a tiny bit cursed?"

Bucky shook his head. "You're mixing superstition in with Christianity—and that doesn't work, Jelly."

"Honestly," Wilson said. "I think she's making some great sense. For once."

Jelly acted like she didn't even hear him. She kept her focus on Bucky, like she knew he was the one to convince. "Can you tell me you've never felt the presence of evil in this place?"

"I've definitely felt it," Wilson said. "My people—"

"I want to hear it from Parker, Wilson."

Bucky looked down, like maybe he was remembering a specific time—or place. "You know I have. But a *presence* of evil isn't the same as a curse. And God is stronger than any present evil. That's what I believe."

"Well, I guess you're just a way better Christian than I am."

"Jelly, hold on—"

"No, *you* hold on." Her eyes were pleading. "You almost got killed in the Everglades, Parker. Clayton *threatened* to kill you if he caught you out there. And now you're talking about snooping around Crawley's place—a guy who looks like he's *already* killed? We've made it this far. There's two more days of school—and then the moving van. Let's not be stupid. Just stay out of the Everglades, okay? Let's not give Crawley, Clayton—or the curse, as crazy as it sounds—a chance at you."

Bucky stayed quiet for a moment. "I hear you, Jelly. Really, I do. And I know the Glades can be absolutely deadly. But not because there's a toll. There's no curse. I believe God is in control. And you're a Christian, Jelly. Deep down you know He's got this, right? Even if there was a curse, God is stronger. You know He can protect me—all of us."

"Sometimes I do." Jelly wouldn't look at him. "But you almost died in the Glades. I can't forget that."

"Almost," Bucky said. "That's the key word. God saved me. That makes me more confident. And if it's His plan, He'll do it again."

"If it's His plan?" Jelly's words came out as more of a wail than a question. "We don't know His plan. He doesn't run it by us—right? So let's use our heads. Play it safe."

The way Wilson saw it? The longer they talked, the wider the gap was growing between them. This was going nowhere.

"There's no safer way to play this than to give this whole situation to God—our safety included—and trust Him," Bucky said. "I know you're afraid, and frustrated . . . but I have to check out this last angle. I don't know if I can live with myself if I don't."

Jelly shook her head. "And I'm afraid you *won't* live if you do."

CHAPTER 57

PARKER'S MOM HAD BEEN BUSY. When he stepped inside the house, it looked more like a warehouse than a home. Boxes stacked almost everywhere. Except Dad's office, and Parker's room. They hadn't been touched.

And somehow, even with all the packing, she'd had time to do interviews and write an article for the local paper. She was amazing.

"You've got two days," Mom said. "Do whatever you'd like to find closure on the Maria tragedy—but Saturday you're all mine."

She was beyond amazing. Somehow, she knew he had some things he had to finish before he left the Everglades. He pulled her into a tight, quick hug. "I'll do a little before school each day. I'll get the rest boxed first thing Saturday." It wouldn't take him much more than a couple of hours. And now he'd have all the time he needed to check Crawley out. Hopefully Wilson was already working on that. He pulled out his phone.

Mom got that serious look on her face. "How are you doing?"

"I'd be better if I just knew."

"We all would, sweetie." She looked like she was ready to cry. "Want to talk about it?"

He knew what that meant. It was all about processing Maria's *death*. And that would have to wait until he was sure she was gone. He shook his head. "Not yet." There'd be plenty of time to talk on the drive north. "I wish we'd never moved here. Bad things keep happening."

"Come here." She drew him into a hug. "It's going to be all right."

One of those things parents said when they had no answers. When they were pretty sure there wasn't a thing they could do to change things. But everything wasn't going to be all right. It never really would—if Parker didn't know what happened to Maria.

The truth was, they were no closer to finding Maria than they were Sunday morning. The Glades were sort of like the black holes in space. Dark. Mysterious. Deadly. The Everglades had a way of drawing people in—and keeping some of them forever. Was Maria one of them? Parker only had two days to find out. The moving van was coming Saturday afternoon, whether they found her or not.

"For months I've wanted to get away from here. To escape. But now that it's really coming, all I want to do is slow it down."

Mom gave him a squeeze. "Funny. When I was in Boston, I couldn't wait to get back to Dad and you. But getting here didn't make my problems go away. I just had more shoulders to help carry them."

And in that moment, he knew that moving away from the Everglades wasn't the answer. Ever since that day on *Typhoon*, Parker had felt like he didn't belong here. He'd known it. He'd believed moving would solve everything. But he was just fooling himself, wasn't he?

So many wanted to escape their situation. *If I only had a different mom. A different dad. Different brother or sister. If I only had a different face. Body. If I only could get out of this school.* If somebody said any one of those things to Parker, he'd have told them they'd never find an escape by going to a new place. And they'd never get more than a temporary escape with more screen time or their music. There were kids at school who were already surrendering to drugs or alcohol to find escape. But like so many things, they were temporary escapes. Dead ends. Parker could have told them that. So why had he believed a change in address would make all the difference for himself?

Escaping wasn't the answer. And honestly, was escape even possible? He looked at the scars on his arm. He'd carry them with him wherever he went. Hadn't Wilson and Jelly told him something like that?

"Did you read my article yet?" Mom said it quietly, like she wasn't sure if she really wanted him to see it or not. "There's a copy pinned to Dad's corkboard. It might bring you a little closure."

"Maybe I'll do that now," he said.

She smiled—in a sad kind of way.

Parker shuffled around stacks of boxes and headed for his dad's office. The local paper was on the desk, opened to the page where the story had been neatly clipped from it and tacked to the corkboard. Parker hesitated in front of it, and the story sucked him in.

Search Efforts End for Missing Girl
By Elizabeth Buckman

Maria Malnatti, honor roll senior at Everglades City School, paddled up the Lopez River just after sunset on September 19 . . . and never returned.

Parker studied her yearbook photo embedded in the column. She was looking directly into the camera. No. Directly at Parker.

Never returned. "Never" was one of those trick words. Like *always*. When one of them showed up in a test question, it was a sure bet the statement was false. But when it came to Maria returning, the word *never* just might be true.

After three days that brought more questions than answers, search and recovery efforts were officially discontinued Tuesday.

A series of captioned photos broke up the story. *Doing Watson's Run . . . wish me luck!* The same selfie Maria had posted on Instagram. Paddle in one hand. Setting sun silhouetting mangroves behind her.

Paddling the deadly route known as Watson's Run has become a kind of unofficial rite of passage for some high school seniors here in Florida's Miami-Dade County. Miles through the black water labyrinth of the untamed Glades. In a kayak. At night. Alone.

Despite warnings from park rangers, school officials, and parents, every year the number of students making the night passage increases. Nobody knows how a thing like this starts. But in Maria's case, this is how it ends. A young girl goes missing . . . and a family is lost.

So, she didn't mention anything about this being an act of desperation on Maria's part. A way to lash back because of how they'd tried to keep her away from Clayton. Mom probably saw no point in it.

Parker skimmed the rest. More photos—and Maria's text about this being a bad idea.

Parker squeezed his eyes shut, but the image of Maria was burned into his retinas. "Definitely a bad idea, Maria," he whispered. "So was going out with Clayton. You deserved better."

He spun in the chair away from the corkboard—and stared at the alligator skull on the bookcase. It had to be the one that tried to kill him.

And if he knew his dad and Uncle Sammy, there'd be another gator skull soon. But it would be on Uncle Sammy's bookcase this time.

What if Maria ran into a monster alligator? What if he thrashed her kayak with his tail—hard enough to tip her? Crawley was definitely out there that night. If Crawley had roared up in his skiff, would she have climbed in?

For sure. She'd have climbed in with the devil himself to get away from a monster gator.

It was nearly ten when Wilson texted.

Found out where he lives. Just got back from scoping it out. Crawley is the king of creepiness.

Parker's heart spiked—and he texted back.

Do you think . . . he hesitated . . . he has her?

Got a ride and did a drive-by. Didn't get close enough to tell. But saw enough from the road to know this guy is seriously demented enough to do anything.

Parker whipped off a response.

We'll go right after school. You in?

Wilson's answer came back in record time.

100%. Your dad green-lighted this?

Parker definitely was getting ahead of himself.

I'll convince him. Somehow. Which was likely going to be tougher now that Mom was home.

Tell your dad we'll go by water. Safer. Quicker. Bring your binoculars and we won't get near the place.

Parker wished they could go now. If Crawley had Maria, how could she take another night with him? He texted Wilson again.

I'll bring the knife. Gator stick. Binoculars. What else?

Parker's phone vibrated almost immediately.

Diapers. We're going to need them.

CHAPTER 58

ANGELICA HAD WAITED UNTIL LONG after dark before kicking her own little plan into gear. It meant riding back out to the *Boy's Bomb* and doing more than just swiping his transom plug this time. She had to stop him from doing something stupid, even if it meant doing something awful to his boat.

And she actually did it . . . she pulled it off, but it gave her no "mission accomplished" satisfaction. Parker loved his boat—and she hated to imagine how this would hurt him. She gave the boat one last inspection, then buried the can of black spray paint in her pack. This had to make her the worst best friend in the world. Suddenly she couldn't get past the feeling she was being watched. What if Creepy Crawley was here somewhere?

She mounted her bike on the run. Angelica had never felt more alone in her life than on that ride back home—or more like a traitor to the best friend she ever had. She pedaled hard—and was soaked in sweat by the time her home was back in sight. She didn't have to worry about Dad meeting her at the door, asking questions. *Why did you go out at ten o'clock? Where were you?* Obviously he wasn't even home. In fact, he was almost never home since he'd rushed off with Parker's dad to search for Maria Saturday night.

But the search for Maria was over. What was Dad still doing out there at night? But then she had a pretty good idea, didn't she? He believed an alligator grabbed her, and he was going to find it. Exact some revenge. This whole thing was such a tangled mess. She wanted to pray. Needed to. But somehow the words wouldn't come.

She pulled into the driveway, coasted her bike to a stop, and turned off the light. She leaned it against the side of the shed and hurried toward the house.

"Well look who finally showed up." A figure stepped out from the darkness shadowing the back door. Clayton Kingman.

Angelica took a step back—panic tightening around her like a strangler vine. "What are you—"

"You and I have a bond." Clayton stepped closer. "Secrets. But I can't have you getting weak and caving on me. We share a secret, you and I. And I want to make sure it stays that way."

"Are you threatening *me* now?"

Clayton grinned, but his eyes were wide with anger. "Am I?"

"You promised to leave Parker alone if I kept Maria's secret."

"Yeah, well I've had a lot of time to rethink that. It just wouldn't be right—letting the ranger's kid think he got away with all he did to me."

"He's moving," Angelica said. "He won't be bothering you anymore."

He stood there for a moment—like maybe he was weighing it out. Dark shadows pooled in his eye sockets like there were no eyes there at all. And if eyes were the windows to his soul, maybe he didn't have a soul, either.

"I'm keeping Maria's secret. *Your* secret." She wasn't going to beg, but her voice definitely sounded like she was already on her knees. "Two days—and he's gone. He won't find out—and he loses. You win."

His jaw clenched, and he gave a single nod. "Keep your secrets—and I'll hold off on my plans for Parker for another day—or two." He backed away. "If you talk," he pointed at her, "you'll only have yourself to blame for what happens." He gave a quick shoulder check and disappeared around the side of the house.

She stood there for a moment, too stunned to move. Then she rushed to the house and bolted the door behind her.

Angelica pressed her back against the door. "You're going to be okay. You're going to be okay." She tried to steady her breathing. Promised herself she'd never talk to him again. "He's gone. Gone." How had she gotten herself into this mess—and how was she going to get out?

Instinctively she pulled out her phone and dialed her dad.

He answered immediately. "Angelica, you okay?"

No she wasn't.

"Angelica?"

"I just needed to hear your voice." What she really needed was to tell him what was going on. But she couldn't. Not yet. "When are you coming home?"

A long pause. "You know what? I think I'm ready to hang it up now. I still won't make it home until midnight or later."

"Maybe I'll wait up for you." Normally being up that late

would never happen. But their home life hadn't been normal in a long time. "But if I'm asleep, you wake me, okay?"

"Count on it."

Just hearing Dad's voice helped. But until he got home she needed to escape. She just wanted to pop her earbuds in and get her mind off Clayton Kingman and his threats. But the thought of Clayton creeping around somewhere was still unnerving. So no earbuds. She had to be smart so she'd hear if someone was outside—and definitely wanted to hear Dad's truck when he pulled in the driveway.

She wished she could tell Dad everything. But that would make things even worse, wouldn't it? The secrets were killing her, but they were the only way to keep Parker alive. And it was for her dad's own good too, wasn't it? He was a good dad. He did the best he could. But he didn't operate with the same set of rules as Parker's dad did. If Dad found out the truth, he'd hunt Clayton down—and likely even Uncle Vaughn wouldn't be able to stop him. Then they'd be in an even worse mess.

Angelica sat at the kitchen table with paper and pen and started writing. Everything. Every thought that came to mind. For the moment, she was safe. If Clayton intended to hurt her, he'd have done it when he caught her outside, right? And she was pretty sure Parker was safe for another day as well—at least from Clayton. But it wouldn't last. She was certain about that.

"Oh God," she whispered. "There's no way out. Clayton's got to be stopped—but I'm not strong enough. I know that now. Help me. Please. Forgive me for the mess I've made." She didn't deserve God's help, but He was the only one who could.

It was nearly midnight before her emotions steadied. But a deep emptiness settled in and clung to her like her sweat-soaked

T-shirt. It was the lies. Deception. The secrets. They were becoming a family thing. Her Dad was keeping things from her. Like the money he'd given to Parker's dad. Not that it mattered now, but what was that all about? And why all the secrecy about his night hours in the Everglades? Why didn't he just admit he was hunting the alligator with Uncle Vaughn? Maybe tonight she'd ask him to be straight with her.

Suddenly she sucked in her breath—and knew exactly why he hadn't told her. To tell Angelica would be to admit he had no hope of finding Maria—and that he'd stopped looking. He wasn't trying to deceive Angelica. He just didn't have the heart to tell her the awful truth.

But the real deception was hers. She'd known Maria's plan but didn't tell a soul. Keeping a secret was its own kind of torture. And she knew for all the searching Parker was doing he'd never, ever, find Maria in the Everglades. Or at Crawley's.

And unless she was able to stop Parker some other way, he was going to check out Crawley—no matter what she said. He wouldn't listen to reason.

And she couldn't tell him the truth.

He'd practically forced her to do what she did to his boat tonight. She had to be out in front, playing offense instead of defense. And that meant sabotaging any possibility of him going into the Everglades to check out Crawley or the Lopez River. Taking the new transom plug was a little too obvious, wasn't it? But it was just as effective as lifting the five-gallon gas tank from the boat—and a whole lot easier to bring home. And it would buy her a little more time.

If that didn't work, maybe the spray paint would throw a scare into him. She hated herself for what she did to the *Boy's Bomb*. He'd never guess it was her.

And she would never tell him.

It would be another lie—another sin. Why would God listen to the prayer of someone who kept lying?

Instantly the claustrophobic sense of complete isolation closed in. She was pretending to help Parker, but secretly working against him. She wasn't just telling lies; she was pretty much living a lie. But she was trapped—and desperate enough to keep doing it. What kind of an awful person did that make her?

One horrible sinner who was desperately trying to save her best friend's life.

CHAPTER 59

PARKER HEARD DAD'S TRUCK CRUNCH up the gravel drive just after midnight. He peered out the window and watched Dad trudge to the house. It was obvious by the way he walked that he didn't have any good news about Maria.

Mom flew out of the house, threw her arms around him, and didn't let go. They stood there holding each other, talking so quietly that Parker couldn't make out a thing they said, even with the window open.

Parker slumped down on his bed, happy the family was all together again, but still feeling a deep sadness that he couldn't shake. Minutes later he heard the microwave ding, and Parker got up and walked into the kitchen.

Dad twirled his fork deep into a pile of their reheated spaghetti dinner. He gave Parker a tired smile.

Parker slid onto a chair across the table. "How about telling me what you've been doing since the search officially ended?"

Dad looked at him for a moment. "Fair question." He glanced at Mom.

She nodded. "Tell him."

"Sammy and I have been gator hunting."

Just as he'd thought. Did it mean they'd totally given up on finding Maria—or were they looking for proof that she was dead?

"At first Uncle Sammy wanted to slaughter any gator he saw," Dad said, "but we've been focused on the Sunday Bay area."

Okay, so they believed there was a monster gator, like the one Maria mentioned in her post. "Did you get him?"

Dad shook his head. "We opened a couple twelve-footers. But they were clean."

Meaning there were no human remains found in their guts?

"We thought Maria was exaggerating when she mentioned the monster gator. We've never seen one that big in that area."

Mom hugged Dad's arm, leaning into him. "I'll be so glad to get out of this place."

Parker knew the feeling.

"But last night we saw him." Dad paused—like he wasn't sure he should say more. "And believe me, Maria wasn't stretching the truth. He's a brute. Every bit of fourteen feet. More like fifteen."

A chill flashed through Parker. If they'd killed it, he'd have given the exact length, wouldn't he? "You will get him, though, right?"

Dad nodded. "He's priority one. We only have two more days—and he didn't grow that big by being stupid. But, yeah. We'll get him."

"Like you got the one that did this." Parker raised his gimpy arm.

Dad and Mom exchanged a quick glance. But it made Parker just that much more sure he was right.

Dad's eyes narrowed. "You think I hunted and euthanized the gator that pulled you off *Typhoon*?"

"Uncle Sammy brought over a skull—the right size—just a couple weeks later. You put it in your office like a trophy. Oh yeah. I'm sure that's exactly what happened."

Dad raised one hand like he was taking an oath. "I'll neither confirm nor deny that allegation. But I can say on good authority that gator will never hurt my son—or anyone else—ever again."

"You're going to get this one, too."

Dad's jaw muscles clenched and unclenched. "He's smart. Really smart. But we'll have Goliath's head."

"Goliath?" Mom shook her head. "You *named* him?"

"The name suits him."

Parker wanted to hunt with them. Wanted to see Goliath roll over dead. Wanted to see Dad and Uncle Sammy take his head. But there was no way they'd let him near this one. Especially when they opened its belly to see if there were any remains there. And Parker had his own things to do anyway. Like getting to Crawley's place.

"What did you name mine?"

Dad looked at him for a long moment. "Dillinger."

"You never told me that," Mom said. "The gangster bank robber from back in the 1930s?"

"He was Public Enemy Number One. On the FBI's Most Wanted list." Dad shrugged. "That gator was number one on *my* list. Sammy's too."

"Dillinger," Parker said. "Great name choice. And you're sure it was *the* one, right?"

"Positive. Found your watch in its gut."

"Seriously?"

Mom hugged Dad's arm again. "I wish we were leaving tomorrow."

"Saturday," Dad said. "But until then, I need every hour I can get."

Parker's thoughts exactly. His mind flashed to the money hidden in Dillinger's throat. Whatever happened to Maria, it obviously had nothing to do with that payment.

But if Dad and Uncle Sammy were hunting an alligator now, and had totally given up on Maria, shouldn't he at least talk to him about the Crawley angle? Had they even considered that Maria was taken?

"Dad." Parker wasn't sure how to start. *Just say it, Parker. Do it.* "Could this be a kidnapping?" He told them all about Crawley—and how the creepy guy had watched Maria leave in her kayak Saturday night.

"I don't know all the details," Dad said, "but the police considered an abduction. They questioned everybody whose trailer was parked at the marina overnight."

"Did they check his house?"

"Honestly? I don't know." Dad took another bite of his spaghetti. "But I'll tell you this much. Every cop wanted to find Maria. If they had any reason to suspect this Crawley character—or anyone else they questioned—they wouldn't have hesitated to do exactly that."

Parker wished he could be as sure as his dad seemed to be that the Crawley angle was a dead end.

"Look," Dad said, "I'll check this guy out myself if I get even a *hint* that there's something more to your hunch, okay? But until I do, I have to stay close to Sammy. He's in a bad place."

Obviously finding the gator was important too. It might hold the answers they were looking for. Literally. Parker's gut twisted at the thought.

"This is a tough time for all of us, Parker," Dad said. "Uncle Sammy is obsessed with finding that gator. I've got to be there. It just isn't safe for him to be out there alone. Especially with a gator that big."

Mom leaned into him. "It's not safe even for two grown men hunting that beast—and you know it."

Dad kissed her on the forehead. "The thing is, if we don't get Goliath before moving day Saturday, Uncle Sammy will keep hunting the thing on his own. That has disaster written all over it." Dad stood and pulled Parker close in a bear hug.

There was so much strength in his dad beyond muscle alone. And Parker would be like him some day. Prayed to God he would be. But even now, at this moment, Parker wrestled. Would he tell Dad more? Wouldn't that be the right thing to do? How was he ever going to be a man of strength and integrity if he compromised and wasn't truthful? But what if Dad said no to him checking out Crawley's place? Honestly—how would he *not* say no?

And if Dad said no—and Parker went anyway—he should just yank that INTEGRITTY sign off the wall. Yeah, then hide it in the closet and "forget" to pack it when they moved north. The idea of asking his dad for permission was like stepping out onto a football field against a team a whole lot bigger than he was. What chance did he have? He took a deep breath. "Dad, how about Wilson and I do some recon on Crawley?"

Dad released the hug and held him at arm's length. "Run that by me again."

"Vaughn." Mom's face had worry all over it. "You handle this. I can't even bear to hear more." She shook her head and left the kitchen.

Not a great start. He was already losing yardage. Parker took a deep breath, blew it out, and told his dad what he hoped to do—and how he'd be super-cautious. He really sold the part about being careful.

Dad listened. Sat back down at the table. "Parker, there's a part of me—a big part—that wants to let you do this. It's important to you. I get it."

He paused, and Parker resisted the urge to blurt out something about how he just had to check this angle. Had to.

"I wasn't wild about you going up the Lopez to help search. If you'd snuck off and did it without talking to me, I wouldn't even consider this. But you followed my guidelines. Never missed a time of texting me. That builds my trust in you, son."

And Parker was determined to continue working on that.

"And I trust God in all this, too. Not perfectly, sad to say, but I'm working on it." Dad seemed to be searching for the right words—or maybe an easier way to say no. "But as a dad, part of my job is protecting you too—even if you don't think you need it."

Parker groaned. Dad. Mom. Even Jelly. Why was everyone so worried that something bad might happen to him? Time to play some defense here. "You said it yourself. I've been building trust, right?" It was a cheap shot, using his dad's own words against him.

"I trust you, Parker. More and more. But it's the devil in others that I don't trust. And if this Crawley guy is half as bad as you've described, it's just not going to happen."

The ball game was as good as over—and Parker knew it. Time to throw a Hail Mary pass and hope for a break. "Dad—before you say no, just pray about it tonight, okay? You always like to pray before making a tough call—right?"

Dad looked him in the eyes for a very uncomfortable and long five seconds. "Fair enough. I'll let you know before school tomorrow. Deal?"

Parker nodded. "Thanks, Dad. Set up any ground rules you want. We'll use the *Boy's Bomb*—so we won't even get close to his house. I'll use binoculars—from a safe distance offshore. If we see anything suspicious, we get word to you."

"Whoa, whoa, whoa. Pump the brakes, son," Dad said. "I'll pray about it—as you asked . . . but don't start making plans just yet. We'll talk in the morning."

It was way too late to stop Parker from making plans. And he wasn't going to let go of them unless he got some kind of rock-solid "no" from his Dad in the morning. And if everything went according to that plan, Parker would be checking out Crawley's after school.

CHAPTER 60

ANGELICA HAD NEVER SEEN WILSON and Parker more hyper. When she pedaled up to Parker's house before school Thursday morning, she found them both around back, stuffing a backpack. Binoculars. Parker's survival knife with the leg straps. Machete—that nasty-looking curved one that Parker had been so excited to get when they moved here. "Packing for the moving van?"

Parker smiled. "You wish. You know what I'm doing." He quickly explained how he'd asked his dad for permission to scope out Crawley's.

Angelica couldn't believe it. "Your dad was *okay* with that?"

"Not exactly." Parker glanced at Wilson. "But I'm still hoping he changes his mind. And if he does, I want to be ready to head out in the *Boy's Bomb* right after school."

"Changes his mind?" Angelica watched Parker's eyes. "Either

your dad green-lighted this thing, or he gave it a red light. It was a yes or a no. I've never known your dad to be wishy-washy."

"I was with Bucky," Wilson said. "Heard every word his dad said. I wouldn't call it a full-on red light."

Were they talking themselves into checking Crawley's place anyway—without his dad's okay? How dumb was that? She stared at him. Parker had been working so hard at the whole integrity thing. Did this mean he was thinking of tossing all that away?

Thankfully, she was one step ahead of them—and if they tried going through with this, they definitely would not be taking the *Boy's Bomb*. She didn't smile, which took more than a little control on her part. "You bring that pack to school and the only place you'll be going is Kingman's office."

Wilson snorted. "We're dropping by the boat on the way, Einstein. We'll stow it under a seat so we don't have to stop home after school. We'll need every minute we can get."

This time she did smile. She was more like two steps ahead of them. And she was going to stay ahead of them until Parker left with the moving van. If he didn't have enough sense to stay out of the Everglades, she'd make sure he did.

Parker slung the pack over one shoulder, and both boys mounted their bikes. His dad's truck was already gone. Uncle Vaughn was likely already with her dad. Two sleep-deprived men hunting a gator the size of a nuclear sub? Angelica didn't even want to think about how dangerous that was. Everybody was taking greater and greater risks.

Parker kicked off. "Try to keep up, loser."

Wilson raced to catch up—and actually got a wheel ahead of him.

"That pack too heavy for you, Bucky?" Wilson smiled. "Maybe I should carry it so *you* can keep up."

"Then you'll be begging me to stop every few minutes so you can rest."

What was it with guys? They turned everything into competition. But it was the first time Parker had seemed like his old self in a while—and it was good to see it. Too bad it couldn't last. Jelly didn't push hard to catch up. There was no point. By the time the boys passed Smallwood's Store, she was nearly fifty yards behind them—and holding her breath for what had to be coming next.

Suddenly Parker stopped pedaling. He shouted something to Wilson and both of them poured on the speed again.

Here we go. She'd have to do some pretty convincing acting. More lies.

The moment Parker got close to the boat he dumped his bike and ran the last few yards.

ValuJet #592 was spray-painted in black across the entire length of the *Boy's Bomb*. She could read it clearly even from this distance on the teal fiberglass hull. Somehow what she'd done last night looked so much worse in the daylight.

Parker dropped to his knees and rubbed furiously at the graffiti. He was still working at it when Angelica pedaled up.

God, forgive me.

"No, no, NO." Parker licked his thumb and rubbed the letters. The paint didn't budge.

Wilson went around to the other side. "Starboard side is clear." He hustled back and dropped down beside Parker. He used his fingernail on one of the letters. "You've got enough wax on this thing. I think you'll get the spray paint off with a little Miccosukee muscle." He cleared an area the size of a dime. "We can do this."

Which made Angelica feel a tiny bit better.

Parker turned to her—pain all over his face. "Do you believe this?"

Angelica shook her head. "I'm so sorry."

"It wasn't your fault," Parker said.

Well . . . actually?

"This was Kingman," Wilson said. "That stinking coward. I thought he left town."

"Looks like he came back to leave me a little message." Parker stood and stared at the side of his boat.

"What does it mean?" Jelly tried to sound like she was clueless. But she had to make sure Parker got the message—or this whole thing was pointless.

Parker's face was as red as she'd ever seen it. "It wouldn't be hard to guess."

"It's obvious, Jelly," Wilson said. "ValuJet #592 was one of the flights that crashed in the Everglades. No survivors."

"What does that have to do with the *Boy's Bomb*?" Angelica looked at Parker. "Or with you?"

"He's warning me that if I take this boat out there," Parker motioned toward the Lopez, "I won't be coming back."

Okay. So Parker got the message. Angelica tried not to look as relieved as she felt.

Wilson stepped back, inspecting the boat, arms folded across his chest. "I've never met anybody who had such a streak of bad luck. And the thing I really don't get? You're the Christian. The boy scout. Always so zeroed-in on doing the "right thing." Ever wonder what you get for all your trouble? I mean, what does it gain you, Bucky?"

"Gain me? Like there's a reward or something?"

"Exactly."

This wasn't about winning a prize for choosing to be a person of integrity. But Angelica kept her mouth shut. She wasn't exactly the poster child for integrity at the moment. She'd let Parker handle this.

"It's not what I get, but what I become. *That's* the reward. And because I try to do the right thing here," Parker said as he fisted his chest, "I build trust." He stopped for a moment like he was remembering something specific. "And that's a big deal."

"I'll tell you what I see, Bucky," Wilson said. "Way back in June, I fed the gator—but *you* got pulled off *Typhoon*. Not me. *You* died on the dock at Wooten's. Not me. *You've* got the arm that's all weirded up. Not me. Who got cornered on Gator Hook Trail? That would be you."

He took a breath and motioned toward the side of the *Boy's Bomb*. "And now this. Don't you ever wonder if it wouldn't be a whole lot easier if you weren't, you know, such a boy scout?"

Jelly snorted. "And be more like you?"

"As a matter of fact, yeah." Wilson smiled. "I'm no Christian. I'll admit it. But I'm not so sure I see the plus for me if I were."

Parker thought for a moment. "So besides the fact that my faith in Jesus promises me a place in heaven someday—and forgiveness from everything I've ever done wrong—and that Jesus will never leave me . . . that I'm not alone . . . ever? You're thinking I should have more advantages besides those?"

Wilson laughed. "I'm talking about all the bad things that happen to you."

"Maybe it's all how you look at it," Parker said. "Sure, I got pulled off the airboat, but God rescued me. There was no other explanation. And my heart stopped on the dock, but it wasn't my time yet—and God restarted it. Sure, I got cornered on Gator Hook Trail, but He got me away from two gators."

"Actually," Wilson said, "I kind of helped on that one. Just saying."

"Even better. God provided reinforcements, and I didn't even have to face the gators alone." Parker shrugged. "As for upsides to being a Christian? The way I see it, they're endless. God reminds me over and over that He's got me—and won't leave me—no matter how messy things get." He rubbed at the spray paint again.

Wilson grinned. "Well when you put it that way . . ."

"So," Jelly said. "What are you going to do now?"

"After school today?" Parker shrugged. "This really messes everything up. I gotta get this paint off the boat before I even think of doing anything else—even if my dad does change his mind about the recon mission at Crawley's. I'm afraid the longer this paints stays on, the more impossible it will be to get it off. I'll never sleep tonight if I don't work on this."

By the time he got the paint off, it would be too late to go out looking for Creepy Crawley. Angelica tried not to look elated.

"I need to tell my dad about this." Parker stepped back and took a couple of pictures with his phone. "I'm not sure there's enough daylight to even get this done after school."

"And after seeing this, I got one more thing to add to your list of things to do today." Wilson pointed to the graffiti on the boat. "Stay clear of Kingman."

CHAPTER 61

SOMETHING INSIDE PARKER SHIFTED the moment he finished talking to Wilson about God. Like some invisible toggle switch flipped in his head. But it was as real as the graffiti on the side of his boat. That urgency to leave the Everglades lost a little traction. He still wanted out—and didn't hate the place less. But wherever Parker was, God was with him. Suddenly that counted—or mattered more than it did before.

The instant Parker locked his bike in the rack at school, he texted his dad about the damage to the boat. He stared at the picture of the *Boy's Bomb* before sending it. He'd hoped Kingman was long gone, like the rumors said. The idea that the guy was still around would definitely keep Parker looking over his shoulder.

First period was a blur. ValuJet. Spray paint. Kingman. Crawley. Parker's mind looped on those four things way more than on anything the teacher said. Even in the hallway after the class was over, Parker couldn't stop thinking about them. Parker was ready to walk in to second period when an incoming text dinged his phone.

Dad!

Go to the office—pronto—and text me after you've talked with the principal.

What?

Principal Kingman met him before he even got to the office. "Ah, Mr. Buckman. Just the one I want to see." He flashed his whitened-teeth smile. Honestly? His nose still seemed to angle off to one side a bit. He'd always had a schnoz for sniffing out "devilry." Maybe this was his secret weapon. With that hook in his nose, maybe he smelled incoming trouble easier—especially from around corners.

"It seems your father needs your immediate services in the worst way. He's asked permission for you to leave, which I have granted in light of the fact this is your last week."

Parker couldn't believe it. Had his dad changed his mind about Crawley's? "Right now?"

Principal K made a brushing motion with both hands like Parker was a pesky fly. "This minute. Vamoose. But . . ." He poked his finger at Parker. "I'll see you tomorrow morning."

Parker turned and bolted for the exit before the principal changed his mind.

"Walk, Mr. Buckman."

He slowed to a power walk and broke into a run again the instant he pushed through the exit door crash bars. He pedaled a full block away before stopping to text his dad—so he'd be out of earshot just in case Principal K called him back.

Moments later his dad returned a text, like he'd had the thing written and was just waiting to send it.

We don't want the graffiti baking on the hull so I thought it best you get on it. Stop at marina on way and pick up rags and rubbing compound. I've already paid. Wish I could be there to help, but call me at the boat and I'll tell you how to use it.

He waited for a second text—saying Dad had a change of heart about the recon mission. But after a long minute, he had to face the facts—and at least be glad for the gift he'd just gotten. His dad probably felt bad about saying no to Crawley's in the first place, and saw this as a different way he could help Parker. He fired off a quick thanks—then a text to Wilson and Jelly saying he was leaving to work on the graffiti.

Wilson texted back in seconds. Want company?

Parker didn't want to encourage Wilson to ditch school, but he wasn't going to turn down the help, either.

Wilson caught up to him at the marina. Ninety minutes later, the rubbing compound did its magic on the *Boy's Bomb*. Way faster than Wilson's earlier method with his fingernail. Wilson and Parker stepped back and inspected the job. The boat looked like new.

Parker snapped a picture and sent it to his dad.

"You know," Wilson said, "I've been thinking about what your dad said this morning. And the other half of my brain has been focused on Crawley. What *if* he's got Maria?"

Parker gave him the side-eye. Was Wilson messing with him? Trying to get him to check out Crawley's behind his dad's back?

"He saw Maria leave—from this very spot." Wilson looked across Chokoloskee Bay. "How hard was it for him to guess she'd headed for the Lopez? He took off for the marina and I saw him launch his boat."

"Tell me something I don't know."

"He was moving, too. Man-on-a-mission pace—in the dark—to go fishing?" Wilson swept his hair back. "It was weird, you know? He lit out fast—full bore . . . like he was on a clock. A guy isn't racing like that if he's only going to fish."

Parker could picture it. "I just wish we knew if he went after her."

"Well, Bucky, sometimes the right answer is right in front of your face."

"You really think he's got her?"

"Don't you?" Wilson gave him a long look. "I say we check Crawley's out."

Parker shook his head. "You heard my dad this morning."

"Yeah—I heard him. But did *you* hear him? He never actually said you *couldn't* go."

"What?"

"His exact words," Wilson said. "Tell me what he said."

Parker thought for a moment. "'Sorry, Parker. I prayed about it—and I still don't like it.'"

"See? He didn't *like* it . . . the same way he didn't like the idea of you joining the search and rescue teams. But he let you do it—with a list of ground rules."

Dad definitely didn't want him doing the SAR thing.

"This morning your dad said he didn't like the *idea* of you going to Crawley's, but did he actually say you couldn't go?"

"Technically, no. But—"

"And what did he say right after he said he didn't like it—remember?"

How could Parker forget? "He said he didn't want me within a hundred yards of Crawley's place."

"So." Wilson smiled. "We take the *Boy's Bomb*. Stay a hundred yards offshore. I'll take the wheel and do a drive-by while you scope the place with your binoculars. You'll still be obeying your dad."

"I'm not so sure he'd see it that way."

Wilson shrugged. "And how would he know? I'm not going to tell him—are you?"

"I'd have to at some point. I mean, if I didn't I'd be—"

"A good friend? Someone who is willing to take a risk to help a girl who might be in real trouble?" Wilson shook his head. "You—being a Christian who is supposed to care so much about others—can you *honestly* tell me that next week you won't be lying in bed in your new home somewhere wishing you hadn't wimped out?"

Wilson was baiting him, wasn't he? But he was also making a lot of sense.

"You'll be kicking yourself for the rest of your life, and you know it. What if Crawley has her? We're her only hope, Bucky. Everybody else thinks she's dead. Nobody's out looking for her anymore. Nobody."

Wilson knew just where to hit him. He'd say anything to get Parker back in the Glades again, wouldn't he? But so much of what he said was absolutely true. If Parker didn't check out Crawley's, would he really be okay with that? Would he ever forgive himself?

"Your dad isn't Superman, Parker. He's trying to hunt down a monster gator so his best friend doesn't do it alone after you all leave. Hunting a thing that size? Alone? It would be a suicide mission—and your dad knows it. He's trying to keep Jelly's dad alive, so there's no way he's got time to check out Crawley himself. But he never actually said *you* couldn't."

Everything Wilson said about the danger of going against Goliath alone was true. Dad thought it was truly too late to help Maria. He'd given up on finding her alive. Dad had been forced to make a choice. Help his best friend stay alive, or check out the long-shot Crawley angle. Dad really had no choice.

"Your dad gave you a loophole, Bucky—if you man up enough to take it. Just don't get closer than a hundred yards from Crawley's. *That's* what your dad said. We both heard that. One hundred yards. We can do that."

It still felt wrong. That hundred yard thing . . . it was an expression of speech. His dad wasn't saying they could check out Crawley's as long as they stayed a hundred and one yards away, was he? But what if they *could* stay a super safe distance away? "I don't know how I'd tell my dad."

"I don't know why you would," Wilson said. "Look . . . we do a drive-by. No harm, no foul. We don't say a word."

"Unless I see something suspicious." Parker imagined that. "Then how do I explain I was checking out Crawley's place?"

"You won't have to. You'll be a hero," Wilson said. "If they find Maria there—alive—you think your dad will be mad at you? He'll be too busy organizing a parade through Everglades City for you. Jelly's dad will have a statue made of you—and put it up in McLeod Park. That's the way I see it."

Wilson was actually making a good case for this. And there was plenty of daylight left today. Where was the harm in taking a boat ride, and just *happening* to head by Crawley's?

"Let's forget about Crawley's," Wilson said. "We'll just go for a little ride in the *Boy's Bomb*. I'll drive. So you can honestly say you didn't take us to Crawley's. It will be all me."

Like that made it right. But still, what was the harm in taking a boat ride? And if Wilson just *happened* to drive by Crawley's, and Parker just *happened* to pull out the binoculars at that moment, was he really doing something all that wrong? "We'd have to stay at least a hundred yards away. At *least*."

Wilson clapped Parker on the back. "Way to man up."

He had made a decision, hadn't he? For good or bad, he was going to check this out. And deep in his heart he knew this wasn't going to be nearly as okay with Dad as Wilson made it sound. But he wanted to believe Wilson's logic. An antsiness swept over Parker. A sense that they needed to get this done and over with. "I'll get the plug. You untie her."

Wilson grinned and hustled to untie the bow line. Parker climbed over the side of the boat and lifted the driver's seat—and stared.

"The drain plug. It's gone again!"

Parker slid the signal flare gun to the side. Shook the towel stashed below it. Another plug . . . gone. "What is going *on*?"

"But it doesn't make sense," Wilson said. "Clayton wants revenge. He practically dared you to go back into the Everglades with his ValuJet message. Why would he take your drain plug to keep you out?"

Parker totally agreed. "Well *somebody* wants to keep me out, that's for sure." And then it hit him. "Hold on. What if Clayton did the paint job—but somebody *else* swiped the plug? And I'm pretty sure I know who that somebody else is."

Wilson sucked in his breath. "Tell me you're not thinking what I'm thinking."

"Jelly sabotaged me," Parker said. It all made sense now. She was still trying to protect him—and with just a couple of days left, she was desperate. "This is one plan that's going to backfire on her, though." He was more determined than ever to get to Crawley's.

He dialed the marina parts department—only to find out somebody had phoned in earlier that morning and bought every last transom plug that size in stock. He gave Wilson the news.

"Looks like Jelly really wants to keep you out of the Glades in the worst way."

"Unreal, right?" Had she been taking his plugs from the beginning?

"We could bike back to the marina," Wilson said. "And scout around for a plug the right size."

"Boosting again?" Parker shook his head. "We have to come up with something better than that—and we're not going to tell Jelly whatever it is we figure out." He wasn't sure if Jelly had any other plans to slow him down, and he wasn't about to risk it. Maybe the marina carried that Gorilla tape. They'd cover the transom drain with that. It was supposed to hold, even underwater, right?

Both of them were quiet for a moment, then Wilson smiled. "I got it. We can still get to Crawley's, and we'll keep Jelly off our trail at the same time."

Minutes later they hammered out a totally solid Plan B. Parker wasn't wild about it, but it would work—and would get them to Crawley's and back faster anyway.

"I'm going to text Jelly," Parker said. "And keep her from suspecting anything."

Good news/bad news. The graffiti came off. But we're missing another plug. Looks like the Bomb couldn't have gone to Crawley's—even if my dad did give the okay.

Her response came back super quick—like she'd been expecting it.

`How awful! What are you going to do?`

Parker laughed. "Wouldn't you like to know?"

He fired back a text. `Got any ideas? Definitely not going back to class. For the moment, I'm camping out right here. Maybe get some food. Do you have any idea how lousy it feels to be outsmarted?`

Okay, he was laying it on pretty thick. Seconds later she responded.

`Absolutely no idea. I've never experienced that. I would think you'd be used to it by now, though.`

She ended with a little smiley face.

Parker laughed. "You're a piece of work, Jelly."

Jelly fired back one more text.

`I'll be there after school.`

Wilson read the texts over Parker's shoulder. "But she won't find either of us here."

Parker sent Jelly a smiley face back. "No, she will not—and she won't be so smiley either."

They left their bikes leaning against the cypress tree and retied the bow line. Parker strapped Jimbo onto his calf and grabbed the binoculars—but left the backpack in the boat. He hated leaving Amos Moses behind too, but he didn't want to tip Jelly off as to what they'd done. What if she decided to leave school early, too? He had no idea how she could sabotage their *new* plan, but he wasn't taking any chances.

Now all they had to do was call for the Uber ride—to take them to *Typhoon*.

CHAPTER 62

WILSON EASED BACK THE THROTTLE. They were as close to Crawley's as he dared go in an airboat. The best he could figure, his place was still a little trek inland, but that was good. He wanted to be sure they were far enough away where their arrival wouldn't be noticed. He absolutely hoped Crawley wasn't home. "This is it. As close as we can get."

Bucky actually stood—binoculars in hand. "I can't see a thing. I thought you said we'd drive by from a hundred yards out."

Wilson avoided Bucky's eyes. "Yeah, well I was guessing a little."

Bucky stared at him. "You knew."

He wasn't going to deny it—but he didn't have to admit it either. Wilson spotted a gap in the brush big enough to nose in and drove the grass catcher up onto the soggy shore. He cut the motor, unbuckled, and stood. "This will have to do."

"This won't even remotely do." Bucky looked like he'd just learned the truth about the tooth fairy. "This isn't what we agreed on. I can't do this."

Wilson stepped off the grass catcher and onto the spongy ground. "Then wait here. I didn't drive all the way out here just to turn around and head back. I'll check the place out myself." Truthfully? There was no way he was going near Crawley's place alone. Not after what he'd seen last night. But Bucky didn't need to know that.

Bucky shook his head. "We should leave." He said the words, but there was no heart in it.

Wilson was pretty sure it wouldn't take much to get Bucky to join him. He picked his way through the brush several yards before looking back. "Toss me the binoculars. I'll still stay a hundred yards out—just like your dad said. I just can't do it from the water like we'd hoped. No big deal."

He'd shame Parker. That was the way to make this work. "You stay here if you want, Bucky, but I'm looking for Maria. You really going to let me do this by myself?"

Bucky stood on the grass catcher now, right on the edge of the bow—and on the edge of an even bigger decision. His face looked a little tortured, and he gripped the binoculars in one hand like he had no intention of letting go. Another good sign. Bucky was going to cave on this if Wilson played it right. "If I'm not back in an hour, you'll only have to come looking for me anyway. I say we stay together right from the start."

Bucky took his phone from his pocket like maybe he wanted to text his dad for permission or something. But he looked like all he needed was one more little nudge to get him off the airboat.

"What if I find Maria and she's hurt—or really weak because

Crawley hasn't fed her? How am I supposed to get her back here by myself?"

Bucky growled and slung the binoculars over his shoulder. He leaped off *Typhoon* and hustled to catch up. "You're an idiot sometimes, you know that?"

Wilson did his best to hide the smile—and the Miccosukee war whoop—that were both busting to get out. "Tell me all about it later. Right now we both need to stay focused—okay?" Wilson pointed toward a coiled cottonmouth not four feet in front of them. "He could ruin your day."

"Wicked eyes on that thing," Bucky said. "I *really* wish I had Amos Moses."

Wilson laughed. "I'm not so sure the Uber driver would have let us in."

They backed up a few feet and took a wide sweep around the deadly snake. Parker scanned constantly. Where there was one cottonmouth there were bound to be more. Wilson pulled a can of yellow spray paint from his pack, and marked trees with a shot the size of his fist so they'd find their way back easily.

Parker looked at the paint—then at Wilson. "You just *happened* to have spray paint to mark a trail? You played me."

Wilson waved him off—and kept walking. "I learned some things about Crawley that I wish I never knew." The guy had quite a reputation on the Miccosukee Reservation. None of it good.

"Like?"

"The guy catches snakes. Mostly venomous. Cottonmouths. Eastern diamondbacks. Pygmy rattlers."

"To sell?"

Wilson shook his head. "Lets 'em go on his land."

Bucky stopped. "Why?"

"He doesn't like fences, but hates trespassers," Wilson said.

"He's insane."

"That's what everybody says."

"I think I'm going to regret doing this," Bucky said.

"Not if we find Maria."

Bucky smiled, and he didn't seem quite as upset as he'd been minutes ago.

They walked side by side. Sort of. They were constantly ducking under branches, stepping over rotting logs, and around trees and brush. They came together again after every obstacle—like they both knew it was safer that way. Twice they heard the warning rattle from a diamondback in the space of fifty yards.

The leafy canopy overhead dialed down the light surprisingly. The sunlight that did filter through came from over their shoulders, casting giant shadows in front of them.

They passed the first No Trespassing sign just as the brush thinned a bit. A shotgun blast had taken out the bottom corner of the sign—and all but the first letter in the last word.

"Violators will be P . . ." Bucky smiled. "What do you suppose the missing word is? Persecuted? Perforated? Punctured?"

Wilson snickered, but Bucky was probably more right than he figured. From all Wilson had heard about this guy, he'd probably shoot first and ask questions later.

CHAPTER 63

ANGELICA BIKED TO SMALLWOOD'S after school—and couldn't help feeling proud of herself. Her little plan had worked. The boat was here. The bikes were here. Even the gator stick. She'd kept them out of the Everglades for another day—and there was only one to go. It was about time one of her schemes didn't backfire.

Taking the plug again last night was risky—and could have tipped her hand—but the gamble had paid off. She'd stayed two steps ahead of them. But where were they? Maybe they were in Smallwood's, buying snacks again.

She ran her hand along the smooth fiberglass hull. They'd done an amazing job getting every trace of the spray paint off the side of the *Boy's Bomb*. Which made her feel a whole lot better.

She strolled into Smallwood's, expecting to find them jawing with the owner.

"I haven't seen those boys in hours," he said. "Not since the car picked them up."

"Car?" Angelica stared at him. "What car?"

"One of those online taxis," the owner said.

"Like Uber? Or Lyft?"

He nodded.

Angelica ran out of the store, texting Parker as she did.

Where ARE you?

She stood outside Smallwood's watching the screen. "Come on, Parker. Answer me." She scrolled through his earlier texts—and stared at the one about how lousy he felt to be outsmarted. And she knew in that instant exactly how terrible it felt.

Seconds later the response came.

Crawley's

She could hardly breathe. Did Parker's dad actually change his mind? How could that be? And the Uber driver . . . did he just drop them off at Crawley's door? She texted back. How did you get there?

Typhoon

So the Uber driver dropped them at the dock. "What have you two done?" If she hadn't been so zeroed in on keeping the stupid secrets, they wouldn't be at Crawley's right now.

She whipped out another text.

Get out of there. Please.

Something bad was coming. She could feel it.

Angelica pictured Parker the day of the attack—lying on the deck of *Typhoon*. How she'd held him to keep him from sliding off while Wilson raced back to the dock. She saw the blood. So much blood. She squeezed her eyes shut, trying to shut out the picture. Bucky hadn't stepped foot on *Typhoon* since.

Until now.

Superstition. Intuition. Maybe a warning from God Himself. But the message was clear. Disaster was advancing—and it was her fault. Again.

Her phone chirped—and she read Parker's text.

`We'll get out the minute we know`

But deep inside she knew it wouldn't be soon enough. Suddenly she didn't feel two steps ahead anymore. Instead, she felt impossibly behind.

CHAPTER 64

PARKER SLIPPED HIS PHONE BACK in his pocket, grinning. "Jelly is NOT happy." And how happy would his dad be if he knew where Parker was at this moment? Deep down he'd known all along what his dad meant with the "hundred yards away" comment. He did his best to bury the thought. They'd come this far. He couldn't abort—even though his heart was telling him to do exactly that. They were too close to answers to turn back now.

Wilson crept forward—on high alert. "Silence that thing, would you?"

Parker turned off the ringer. They picked their way another thirty yards through dense thickets and suddenly found themselves staring at the grill of a rusting Ford pickup. Late sixties, maybe. Hood dented. Cab crushed. Tinges of green showed through the rust. Parker wasn't sure if that was the original color or if it was just some swamp slime that had taken over. The floor was completely gone in the bed—and trees grew right through it.

There was no path. Not even a trail. To find this in an open field would make sense. But in the dense jungle? "How'd this even get out here," Parker said, "with all the trees and brush?"

"There must have been a road—or the area was clear once." Wilson looked back over his shoulder toward the water. "But the jungle keeps coming back. Taking over."

Parker stepped closer to the pickup.

"Easy," Wilson said. "The thing's probably filled with snakes."

He backed away immediately. "Good call."

In the next few minutes they ran across the metal hulks of another six clunkers. Cars mostly. A couple of pickups. All of them totally shrouded in vines and rust. Windshields, what could be seen of them, fogged over in grime. Tires dry-rotted and flat—or riding on the rims. Doors open and vines twisting out of them. The headlights missing—and staring at them like the empty eye sockets of a skull.

"It's like a graveyard—for cars," Parker said. "Unreal."

Wilson cut a wide path around them like it was a burial ground—and sacred somehow. "Makes me wonder what else Crawley dumped out here."

Parker was thinking the same thing. "Trespassers?"

"Just keep your eyes open," Wilson said. "We should be getting close now."

Parker had hoped they would have seen Crawley's place long before this. "As long as we stay at least a hundred yards away." But with the dense, jungle-like growth around them, how far away could they stay and still see the place? But somehow he would.

Right. And maybe if he told himself enough times he'd actually believe he could stay a hundred yards away.

As spooky as this was, it still beat coming in from the road where they could be spotted.

They reached a clearing—and an ancient Plymouth sat dead center in the middle of it. Late forties, maybe. Early fifties. It looked like the old four-door had been parked there generations ago. As if somebody had pulled into the meadow for a picnic—and never left.

Parker stepped into the clearing and moved in for a closer look. It was amazing that the car hadn't completely disintegrated after all these years, but they used a lot thicker gauge steel in those days. The Plymouth's skin showed definite age spots of rust, along with dull patches of the original black paint.

Wilson stopped a good ten feet away from the car. "Oh, that's sick."

Definitely sick. And Parker was getting a sick feeling in his gut, too. Inside were two mannequins—a man behind the wheel, and a redheaded woman in the passenger seat. A bullet hole sat smack dab in the middle of the lady's forehead.

Her eyes were wide, frozen in an eternal look of surprise—or horror. She stared directly at them in that spooky way where it totally looked like she was watching their every move . . . following them with her eyes.

Another metal No Trespassing sign was screwed to the outside of her door.

"Okay—this is really getting creepy now," Wilson whispered.

Parker felt it too. Like they really shouldn't be there. For an instant he heard his dad's voice replaying in his mind. *I don't want you within a hundred yards of that place.* So how did he get here—on the private property of a guy who shot trespassers? But Parker knew exactly how he got himself into this. One little step—no—make that one little compromise at a time.

Parker inched closer to the Plymouth. Peered inside. The driver wore a latex mask of a former United States president—and there was a hole between his eyes, too. "Doesn't look like Crawley is a big fan of government." A human skeleton leaned up from the back seat, its boney arms covered in mold and draped over the front bench seat.

"Either the guy in the back seat had three eyes, or that's a bullet hole," Parker said. "Think that skeleton is real?"

"I don't want to know," Wilson said. "But it sure looks like it."

Parker stepped around the car—and stopped dead. Not more than one hundred feet away sat a trailer home. So much for the hundred yards plan.

"That's it," Wilson said. He crouched low in the brush.

Parker dropped on one knee beside him. The trailer home hunkered down in the shadow of a massive cedar with strangler vines hugging the trunk. Just beyond the trailer home, Crawley's pickup was parked on the crushed shell driveway. *Night Crawler* was strapped down on the trailer behind it. "He's here."

Wilson groaned. "Lets do some quick recon and get out."

Exactly Parker's thoughts. He swung the binoculars to his eyes and focused on the trailer. He listened for Maria's voice. And he couldn't stop staring at the trailer. Some kind of black mold grew over every surface of it, giving the whole thing a deathly gray look. At first Parker thought the windows had been painted over. But it was the mold—and grime. Parker refocused the binoculars on the glass, but couldn't see a thing through them.

"Parker." Wilson pointed to the hair on his arms, doing that Miccosukee warning thing. "We gotta get out of here."

Wilson . . . wanting to turn tail and run? Parker reached inside his collar and pulled out the gator-tooth necklace Wilson had given him that day at Gator Hook Trail. "You want this back?"

Wilson gave a quick scan around him. "The evil here is too big. Let's get back to *Typhoon*. Now."

In his gut, Parker couldn't wait to get out of there, but something kept him welded in place—with his eyes locked on the trailer. "But what if she's in there?"

"Stay right where you is, boys."

Parker spun toward the direction of the man's voice.

"Who you be thinking I done got in there?" Crawley stepped out from behind a cypress—pump-action shotgun pointing right toward them. At this range he couldn't miss. Sagging jeans. Faded black T-shirt with a Harley logo. The beard . . . long, but not thick enough to cover deep pockmark scarring. One cheek bulged out with chewing tobacco. He advanced slowly. "Lookee here. A couple of tourists. Missed the trespassing signs, did ya?"

Instinctively Parker raised his hands. Wilson did, too.

"I done asked you a question, boy." His voice had a hoarseness to it. Like a forced whisper.

He'd compromised on what he knew was right. And now he was in a mess. "We don't want any trouble," Parker said.

One corner of Crawley's lip twitched into a snarly smile. "Too late for that, fellers." Brown spittle trickled out one side of his mouth. "Trouble done found you."

CHAPTER 65

ANGELICA FIRED OFF ANOTHER TEXT and waited. Were they deliberately ignoring her?

But somehow she had the sense that Parker wouldn't do that to her. He'd already admitted to being at Crawley's. There was nothing to hide.

They were out of range. That was all. Probably in a dead spot.

Immediately she cringed. *Dead spot.* Sometimes the Everglades was one massive dead spot. A place of death.

But what if they weren't in a "no service" zone for the phone? What if something bad happened to them? She grabbed Parker's backpack from the bottom of the boat. She rummaged through it a bit. Machete. Flashlight. Water. Granola bars. Insect repellant. Quick charger. She stared out over the water. "What were you thinking, Parker? Why didn't you take your gear? You're going to need this stuff."

But she knew why. They'd deliberately tried to mislead her. They wanted to keep her from knowing their real plans until there was no chance for her to stop them. Swiping Parker's transom plug last night had been risky, but she'd rolled the dice—and lost. She'd gone too far. They'd obviously figured her out.

Angelica shouldered Parker's backpack. There was no way she was going to stay here to wait for them. She dialed for an Uber ride to take her to the dock where *Typhoon* was normally tied. And maybe by the time she got there she'd figure out exactly what to do next.

CHAPTER 66

"PLEASE—WE CAN EXPLAIN," Parker said, careful to keep his hands in the air. His bad arm was already prickling. "There's a girl. From Chokoloskee. She's missing."

"I seen the paper." Crawley's eyes narrowed. "You thinking I got her in there?" He nodded in the direction of the trailer.

What was he supposed to say? The answer was obvious.

"No," Wilson blurted. "Just asking if people saw her."

Crawley swung the shotgun toward Wilson. "Do I look stupid to you, boy?"

Do not answer that. "You're right," Parker said. "We came here to see if she was here."

"And what makes you figure I got me this girl?"

Parker swallowed. His right arm felt heavy. Weak. "You were

on the water that night. And earlier—you offered her sister a ride, but not me. On the causeway. Remember?"

His eyes were barely more than slits now. "I do." He smiled real slow. Enough to show the tobacco-stained teeth. "She was put together real fine." He circled around them—always keeping the shotgun aiming their way. "But I didn't take no girl."

Parker's mind raced for a way out of this. If they rushed him, they'd both be dead before they got close. If they ran for *Typhoon*, they'd never get past the old car. He'd blast a hole through each of them the size of the Plymouth's hubcaps.

"You want to have a look around my place?"

Wilson shook his head. "No sir. We'd like to leave."

Crawley laughed in a wheezy, gaspy way. "I'll just bet you do." He eyed Parker. "How 'bout you, boy?"

His heart thudded in his chest like a caged animal trying to get free. He'd never seen Wilson spooked like this. But how could they leave without knowing? "I'd like to make sure she isn't here. Yes, sir."

Again, that laugh. "That ain't gonna happen. It wouldn't do you a lick of good anyways. If I had me that girl they's plenty of places to hide her. I wouldn't keep her in no trailer. But like I said," he showed brown teeth, "I don't got her."

Wilson nodded. "Okay. We're sorry for trespassing. We'll just leave the way we came."

"Get your foot off the gas, boy. You trespass on my land. You accuse me of taking some girl—and then figure you can fly away just as free as a jaybird?" Crawley circled them again. "It don't work like that."

If the guy let his guard down, Parker would rush him. What else could he do? But he felt weak. So incredibly weak.

He gave Parker a long, hard look. "You're the ranger's boy."

Parker hesitated, then nodded. His phone vibrated in his pocket.

"I hate rangers." Crawley spit. "They's always nosing around, getting in the way." He bobbed his head. "All high-and-mighty with their o-thority and all." His eyes darted from one side of the clearing to the other as if he thought rangers were advancing at that very moment.

"My dad isn't like that. He has to come down on poachers but—"

"Poachers?" He shook his head. "Poaching is taking what ain't yours. But this land *is* ours. My grandpappy done took alligator skins from the Glades whenever he wanted. My pappy, too." His face got darker, the pockmarks redder. "The way I sees it? They's nobody who can stop me from taking gator skins—or anything else I want—in the Glades."

Parker's mauled arm was tingling so bad, he wasn't sure he could hold it up much longer.

"The rangers don't own the land. Never did," Crawley said. "They just like ta zoom in with their fancy unee-forms and tell us folk what we can and can't do on our own land."

Crawley stepped to within two feet of Parker without lowering the shotgun. "That seem right to you, boy?"

He shook his head. Actually, it didn't seem right at all. "I don't make the rules."

"But your pappy, he makes sure people follows 'em, don't he."

Parker nodded.

"A man has got to enforce the rules, yes sirree." Crawley leaned in close. "And you boys done broke my rules when you walked right past my trespassing signs."

The liquor on his breath—mixed with the tobacco—almost made Parker gag.

"Look, our friend knows we're here. She's a ranger's kid too. I've been texting her."

Crawley's eyes narrowed. "You expect me to believe that?"

"My phone is right here." Parker pointed at his pocket. "I can show you."

Crawley nodded. "If you're bamboozling me, boy, you'll be soon a-wishing you done told me the gospel truth." He jabbed the shotgun. "You're going to show me the phone. You right-handed or a southpaw?"

"Right."

"Alrighty. Left hand. Show me the texts. Nice and easy like."

Parker did as he was told. He held out the phone so Crawley could see the screen.

The man glanced at it quickly, and nodded. "Put it away. You was telling the truth. Lucky thing for you both."

Wilson looked relieved. If they ever got out of this, maybe Wilson wouldn't be so quick to doubt the payoffs of integrity again. Then again, if Parker hadn't compromised, they wouldn't be in this position to begin with.

"I could feed your sorry hides to the gators. Won't nobody ever find you."

Parker had to keep Crawley talking. "You absolutely could. We trespassed. But Maria's my friend. Everyone thinks she's dead."

"Exceptin' you," Crawley said.

Parker nodded.

"Smart kid."

What did that mean? Did he know something? "People think she ran into some monster gator in Sunday Bay."

"And they's a big 'un out there." Crawley nodded. "I seen him."

Parker stared at him. "You saw the gator—I mean—"

"You said it yourself," Crawley said. "I was out there Saturday night."

Parker could hardly breathe. "Did you see Maria?"

"I seen that missing girl," he said. "But she never saw me."

"Did you see the alligator attack her?" Wilson said.

"Weren't no gator attack," Crawley said. The man seemed to be enjoying this. He took a step back—but kept the shotgun steady.

"Sir," Parker said. "I can't hold my arm up any longer. I've got to lower it. Please don't shoot."

Crawley squinted, like he was studying the scars. "Gator tats, looks like."

Parker nodded.

"Bring it down real easy like."

Parker lowered his arm. Slowly. He opened and closed his fist to get the circulation going. "You said Maria wasn't attacked. If you know something, please—"

"I know plenty." He stared at Parker for what seemed like a full minute. "Maybe nobody found that girl because she don't want to be found."

"What are you saying?"

"You got ears, don't you?" Crawley laughed. He stepped closer and gave Parker's forehead a two-fingered poke. "If you got any brains in that hat rack mounted 'tween your shoulders you'll figure it out."

"You mean she's alive?" Parker glanced at Wilson. He wanted to be sure Wilson was hearing this. "She's still out there?"

"'Course she's not still in the Glades." Crawley spit to one side without taking his eyes off them.

"Then—where is she?"

Again, Crawley laughed. "You're a funny one, you is. Sneaking onto my land, thinking I took that girl. Now you want my help finding her?" Crawley took a step back. "You don't need me. They's eyes all over the Glades, if you know where to look. And they's all the help you need. One was there. Right there—and it saw plenty. I'm guessing those college-boy rangers done missed that. The answer was just a staring right back at them."

Oh, yeah. Crawley definitely knew something. "Just steer us in the right direction."

Crawley pointed his shotgun toward the trees. "The right direction is off my land. Right now." He looked toward the brush and back at Parker. "You was honest with me, boy, from the get-go. And I respect that. So you done bought yourself and your friend here a chance. Sixty seconds. How's that?"

"You mean," Wilson said, "you're going to let us free?"

Crawley shook his head. "Just giving you a head start. Then I'ma gonna follow—and make for certain you ain't circling back for another look-see."

"We're leaving," Parker said. "Promise."

"By golly you better haul your sorry tails all the way back to your fancy-pants, rich-boy airboat. Yeah, I saw you boys come in."

He was just putting a good scare into them, right? If he was going to shoot them, he'd have done it already, right?

"Iffen you haven't fired up that swamp skimmer by the time I gets to the waterline, I just may put a hole in the hull and let you boys swim home. Are you gettin' my meaning?"

Parker could do the fifty-yard dash in eight seconds flat. And a shotgun behind him was better than a stiff tailwind to better that time. But still—the jungle was thick. He wouldn't be breaking any speed records once they got to the tree line.

"When you get in that swamp cruiser—you better by golly hightail it out of here. Don't never come back. You hear?"

Wilson and Parker both nodded.

"Say it."

"We won't come back. Ever," Parker said.

"If you change your mind," he smiled and jabbed the shotgun toward the black car, "you'll get a ride in my grandpappy's Plymouth." He pumped the shotgun and chambered a cartridge. "Sixty seconds." He jerked his head toward the trees. "Better git running—cuz maybe I can't count past ten."

Wilson bolted for the brush.

"Thank you," Parker said, then took off after Wilson. They crashed through the brush, leaping over logs and plowing through dense patches of vines rather than around them.

Parker caught up to Wilson. "What about snakes?"

"We're making noise. They'll get out of our way. I hope."

The most dangerous snake was the one following them, anyway.

"Ready or not," Crawley's voice shouted from somewhere behind them.

That was no sixty seconds.

"This way." Wilson pointed.

The yellow spray paint dots marked the route back clearly. But it would lead Crawley right to them, too. Branches and vines slapped at Parker's face like they were trying to slow him down for Crawley.

There was no point trying to be quiet. Parker pounded through the brush. "God help us. Please. Help."

"Keep praying," Wilson said. "Almost there."

Parker didn't even realize he was praying aloud. The ground was spongy, and the mangroves grew thick at the water's edge. They busted through the brush not fifty feet from *Typhoon*.

"I'll start her." Wilson took the lead. "Push us offshore."

Wilson leaped aboard and scrambled for the driver's seat. Parker grabbed the front of the airboat and pushed, his feet sinking to his ankles in the swampy oobleck.

Wilson fumbled to get the key in the ignition. "C'mon, c'mon."

Parker's gimpy hand was still tingling like it was plugged in. He let it drop and shouldered the boat away from shore. When the water was up to his knees, he pulled himself aboard with his good arm. "I'm in. Get us out of here."

Crawley crashed through the brush behind them.

"Well, lookee here." Crawley smiled like this was more fun than he'd had in years. "Seems to me you need a little something to remember how local folks don't take kindly to trespassing." He raised the shotgun.

Wilson cranked the engine and it roared to life. He pulled the stick and stood on the gas.

Parker made his way back to his seat on all fours. Chanced another look back.

Crawley waved goodbye, then took aim—but clearly too high. A bright orange blast exploded from the barrel.

The airboat shuddered with the hit. Obviously Crawley intended to scare the living daylights out of them. He was doing a good job of it, too.

"Floor it!" Parker shouted. "Move!" He pulled his cap lower on his head, as if that would give him any protection. Crawley could have taken Parker and Wilson out if he'd really wanted to—and he still could.

Wilson swung the back end around and picked up speed.

He was sure he heard another blast from the shotgun, but with the sound of the engine it was impossible to know. Parker ducked instinctively. "Keep your head down!"

"I'm trying," Wilson said, "but if I don't watch where I'm going we'll both end up in the water."

Parker looked behind them, but couldn't spot Crawley through the engine cage. He held his breath—unsure if they were out of the shotgun's range.

Wilson plowed through patches of grass. Grazed a log. It took everything Parker had to hold on.

It had to be a full five minutes before Wilson eased up on the gas. He did a side-slide, came to a ratcheting stop, and cut the engine.

"What are you stopping for?"

Wilson jumped from his seat, leaned over the side, and puked. Moments later he rocked back on his knees, took a breath, and smiled. "Much better. And don't let anybody—not even me—ever give you a hard time about being a boy scout. I think you telling Crawley the truth back there saved our lives."

But he hadn't been honest with his dad, had he? He'd have to do something about that. And he would. He'd tell him everything. Parker dreaded the thought of how disappointed his dad would be.

Parker scanned the waters behind them. He should have felt terrific at this moment. They'd escaped, right? An unnamed fear crawled up his throat. Crawley? Definitely. But there was something more. The Everglades themselves. The Glades were alive— and on the hunt. Parker felt like he and Wilson were the main course, and something was moving in. "Let's get out of here."

CHAPTER 67

IT WAS JUST AFTER SUNSET before Angelica heard the sound of an airboat approaching. The sky absolutely glowed with a deep orange—and reflected off the black water. She stood on the dock, up on her tiptoes to see above the sawgrass. "Be *Typhoon*. Be *Typhoon*."

The airboat skimmed around the bend and banked toward her. The red hull and rudders were a dead giveaway. She counted two heads and practically squealed with relief. They were both alive.

The moment Wilson cut the engine and glided to the dock she noticed the damage just behind the propeller cage. The top of one rudder was gone—like it had been blown off by a cannon.

She pointed. "What *happened*?"

"Crawley gave us a little souvenir to remember him by," Wilson said. He slid off the seat and tossed Angelica the dock lines. "Isn't your dad worried about you being out—and on a *school* night?"

"He's out in the Glades somewhere with Parker's dad. And it's still early," she said.

Parker stepped off the airboat onto the dock, and Jelly had his cap on her head before he could stop her.

"Tell me what happened out there," she said.

Parker helped Wilson secure the airboat to the dock and quickly filled her in on Crawley's bizarre place and everything the man said.

"Don't you see?" Parker said. "Crawley thinks Maria's alive."

"Thinks . . . or knows? Did he actually see something to prove it?"

Parker gave her a questioning look. "He sounded like he *knows*."

Wilson turned from inspecting the rudder. "The Everglades have eyes. That's all he'd tell us."

"Eyes? What does that even mean?" She looked from Wilson to Parker.

"He saw something," Parker said.

Jelly's head was spinning. She had to end this, or Parker would only want to do more searching. Tomorrow was Friday. All she had to do was keep him out of the Everglades that one last day. Saturday Parker would escape Clayton Kingman, Everglades City, and the Glades themselves for good. She had to discredit Crawley—and Parker would give up the goose chase. "If Crawley saw something, why didn't he come out and say it? And besides, I wouldn't pay attention to anything that deranged man says."

Parker looked frustrated. "But what if he *did* see something?"

Angelica shook her head. "He was messing with you. Playing a game. Yeah, there are eyes everywhere in the Glades. Alligators. Snakes. They all have eyes, but they don't talk much."

"Maybe it was a skunk ape." Wilson grinned. "Sasquatch see a lot, but I'm pretty sure they don't talk much either."

Angelica didn't even grace his joke with a comment. "Look, I don't want to be Suzy Skeptical here, but I wouldn't exactly call Crawley a reliable source."

"But he definitely made it sound like there's something out there that the rangers missed," Parker said. "Answers. And he's the first one who has admitted to seeing anything that might give a shred of hope. That's got to be worth something, right?"

"Not in my opinion," Angelica said. She had to squelch any hope Crawley's cryptic message gave Parker—without raising his suspicions.

Parker didn't say anything, but he had that determined look on his face like he was processing. Wilson went back to checking out the rudder, manually turning it back and forth.

Angelica opened the Uber app and set up their ride back to the *Boy's Bomb* and their bikes, then pocketed her phone. Parker still looked deep in thought—and he hadn't tried to get his hat back once. If she truly hoped he was going to let this go, these were not good signs.

"What are you thinking, Parker?"

He stood there, staring out at the black water of the Everglades.

"Parker?"

He didn't turn. "Five things keep looping around in my mind ever since we got away from Crawley," Parker said. "Make that six. One. I messed up good by doing this behind my dad's back." He gave Wilson the side-eye. "It will be really hard to talk me into compromising what I know is right again."

Jelly glared at Wilson. "I knew you were behind this." She focused back on Parker. "And number two?"

"Maria didn't get eaten by an alligator," Parker said. "Three.

Maria isn't at Crawley's place. Four. That 'eyes' comment he made . . . somebody knows something. Five. I'm going to figure it out."

Angelica tried to stay calm. There were things she wanted to tell him. Was dying to tell him. But she couldn't do that. Not until he was on his way to his new home up north. When there was no chance he'd go back in the Glades. "And number six?"

"I am *never* stepping foot on Crawley's property again."

Wilson laughed. "I'm with you on that one, Bucky. One hundred percent."

"I am sooo glad to hear that, too," Angelica said. And she believed Parker would stay away. But it was his wild-card comment about figuring things out that had her worried. "So now what?"

"I want to get home and hit the shower," Parker said. "I've got a lot of thinking to do."

Angelica nodded. So did she.

Parker reached for his cap, but Angelica ducked and stepped back. "You'll get it back tomorrow. On the way to school—as long as you don't try another stunt like this."

The two guys paused to look at *Typhoon*.

Angelica followed their gaze. "Are you seeing a pattern here? Every time you take your uncle's airboat out, it has to go in for repairs. What do you think he's going to say about that?"

"I think," Wilson said, his face suddenly serious, "he'll just be glad Crawley only gave us a *warning* shot. Any lower and it would have been my head."

Actually, it would have been Parker's more likely—based on where he was sitting. Parker had cheated death again.

And he would tomorrow, too, with her help. All she had to do was keep him out of the Everglades one more day.

CHAPTER 68

INTEGRITTY. Parker's eyes had long adjusted to the dim light filtering through his bedroom windows. He stared at the sign. If he really wanted to be a person of integrity, he'd have to confess to his dad about going to Crawley's today. He'd messed up good, hadn't he?

Parker's stomach had been hijacked by a massive knot of dread. Just the thought of telling his dad how he'd messed up cinched the knot tighter. He'd sent him a text with the short version—which made him feel a tiny bit better. But if his dad was out on the Lopez with Uncle Sammy, he wouldn't get that text until he got within range of a tower—which probably wouldn't happen until morning.

INTEGRITTY. Not that it mattered all that much to him right now, but what was his Grandpa trying to say with that misspelling? It had to take a lot of hours to carve the sign. Why would he wreck it by purposely spelling the word wrong? It had to be something important. But if it was that important, why not just tell him what it was? Even Dad wanted Parker to figure it out on his own.

He slid out of bed, took the sign off the wall, and climbed back in bed. He flicked on his flashlight and read the back side again.

"Even in darkness light dawns for the upright, for those who are gracious, compassionate, and righteous." Psalm 112:4-6

Except for the Crawley fiasco, he'd been trying to be the kind of son who did the right thing, hadn't he? Yet he'd never been in a darker place. "God," he whispered, "I'd definitely like to see some dawning light here."

Parker looked at the Sharpie message Grandpa had written below the verse.

I've found this verse to be true for a man of INTEGRITTY, Parker. If this is the kind of man you'll dedicate yourself to becoming, I know you'll find it true as well. It won't come naturally, and it won't come easy. It takes something you'll find embedded in the word itself.

Lots of love, Grandpa.

Parker wasn't so sure he had what it took to be that man. But Grandpa said he'd find it in the word. As in the misspelled word, integritty? Or did he mean *the* Word—which would be the Bible. All throughout the Bible it showed what it meant to be a person of integrity—and what happened when you compromised, as Parker did today. But if Grandpa was referring to the Bible, didn't that seem a little too obvious? And what did that have to do with spelling integrity the way he did, anyway?

"Why the misspelling, Grandpa?" He'd added that extra "T" in integrity here on the back of the sign, too. Whatever Grandpa was trying to tell him was a puzzle for another day. Right now he had to get back to the real mystery. That puzzling message from Crawley.

He set the sign next to his bed and turned off the flashlight. He lay back and stared at the ceiling, picturing the bizarre encounter at Crawley's place.

"They's eyes all over the Glades. They's all the help you need." Parker tried to remember Crawley's exact words. He knit his hands behind his head and stared at his dark bedroom ceiling. "The answers were staring back at the rangers" or something like that. Crawley made no sense.

And his comment that maybe Maria didn't want to be found. How insane was that?

"Parker?" His mom opened his door and hesitated. Dim light filtered in from the hall, silhouetting her slightly. "You still awake?"

He was pretty sure she knew he was. He raised himself on his elbows.

"It's after midnight," she said. She tiptoed in and sat on the edge of his bed. "Can't sleep—or bad dreams?"

He lay back down and held out his bad arm. "You going to tell me there's no such things as monsters?"

She smiled at him with kind of a sad smile. "No. I'm not going to tell you that at all." She stroked his mangled arm. Traced the scars with her fingertip. "You know monsters are real. Your Daddy and Uncle Sammy are hunting one right now."

"Goliath."

Mom bit her lip. "Yes, honey. They've been at this for too many hours today already. He'll be home by six, catch a few hours sleep, then head out again if they don't get him tonight. There isn't much time left, but they want him real bad."

"He's a real bad gator."

She nodded. "I wish they'd leave it be. I just fear they're—" Mom caught herself. She took a deep breath and smiled. "I wish we'd skip the moving van. I'd like to hop in the pickup, leave all the baggage here, and make our escape. Just between you and me, I can't wait to get out of this place. And get my boys out in one piece, too."

He flexed his hand. God knew he wanted out of this place. But he seriously doubted it would make as much of a difference as he'd once thought. How do you escape the baggage in your head?

"Do you think Maria's alive?" If someone else believed, it would make it easier for Parker to believe it himself, wouldn't it?

"I can't believe she's dead," Mom said. "But that's not the same as believing she's alive." She brushed the hair out of his eyes and stood. "Only God knows. Let's talk about it after school tomorrow." She smiled. "Last day, right?"

One last day of school. One last day to find Maria—or the answers to what really happened that night on the Lopez.

She leaned over and kissed him on the forehead—just about where Crawley had given him that two-fingered poke. "Sleep good."

He'd be happy just to sleep. No, that wasn't true. He couldn't sleep, even if he wanted to. He had to figure this out. Mom was right, though. Only God knew if Maria was dead or alive.

The hall light flicked off, and he heard his mom's door close.

"God," he whispered. "It's me again. Thanks for rescuing us from Crawley—even though I shouldn't have been there in the first place. And now I need another big favor. I need your help to figure out what Crawley was hinting at." How long Parker prayed, he wasn't sure. When he'd said everything on his heart, he went back to Crawley's riddle.

Eyes. Somehow all over the Glades. Watching the rangers.

Alligators? They were definitely all over—and watching. But how could they tell the rangers anything? Crawley made it sound like the rangers *missed* something.

He pictured the image from Dad's camera again. Sunday Bay. The upside-down kayak in the short grass. The cypress tree with the strangler vine wrapping itself around the trunk like a python. Branches hanging over the water's edge. The water itself black as the gates of hell.

What did the rangers miss? What was Parker missing?

Eyes. Eyes. Watching. But not eyes from an animal—or a sasquatch. Eyes that belong to someone or something that can communicate back. If the eyes belonged to a gator or something that couldn't talk, why would Crawley make such a big deal of the rangers missing it?

If someone else was there—an eyewitness—why didn't they come forward and tell what they knew? Unless it was a poacher—like Crawley. There were probably dozens of guys poaching in the Glades that night. Eyes all over the Everglades, right? That's what Crawley said. Had the rangers questioned guys with prior records of poaching? Maybe that's how the rangers had missed what really happened to her.

Parker's heartbeat shifted into a higher gear. Could that be the answer? The rangers needed to do more questioning? And what did Crawley mean about Maria not *wanting* to be found?

Maybe talking to the right "set of eyes" would answer that question.

Parker stood and paced his room to stay alert. To keep blood flowing to his brain. He tried on his theory like a new pair of shoes. Eyes. Poachers. Seeing something happen but not telling. If they were poachers, they didn't like rangers any more than Crawley did. Why would a poacher suddenly want to help? How would they explain what they were doing out there in the middle of the night?

Crawley made it sound like the information was right there in front of the rangers. Free for the taking. Something they missed.

That didn't sound at all like a poacher. Maybe the poacher theory wasn't as good a fit as Parker had hoped.

He flopped onto his bed again and went back to staring at the ceiling. Talking to God again. Nothing fancy. "God . . . you see everything. Know everything. And you know exactly what happened to Maria. Show me what I'm missing, okay?" It seemed all his prayers lately were desperate, get-me-out-of-a-jam prayers. But he wanted it to be more. He would work on that when this was all over.

He replayed Crawley's crazy talk about eyes.

Eyes. Everywhere. One right there—staring at the rangers. Something they missed.

Wait.

One eye. Not eyes—plural. Technically, Crawley said there was *one* right there. Not a *set* of eyes. Then again, Crawley wasn't exactly the grammar king of the Everglades either. He could have meant a set of eyes.

But he said *one* was right there. Staring at them. An eye that saw Maria. An eye that stared at the rangers. An eye that held the answers. Something they missed at the scene.

Parker closed his eyes. Pictured the Sunday Bay scene again just as he'd memorized it from the shot on Dad's phone.

An eye. An eye. Seeing everything. Staring back at them.

Parker forced his mind to zoom in on the picture in his mind.

The water was black. Still. Nothing breaking the surface at all. He moved to the shoreline. Slowly. Carefully. Looking for any detail he may have overlooked before. The log. Cypress knees. Nothing seemed unusual. Certainly nothing that had eyes.

What was he not seeing? Or was it Crawley who was missing something? The guy lived in the Everglades, right? How sane could the guy be? The guy was working with only half a prop on his airboat, so to speak, right?

He forced his mind back to the picture from Sunday Bay. Left to right, he scanned the picture in his mind. He checked each tree.

Suddenly Parker stopped at the cypress with the choker vine. There was another cypress behind it. Much smaller—with a greenish vine hugging its trunk.

He looked closer at the vine. Not green . . . *camouflage.*

Parker jumped out of bed. Shook his hand to get the feeling back. "God . . . that's it, right? It has to be."

Eyes. All over the Everglades. Yes, of course. Exactly right. And one *was* right there. Not a pair of eyes. *One.* It had seen everything— and was staring back at every ranger who'd missed it.

He checked the picture in his mind one more time. The vine was definitely camouflage. And it wasn't a vine. It was a strap . . . just like the one on Jelly's wildlife camera.

CHAPTER 69

ANGELICA ROLLED OVER and swept the nightstand for her phone. Who was texting so early in the morning—before her alarm?

Parker. Who else?

Sure enough. And it was a group text—to Wilson too.

`You two awake?`

She texted back.

`I am now. It's only 6`

`I waited as long as I could to tell you`

His text came back super-fast. Apparently his fingers were working a lot faster than hers.

`I figured it out last night.`

She stared at the words. Sat up slowly, like her world might tip off its axis if she didn't stay controlled. Calm.

Deep breath, Angelica. Take a deep breath. She texted back.

Figured what out, exactly?

The eyes—or rather EYE that everyone missed

She tried to steady her breathing.

Enlighten us.

Wilson—you there?

Angelica waited a half minute then fired back. Just tell me.

She fought back a sense of unexplained dread. What did he figure out? What did everyone—including herself—miss?

I studied the picture again—from my Dad's phone

She texted back. The real picture, or the one in your head?

Parker texted back in seconds.

Head

Angelica found herself counting off the seconds, waiting for his explanation as to what this was all about. Twenty-six. Twenty-seven. Twenty-eight. This was ridiculous. She fired back a prompt.

I'm going back to sleep if you don't spit it out.

But there was no going back to sleep for her. And he was back in seconds.

It's one of those cameras wildlife photographers strap to the trees.

She stared at the text. No. No. No. No.

Night vision. Motion sensitive. We get that camera—we find out what really happened to Maria.

Oh, yeah. They absolutely would.

Can't reach my dad by phone—or yours. Tried for hours. I'm going to explain to him as soon as he gets home. You tell your dad. They'll grab the camera.

Angelica fought back a sense of panic. If there was a camera, the thing had to be buried before her dad—or anybody else—found it. Because if there was a camera—and it captured what really happened . . . the truth would come out. The secrets Angelica had been hiding since this all started.

That Maria was alive.

That Maria hadn't been mauled by an alligator.

That another boat had been there in Sunday Bay . . . waiting for her.

That Clayton was in that boat.

That together they'd staged her death so she'd be free to be with him.

That Clayton's search efforts and his "desperately grieving boy-friend" act were all a diversionary tactic.

And once that news got out, her dad would be looking for Maria again—but not in the Everglades. If the *real* story about what happened to Maria came out, her sister would think Angelica deliberately leaked it. She'd see her as a traitor.

Then things would *really* hit the fan. Maria would think Angelica snitched—and Clayton would consider it open season on Parker. She had no doubt. Clayton would kill him. And when her dad found Clayton, he'd do something that would land him in jail for life.

She looked out her window. Her dad wasn't home yet, which meant she had a little more time. And she'd need it if there was any hope of avoiding this disaster.

How can you keep deceiving your dad, Angelica? The thought had tortured her from the beginning. But she was protecting him, too. If he knew the truth . . . he'd do something awful.

Another text. Wilson.

Just catching up. Brilliant work, Sherlock. We should totally ditch school and get it ourselves.

"Wilson—you're going to get someone killed." But she couldn't text that. She pecked out a message and fired it back.

Go back to sleep, Wilson. Let our dads handle this.

A text from Parker dropped in right after she sent hers. I'll explain more later. Have to get some things done for the move before school—so no time to bike with you. Will get my mom to drop me and my bike at school. See you both there.

She was relieved he was going to school on his last day. At least that was something.

Wilson's face popped up on her display. Why not get the camera ourselves?

What was Wilson thinking? Her thumbs hovered over the keys as she tried to figure out how to talk them out of it without looking obvious.

Parker's response came up first.

She's right, Wilson. Let my dad handle this. Besides, ranger boats have something mine doesn't

Wilson weighed in. Bigger engine—or guns?

Parker's text dinged. Ha! Drain plug.

Angelica gave a half smile and glanced at the row of plugs on her dresser. She picked one up and kissed it.

Her phone whistled again. Parker.

I'm behind—see you both at school

She sat there, racing through her options. But she had no options. Nothing good anyway. Just a decision to make.

"Do you want that camera to be found by Dad or not?" Hearing her own voice made the answer to the question incredibly obvious.

Definitely not.

So, the decision was really made for her. She had to stay on autopilot here. Every decision absolutely had to orbit around the goal of keeping her secret—and keeping everyone safe in the process.

Angelica scrolled through her phone contacts. Found the one she'd hidden under a ridiculous alias.

Were her hands actually shaking? She held them out in front of her. Oh, yeah. They were shaking. And so was everything inside her. Her eyes burned, vision blurred, and she blinked back tears.

"You've got to do this, Angelica. You know it. Do it. Just do it and get it over with."

She took a deep breath. Pressed the contact number. Heard it ring on the other end.

What are you doing, Angelica? What are you doing? Hang up before it's too late! She squeezed her eyes shut. Felt blind tears feel their way down her cheeks. Chin.

He answered on the third ring.

"This is Clayton. Talk to me, *Angel*."

CHAPTER 70

WILSON LEANED AGAINST THE BRICK WALL of Everglades City School and sighted down School Drive. "What is taking Parker so long?"

"He said he was behind. We should go in." Jelly adjusted Parker's cap on her head. "The bell's going to ring."

Did she really think he cared about the bell? "I'm due for a tardy. I'll wait."

Jelly shrugged. "I can't afford one." She reached for the door and looked down the road one more time. "His last day—and he's late. Perfect."

"Yeah, well I'm sorry he's even coming to school," Wilson said. "I told him we should ditch school and get the camera—"

"I read the text, and I am sooo glad he doesn't take advice from you." Jelly smiled. "See you guys third period."

He nodded, but kept his eyes on the road. How long did it take Bucky to explain the camera theory to his dad? Maybe Bucky's dad let him ride along to get the camera.

Not a minute after Jelly disappeared inside, the tardy bell rang. Wilson's phone vibrated an instant later.

Parker.

Just found note left for me in kitchen from my mom . . . my dad was out all night—still didn't get Goliath . . . but early this AM on drive home my dad had accident—fell asleep at wheel—drove right off the road.

Wilson stared at the text for a moment before replying.

Is he okay??

Thankfully. He's at the clinic. Stitches. Bruises. Truck towed.

Wilson relaxed a bit. How crazy to be in a serious accident—his last day on the job? Like a soldier wounded just before getting leave.

Wilson texted back.

What did he say about the camera?

Parker answered immediately.

Still can't reach him—I'm trying—not sure when he'll be home

And the texts kept rapid-firing in—with no time for Wilson to even answer in between.

All I know is what my mom's note said. She rushed to be with him before I was up—so I couldn't even tell her.

Tried Jelly's dad—he's obviously with my dad—nobody is answering their phones.

I left detailed voice messages on Dad's phone, Mom's, and Uncle Sammy's about the camera—but I'm not even sure he'll be in good enough shape to go get it when he gets back anyway—or if there'll be enough time.

Wilson whipped off a text.

What now?

Instantly Parker was back.

Is Jelly with you?

The moment Wilson read the text he knew what Bucky was thinking. He would have let out a whoop if he hadn't been just outside the school doors.

She's already inside.

Wilson had never seen Parker text so fast.

We need that camera. Now.

Wilson's heart danced a little happy jig in his chest. His phone rang an instant later.

"Bucky?"

"I'm going in." Parker sounded out of breath. "If I wait much longer, I won't be able to get back before dark—and Dad wouldn't want that. Uncle Sammy deserves to know what happened to Maria. The moving van comes tomorrow. And who knows when the owner of that camera may come and move it to another spot. It could already be gone. This is my last chance."

"Ditching school?" Wilson kept his voice down. "I'm impressed. No more boy scout, eh?"

"I already called the school—thankfully got the receptionist instead of Principal Kingman. Told her the truth . . . my dad had an accident and now some things fell on my shoulders—and I'm not coming in. She told me I was doing the right thing— and that they'd make arrangements later for me to empty my locker."

Wilson shook his head. Parker was crazy. "You're even more

of a boy scout than I thought." But at least he was going after the camera. "Hold on for a second, Bucky."

Wilson checked over his shoulder—through the school doors. No teachers. No Principal K. And there was going to be no Wilson in school today either—and he wasn't going to call anybody for permission.

He made his way to his bike. Casually. Like he forgot his lunch or something—just in case a teacher was watching out a window. His absence would be discovered soon enough, and Principal Kingman would make a call to Wilson's dad—who really wouldn't care. He'd probably be calling Parker's dad, too, even though the lady in the office said Bucky was good to go. *Good luck with that, Principal K.* "Bucky, don't you dare leave without me."

Parker laughed. "Why do you think I'm calling?"

"You need a Miccosukee guide, eh?"

"More like a drain plug. I just called the marina. They're still out."

"I know just where to borrow one."

"But the instant we get back—we return it," Parker said. "Got it?"

If it was that important to Bucky, why not? "I promise."

Wilson yanked his bike free from the rack. They were getting one more adventure together. And it would be their best. He could feel it.

"I'm there in twenty-five minutes—max. And Bucky . . . I guess ValuJet 592 is making one more flight into the Glades after all!"

CHAPTER 71

ANGELICA NEVER FELT MORE MESSED UP. She'd kept Maria and Clayton's dirty little secret. Their insane plan for Maria to run away—and their scheme to keep anyone from following. All they needed was a good place for her to hide out until she turned eighteen, and they could legally get married without Dad's okay. Clayton claimed he had the perfect place for her to lie low. And with everyone thinking she was dead, it wouldn't be hard for her to pull it off. Nobody would be looking.

Maria had played her part well. The Rod and Reel Club. The speeding. The reckless "death wish" stunts and doing Watson's Run solo. Only she wasn't alone. Not for long anyway. Clayton met her in Sunday Bay—but not before she'd thrown everyone off with her posts. And Clayton used the whole Gator Hook Trail thing as an alibi—to look like he had no idea where she was that night.

But he'd had everything planned to the minute, and when he left the trailhead in a rage, he was really racing to his boat—which he was launching from some remote spot. They broke the paddle, swamped the kayak, and took off in *King of the Glades* for Flamingo City—right according to plan.

Angelica kept her end of the bargain—in exchange for the promise that Clayton would stay away from Parker. She was absolutely convinced that the only thing keeping Parker alive was the fact that she could blow the whistle on Clayton—and her dad would find Maria and keep her away from him for good this time.

In a way, Maria and Clayton were blackmailing Angelica—and she was doing the same back to them. It worked. And it would keep working indefinitely as long as Clayton got that camera out of there.

She was almost glad she didn't see Parker in the halls after first period. He would take one look at her and know something was wrong. He'd sense that somehow she had betrayed him. Right now, it felt like the word "traitor" was written across her forehead with a permanent marker. She'd probably need until third period to get her game face on.

Wilson, on the other hand, wouldn't notice if her nose was missing. But she hadn't seen him either. With only 165 students in the entire school, it seemed strange that she hadn't seen either one of them.

Between second and third period she actually started looking for them—and waited for them in the hall outside class. Her phone chirped, and her dad's name came up on a text. She swiped it to the side without reading it so she could watch the halls for Parker and Wilson.

When the bell rang and neither one of them were at their desks, a sick feeling seeped into her stomach.

She shouldered her pack and practically power walked to the girl's room. She stormed into a stall, locked the door, and dialed Parker.

No answer.

She tried Wilson.

Right to voicemail.

Maybe they left a message. That's when she saw her dad's text again—and read it this time.

Parker's dad dozed at the wheel early this AM. Put his truck in the ditch. Bumps. Bruises. Stitches. But okay. I'm still at the clinic with him. Sorry—my phone was off until now. Should be leaving the clinic any minute. Didn't want you to worry if you heard something . . . I'm fine.

Relief flooded over her that they were both okay. But guilt did too. Her dad and Parker's wouldn't have been searching for Goliath all night and exhausting themselves if she hadn't covered for her sister.

At least now Parker's disappearance made sense. "Of course." Parker ditched school to be with his dad. But where was Wilson?

Angelica dialed her dad's phone.

"Angelica?"

"Dad—is Parker there?"

A slight pause. "No. His mom is, but not Parker."

Her stomach tightened. Parker's dad had the accident on the way home from work. How could Parker have told him about the camera if he wasn't with him?

"What about Wilson?"

Another pause. "Why would Wilson be here? They should both be in school, which is where you are—right?"

She pushed through the stall door and opened the bathroom door a crack. The coast was clear. "I'm here." She glanced down the hall again. "But they're not." And she had a pretty good idea where the boys were. She fought back a sense of panic. She walked out the bathroom door and trotted for the exit nearest the bike rack. She needed to be sure.

"You sound out of breath. You all right?"

"No." She half wailed it. "I don't know. I think I really messed up."

"It's going to be okay."

But how could he be so sure it would be okay *this* time? He didn't know what she had done.

"Angelica?"

She ran the last thirty feet to the glass doors, hit the crash bars—and stopped the moment she got outside.

Wilson's bike was gone. They were going for the camera themselves. "No. *No.*"

"Angelica . . . talk to me." The concern in his voice was unmistakable now.

"I can't." *Tell him. Tell him.* He's your dad. He's there for you. You can't handle this anymore.

"Baby—you're scaring me," Dad said. "What's going on?"

She shook her head. Tears burned in her eyes. *Tell him. Tell him.*

"Let me help you. Are you in some kind of trouble?"

"Big trouble. I've been keeping things from you. Lying."

A slight pause. "But you're talking to me now. That's all that matters."

She glanced back at the school entrance . . . afraid Principal Kingman might stop her. "I can't talk to you over the phone."

"I'm out in the hospital hallway," her dad said. "Nobody is around. It's just you and me. No twenty questions this time, baby. What have you been keeping from me?"

This was it. A direct question. The lies needed to stop. *Tell him.*

"Angelica . . . you have to tell me what's going on. I can help you. I *want* to help you."

And she desperately needed help. If she really believed Clayton would hurt Parker, how long would it take for him to really hurt Maria too? She took a couple of deep breaths.

"Maria . . . is . . . alive."

Silence.

"I can explain, but there's no time."

"We've been through this, baby."

"No—she's alive. She ran off. She's hiding somewhere until she can marry Clayton."

Silence again. "Are . . . you . . . sure?" His words sounded choked. Forced.

"Maria—Clayton—they set the whole thing up. I couldn't tell you because he was going to do something bad to Parker if I snitched, but now he's going to do it anyway—and he'll hurt Wilson, too."

Hurt him? With the way Clayton's voice sounded on the phone this morning? "He'll kill them, Daddy. He'll do it." The words gushed out. "They're on a collision course and don't even know it. And it's all my fault."

"Where are they?" His voice was low—like he didn't want someone nearby to hear.

"They won't answer my texts—but I think I know." She

sprinted for her bike. "I'm leaving school for the marina now—meet me there and I'll tell you everything."

"Where are the boys?" The urgency in her dad's voice was clear. "Your best guess."

"I'm sure they're heading to Sunday Bay—but so is Clayton."

"I'll bust Parker's dad out of here," Dad growled. "We'll be at the marina in twenty minutes. You wait for me there. Got that?"

"Just hurry."

She pocketed her phone, jerked her bike from the rack, and swung a leg over. She pedaled off school property like a crazy person and didn't look back. And she prayed—like she'd never prayed before. The same seven words, looping over and over in her mind in rhythm with the pedals.

Dear God—don't let Clayton kill them.

CHAPTER 72

IT FELT GOOD KNOWING he'd be taking the *Bomb* out one last time before the move, even if it meant they'd be going back up the Lopez River. It had taken Wilson longer to "borrow" the right size plug than he'd figured, but in the end, he came through. He'd also stopped at Subway on the way to Smallwood's Store for a Santa-sized bag of stale French bread.

"Don't worry, Bucky," Wilson said. "This isn't about coaxing an alligator to the boat."

Parker wasn't buying it.

"We've got to get that camera—and we can be pretty sure we won't get the boat that close with all the trees there, right?"

That made sense.

"Which means one of us is going in the water," Wilson said. "And if Goliath really is nearby?"

"Got it. We'll lure him *away* from the tree."

Wilson grinned. "I'll make an Everglades guy out of you yet."

"Don't count on it."

By the time they got the gas can and a spare filled, Parker had a growing fear that Principal Kingman would show up and haul him back to school before he could get away—as ridiculous as that sounded. Even though the school receptionist assured Parker his absence was okay, Principal K wouldn't want anyone leaving his kingdom without getting permission from *him* first. Parker stowed everything in the boat. "We've got to get out of here."

His phone dinged—and he skimmed the text.

"It's Jelly again. Says she needs to talk to us—that it's important. Life and death."

"Nice try, Jelly," Wilson said. "Don't even answer it. We are *not* letting her talk us out of this."

If it was news about Parker's dad, the text would be coming from Mom.

Wilson's phone chirped a moment later. He checked the screen. "Oh yeah. She's on to us. I'm not even going to open it. Then I can honestly say I never read her text."

Parker's phone dinged again. Jelly. "She's persistent." She'd do—or say—anything to keep him out of the Everglades. She'd stall him until she could sabotage his plan somehow. They'd already taken way more time than he'd hoped to get ready—and they still weren't out on the water. He glanced down the road by Smallwood's Store, half expecting to see Jelly pedaling their way.

"Give me that phone," Wilson said. He held out his hand.

Parker slapped it into his palm.

"I'll just tuck these away where we won't hear them." Wilson stowed both phones in the compartment below the driver's seat.

"Hold on." Parker reached for his phone.

Wilson blocked him.

"If my dad calls—"

"Look," Wilson said. "You left him a message—told him about the camera?"

And when he didn't hear back, he'd messaged that he was going after it. "I told him everything." That he'd wanted to wait for him—but knew if he waited any longer they'd miss their chance. Losing their one opportunity to find out what happened to Maria didn't seem like the right thing to do. He told his dad he'd be careful—he wasn't going in alone—and he'd be back long before dark. He was following the ground rules Dad set up when Parker joined the SAR teams.

"Okay, then," Wilson said. "Let's focus on getting out of here. You still going to text your dad every thirty seconds like he made you do before?"

"Thirty *minutes*, wise guy," Parker said. "That's my plan." Although he wasn't sure there was a point to it. Once out on the Lopez, there'd be no signal anyway. His dad wouldn't get his texts—and Parker wouldn't get Dad's.

"So you can leave the phone alone until then. I'm not worried about your dad trying to stop you. As long as you're giving him updates, you're good. It's Jelly's texts I don't want messing with your head."

Not even Jelly could stop him now. Parker untied the bow line from the cypress. "Let's get this baby in the water before she comes looking for us."

Wilson laughed. "If I know her, she's already on her way."

Together they slid the boat off the beach and into deeper water. The motor fired up on the first try. Parker steered for the Lopez

River—and rammed the throttle nearly all the way forward. He chanced a look back at the beach. No Jelly. But even if she had been there flapping her arms like flamingo wings, Parker wouldn't have turned back.

Wilson sat in the bow seat, arms spread along the backrest, facing Parker. He looked like a wild man the way his hair whipped around. "I'm going to remember this sight," Wilson said. He never looked happier.

"What?"

"This." He pointed both hands at Parker. "This is the last time you're ever going in the Everglades," Wilson said. "Am I right?"

"Absolutely. Last time out, too."

Wilson grinned. "You *hope* you're getting out. It said *ValuJet* on the side of this boat, remember."

Parker laughed and cupped his hand around his mouth. "This is your captain speaking. In the unlikely event of a water landing, please use the seat cushion as a flotation device." He opened up the Merc to full throttle. "And buckle your seat belts."

"This thing doesn't have seat belts, Bucky."

It was true. There was nothing holding him back—or holding him down. "Then you'd better hang on tight. We're going to fly."

CHAPTER 73

PARKER WAS NEARLY DRENCHED with sweat by the time the Lopez opened up into Sunday Bay. He'd manned the wheel the entire time—and kept his speed up as much as the Lopez had allowed. Wilson took Parker's phone out every thirty minutes and dashed off a quick text to Dad that they were okay, even though they weren't getting a signal. Dad would get the texts eventually, and he'd know Parker had kept his end of the bargain.

Wilson insisted on keeping the ringer off on both phones, even after the signal was lost—which was probably just as well. He didn't need a call from Jelly getting through by some freak chance, dividing his attention. He'd felt like he and Wilson were in a race, and they needed every bit of focus to shave seconds off their time.

The *Bomb* handled the Lopez like a champ. The water was high, which meant they could keep up their speed without as much worry of clipping a submerged log or snagging the bottom. There was a fine balance between taking calculated risks and just being plain stupid. He couldn't chance damaging his prop, or worse—sheering the pin holding it in place. At least a half dozen times, in super-tight or shallow places they killed the engine and raised the outboard to protect the propellor. They used Amos Moses and a gaffing hook to gondola their way through.

Something had spurred him on—beyond the fact that he was totally juiced to find that camera. He had pictured one of those hourglass gizmos—with sand pouring through a narrow opening. He'd wrestled with the definite sense that there was very little sand left, and it had nothing to do with leaving for Boston—or the hour. It was like deep down he knew the owner of that camera was going to move it—unless Parker got there first. The moment they finally reached Sunday Bay, the feeling grew stronger.

"Let's switch," Wilson said. "I'll drive so you can concentrate on finding the right spot with that freaky memory of yours."

Parker swapped places and kneeled at the bow, mentally reviewing the way the trees looked in that shot on his dad's phone. Wilson steered the *Boy's Bomb* parallel to the shoreline—which really wasn't a shoreline at all. It was more of a thick tree line with an endless swampy, jungle-like interior behind it.

He shook his bad arm and worked the prickles out of his hand. "I can't see how Maria could survive out here without a boat for nearly six days." He had to admit, it just wasn't possible. Still, he felt a lightness he hadn't felt in a long time. He was going to finally have an answer. A poacher *must* have picked her up.

"She wouldn't last six hours out here," Wilson said. "I, on the other hand, could stay out here six months. No problem." He thumped his chest. "Miccosukee blood."

Parker grinned. "Only *half* Miccosukee."

"Okay." Wilson stood at the console, both hands on the wheel. "We'll make it three months."

Parker kept his eyes on the trees. It was like he was traveling back in time. There was absolutely no sign of man. The place probably looked pretty much like it did in prehistoric days. And it was infested with the closest things to dinosaurs on earth. Alligators.

"There!" Parker pointed to a spot on the tree line. "That's it!"

Wilson eased back on the throttle. "You sure?"

Parker studied it again. Compared it to the image in his mind. "One hundred percent. See the cypress with the strangler vine?"

"Nice navigating, Bucky." Wilson cut the wheel hard toward shore and peered over the side. "Lots of submerged logs, though. I say we kill the motor and pole in."

Together they raised the Merc and locked it in place.

Parker grabbed Amos Moses and used the blunt end to push along the bottom until the bow got hung up in the roots and reeds.

The massive cypress with the strangler vine rose out of standing water, maybe twenty feet ahead.

Wilson bent low, trying to get a line of sight on the cypress farther back. "I can't even see the camera yet. You sure this is the spot?"

Parker leaned out low over the bow. "This is it. I see the strap!" And it *definitely* was a strap. Nylon. Camouflage. And well-hidden. He pointed right at it.

Wilson whistled. "Sure enough. No wonder the rangers missed it."

How many times had Parker studied the picture in his head and not seen it?

"Creepy vibe about this place, right?" Wilson looked around like he suddenly felt on edge.

The place definitely had a dark feel. Was it because this was the very spot where so many thought Maria had been killed? For some crazy reason, his mind flipped back to the verse Grandpa had left him. Yeah, Parker definitely wanted a little light dawning in this darkness. "Let's get the camera and get out."

"Okay." Wilson looked out into the bay and back to the cypress. "How do you want to play this?"

There weren't a lot of options here. "One of us grabs the camera. One of us mans the boat."

"Let me do the wet work," Wilson said. "Miccosukees are invisible to gators. Did you know that?"

Parker had been bracing himself to go in the water. Wilson had just handed him a gift. "You're still only half Miccosukee, so you're only half invisible at best. We've got to be smart about this."

"Noted," Wilson said. "Before I step out of this boat we'll sit here a few minutes to make sure everything is clear. I would not want a visit from Goliath when I'm up to my belly button in swamp water."

"Agreed." The way his dad—and even Crawley—talked about the beast, seeing Goliath was the last thing they needed right now.

"You take port side," Wilson said. "I'll take starboard. We'll watch for a couple minutes. Then switch. Look for bubbles. Movement. A swirl in the water."

"Or a set of eyes surfacing?"

Wilson gave a half smile. "That too."

The water was dead still. Not a ripple. Not a bubble. The sun's glare made it nearly impossible to be certain if the area was clear or not. And alligators could lie on the bottom—perfectly still for what? Hours—if the conditions were right. Would they even see any bubbles?

"As much as I'd like to see that monster gator," Wilson said, "I kind of wish your dad and uncle would have bagged Goliath last night."

It definitely would have made the job of grabbing the camera easier. "Me too." He wondered how his dad was doing. Mom's note said he would be fine, but—

"Time to switch." Wilson took his turn battling the sun's reflections. "Think we'll find out what happened to Maria when we snag that camera?"

"Crawley sure seemed to think so."

Parker scanned the brush line. Stared into the dark waters. And he listened. Wilson was quiet too, and when Parker glanced over, he was studying the hair on his forearms.

"What are you doing?"

Wilson didn't look up. "My hair is standing up, see?" He raised his arm a little. "Just like at Crawley's yesterday. My Miccosukee—"

"Early warning system," Parker said. "I get it." His heart felt like it was beating in his lungs. "And you got that same sensation just before I got mauled." He took a step back from the edge of the boat.

Wilson nodded and studied the water. He walked slowly around the boat as if he sensed something rather than saw it. Wilson rubbed his forearms down, then held his arm out in front of him again. The hair began to rise.

Wilson stopped and looked at Parker square on. "He's here." Wilson studied the water again. "Somewhere close."

"Goliath?"

"I'm sure of it."

Parker grabbed Amos Moses and pulled off the sheath with shaky hands. "We can't risk you going in. We need a new plan."

"The French bread," Wilson said. "We chum the water away from shore—just to put a little insurance on this. Then I'll slip over the side and get the camera."

"I don't know. This whole thing doesn't feel right." Parker hunkered over to get a visual on the tree with the camera. Whoever had placed the camera was good at it. They'd strategically tucked Spanish moss around the camera itself so the thing looked more like a nest.

"Help me chum." Wilson twisted a loaf in half and tossed it into deeper water. "Come and get it, big guy."

They tossed a few more hunks of bread out there, but left enough for later if they needed it.

The air felt thick. And heavy—with something. "There." Parker pointed. The head of a massive gator surfaced behind the floating bread.

"Whoa," Wilson said. "Hel-lo, Goliath."

Parker's scars tingled. Maybe he had some kind of mortal danger warning built into his mauled arm. Weird. "I've never seen one so big. You?"

Wilson shook his head. "Time for me to go." He walked to the front of the boat, toward shore.

"You're not still going in? With *that* guy out there?" Parker looked at Goliath, then back at Wilson. "Don't be crazy."

"As long as he's busy—and you can see him—I'm okay," Wilson whispered. "Besides, I'm a Miccosukee, remember? I'm invisible."

"Half," Parker said.

Wilson smiled, but it looked forced. "If he goes under—"

"I'll let you know." Parker grabbed the gator stick. "Take Amos Moses."

Wilson looked like he was thinking about it. "I'll take Boomer instead." He held up Parker's SOGfari Kukri machete. The twelve-inch carbon steel blade had a wicked edge on the business end—and a saw-back that could cut through anything. The first time Wilson saw it he said it reminded him of a boomerang. Parker had been calling it Boomer ever since. "I'm not taking the time to untie that camera strap." He made a chopping motion with the machete. "I'll cut the thing free."

"Good choice." Parker lowered the engine, fired it up, and nosed the bow in as close as he could to the trees before cutting the motor. He gripped Amos Moses and took his post at the stern. Wilson sat on the bow and slowly lowered himself into the water without making a ripple.

Parker twisted off another hunk of French bread and heaved it past the alligator's ugly head. "Go the other way, Goliath. The bread is behind you." The thing didn't move. Just stared at Parker.

Could alligators smell humans—or somehow sense if someone was from the same family, like a kind of DNA scent? Did Goliath know Parker's dad had been hunting him—that they were related?

He glanced over his shoulder. "How you doing?"

Wilson waved one hand, but didn't speak. He was just beyond the cypress with the strangler on it. He moved slow—obviously trying not to slosh the water and get Goliath's attention.

The gator moved closer. Five feet maybe. And it wasn't just his head visible now. His whole body surfaced. Parker stared—absolutely stunned at Goliath's size. The scutes on his back were massive. Black. Glistening. The serrated edge on his tale—truly like something from the dinosaur era.

"Keep moving, Wilson. I don't like this. He's staring me down."

A sharp thwack came from the trees. Then another. Parker stole another look over his shoulder. Wilson grinned and held the camera in one hand, Boomer in the other.

Parker turned back to Goliath. The gator was gone.

"Hurry—he went under!"

Wilson sloshed through knee-deep water, seeming to forget all about not making a sound.

Parker gripped Amos Moses—ready to strike—and ran along the inside of the boat, looking for any telltale sign of Goliath or a shadow passing underneath.

"You see him?" Wilson passed the cypress with the strangler vine. "Anything?"

"He could be anywhere. Hurry!"

Parker hustled back to the stern, reached for the control console, and turned the ignition key. The Merc fired up immediately. Keeping it in neutral, he revved the motor—hoping that would send Goliath swimming for its lair. Parker raced back to the bow, still holding Amos Moses.

Wilson was five feet away. He tossed the camera to Parker, but kept Boomer.

"C'mon, c'mon!" Parker dropped Amos Moses in the boat just as Wilson lunged for the bow. Parker grabbed handfuls of shirt and pulled Wilson over the side even as he clawed his way in.

In a final thrust, Wilson tumbled inside and tucked in both feet, falling to the floor.

Parker dropped down beside him. "That was insane!"

Both of them laughed—that hysterical type that only happens when you've just had five years scared off your life.

"I made it," Wilson said. "I made it."

"Tell me you didn't pee your pants," Parker said.

"When you started that engine," Wilson said, "I almost did a lot more than that."

They burst out laughing again.

"I didn't know if you were trying to scare away the gator, or if you were going to leave me behind."

"It was a toss-up."

They both rolled on the floor of the boat laughing until Parker's side ached.

"No more," Parker said, driving a fist into his side. "I got a massive side-cramp."

They both lay on their backs, catching their breaths, looking up through a canopy of overhanging branches at a sky that was getting darker with an incoming squall. "Okay, let's get out of here."

"We going to look at this thing or not?" Wilson held up the camera.

"Definitely." Parker scanned the surface of the water. "But I'm thinking we'll drive a good mile or so away from here first—*then* we'll stop and look at it."

"Because of Goliath?" Wilson shook his head. "We're in a boat—and that puts us at the top of the food chain here."

Parker didn't feel at the top of *anything* at that moment. "If Goliath is fifteen feet, he's longer than the *Boy's Bomb*. Let's not test your top-of-the-food-chain theory."

Wilson reached over and turned off the key. The Merc shuddered to a stop. "I'm the guy who just went in the water to get this thing. Before we pull away I want to see what I risked my life to get."

The surface of the water was absolutely still. The bread, what was left of it, clumped together in a soggy mess. No sign of Goliath. "Just a quick look."

The pictures were organized by date and time. Within seconds Wilson scrolled back to the night Maria disappeared. The first frame was time-stamped shortly after midnight. The frame was almost entirely black except for a small light in the center.

"What is that?" Parker said.

Wilson whipped through more frames. The light got bigger. Closer. "It's a lantern. On a pole mounted on a skiff. Somebody's out there fishing."

"Poaching?"

"Could be that, too."

There was something entirely creepy about looking at the pictures. He had believed Maria was alive—but that was more hope than anything, wasn't it? What if he saw something on the camera that he really didn't want to see? What if Goliath showed up? What if the beast attacked? Or what if the mysterious person in the boat had something to do with her disappearance?

More frames slid by. The boat drifted closer to the camera. A smudge of a face appeared. Parker moved in closer. "Can you make him out? Is it Crawley?"

The image was too faint to tell. Wilson whirred through more pictures so fast that the images seemed more like an animated movie. The light ratcheting left and right, closer and farther. He stopped as the light got bigger than they'd seen it yet.

The man was clearer now. Not fishing—but sitting there. "It's like he's waiting for something," Wilson said.

"Or someone." A sick feeling twisted Parker's gut. "It's Crawley, right?"

Wilson scrolled ahead—and then something changed. "Go back, go back."

Wilson backed the images up—and gasped. The man was

standing now—leaning over the side of the boat. The nose of a kayak poked into the frame. "Maria!"

He advanced one. Two. Three pictures. Maria pulled up alongside the boat. Reached out and the man hugged her and helped pull her aboard. Her face looked happy. Relieved. And she should be if she'd just escaped a monster gator.

"Her paddle," Parker said. "It's not broken."

"That's weird."

The man grabbed the front of the kayak like he was going to pull it into the boat, but twisted it upside down instead and dropped it into the water.

"He deliberately swamped her kayak," Parker said. "Why is she not trying to get away from him?"

Wilson shook his head. "This makes no sense."

The man used her paddle to pole him closer to shore. He hauled back and split the paddle against the cypress with the strangler vine. Maria still sat in the chair—not making any move to stop him.

Wilson advanced one more frame. Maria was on her feet—coming up behind him. "Here we go. She's on to him. I'll bet she pushes him right over the bow."

He swiped to the next frame. Maria reached out and hugged the guy from behind. The guy turned and hugged her. It looked like he picked her up and half twirled her—and for one frame his face was visible.

"What?" Parker pulled the camera closer. Cupped his hand around the display screen to cut some light from overhead. But the face was unmistakable. "Clayton Kingman."

Wilson stared at Parker in a kind of stunned silence. "This whole thing was a setup. They faked her death so nobody would suspect she was actually running away."

"He's an absolute scumbag."

There were only three more images of the night encounter. Clayton's boat moved off the scene. The next picture was taken in daylight—of Parker's dad and Uncle Sammy in one of the ranger boats.

Wilson lowered the camera, and Parker lay back staring at the darkening sky. "This changes everything." She *wanted* to go with him. She was willing to let her dad be in agony—and everybody else—just so she could be with that moron?

"I thought we were keeping them apart," Wilson said.

"They played us." How could Maria do that? To Parker?

A massive cloud bank boiled silently overhead. Thunderheads. Dark, with flashes of lightning trapped inside—and threatening to break out. The wind—definitely moving at a frantic pace up there. The clouds crept lower, like they'd been stalking them. Storms rolled in fast off the ocean, and it looked like this one was going to bust open. "We have to get out of here."

Wilson agreed, and pointed at the camera. "What do we do with this?"

"We get it in the hands of my dad. And Uncle Sammy. The sooner the better. They'll know what to do." Parker slipped the memory card out of the camera and zipped it in his pocket. That was all they really needed. But there was no way they were going to retie the camera around the tree. Not now, anyway. Likely the owner had his name on it somewhere. They'd contact him later. "Let's go."

Wilson hesitated. "Do you think Jelly knew—about Clayton meeting Maria here?"

Something big and solid thudded into the engine. Like they rammed into a submerged log, except the boat wasn't moving.

Both of them grabbed the sides to balance themselves, then

held perfectly still. "*What* was that?" But Parker knew. And by the look on Wilson's face, he did, too.

Another thump, this time directly below them. Then a thwack, thwack, thwack, thwack, thwack—like a heavy anchor chain being dragged from port to starboard along the bottom of their boat. Parker could feel every vibration through the thin fiberglass hull.

"I've never heard of a gator doing something like that," Wilson whispered.

Suddenly the entire outboard motor shook and lurched so hard that Parker feared it was going to get ripped right off the transom. The water churned, throwing spray onto both of them. "What's the thing *doing* to it?"

Wilson rubbed down the rising hair on his arms. "We gotta get out of here. Now."

Parker scrambled on all fours toward the wheel and cranked the engine. It caught immediately. He revved it a couple of times—just to scare the beast away. He shifted into reverse and gave it some gas.

The boat didn't move. Parker gave it more gas.

Wilson rushed to the transom and looked over the side. "Your prop . . . it's gone."

"What?"

Parker chanced a peek over the stern into the water. "He must have sheered it. I can't imagine how much force it took to do that." With a shaking hand, Parker turned off the ignition.

Wilson dropped onto his knees, staring over the transom at the useless motor. He looked at Parker, eyes wide with disbelief. "We're stranded."

CHAPTER 74

ANGELICA STOOD NEXT TO HER DAD as he negotiated the hairpin turns of the Lopez. Her tears had dried, but her dad still had fresh lines running down his cheeks. He looked livid. Hopping mad—like she'd never seen him before. But the love in his eyes when he looked her way made it clear he wasn't upset with her. Her dad was amazing.

They'd made record time, but it still seemed they were torturously behind. Dad drove the Lopez River faster than Angelica thought humanly possible. Parker's dad knelt in the bow and used a pole to help them steer clear of the worst of the obstacles in the tight turns. "Hurry, Dad."

He reached over and squeezed her hand, then went back to his two-handed grip on the wheel. She pulled the visor of Parker's cap lower on her forehead and strained to see ahead.

Why did she keep the secrets? Why did she not believe her dad could have kept all this from happening? Her secrecy all seemed so stupid now. She should have told her dad so much sooner. She ended up telling him anyway—but too late.

"I'll never keep a secret like that again, Dad." She wished making that promise would make her feel better, but it didn't. It never turned out good when people were pressured into keeping secrets. She'd learned that the hard way.

"If a family member—or a friend—pressures you to keep a secret that shouldn't be kept at all?" Dad kept his eyes on the river. "They aren't acting like a friend at that moment. Remember that."

It was a lesson she'd never forget.

"It won't be long now," Parker's dad said. He pulled the shotgun out of the case and thumbed cartridges into the chamber. Whatever injuries he had from the accident this morning weren't slowing him down a bit.

She looked at her dad. "What are you two going to do to Clayton?"

His jaw muscles tensed and relaxed. Tensed and relaxed. "What we do to any monster who hurts our kids."

Exactly what she was afraid of. "Dad—you're not going to jail over Kingman. Maria *wanted* to run away. She threatened me to keep me quiet. Remember that."

He kept his eyes on the river. "Clayton is a coward. There isn't an honorable bone in his body. He messed with her head. But she'll come around once he's off the scene."

Off the scene? What did that mean? "We *need* him."

For a moment, he just looked at her. "I'm not going to kill him, Angelica." He glanced back at the river and then at her. "I'd never kill another human being unless I truly believed that was the only way to stop him from hurting one of my kids. Although I guarantee you he'll never get near Maria again."

That was a promise she absolutely wanted Dad to keep.

"You said we needed him. Why?"

Angelica stared at the twisting Lopez in front of them. "Because he took Maria someplace. Far from here—and Maria wouldn't say where. Clayton knew a place she could stay where she'd never be found—that's all Maria told me. She left the phone in the kayak to throw everyone off. If something happens to Clayton, how will we ever find her?"

CHAPTER 75

FOR A MOMENT WILSON THOUGHT about the fiberglass skin on the hull. What was it, an eighth of an inch thick? A gator this size could punch a hole through it with one sweep of its tail. Easy. Goliath had to weigh well over a thousand pounds. That was more than Parker's boat, motor, and the two of them in it combined. Maybe on an aluminum airboat with a Chevy 350 they'd be at the top of the food chain out here . . . but in this skiff? He kept his thoughts to himself. It wouldn't do Parker any good to know how bad this could really get. "You have a backup prop?"

Parker nodded. "A cheap aluminum spare—and tools. Under my seat. But neither one of us is hanging over the transom to swap it out while Goliath is around, even with the motor raised."

"Got that right." There was a limit to how far Wilson would take that Miccosukee invisibility claim.

"We'll use Amos Moses as a pole . . . push ourselves to deeper water."

But Goliath would follow. And if he battered a hole in the fiberglass out there, their chances to get to the trees for cover were out the window.

The boat lurched, like the beast came up underneath and tried to surface. Wilson grabbed the side to steady himself. "It's just trying to scare us."

"Or he's looking for a meal," Parker said. "And he sees our boat as a little package he's got to open first."

The phones. "Think there's a signal out here?" Wilson already knew the answer to that.

Parker didn't look hopeful. He reached for the storage compartment to check the phones anyway—then stopped and angled his head slightly. "Listen."

Wilson held his breath. He could hear it now. An outboard motor.

Parker scrambled to his feet with Wilson a half heartbeat behind him. "There."

A lone fisherman in a Boston Whaler sped along the shoreline from the opposite direction of the Lopez—heading roughly their way.

"Hey!" Wilson raised both hands over his head and waved. "Over here!"

Parker let loose a piercing whistle. "Help!" He picked up Amos Moses and swung it back and forth.

The boat altered course slightly so it was coming right at them. "Finally catching a break." Wilson looked into the dark waters. "Where'd Goliath go?"

Parker scanned the water. "Not far, I'm sure." He slid Amos

Moses into the water and pushed off the bottom and away from the line of cypress trees. "Maybe this guy can tow us far enough away so we can change the prop and get back to civilization."

It definitely beat staying here. Wilson nodded. "That's a solid plan."

The driver of the boat slowed, the bow raised, and he stood at the console.

"Wait a sec," Parker whispered. He shielded his eyes and stared at the approaching skiff. "Isn't that—"

"Clayton Kingman." His royal highness himself, driving *King of the Glades*. It felt like an anchor dropped in Wilson's gut. "Right now I'd rather take my chances with Goliath."

CHAPTER 76

PARKER'S MIND SPUN INTO HIGH GEAR. "Grab Boomer. We need him to see we're armed."

"I like that idea." Wilson slid the leather strap around his wrist and let the black machete dangle.

Parker dropped the trail cam into the storage compartment and rolled up his pant leg so Jimbo—strapped securely to his calf—showed. He picked up Amos Moses and held it there, blade pointing to the tumbling thunderheads above them.

Wilson nodded. "Boomer. Jimbo. Amos Moses. You. Me. That's five against one by my math."

Kingman eased his boat into neutral when he was thirty feet away. Slid it into reverse and goosed the gas to stop all forward movement. He cut the motor. Smiled. "This is definitely a surprise. Gator-bait and Cochise. What are you boys doing *miles* from any living soul?"

The real question was what Kingman was doing—here at the scene of the crime. There was no way he knew about the camera or he would have gotten rid of it days ago.

"There's a monster gator here," Parker said. "Honest. Our prop is sheared off."

Clayton raised his eyebrows. "What's the boy who is *so* pee-pants-scared of alley-gators doing way out here? I think we both know you aren't hunting for some imaginary monster gator."

"Right now, we just want to get away from this spot. I saw the gator, Clayton. It's a fifteen-footer," Wilson said. "We just need a tow away from that thing so we can put on the spare."

"Now why would I do that?" Clayton looked at Parker. "You still haven't told me why you're out here. At the very spot Maria's kayak was found. Coincidence?"

Parker couldn't get the images out of his mind . . . seeing Maria . . . here . . . in Kingman's arms. "And how would you know *this* is the exact spot? Coincidence?"

Clayton spit in the water. Sized Parker up and down real slow. It was probably supposed to be intimidating.

And it was.

"Game time is over." Clayton scanned the cypress trees behind them. "Where's this wildlife camera I heard about?"

What? Besides Wilson—and the messages he'd left his parents—Jelly was the only one who knew. There was no way she would say anything. Absolutely no way. "What are you talking about?"

"Judging by the way Cochise is soaked from the waist down, I'm guessing you already found it." Kingman smiled. "Let's have it."

Parker didn't move.

"You boys going to make me come over there and take it?"

Wilson tapped the flat side of the machete blade onto his open palm. "That would be a dumb choice, but then you've made a lot of stupid moves lately. Yeah, we have the camera—and we saw the pictures. Your little charade is over. Where's Maria?"

"Now *that's* what I like," Kingman said. "An honest Injun."

Wilson tightened his grip on Boomer.

Maybe it was all Wilson's tough-guy talk, but Parker had a surge of something flash through him. He reached into the storage compartment and held up the camera. "Wilson's right. It's over. Where did you take her?"

"No place she didn't want to go," Kingman said. "Now, why don't you toss that camera over?"

He dropped the camera on the floor of the boat. "I don't think so. We'll see what the police have to say about this."

"Don't make me take it from you."

"You and what army?" Wilson raised Boomer over his head. "My people were never conquered—are you forgetting that?"

Clayton bent over and picked up his shotgun. "I hate to sound so cliché, but leave it to a couple of boys to bring knives to a gun fight. Toss me the camera."

Neither one of them moved.

"I launched my boat in a little spot nobody even knows about," Clayton said. "Everybody thinks the poor grieving boyfriend is miles and miles away. Nobody has seen him in days. I've got an alibi big enough to drive your boat through. What's to stop me from taking the camera? I'll fill you with so much buckshot the alligator that eats you will die of lead poisoning." He brushed his hands like he was dusting off. "Easy-peasy. After the gators finish with you, there won't be enough left of either of you to fill an evidence bag."

Wilson lowered the machete. Shifted his weight from foot to foot—like he just might do something crazy.

"You could shoot us where we stand," Parker said. "But the buckshot would blow away chunks of fiberglass. The boat will be found eventually—no matter where you hide it. With the boat all shot up, they'll know it was murder. Who do you think will be the prime suspect? Jelly knows you threatened me."

"Angelica? She'll cover for me. Who do you think tipped me off about the camera? She's in way too deep. She'll never squeal on me."

Parker felt like he'd taken a load of buckshot in the gut. "No way."

Kingman seemed to enjoy Parker's disbelief. "*Yes* way. After I found out about the tires and texts, Angel had this *crazy* idea I was going to kill you. Somehow she uncovered Maria's plan to fake her disappearance. So, we made a trade. Angelica kept quiet to save your hide."

Jelly *had* been protecting him—just like he'd thought. But until now, Parker had no idea how many secrets she'd been keeping to do that. *Oh, Jelly.*

"And naïve little Angelica was still trying to protect you when she tipped me off about the camera. She thought if I got here first and got the camera, our little secret would be safe—and so would you. You'd leave Everglades City in one piece and everybody would live happily ever after. Pathetic, right?"

"You're the pathetic one, Clayton," Wilson said.

"I agree. I was pathetic to agree to Angel's little deal," Kingman said. "I hated the idea of you leaving town free as a bird. People who mess with Clayton Kingman *need* to be taught a lesson."

Parker's mind raced. What chance did they have against a shotgun? *God help us! Please!*

"But it looks like fate didn't want you leaving any more than I did," Kingman said. "I heard all about the Miccosukee Everglades Toll. And I'm going to collect it."

Wilson looked like he was ready to dive over the side. And he might make it if Parker kept Kingman distracted.

"So where is Maria?"

"What difference does it make? Whether you hand me the camera or you make me come and take it, neither of you are going home tonight."

Parker had to stall for time. Slap together an escape plan. "So what's the harm in telling us?"

Kingman angled his head slightly, his lips twisting into a royal smirk. "No harm at all. Flamingo City. My aunt lives there all alone. My dad told her that Maria's parents live out of state—and she needs a place to stay until the wedding. My aunt is thrilled to have the company."

Principal K was part of this? "Your dad *knew* Maria was alive?"

Kingman shrugged. "When Maria's dad busted us up, he basically declared war on the Kingman clan. That's how my old man saw it. He suggested Maria stay with my aunt. Even had my boat ready at that remote little launch site so I could be waiting right here for her when she paddled up."

Parker wanted to puke.

"She'll stay with my old man's sister until Maria turns eighteen." Kingman was bragging now. Like he had a failsafe plan. Like this whole thing was already in the bag. "Then I'll drive to Flamingo, we'll walk into the justice of the peace, and two minutes later we'll be married. Once that happens, nobody will ever stop us from being together again."

If Maria was so set on marrying a guy like *him* . . . maybe it was better that she did disappear.

"Now here's how this is going down," Kingman said. "I'll give you a fighting chance—if you do exactly what I say." He glanced at Wilson. "In the water. Now."

The bow was pointed toward the tree line, but the boat itself was a good thirty feet away from the cypress with the strangler vine. Wilson would be totally exposed.

Wilson stared at him. "The gator—I told you."

"I'm going to blow a hole in you big enough for the gator to crawl through if you stay on the boat."

"Hold on." Parker raised both hands. "Please, Clayton—don't do this." But he *would* do this. There was no way Kingman intended to let them live to tell what they knew. Obviously Kingman wanted to get Wilson in the water and let nature do the killing—or blast him when he was clear of the boat. There'd be no buckshot in the *Boy's Bomb* hull that way. Nothing pointing to Kingman's role in this.

God, help me. Help me know what to do. Instantly his mind went back to the conversation when Kingman stopped for Snak-pak. Somewhere there was a little bit of kindness in him. "Listen. You don't have to do this. It's not too late to change directions."

"I'm going exactly where I want to go."

"Jail?" The word came out before Parker even thought about how Kingman might react. "Look, help Wilson and me out. Tow us away from this gator and use your shotgun to stand guard until we get the prop fixed—and you're a hero. Everybody will see it that way. Tell the rangers about Maria. She went with you willingly—the trail cam proved that. You didn't force her. She was running away, and you helped her. No harm no foul, and no crime you can be charged with. Nobody has to get hurt here today. Bring her home—and you're a hero again."

Kingman's eyes narrowed. Was he processing—or getting ready to shoot? *God, what do I say next?*

"You're angry at your dad. Maybe the world," Parker said. "But if you take it out on us, you're only going to make your own situation worse. Look, Kingman . . . Clayton . . . I know you can be kind. I saw it on the Tamiami Trail—when you stopped for that dog. You *wanted* to help Snak-pak. I saw kindness in you again when you told me about your puppy, King. How you tried so hard to keep it from barking—and had the Cheerios ready."

For an instant the fire in his eyes dimmed, just a bit. Did he lower the shotgun a hair? Parker held his breath. It was like Kingman was balancing on the top of a fence. The slightest move—the wrong word—and he'd topple the wrong way. Wilson must have sensed it too. He stood beside Parker like a statue—with a machete.

Kingman shook his head, like he was trying to clear it. He regripped the shotgun. Raised it back up. "Nice try, Gator-bait. Being *kind* is being weak. And wimpy isn't exactly something I'm shooting for."

Not good. Not good. "Look, be the hero here, Clayton. Otherwise you'll be living with a dark secret the rest of your life."

Kingman snickered. "I crossed to the dark side a long time ago."

God, what do I say to him? "It's not too late to change where this is going. There's still some light in you."

Kingman smiled. "I like the darkness, gimp. I prefer it." He aimed the barrel toward the clouds and pumped a round into the chamber. "Out of the boat, Cochise."

"Please," Parker said. "Help us. Bring Maria back. It's the right thing to do, Clayton."

"I am so sick of being told about what's right and what's wrong."

The way Kingman said it . . . like there was some kind of rage boiling up from deep inside. "My old man goaded me with his stinkin' Star of Integrity talk. I got more scars from that star than that gator left on your arm. Now *I* decide what's right and wrong."

No, God decides. Parker wanted to say it, but clearly, the talking was over. And obviously the darkness had done a better job of convincing him than Parker had.

Kingman scanned the surface of the water. "Looks like your make-believe monster gator is a no-show. Surprise, surprise." He looked directly at Wilson. "Now you can take your chances with the imaginary gator—or with my aim. You have five seconds."

The look in his eyes said Kingman wasn't bluffing. Parker pulled the alligator-tooth necklace from around his neck and tossed it to Wilson.

Wilson caught it, locked eyes with him for an instant, and slid it over his head.

"Four."

Wilson looked at Parker. "I have to, right?"

"Three."

Wilson looked more scared than Parker had ever seen him.

"Two."

"Head for the cypress," Parker whispered. "He won't get a shot—and he sure won't chase you. You're half Miccosukee. You could last months out here, right?"

Wilson gave a half smile. "Easily."

"One." Kingman raised the shotgun. "Time's up, Cochise."

"I'm going." Wilson raised his hands. "I'm going." With a warrior battle cry, Wilson leaped off the bow—machete in hand—and splashed into Sunday Bay. Immediately he waded through waist-deep water for the cypress with the choker vine.

Kingman tracked him with the shotgun. "Hold it right there, smart guy."

Wilson stopped—held Boomer up like a club—and scanned the water.

"I want your transom plug, Buckman. Then the camera," Kingman said. "Toss them to me—and I'll let Cochise get to the tree line."

"Once he gets that camera," Wilson said, "He'll—"

Kingman fired a round in the air. "Another word and I'll fill your mouth with buckshot."

He glared at Parker. "Pull the transom plug. Now."

Parker hesitated.

Kingman swung the shotgun halfway between Wilson and the trees and fired another round. A water geyser exploded not ten feet from Wilson. "Think I'm playing games?"

Instantly Parker twisted free the plug—and the Glades poured in. He held up the plug so Clayton could see it and lobbed it to him.

Clayton caught it with one hand and stuffed it in his pocket.

"Please. Let him get to the trees," Parker begged. "That gator was huge."

Kingman appeared totally unmoved. "I want that camera. Then Cochise can head for the cypress. I'll catch up with him later. Tracking a real live Indian will be fun." Kingman pumped another round into the chamber and stared at Parker. "But after I get that camera, I'm coming for *you* first."

CHAPTER 77

THE INSTANT ANGELICA HEARD the second shotgun blast, she felt the tears streaming down her cheeks again. But with all the twists and turns of the Lopez, her sense of direction was off. "Which way is Sunday Bay?"

Her dad didn't answer. She looked to Parker's dad. Fresh tears wet his cheeks as well. That was all the answer she needed. Why did she wait until third period to find out where the boys were? Maybe if she'd called her dad five minutes earlier they would have been there by now. Why did she trust anything Clayton promised her? She'd made an impossible mess. Of everything. She'd made a deal with the devil—and now she was paying for her sins.

It was a little late to realize that. She only hoped they weren't too late for Parker and Wilson.

CHAPTER 78

SWAMP WATER ROSE above Parker's ankles as the stern settled lower in Sunday Bay. He'd give Kingman the camera—but not right into his hands. He needed to buy Wilson—and himself—a few seconds. Enough time for Wilson to duck behind a cypress. And hopefully enough for Parker to find cover himself.

Wilson stood in waist-deep water, Boomer still over his head. But Parker could tell he was inching backward slowly, toward the trees. *Keep going, Wilson. Keep going.*

"You should have stayed out of the Glades, Gator-bait," Kingman said. "Angelica tried to stop you. Even spray-painted your boat to scare you. And here we are. ValuJet #592 sinking into the Everglades all over again. No survivors this time either. Fitting, right?"

Jelly? No way. "You're sick, Kingman. You don't have to do this."

"But I *want* to, Gator-bait. I really, really want to." He wiped his hands on his shirt and took a fresh grip of the shotgun. "Camera. Now. Final warning."

Parker grabbed the bag of French bread and pulled out two loaves. He wrapped what was left of the camo strap around and around the bread and tucked it through twice so it wouldn't shake loose. He held up the camera with the French bread pontoons. "Okay—the bread floats. I'm going to toss this to you."

"What, can't throw the camera all the way over here with your freak-show arm?"

"Maybe I'm afraid you'll miss the catch," Parker said. "And you'll blame it on me."

Kingman smiled. "Somewhere in this I sense a strategy. Something that will increase your odds of survival? Good luck with that." He held one arm up like it was twisted and deformed— obviously mocking Parker's injuries. "But then you never were very lucky when it came to the Everglades—Gator-bait."

"I'm not trusting in luck. God protected me before." Parker tried to sound strong. "He can do it again." *Please God . . . help me.*

Kingman glanced up at the dark clouds. "Looks like your God is a no-show . . . just like your mythical monster gator."

Parker glanced at Wilson, who was searching the water frantically. They locked eyes for a moment. "Toss the bread, Parker. Give him what he wants."

Goliath is here. He's here. Parker tossed the bread and camera toward Kingman—but deliberately short. The camera slapped the water and disappeared, and the bread smacked the surface a fraction of a second later and bobbed in the water, the strap tugging it downward. But the bread worked perfectly as a buoy—at least for now. Instantly Parker snatched up Amos Moses.

Kingman kept the shotgun trained on him. "Going to try to spear me with that gator stick?"

He shook his head, inching his way toward the bow. The top edge of the transom was halfway to the waterline now, angling the deck. He grabbed the gunwale to steady himself with one hand—still gripping Amos Moses in the other. All he had to do was get over the side. "I'm not going in the water unarmed. There's a gator here. His name is Goliath. I don't think you're going to want to stick your hand in there to get that camera." He grabbed another loaf and tossed it in the water, near the loaves with the camera.

"Chumming the water?" Kingman actually looked like he was enjoying this. "Why don't you throw a few more?"

Parker grabbed the last of the loaves in the bag and lobbed them over with a high arc. They pancaked down with a muffled plop.

Suddenly Parker felt the vibrations of the serrated tail rubbing the bottom of the boat. But going which way? "Did you hear that? Seriously—he's here."

"The gator is talking to you now?" Clayton snickered. "You think I'm stupid? You think I'll just leave the camera?" He knelt down and leaned over the side of the boat. "The instant this is in my hands, I'm going to collect that toll."

This was his chance. "I'm not lying. The gator is here—I'm giving you fair warning."

Kingman paddled with one hand to coax his boat closer to the camera. He gripped the shotgun with the other. "Now I'm going to give you a warning. I'll have this camera in five seconds. Then

I'm going to hunt both of you down. I'll feed you to the gators myself."

The *Boy's Bomb* was sinking fast. The bow still pointed toward the tree line, the stern toward the open waters of Sunday Bay. The Merc was over halfway underwater now, the weight of it pulling the boat down fast. Once the top of the transom sunk below the surface, he'd be in the water anyway. Parker had to move, but the thought of jumping into the black water made him lock up.

Kingman—and his boat—got closer to the bread with every stroke. "I'm really enjoying this, Gator-bait. How about you?"

Go, Parker. Move! "God—help me!"

Wilson sloshed his way to the cypress. "C'mon, Bucky. You can do it!"

Taking a fresh grip on Amos Moses, Parker splashed toward the front of the boat and leaped off the raised bow—into the dark waters.

Wilson motioned frantically. "C'mon, c'mon."

Only when Parker ducked behind the first cypress did he dare look back again.

"Almost there, Gator-bait." Kingman was stretched over the side of his boat, dog-paddling to the bread buoy. "A hunting we will go, a hunting we will go . . ." He sang the little song eerily slow, and pointed the shotgun right at Parker for a moment before paddling again. "Heigh-ho the dairy-o, a-hunting we will g—"

Suddenly the water exploded in front of Kingman. A massive black head burst out of the water and clamped onto Clayton's arm. The shotgun dropped into the water immediately.

With a jerk of its head, Goliath plunged back below the surface, ripping Kingman from his Whaler.

Wilson screamed. "It got him, Bucky—it got him. That thing's a monster!" He held the machete at the ready and backed deeper into the flooded cypress forest.

Parker sloshed up beside him, holding Amos Moses out in case Goliath came their way. Flooded cypress forest behind him— crawling with venomous snakes no doubt. The gator-infested waters of Sunday Bay—and the sinking *Boy's Bomb* directly in front of him. There was no place to go. And the idea of swimming all the way out to Kingman's empty boat? Not a chance.

Goliath rolled to the surface with Kingman's arm still in its mouth, churning the water into a bloody foam. The monster's white belly showed for an instant, then Kingman and Goliath went under for round two.

Water up to their waists, Parker and Wilson stood shoulder to shoulder, weapons at the ready.

"Keep your eyes peeled, Bucky! This place will be crawling with gators—looking for their share of meat!"

CHAPTER 79

THE MOMENT THEY BROKE FREE of the Lopez River and into Sunday Bay, Jelly was at the bow alongside Parker's dad.

"There!" She pointed toward an empty boat a good two hundred yards away. "It's Clayton's."

Uncle Vaughn squinted. "And a second skiff is swamped. It's the *Bomb!*"

Even from this distance she picked out the teal bow barely nosing out of the water. The stern and motor were on the bottom. She whipped Parker's hat off her head, clutched it with both hands, and pressed it to her lips. "Let him be okay, God. Let them both be okay." She said it aloud—but only God would have heard it over the roar of the outboard.

Dad had the ranger skiff wide open. "Where are they?"

Jelly strained to see any movement. Any sign of life.

The water erupted in front of Clayton's boat. A monstrous alligator rolled its victim below the surface with a blur of fierce speed.

"No," Jelly wailed. "No!"

In her heart, she knew it was Parker—and the curse had found him again. But this time the toll would be paid. There'd be no way they'd get to him in time.

CHAPTER 80

RIPPLES FROM THE FIGHT RUSHED past Parker, like the water itself was afraid and wanted out of there. Goliath and Kingman steamrolled to the surface. Kingman pummeled Goliath's snout with his free hand. He got whipped under again.

"We can't stay here," Wilson said. "We have to get to Kingman's boat."

He was right. They were at the bottom of the food chain as long as they were in the water. But moving toward Goliath seemed unthinkable. Kingman's boat drifted closer to shore and bumped past the nose of the *Boy's Bomb* now. Thirty feet away. Maybe thirty-five. There would never be a better chance. "Together?"

Wilson took a couple of quick breaths and gave a single nod.

Parker lowered Amos Moses so the point cut through the water ahead of them. Wilson walked backward, machete raised, to guard against a rogue gator making a rear attack. The first step was the hardest—but once they got moving, they picked up speed.

Goliath slapped Kingman under again.

"Ten more feet," Parker said. The water reached his chest. Submerged branches and logs hooked his feet. Snagged his pants.

Goliath surfaced—alone this time.

Kingman broke the surface an instant later, gasping for breath. His arm bloody and shredded. Lots of bone showing—but the arm was still there. Barely. "Ahhh—ahhh—ahh!" Wild-eyed, he clawed at the water with his good hand, trying to get to the tree line.

Goliath ignored him—like it knew Kingman was already in the bag. It swung its massive head toward Parker and Wilson.

"He's seen us," Parker shouted.

Goliath stared at Parker for an instant—and with a powerful snap of its tail, bore down on him with terrifying speed.

Even then Parker knew it was too late. He'd never pull himself into the boat in time with his gimpy arm—not with the extra weight of his wet clothes. He'd likely be in Wilson's way, delaying him too. If Parker stayed in front, the gator would get them both. But if Wilson went first? He pushed Wilson past him. "Get in! Get in!"

"But what about y—"

"My arm—I'll slow you—wouldn't be right. Now go—I'll hold him off!"

CHAPTER 81

SEVENTY-FIVE YARDS OUT—and Angelica's dad had the ranger skiff wide open. Clayton staggered toward the cypress like a one-armed zombie. The monster gator shot like a torpedo toward Parker and Wilson.

"Parker!" Angelica screamed.

He stood there—Amos Moses in front of him like a harpoon, just like he did on Gator Hook Trail. Only this gator was terrifyingly bigger. With what looked like an angry roar, Parker took a step closer and attacked—rushing the monster gator while Wilson dragged himself over the bow of Clayton's boat.

Uncle Vaughn crouched in the bow, shotgun at the ready. "Bring me in between the boats—right on top of him."

Angelica's dad banked hard and bore down on them at full speed.

She judged the distance, her panic rising. "Faster, Dad. Faster! Dear God—please save him!"

Safely aboard Clayton's boat, Wilson leaned out and reached for Parker—but he wasn't even close.

Parker jabbed at the gator like a madman—but each time the beast forced him backward toward the trees. Goliath raced in for the kill—and opened its mouth.

She couldn't watch—but couldn't turn away either. "Parker—noooo!!"

CHAPTER 82

WICKED, EVIL EYES. Black. Smoldering. Parker thrust at the beast over and over with Amos Moses. Each time the gator stick made contact, the monster drove him farther from the boat and Wilson's outstretched arms.

"Die, die, die!" He speared Goliath again and again. It was like attacking a log. The knife never penetrated the tough, bony hide. Goliath kept advancing with easy, unhurried sweeps of its tail—like Parker was a sure thing. An easy meal.

"That's it," Wilson shouted. "Keep that gator stick in front of you."

Parker had the knife point firmly against the gator's shoulder, creating a buffer of space between man and beast. If Goliath got past the blade, Parker was dead.

He picked up movement in his peripheral. *Kingman.*

Kingman stumbled toward the cypress—cradling his mangled arm. "Help me, help me, help me . . ."

Maybe Kingman was in shock—and unless he got help, he'd be dead soon. Parker wouldn't be far behind him.

Goliath ignored Kingman, despite him chumming the water with his own blood. The gator's primal instincts should have made him back off Parker—and go for the easy prey. But the beast didn't veer away from Parker. Like it knew Kingman wouldn't get far. Like the beast just wanted another kill.

Mouth slightly open, water rushed between yellowed, dagger-like teeth. Goliath clawed at the water and swept his tail side to side with more force now, pushing Parker back with tremendous power.

Parker's foot hooked on a submerged root, and he stumbled backward. He struggled to keep the knife point on the gator's hide. If it slipped off, there'd be no stopping the thing.

"Bucky!" Wilson's voice—sheer terror.

Goliath stopped. Its jaws opened wider in a hideous, mocking smile. Like it knew it had him and wanted to relish the moment.

Parker got his feet back under him. Kept backing up while Goliath floated in place and watched.

"Get to the trees," Wilson shouted.

But there was no turning his back on Goliath to retreat. The monster would have him before he got to the nearest cypress. And there was no getting past the gator to the safety of the boat. Parker was pretty sure Goliath knew that too.

Wilson leaned over the side of the boat, slashing at the surface of the water with his hands. "Hey Goliath—look at me. Over here. Easy meal."

But Goliath kept his eyes on the meal in front of him—and advanced.

Kingman whimpered from someplace behind him—like he knew Goliath would be coming for him next.

There was no escape. No rescue. The water—waist deep. But that was an illusion. He was in high water now. Way over his head. "God help me! Jesus, please!"

Parker backed up until the butt end of Amos Moses bumped the cypress with the strangler vine. *Stand your ground and fight, Parker.* He planted the back end of the solid oak gator stick firmly against the cypress behind him. He crouched low, and took a fresh grip on Amos Moses.

Goliath showed his teeth. The pink insides of his mouth.

"Been there, big guy," Parker shouted. "See these scars? We got the skull of the gator who did this—and God help me, I'm going to have your head, too, Goliath!"

Careful to keep the blunt end of Amos Moses anchored against the tree, Parker positioned the dive-knife tip directly in front of Goliath's nose, where a gator's vision is the worst.

Mouth gaping, Goliath lunged with a mighty thrust of its tail.

Parker lowered Amos Moses slightly—aiming for the trap door in the back of its throat. He felt it slice through the soft flesh.

The pink insides of Goliath's mouth turned bright red as blood spurted from its throat and out from between its teeth. The monster drove forward and thrashed to get at Parker, impaling itself on the gator stick.

Parker ramrodded Amos Moses deep down Goliath's throat with all his might—his hands getting closer and closer to the lethal incisors with every thrust.

"Stick him, Bucky!" Wilson jabbed the air like he held Amos Moses himself. "Stick him good!"

A ranger skiff raced toward them. *Dad!*

Goliath writhed, flailing its head from side to side like a dog shaking a rag doll.

The force of the gator's frenzied head swings ripped the gator stick from Parker's hands.

The alligator whirled around toward deeper water, plunging below the surface—the last two feet of Amos Moses still sticking out of its mouth. His wicked tail slashed back and forth as it dove into Sunday Bay, the tip clipping Parker across his cheek. He stumbled backward a few steps, but never lost his footing. He reached for Jimbo—strapped to his calf—pulled it free from its sheath, and held it at the ready. Warm blood streamed down his cheek and onto his shirt.

Suddenly the ranger skiff was there, blasting between Clayton's boat and what was showing of the *Boy's Bomb*. Uncle Sammy threw the outboard into reverse, the engine screaming and the backwash pushing Parker back a couple of feet.

Dad leaped over the side—shotgun in hand—and splashed to Parker's side.

"I see him," Jelly's dad shouted. "Toss the gun!"

Dad heaved the shotgun back to the boat.

Uncle Sammy caught the weapon in mid-air and pumped four rounds into the water along the port side of the skiff—and hopefully into Goliath himself.

Dad gripped Parker's shoulders. Patted him down to his ribs. "You okay?"

Parker smiled. "Better than I've been in a *really* long time. But Kingman isn't doing so good." He shot a glance at Kingman's mangled arm, and instantly relived his own gator death roll. Somehow Kingman had cinched his nylon belt around his upper arm, effectively stopping the bleeding.

His dad's eyes followed Parker's and narrowed in obvious concern. "We've got the satellite phone. He'll need an airlift."

The nose of the ranger skiff had drifted close enough to touch now. Jelly slipped over the side and rushed to Parker. She wrapped her arms around him, tears streaming down her cheeks.

"This was my fault," she said. "I'm so, so sorry. I have a lot of explaining to do."

Dad wrapped his arms around both of them. "Plenty of time for that on the ride home. Let's get you two in the boat, and that rescue chopper for Clayton. And then we've got your sister to pick up."

She looked up with a trembling smile and nodded. "It's going to be a busy day."

Wilson stood in Kingman's boat. He grinned at Parker and shook his head. "For a guy who hates alligators, you're sure in no hurry to get out of the water."

"So, let's get out already," Jelly said.

"And about that Everglades toll?" Jelly pointed at Wilson. "I think we can put that superstitious mumbo jumbo to bed. God is more powerful than any curse."

Wilson raised both hands, still gripping the machete. "No argument from me. Any guy who squares off against a fifteen-foot gator—and comes out with only a scratch—is *blessed*, not cursed." He pulled *King of the Glades* alongside the ranger skiff and climbed aboard.

Jelly laughed in that shaky way that people often do after they've had a brush with death. "God answered my prayers—can you believe it?" She slapped Parker's cap back on his head. "But get out of the water. I'd rather not have to ask for a second miracle today."

Uncle Sammy held the shotgun in one hand and pulled Jelly out with the other.

"You're next," Dad said. He reached for Parker's survival knife and motioned toward the boat. "I've got your back."

Like he always did. Between the wet clothes and his gimpy arm, Parker struggled a bit to drag himself over the side. But he did it—and all on his own.

Jelly slugged Parker in the good arm the moment he got inside. "Promise me you'll never go in the Glades again."

"Never again. There's no reason to anymore." He looked around him just as Dad hoisted himself into the boat. A break formed in the thunderheads and beams of sunlight filtered through. For an instant the verse Grandpa wrote on the back of the plaque jumped into his head. *"Even in darkness, light dawns for the upright."*

"You were right all along, Parker," Jelly said. "This is a place of death."

Parker instinctively scanned the water—searching for any sign of Goliath.

Kingman was looking too—cowering to one side of a cypress. "Help. Me." His eyes wide—like he expected Goliath to circle back for him.

Kingman reached toward the ranger skiff with his good arm. "Don't leave me here."

This from the guy who minutes earlier intended to keep Parker and Wilson from ever leaving the Glades.

"Goliath isn't the only monster here." Uncle Sammy jabbed his finger toward Kingman. "You're a predator. I should let you die."

Kingman took a step toward their boat. "You can't leave me." He spoke through clenched teeth—like maybe the pain was beginning to register.

"Leave him, Mr. Malnatti," Wilson said. "You'll be doing God a favor. He won't have to bother zapping him with lightning."

Kingman waded closer. "You could never live with yourself."

"Oh, I can live with myself." Jelly's dad pointed at Kingman. "Even if I leave you. Believe me."

After all Kingman did, there was a part of Parker that wanted him gone. The world would be a better place. And here, in the Glades, frontier justice had likely been exacted more times than anybody could ever guess. But to leave someone to *die*—even an enemy—would go against everything Dad had taught him.

"We *need* him," Jelly said. "We don't even know where Maria is. For all we know—"

"Where's my daughter, Kingman?" Uncle Sammy's voice came out more like a growl.

"She's in Flamingo City—and we know how to find her," Wilson said. "We don't need this swamp scum. Let's tow his boat to the middle of Sunday Bay and let him swim for it."

Parker glanced at his own mutilated arm. "No—not that." It would be barbaric. He caught Jelly's eye. She smiled—and gave a nod so slight he might have imagined it.

"You can find her," Uncle Sammy's eyes bore into Wilson, "for sure?"

Wilson nodded. "Absolutely. He told us everything we need to know. Bragged about it. Let's just let Goliath finish what he started."

Uncle Sammy glared at Kingman. His eyes blazed with an intensity like Parker had never seen before. Was he really going to leave Kingman?

"You'd be no better than me." Kingman managed a lopsided grin.

Dad put a hand on Uncle Sammy's shoulder—like everyone knew the life and death decision rested with him. "He's not worth it, Sammy. Let the courts deal with him."

Uncle Sammy's hands clenched and unclenched. He nodded, finally, and fired up the outboard. Nudged the gearshift forward. The skiff glided closer to Kingman. "Let's get him in the boat—and call for an airlift." He looked directly at Kingman. "We'll get you to a hospital. Then you'll be put in a cage—where monsters belong."

Parker let out a deep sigh, like he'd been holding his breath without realizing it. "Good call, Uncle Sammy."

"Get him in here before I change my mind."

Kingman was still losing blood. How he stayed on his feet was beyond Parker. But if they didn't get him help, he'd go downhill fast.

Kingman, smirking, waded to one side of the bow, his mangled arm dragging and twisted at a weird angle. He grabbed hold and struggled to pull himself over the side. Wilson took a step back toward the stern, arms crossed, refusing to help.

Dad grabbed Kingman's good arm while Parker took a handful of his shirt. Together they dragged him into the boat, with Kingman yelping and howling the whole time. He landed on the deck with a heavy thud—on the arm Goliath had been gnawing on.

"My arm! My arm!" Kingman writhed in fresh pain, clutching at the maimed arm.

"Sticking your arm out there over the water like you did?" Wilson said. "Somebody needs to school you on living in the Everglades." He shook his head and leaned in close. "Now who's the real gator-bait?"

Parker looked at his own arm . . . grateful for every scar . . . every stitch that had held his arm together. Right now his 60 percent mobility looked really good.

"That was incredibly insensitive, Wilson," Uncle Sammy said. "But thank you."

Wilson did a little bow. He lifted the alligator-tooth necklace over his head and held it out to Parker. "Thanks for loaning this to me. But it's yours now. The way you went after Goliath? You were insane."

"Maybe you should keep it," Parker said. "I'm done with the Everglades, remember?"

Wilson shook his head. "You earned this, brother. Besides, without me helping you out of jams after you move up north, you're going to need this for a little Miccosukee luck." He pressed the necklace into Parker's hand.

"Luck had nothing to do with how this turned out." Parker smiled. "And I think you know that. But I'll wear it with pride—and think of you every time I do."

Dad got on his satellite phone to call for a Coast Guard rescue chopper. Uncle Sammy climbed aboard *King of the Glades* and threw anchor. "We'll send rangers to tow this back. And see about the *Boy's Bomb*, too."

The sight of his boat—with just the nose above water—should have crushed him more, shouldn't it? But he was alive—and eternally grateful.

Jelly studied Parker for a moment. "Something is different about you. At first I was going to say your fear of the Glades was gone . . . but I think that's been gone for a while."

"Gator Hook Trail," Wilson said. "I cured him of that back then."

Parker did *not* want to think about Gator Hook Trail.

Jelly shook her head. "It's something else."

In a weird way, Parker felt it too—but even *he* wasn't sure what it was.

"You've grown," she said.

"He's about a foot taller in my book," Wilson said. He turned to Parker's dad. "So maybe now that we know this guy is blessed, not cursed," he jerked his thumb toward Parker, "maybe you'll want to skip that transfer and stay."

Dad laughed. "Not going to happen, Wilson. It's time—and we're going."

Parker totally agreed. But he could *walk* away now. He didn't feel the need to run.

EPILOGUE

PARKER WAS THE FIRST ONE to the beach by Smallwood's for the celebration two weeks later. A National Park Service picnic table sat right where the *Boy's Bomb* had always been, thanks to Dad and Uncle Sammy. Thankfully, the *Boy's Bomb* wasn't still resting on the bottom of Sunday Bay. Rangers had towed the skiff back to Chokoloskee—and they'd even pitched in to outfit it with a rebuilt motor to replace the water-damaged one. So, the *Bomb* would ride again—but along the New England coast just north of Boston.

Parker's dad got a two-week extension on the transfer. There had been too many loose ends to clean up here—and of course there was a party scheduled.

Thanks to the airlift, Kingman survived. But his arm was too badly mangled to be saved. They'd amputated it just above his elbow. Parker didn't want to think about it.

Parker gripped Wilson's gator-tooth necklace and looked out over Chokoloskee Bay. The cypress were magnificent. Amazing how they grew right out of the water and didn't rot. A blue heron flew overhead—like it was enjoying the view as well.

So much had happened. He'd wanted out of this place ever since Dillinger pulled him off the airboat. Over and over he'd prayed to escape the place, but God just didn't let it happen. Parker had been so convinced a change of geography was the answer. But if God had made the transfer click in place right away, Parker's problems would have gone with him. No, instead of getting Parker out of the place, God allowed things to get worse and worse until he realized what he really needed.

He hadn't needed a change of address nearly as much as he thought. He needed a change of *heart*. Getting far away from the Everglades was never the answer. He needed to get closer to God. He needed to remember that even living in the worst place on earth wasn't Godforsaken . . . because God would never leave him.

Was Parker glad to leave? Oh, yeah. But the desperate need to escape was gone. God had actually been really good to him when he kept the transfer from going through all those months. The delay was just long enough for Parker to figure out that running away from this place wasn't the answer. Actually, he did need to run, but it was all about *who* he was running to—not where.

He looked down at his scarred arm. Flexed his fingers. Turned his hand over and did it again. Life created scars. He got that. And when he left the Everglades and headed north in the morning, he'd take those scars of experience with him. He wouldn't be carrying any invisible baggage, though. Big difference.

Mom said Dad and Uncle Sammy had reached some kind of legendary hero status within the National Park Service for their tireless dedication to the job. After how things turned out, the Boston office was chafing to get Dad up there—and now they were hoping to get Uncle Sammy, too. Mom wouldn't tell Parker more than that, but she seemed really, really excited about it.

Dad and Uncle Sammy had always been heroes in Parker's book—for as long as he could remember. The minute Dad and Uncle Sammy got back to the marina after rescuing Parker and Wilson in Sunday Bay, they raced to Flamingo City to find Maria. The way Parker heard it later, there was never a girl more shocked to see her dad show up at the door. But at least she didn't try to run. Kingman had only gone to see Maria twice while she was at his aunt's place—and they'd argued both times. Maria found out he wasn't beyond hitting her—and she had the bruises to prove it. Her head still wasn't screwed on right, though, and they drove her straight to some kind of home in Fort Myers for people escaping cults—or toxic relationships.

"Bucky!" Wilson pedaled up with Jelly a couple of lengths behind him.

They dumped their bikes at the cypress tree and hustled over.

Jelly snatched Parker's cap and slapped it on her head in her signature move. "What are you doing out here all by yourself?"

Parker shrugged. "Saying my goodbyes, I guess."

"Going to miss the place bad, eh?"

"Not the place," Parker said. "Just the people."

Wilson slung his arm around Parker's shoulders. "That would be *me* Parker is talking about, Jelly."

"Right." She pointed down the road leading to Smallwood's Store. "Here comes the food."

Dad and Mom were in one pickup, Uncle Sammy in the other.

"Tell me you didn't make the meal," Wilson said. "I do *not* feel like PB and J."

"Ha." Jelly's eyes sparkled in that teasing way. "You'll have to wait and find out."

Wilson groaned. "Don't you ever get tired of it?"

"Never."

Wilson watched the men park their trucks. "I thought Maria would be with your dad."

Jelly shook her head. "She's still in the detox program. It'll be a long haul."

"She okay?"

"No," Jelly said. "But she will be. When she finishes in Fort Myers she'll go to a live-in situation with a counselor in the Chicago area for a while."

Wilson gave her a sideways glance. "All the way to Chicago? Sounds a little extreme."

It did seem like a long way to go for a shrink.

"She'll be with Amy Baker—a friend of a friend. Amy did wonders for her—and she'll do the same for Maria."

"I can't imagine how relieved that must make you," Parker said, "and your dad."

Jelly nodded. "These last two weeks she's already made great progress. We've talked on the phone. In fact," she looked at Parker, "she wanted me to give you a message."

Maybe there was a time when Parker would have been more interested, but now?

"She said she's beginning to see you were right about monsters being real. And that the worst kind walk on two legs."

"Sasquatch," Wilson said. "Better known as skunk ape down here. Am I right?"

Jelly slugged him in the arm. "She's talking about Clayton, idiot."

Wilson rubbed his arm, grinning. The guy was in fine form today.

"She also said when she gets back she thinks she owes you an apology—and maybe even a hug and a kiss for all she put you through."

"What about me?" Wilson looked like he'd been slighted. "I helped, too. A lot."

"She never mentioned you, Wilson." Jelly kept her eyes on Parker—like she was watching for his reaction.

"Her apology is accepted," Parker said. "But she can give the hug and kiss to Wilson."

"Oh, Parker." Jelly's eyes were as alive as the sun dancing on the water. "You really *have* changed."

Parker wasn't exactly sure what to do with that.

"So," Wilson said, "did we ever find out what that mysterious payout was all about?"

Jelly nodded. "My dad was going to hire some guy who extracts kids from cults—and deprograms them. Parker's dad was handling the payout."

Wilson almost looked disappointed, like he'd wished the men were doing something more risky. "So nothing that could have landed them in jail, eh?"

"Technically no," Jelly said. "But Maria wouldn't have gone willingly—so it would have looked like a kidnapping. That was bound to lead to trouble."

Parker didn't even want to think about how many ways the plan could have gone south, especially if Maria was with Kingman when the snatch took place.

"*That's* desperate," Wilson said.

She shook her head. "That's a dad who desperately loves his daughter."

Wilson shrugged. "I liked the idea of a hit man better."

"You're insane, Wilson," Parker said. "I'm just glad Kingman will go to prison. He's one guy I hope I never meet again." Especially not alone.

"I think that's a sure thing," Jelly said. "Two counts of attempted murder. And there's more they'll be investigating. It seems Clayton bragged to Maria about some things he did—and she's just starting to talk about them." She shuddered. "Awful things."

Stories Parker didn't want to know. He'd already seen and experienced enough to fuel bad dreams for a long, long time.

"So," Wilson said. "What about Principal K? He helped Maria pull off her great escape—even lined up a nice couch for her to sleep on at his sister's house. Does he get to write himself a hall pass on this?"

"Technically he didn't break a law," Jelly said. "But the way I heard it, the school board voted to boot him—and his fallen Star of Integrity—right out of a job."

Wilson grinned. "I'm actually looking forward to going to school Monday."

If the new principal was anything like the ones Parker met at other schools he'd attended, Everglades City School—students and teachers included—was going to be a ton better off.

"There's just one thing I'm dying to know about Clayton's arrest," Wilson said. "And I'll bet Bucky here wants to know, too."

Parker had no idea where he was going with this.

"But Parker, being the fine Christian that he is, probably is too kind to ask the burning question."

Now Parker was pretty sure he didn't want to know.

"When the police took Kingman from the hospital, how in the world did they handcuff him—with him having only one hand?"

Parker didn't want to laugh—especially since he'd almost lost an arm to an alligator himself. But the goofy expression on Wilson's face made that almost impossible.

Uncle Sammy walked by carrying a cooler. "Clayton Kingman is going to be in jail a long, long time. That's all I care about. "He'll never lay a hand on my girl again."

"Not his right one, anyway," Wilson said. "The gator saw to that."

Yeah, Wilson was on a roll today. Parker looked down at his own messed-up arm and breathed a silent prayer of thanks—again. Even if he never got full use of his hand again, it was still attached—and for that he was grateful.

"Parker." Uncle Sammy stood at the bed of the pickup. "We got something for the guy who never gave up on my Maria."

A moment later Uncle Sammy held up the gator stick.

"Amos Moses?" Parker rushed over, with Wilson and Jelly right on his heels. "How in the world did you find it?"

Parker took his gator stick and inspected it. The dive knife was still secure. Some deep scratches and scrapes—but otherwise in great condition. Had Goliath somehow upchucked the gator stick? He held it out in front of him, like he did when Goliath had charged him. Amos Moses felt good in his hands. Right, somehow.

"One more thing." Uncle Sammy nodded to Parker's dad—who was already reaching into the bed of the pickup.

Dad held up the most massive alligator skull Parker had ever seen. Bleached-white bone with wicked-looking eye sockets big enough to slide a tennis ball through. The teeth . . . yellow with streaks of brownish-orange—and ginormous.

"Is that *him*?" Parker looked from his dad to Uncle Sammy, and back. "Goliath?"

"Oh yeah," Uncle Sammy said. "What's left of him."

"You got him!"

"No," Uncle Sammy said. "*You* got him. You rammed that gator stick of yours down his throat. *That's* what did him in. That flap in the back of his throat—to keep water out—wouldn't close. He must have tried to shake Amos Moses loose, but he drowned himself in the process."

"Seriously?"

Dad grinned. "He was dead when we got to him."

Wilson squeezed through for a closer look.

"I'll never forget the sight of you facing off against Goliath," Uncle Sammy said. "That took some real grit."

"Grit?" Jelly shook her head. "What are you talking about, Dad?"

"Courage. Perseverance. You, know. *Grit*." He said it like he was surprised it wasn't in her vocabulary. "But all through this, Parker, you demonstrated a grittiness like I've never seen before—except maybe in your dad. And the way you kept looking for Maria and didn't quit? Definitely gritty."

Grit. Gritty. Parker looked at his dad. "How do you spell gritty . . . with one T or two?"

Dad held up two fingers.

Suddenly it all made sense. *That's* what Grandpa was trying to say about integrity. Sometimes doing the right things take courage. Perseverance. "Grandpa's sign."

Dad smiled. "I knew you'd figure it out."

"I figured something out, too," Wilson said. "I teased Bucky a lot about being a boy scout—because he was always trying to do whatever he thought was the right thing. It drove me nuts."

"I think you said it would get us in trouble someday," Parker said.

Wilson nodded. "But when Goliath was bearing down on us, somehow he figured the right thing was letting me get in the boat first." He turned to Parker. "If you'd gone first, I'd have been in water facing Goliath. And with just a machete?"

"You've got Miccosukee blood," Parker said. "You'd have been okay."

"Of course," Wilson said. "Definitely. But there's also this teensy-weensy little chance that you saved my hide."

"Wait," Jelly rubbed her ear. "You're finally realizing that doing the right thing is a good thing?"

"All I'm saying," Wilson said, "is that I'd follow this boy scout anywhere."

"It's about time you wised up," Jelly said.

Uncle Sammy brought the skull to Parker and handed it to him. "I'm proud of you, son." He swung his arm around Parker's shoulder and turned to face the others. "Ladies and gentlemen, meet Parker Buckman . . . a boy who faced his monster—and became a man in the process."

Cheers, whistles—and some really stinging claps on the back from Wilson. Jelly turned away from him, dabbing her eyes.

Wilson raised his hand. "Hold on just a second, everyone. I'm not so sure Bucky deserves *all* the credit for killing Goliath. I think you're forgetting one gigantic factor."

"Give it up, Wilson," Jelly said. "You were in the boat when

Parker rammed Amos Moses down Goliath's throat. Don't even try to claim credit."

"You want to hear my theory or not?"

"Not." Jelly smiled.

Wilson waved her off. "I think Goliath was poisoned."

Everyone laughed.

"Think about it," Wilson said. "Kingman is toxic, right? Totally bad blood. Now remember, Goliath swallowed a *mouthful* of that poison when he chomped on Kingman's arm. I say *that's* what killed Goliath."

Again, the laughter. Full. Unfiltered.

The attention circled back to Goliath's skull.

"I gotta get me a skull like that," Wilson said. "Maybe sometime you can come back for a visit—and you and I can go out in the Glades and—"

"No!" Jelly said. "If you want to see Parker, *you're* the one who's going to have to travel. And he'll be in Rockport, a little town north of Boston."

"I can do that." Wilson smiled. "Can you imagine what it would be like to bag a shark? I mean a really b—"

"Wilson!" Jelly shook her head. "Give it a rest."

The whole group of them busted out laughing. Dad and Uncle Sammy went to get the grill out of the pickup bed. Mom opened the coolers and started putting food on the table.

Wilson took the alligator skull from Parker. "I'll bring Goliath back in a minute," he said. "I need some selfies with this guy."

"That is so vain," Jelly said.

"They're not for me," Wilson said. "I was thinking of sending one to Clayton."

"I have something for you, too, Parker." Jelly reached in her pocket and held out a handful of brass plugs. "Forgive me?"

Parker smiled and stared at them for a moment. She was a good friend—and risked so much to keep him from getting hurt. But honestly, only God could have kept him safe with all he'd been through. "And while you're in the mood for returning things, can I please have my hat back?"

"No can do." She held the visor of his Wooten's Airboat Tours cap like she thought maybe he'd try to snatch it off her head. "I'm keeping this until I see you in Rockport. I'll give it to you then."

"That could be months." The transfer process could be maddeningly slow—and totally unpredictable.

She raised her eyebrows and tilted her head slightly, like she knew something he didn't.

"What?" Parker locked eyes with her. "Did your dad get the transfer?"

Jelly locked her lips with an invisible key, and pretended to toss the key over her shoulder.

"You're not going to tell me?"

Jelly shook her head. "Can't."

Obviously she was really enjoying this. "I thought you were done keeping secrets."

"For *others*," Jelly said. "I won't let anyone pressure me to keep *their* secrets anymore. But a girl can have a few of her own."

"What?"

"Besides . . . this really isn't a secret."

"Really. And what would you call it?"

Jelly smiled. "A surprise."

That seemed like a pretty fine line to Parker. "How about a game of twenty questions?"

Jelly laughed and pointed at her sealed lips. "Sorry," she said out the side of her mouth.

"Okay," Parker said. "Just one question. When am I going to get my hat back?"

She looked up at him in that teasing way of hers and smiled. "Soon."

CP1706